Too Many Secrets Too Many Lies

By

Sonya Sparks

RJ Publications, LLC

Newark, New Jersey

RJ Publications

secretillusion4u@aol.com

www.rjpublications.com

ISBN-10: 0978637305

ISBN-13: 9780978637309

Printed in Canada

October 2007

1 2 3 4 5 6 7 8 9 10

DEDICATION
I would like to dedicate my first novel to my Mom and Dad

In loving memory of my sister Cheryle Elaine Styles

ACKNOWLEDGEMENTS

First and foremost, I would like to give my thanks to GOD for making this book possible.

Thank You so much Pastor Maddox and Church of Deliverance for opening your doors and your hearts.

Thanks to my family for all of their loving support and encouragement.
Husband Jeff, my two beautiful daughters Sennamon and Kierstin, my three handsome sons Mike (wife Angel), Chris and Tyree. My brothers Bryan, Roy, Vernon, Tony and Jr..
My sister-in-laws, brothers-in-laws, cousins, nieces and nephews (especially Stephen who is more like a son or brother) My beautiful granddaughter Akeemie (G-Ma loves you!!!)
Oh yeah and you too Mack (I couldn't leave you out)
Stanley, Charmaine and to everyone who's ever shown me love and support!!!

My Special friends, Vonda Parker, my oldest and dearest friend, I love you. My Shoe Diva, Colette Muhammad, you know you're my girl!!! Brenda Pounds, Girl, we gotta get to StarBucks!!! Sonja Thompson and Alberta Alexander, I love you both so much!!! Natalie Nash and Leigh Hardaway, wherever you are I Miss You!!!

A VERY SPECIAL THANK YOU TO RICHARD JEANTY OF RJ PUBLICATIONS - YOU ARE THE BEST!!! WORDS CANNOT EXPRESS MY GRATITUDE FOR GIVING ME A CHANCE AND FOR ALL OF YOUR HARD WORK. YOU ARE EXTREMELY APPRECIATED. MAY GOD BLESS YOU AND EVERYTHING YOU TOUCH.

And whoever is reading this book, THANK YOU.

Chapter One

"Sorry Mrs. Kendrix, I tried to stop her." Kari, Bianca's secretarial temp said helplessly. "Do you want me to call security?" She asked hesitantly.

"No Kari, I do not need security. That will be all." Bianca smiled toward her temp as she watched her close the door to her office slowly. Bianca leaned back in her chair and directed her attention to her uninvited guest. "What a surprise to see you today. Please have a seat and tell me what brings you by." She said pleasantly.

"You sneaky little, conniving, bitch. You slept with my husband, didn't you?" Annetta Howser said between clenched teeth as she continued to stand outrage shaking her entire body.

Bianca frowned, "Excuse me? Annetta, what in the world are you talking about now?"

"Don't go playing that innocent crap with me. I know all about you and Matthew's little rendezvous. You keep fucking around and somebody's going to end up with *your* husband."

Bianca laughed, "I must admit I'm no angel but honey I never slept with your husband. But I am curious to know where you got a crazy idea like that from?"

"You lying bitch. Laura saw his car parked at your house and Marcus' car was no where in sight." Annetta looked as if she was ready to attack Bianca at any moment.

"Laura" Bianca laughed again, "As in my nosey neighbor, Laura? The same Laura who started that vicious rumor about you and the good reverend, just because the two of you had lunch one day? Let me enlighten you. *Yes,* your husband was at my house, and *no,* Marcus was not home at the time, however, Ashland *was* there. You see Matthew stopped by looking for Marcus and after seeing that Ashland was home visiting, he talked with her for a few moments before leaving. Did Laura mention anything about Ashland?" Bianca questioned calmly.

Annetta sat down in the chair like a defeated woman,

"No, she never mentioned Ashland." Annetta smiled weakly, "How is she by the way?"

"Wonderful as always let her tell it." Bianca said then stood to walk around her desk to lean against it, "Annetta, are you ok? Look, we've been really good friends for over thirty years. I know I've done a lot of things, but I'm not that bad and I do value our friendship."

Annetta looked up at Bianca with tear strained eyes, "I'm sorry I guess I let my imagination along with Laura get the better of me."

Bianca walked over to pour them both a cup of coffee, "Yes you did but you're forgiven."
She handed Annetta the cup and sat in the chair beside her.

"I think Matthew is cheating again." Annetta said softly.

"Honey, I'm so sorry. How about we have lunch today and talk." Bianca said as she reached over to hold her hand.

Annetta squeezed Bianca's hand gently then released it. "That would be great. Are you free around two?"

"Two would be perfect. I'll make this a short day for me here at the office since I've finally caught up on everything pressing."

Annetta stood to leave, so Bianca followed suit and hugged her and said, "It's going to be all right. Don't worry. How about we meet at the nail salon and we'll go from there?

Annetta laughed, "You never miss a thing, do you?" As Annetta looked down at her hands, she said, "Yes that would be perfect. You know I broke a nail on my way over here. You can't imagine what I would've done to you if that had been true about you and Matthew."

Bianca laughed then walked her down the hall to the elevator. When Bianca returned to her office she never glanced at Kari as she passed her by. Bianca thought how she missed Evelyn, her no non-sense personal assistant, and could hardly wait until she was back at work from sick leave. Evelyn would *never* allow anyone to just barge into her office. *Kari had to go,* Bianca thought to herself as she closed the door to her office then picked up the phone to call the temp service.

After making her call, Bianca sat tapping her fingers on her desk thinking of what her husband had said earlier this morning. She had only suggested that they have a party and invite their daughter Ashland, and her friend Nick, to fly up for it. Who knew maybe they would get back together. Marcus had become enraged at that simple gesture and responded angrily before storming out for work by saying, 'I don't blame Ashland for being angry with you. For the life of me, I can't figure out why you continue to interfere in her life, she a grown woman for goodness sake. Aren't you happy with the fact that Jordan is no longer a part of it? She doesn't want to get back with Nick so just let her be. Haven't you caused her enough misery over the years?" Bianca was a little shocked at the raw anger that Marcus had in his eyes.

"I guess that means there will be no party," she mumbled to herself.

Bianca made a crude noise as she thought about Jordan's grandfather. She hated him with a passion, so what if she messed up her daughter's relationship, but the idea of Ashland being married to Jordan aggravated the hell out of her. All Ashland needed was to get over Nick's little indiscretion and move on. She really needed to learn that people cheated all the time, but that didn't necessarily mean they didn't love their mates.

Bianca thought how Ashland had flown in town to surprise them a few weeks ago. Just as Marcus' partner, Matthew, was about to leave Ashland had arrived, so they chatted a few moments before he left. She told Ashland he was there looking for Marcus but she wasn't fooled, it was too obvious as to what they had been doing. Ashland avoided her as much as possible and cut her visit short. Bianca smiled thinking she didn't really care because Ashland couldn't prove a thing and she wouldn't dare tell her father.

"But I did cross the line with Annetta and our friendship," Bianca said out loud feeling only a small degree of guilt, then thought, *Oh well, Matthew's going to cheat on her no matter what.* Dismissing Annetta from her mind completely, she smirked as she thought of Laura briefly and wondered if she had seen her husband sneaking from her pool house last summer. She picked up the phone to call her daughter.

Damn I do not need this today, Ashland thought to herself as she heard her mother's voice.   "Hello mother how are you today?"

"I am doing fine, as I'm sure you are. I noticed how stunning you looked when you were here. I also noticed that locket. Why are you still wearing that thing?" her mother casually asked as she struggled to hold her emotions in check.

They had this conversation a thousand times so Ashland only closed her eyes and inhaled deeply.

"Ashland, I don't know why you still wear that thing after all these years. You should know by now he never gave a damn about you. I hope he's not the real cause of you and Nick not being together. You really need to move on with your life. Get married and have a couple of kids. And get rid of that necklace. My goodness, don't you think you've worn it long enough?" Bianca said heatedly.

"Mother, please don't start. Not today." Ashland pleaded.

"You know that can't be healthy for you, he's gone. Or have you forgotten how he just forgot about you and his unborn child?" Bianca said deliberately, hitting a sore spot.

"No I haven't forgotten." Ashland said hotly. She had started to remind her mother of her little indiscretion with her father's partner, but she knew it was useless. Her mother would never admit to anything. Besides, she also knew how useless it was to argue with her, so she just sat back in her chair being forced to think of Jordan as her mother went on her usual rampage.

Kayla buzzed her on the intercom to let her know she had a call waiting. Breathing a sigh of relief Ashland said, "Mother I'm sorry to cut you off but I have a call on hold and it's very important that I take it."

"I have to go any way, just remember what I said, and I'll be sure to tell your father hello for you." Bianca hung up as usual before Ashland could say goodbye.

Ashland buzzed Kayla on the intercom, "Who's on hold?"

"It's the office of Mr. Whitfield; they were referred by Professor Faulkner. They want to speak with you in hopes of contracting us for renovating a building for his business and decorating his home." Ashland heard Kayla shuffle some papers, "But he has requested for you to personally handle the project. Do you want me to set something up or do you want me to let her know that your schedule is tight for the next couple of months?" Kayla inquired.

Ashland leaned back in her chair rubbing her temples. She really didn't feel like getting personally involved in a large project, but Professor Faulkner had helped her get everything started with her company. "Kayla, please schedule the meeting, then print me a spreadsheet for all of the projects we're working on and their scheduled deadlines for their anticipated completion," she said.

Ashland stood up to look out her window and thought this might be exactly what she needed. She was beginning to have too much free time if she was sitting here thinking about him. She grabbed her locket and thought, *Who really believes in love anyways?*

Chapter Two

Ashland was on her way to meet Mr. Whitfield for the second time. On their previous meeting he was called away on a family emergency. His assistant fortunately filled in for him, taking care of all preliminary documents and explaining everything their company required. Her company was contracted to begin work immediately.

Driving slowly up the driveway, Ashland smiled, thinking it was the most breathtaking view she had ever seen. Everything was so lush and green; it all seemed to have a calming effect on her. There were several vehicles parked out front so she took the space between a black Mercedes and a blue ford pick up truck. Poised and confident as usual, Ashland stepped out of her silver Jaguar and walked toward the front porch.

There were men all around working on various jobs, planting flowers, cutting hedges, and everything else. She admired all of the different flowers. Even though they were weeded and overgrown, she still managed to see the beauty of it all. She was about to knock on the door when an old man with a cigar hanging out of his mouth said "Ma'am, he says to tell ya to go right on in. He'll be waitin' for ya. As you walk around the house, you'll more than likely run into him somewhere." He turned and walked away before she had a chance to say anything.

Ashland walked into the house and immediately fell in love. She knew she was going to enjoy this project very much. The hard wood floors in the foyer were immaculate. She especially loved the two spiral staircases. One immediately to the left just past the first large room, which was extremely sunny and bright, and the second stairway was located straight ahead. Ashland went about her exploration of the house.

In the study, Ashland stood staring out the large balcony doors when he entered. He leaned against the doorway admiring how sexy she had become. *Damn, she's beautiful*; he thought as he remembered how soft her honey colored skin was. She was wearing a white blouse and short pale pink skirt that brought attention to her shapely legs. To his surprise, he briefly wondered how many men had there been after him. Pushing that thought aside, he felt despite everything her mom had said to him all those years ago; he knew he still had some feelings for her. He cleared his throat "It's been way too long, Ashland."

Ashland heard the familiar voice and was immediately dazed and disoriented, she willed herself to move, but it took her a few minutes to get her bearings together. She was suddenly taken back to when she was seventeen.

Ashland was young, in love and pregnant by Jordan Alexander, her first and only true love. Jordan had been nineteen and was the cutest boy she had ever seen. They were to be married, even before the pregnancy, as soon as she turned eighteen; unfortunately things had a way of turning out differently.

Ashland thought about when her parents found out about her pregnancy, she had never witnessed so much anger before, especially from her mother. Jordan's grandfather had come over to talk with her parents, but by the time her mother finished with him, he had decided to send Jordan away to start his internship in their family business overseas and complete his schooling there. A Trust Fund would be set up for the child when she gave birth; unfortunately she had miscarried six weeks after Jordan left. She never knew what had actually been said behind her father's office doors that miserable day, but whatever it was put Jordan's grandfather in a rage, he hadn't been at their house twenty minutes before he had left slamming the door with a boisterous bang.

Ashland unconsciously grabbed the locket Jordan had given her only days before he'd left, when she opened it, there was a picture of her and Jordan on the right side, and inscribed on the left side was, *"I love you. I'll be back."* The night Jordan was to leave she had called but it was too late, he was gone. She was devastated as she cried to Jordan's grandfather, "Grandfather, please tell Jordan I love him and to please call me. I need him so bad to be with me right now it hurts." She thought about the promise Jordan had made her when he had given her the locket, he had smiled then said, "Ashland, please try not to be sad I promise I'll call you all the time and besides, before you know it, you'll be eighteen and we'll be together again. Don't you ever forget that I love you always and forever, no matter what." She thought how that had taken place ten years ago and to this day Jordan has never called.

Ashland thought how she had always been a straight A student, but after he left, she had devoted herself completely to her studies, trying anything to keep Jordan off her mind. When studying wasn't enough she had taken an after school job at a department store. By the time she turned eighteen, she decided to move as far away from home as possible. Her dad was pretty cool but her mom would never let her forget the pregnancy. She always threw it up in her face about Jordan being no good, telling her how silly she was for loving someone who didn't love her in return. Her mother seemed to thrive on her unhappiness regarding Jordan. Ashland remembered how she couldn't take it anymore, and ended up moving to the Atlanta area.

Ashland remembered the fact she didn't have a lot of money left after renting an apartment and paying for the down payment. She ended up working days at a Filbert's, a paint store, while going to college at night majoring in business. Ashland smiled thinking of Filbert's and the time she and Kayla met and instantly bonded. They both had been struggling to survive and became great friends in the process. It was almost as if they were sisters.

Ashland was consumed with her classes, tuitions, bills and getting beyond Jordan, and Kayla with raising her two children, D'Neko who is now ten and Tymera who is nine years old. Kayla had to raise them alone after she put her boyfriend DeShun out. Then one day Kayla offered a room to Ashland to stay with her family in the house. They both needed the help during that time.

Although Ashland's grandmother had left her a Trust Fund, she had to wait until age twenty-one to receive it, her parents had offered to help her financially until that time, but she refused. Ashland Kendrix wanted to owe nor be obligated to no one but herself. Even after Ashland received her Trust Fund she continued to stay with Kayla and the kids for a while, but she had become a very wealthy woman, so with the help of her college professor she had begun the process of starting her own business. It had taken her two years, but her company was finally born, Ultimate Renovations.

Ashland knew Kayla was confident, direct and hard working, she hired her on as her personal assistant and paid for her schooling and even kept her kids at night at times when her mom couldn't. Kayla thought that was too much, but Ashland always joked by saying she was in training, because one day she too would be a mom. She didn't move out of Kayla's house until Kayla finished school. They stuck together truer than most families.

She thought of her twenty-first birthday, her dad and Jordan's grandfather were the only people who called her. Ironically enough, her mother was too busy to pick up the phone on her birthday. She always felt her dad's love for her and as brief as Tylen's calls were, she knew he cared, always calling her on all major holidays and sending flowers for her birthday. It was a bittersweet moment when twenty-one long stem roses were delivered to her job, and she excitedly read the card as she thought of Jordan. Ashland thought how something had happened to her that day and her life was never the same. She vowed never to ask about Jordan and the necklace was now only a reminder for her to never lose her heart and soul again.

Ashland forgot about the past, took a deep breath and slowly turned around. At first, she was busting with joy. She could barely stand the feeling, she felt as if she was floating, moving in slow motion. Standing there with his hands in his pockets, gone was the boyish good look. He was now an extremely handsome man, with skin like sweet rich melted caramel. He seemed to be taller than she remembered, maybe six feet two or so. She found herself staring into his dark silvery gray eyes that still held the power to render her speechless. The only word to describe Jordan was magnificent, she thought to herself, and then suddenly she became very angry. She spoke slowly to maintain control of her feeling, "Hello Jordan." she said tightly, and then added, "Yes, it has been a very long time."

Noticing the changing expressions on her face, Jordan walked in and closed the door behind him. For a brief moment, he actually thought she was happy to see him. He motioned for her to sit in the wing back chair in front of his large cherry wood desk. She crossed her legs after she sat, unaware of giving him a very nice view of her thigh in doing so. Jordan continued to stand, and then leaned against the front of his desk with his arms folded.

Just as he began to speak, Ashland interrupted him, "So, I take it you're Mr. Whitfield?"

Jordan smiled, "I figured if you knew who I really was you wouldn't have even considered the job. I only want the best and from what I hear, that's you. This house should be fairly simple; it's in excellent condition, it's just a matter of decorating." Jordan again smiled then continued, "But as you know I've expanded my business to Georgia, you've already seen the specs for everything I need. I have five months to have this company up and running in full force. So," he said uncrossing his arms and putting his hands in his pockets, "I need you," he paused briefly then continued in a very businesslike manner, "So, here we are."

The nerve of him, she thought to herself. *What about when I needed you.* She was getting pissed and was about to lose all perspective on things and she knew she had to keep cool. If this had been anyone else she would not be having any regrets, he actually offered more than she usually charged, even on a short notice. At that thought, Ashland unconsciously brushed against his pants as she uncrossed her legs to stand. Feeling once again in control, in spite of all she was feeling, she managed to sound professional when she spoke, "We have a contract and my company will honor that contract. We will deliver everything you expect and more. Now," she paused briefly, "if you'll excuse me I'm running late for another appointment."

Ashland turned to leave but Jordan grabbed her arm lightly, "Ash-"

She felt the attraction as soon as he touched her and hated herself for it. She looked up with a raised eyebrow and cut him off before he could say anything, "Let's just keep it strictly business, and get the job done." She angrily pulled her arm free and left.

Jordan was thinking about the letters he had sent her, all returned back to him unopened and the calls he had made, only to have her mother insisting that Ashland never wanted to see him again. He would never forget the last time he had called Ashland, her mother told him never to call their house again because Ashland had decided to have an abortion. He had felt so much anger, hurt and disappointment that he never called back, actually hating her for a long time after that. Although it was hard for him to imagine Ashland doing anything like that, the reality was, she never gave birth to their child. That loss was the reason he graduated top of his class. Driving himself to work until all thought of Ashland and his unborn child became only a dream. He never allowed himself to get seriously committed to another woman.

Over the years, his grandfather had tried to talk to him about Ashland, but the thought of her rejecting him and killing their baby was too much for him. He learned to ignore his grandfather when her name was brought up. Only curiosity brought him here after his grandfather casually left a picture and an article on Ashland in some legal documents that had required his immediate attention, he realized he wanted to see her. He had been debating for years whether to expand the company south, now the decision was made.

Jordan sat in the same chair Ashland had just sat in. He leaned his head back and closed his eyes. He thought if things had been different they would be married and their child would be almost ten. Who knows? They would've probably had three or four kids by now, he smiled. Then he thought, maybe they had been too young at the time to have a child. So much was going through his head that he stood to pour himself a stiff drink.

***

Ashland was happy to be home after her encounter with Jordan. She had lied about the appointment because she needed to get away from him, feeling as if she couldn't breathe. She was angry with him for walking back into her life so casually after all these years. Maybe now she would finally have some closure on that part of her life, at that thought she called Kayla to let her know she would be unavailable the rest of the day. She finally began to relax after soaking in a hot bath. She didn't bother to dress just threw on a tank top and a pair of sweat shorts. It was still early, only about one fifteen in the afternoon, so she decided to read over the specifications on the projects she had for Jordan.

She dosed off and was awaken when her cell phone rang.

"Hey sunshine" It was Nick Balinsky, CEO of his family owned business, Balinsky's Fine Jewelry, the largest imports of rare jewels around the world. He was a very nice specimen to say the least, six feet one, with a smooth mocha complexion and had the thickest eyelashes and dark sexy eyes that could make a woman melt like butter. They had been an item at one time, at least until he slept with Sheila, a real-estate agent and a so-called friend of hers that she had met when she first arrived in Atlanta. She thought with a laugh, Sheila had actually helped Nick find his current home. Considering everything she and Nick had been through, she was surprised they managed to remain friends. Of course, Nick was a charmer and always fun to be around.

"Hi Nicky," Ashland said stretching.

"I just got back in town and decided to check on you and to see if we could get together and have a few drinks tonight," Nick said.

Ashland leaned back on the couch and closed her eyes, "I don't think so."

There was a long pause, "Where are you? I hope I'm not interrupting anything. When I called your office Kayla told me that you were unavailable." He laughed then added softly, "I still remember our afternoon meetings."

Ashland smiled thinking he made everything seem so easy, "I'm working from home that's all. So, how are things with Stephanie?"

"I think I'm going to ask Stephanie to marry me. That's really why I called to see if you wanted to hang out with me before I officially become an engaged man."

Ashland couldn't help but laugh, "Nicky, you're joking, right? In the past year, you've been in three different relationships, and I'm not even going to begin to count all the other women you've bedded. Now, all of a sudden you think you're ready to settle." Ashland laughed so hard; Nick couldn't help but laugh too.

"I've been faithful to Stephanie." Nick said defensively then asked, "Ashland, just out of curiosity, would you have married me if I had asked?"

"Marry you? Hell no! I-"

Nick interrupted her, "I'm serious, Ashland. We were pretty intense at one point."

Ashland thought for a moment, he had become her safe haven for a while. Thoughts of Jordan didn't come very often when Nick was around. They might have ended up married or at least engaged. Ashland smiled, thinking she had been crazy about her some Nicky back in the day. Everything was always spontaneous, fun, but she didn't trust him anymore, and she couldn't deal with that. "I honestly don't know. Maybe."

They both were quiet for a moment, and then Nick cleared his throat, "Well, Stephanie understands me. She…"

It was Ashland's turn to interrupt, "No Nicky, don't even try it. She lets you do whatever you want and believes everything you say. She's like a puppet and you're in complete control."

Nick saw the truth in her words, "I really do care about her. I'm actually content with only her." He said earnestly.

"You mean for now, unless another Sheila comes along or if she starts complaining about your business trips and meetings. You'll be ready to move on to someone else," She said carelessly.

"Sheila was the biggest mistake I've ever made and it cost me big time. And you damn well know it. I don't know why I even bother to call you." Nick was annoyed at her for bringing up Sheila.

Ashland thought she was glad he called, he always lightened her mood but he could stop with the attitude because she never told him to mess around with Sheila. "Don't go getting all mad. I'm only telling the truth and you know it. Besides, I wouldn't be scared to bet that within six months there will be someone else to replace Stephanie."

Nick laughed, "Damn I hope not. This ring cost me a small fortune."

Ashland busted out laughing, "I would love to have drinks with you AND Stephanie tonight."

Nick cleared his throat, "Stephanie can't make it. She's out of town"

"I don't think I understanding. What do you really have on your mind?" she asked.

Nick inhaled deeply and laughed, "I just wanted to be the one to tell you. I don't know, maybe I just need to know how you would feel if I became engaged to another woman. I was kinda hoping it would bother you. I asked you out for drinks because I really miss hanging out with you, and honestly I just wanted to spend some time with you, just having fun that's all, I swear."

Ashland briefly thought about going but decided it would be best if she didn't. Nick was one of those brothers that made you have chills just by thinking about him, and right now his voice and laughter was a little too sensual for her to handle especially with so much history between them. Damn, he was one hell of a lover, she thought all of a sudden. She laughed as she pushed those thoughts aside, besides, she thought, I won't be the one to ruin their relationship. "I see. I'm not up to drinks tonight, but if you think you're ready for marriage, then I want to be the first to say congratulations. I really am happy for the two of you."

"Thanks" Nick said quietly not quite sure if that's what he'd really wanted to hear.

"I've got some things I really have to finish, but call me later, ok. Bye Nicky."

"Bye sunshine" Nick said after she had hung up. He regretted the day Sheila ever walked into his life, Ashland never believed him, but that was the only time he ever cheated on her.

Chapter Three

Wednesday morning Ashland was in a rather good humor when she got off the elevator "Good morning, Kayla. How are you today?"

Kayla smiled, "I'm fine and I see you're looking very refreshed this morning. You really need to take more time off." Kayla suddenly frowned as a thought occurred to her, "I hope Nick has nothing to do with your mood."

Ashland smiled brightly, "I couldn't be any better. And No, Nicky has nothing to do with it." Ashland went into her office and closed the door. She didn't come out until around ten thirty, "Kayla, do me a favor and get in touch with *Mr. Whitfield* and set up a lunch meeting for one forty-five today at Bennigan's. "

"What if he's unavailable at one forty-five? Would you like it for later today?" Kayla questioned.

Ashland smiled mischievously, "If he's unavailable today, tell him I'm not available until next Friday at one forty-five."

Kayla laughed out loud thinking it was rather short notice, Ashland usually made her lunch appointments before nine, but Kayla didn't question her, knowing Ashland the way she did, she knew she had her reasons. She would wait and let Ashland call her whenever she was ready to talk.

* * *

Ashland arrived at the restaurant a few minutes early and frowned. Jordan was already sitting in a secluded corner with a window view. She was surprised, she really didn't think he would make lunch because all she really wanted was to get him riled for coming back into her life the way he did. Jordan stood while she took her seat. "Hi. I'm glad you could make it on such short notice. I have a few things to discuss with you before getting started tomorrow. I hope I haven't disrupted your schedule today." She smiled sweetly. Jordan returned the smile and said, "Nothing that couldn't be postponed for later" He was actually irritated she called at the last minute, but considering everything, he wasn't surprised. He had to admit he needed a break. He'd been working through his lunches lately, and he really wanted to see her.

The waiter arrived, "Would you care to order drinks while you look over the menu?"

"Yes, two sweet teas please," Jordan stated.

The waiter nodded, "Very good, sir. I'll return with your drinks in a moment."

Neither spoke until he walked away.

"You could have asked me what I wanted instead of ordering." Ashland said while pretending to be studying the menu, being careful to avoid his eyes.

Jordan smiled, "I'm sorry, Ashland. I just assumed you still preferred tea."

He remembering something so small momentarily struck Ashland speechless. When she was younger, she liberally drank sweet tea by the gallons. "I wanted a glass of white wine but I guess the tea will have to do."

Jordan looked at her and could not help but grin. He got the waiter's attention while she continued to look over the menu.

"Yes sir," the waiter said.

"I do apologize but we would like a bottle of your best white wine instead." Jordan said smiling.

"As you wish. Will there be anything else, sir?"

"No, that will be all for now, we'll both be having wine."

The waiter nodded and smiled mischievously at Jordan, while Ashland just glared.

"You really didn't have to order a whole bottle." She stated a little irritably then added, "I'm just used to ordering for myself or at least being asked what I want."

Jordan nodded. "I'll remember that next time."

After their wine arrived, Ashland leaned forward and said teasingly "Admit it Jordan. Isn't this better than sweet tea?"

Jordan couldn't help glancing at her breasts. When he saw her locket, he was wondering if it was the same one he had given her all those years ago.

"Are you ready to order now, sir?" The waiter asked looking directly at Jordan.

Jordan cleared his throat, "Ashland, are you ready?"

She smiled brightly, "Yes, I think I'll have the Caesar Salad" She politely handed the menu to the waiter.

"Good choice ma'am" then he turned back to Jordan "And you, sir, what will you be having? If I may suggest the salmon it's quite excellent today."

Jordan nodded. "Salmon it is. Thank you." Jordan studied Ashland for a moment and realized there was so much about her he didn't know. A part of him wanted to hold her once more, wishing they could go back to the way they were. However, he knew it was too late for that. They were not teenagers anymore and he could not forget, as hard as he tried, how she aborted his child.

Ashland didn't like the way Jordan was looking at her because it was always so difficult to tell the mood he was in until it was too late. However, one thing was for sure and that was his eyes still held the promise to make her forget or remember too many things. Ashland turned away and pretended to be interested in the people surrounding them.

"Ashland," Jordan said bringing her attention back to him, then picked up his glass, "A toast to us and strictly business."

* * *

Jordan sat at his desk and grudgingly admitted he had enjoyed his lunch with Ashland, even though it had been very tense, but they kept it strictly professional. He had almost forgotten how intelligent she was. He smiled thinking she really knew her business. His only concern was if he would be able to keep his personal feeling under control until the job was completed. He wasn't sure if working with her day in and day out would work out and wondered if it was the smart thing to do, but hoping they could at the least become friends again. The longer he sat in the restaurant talking with her and listening to her laughter, the more memories it brought back, which made one thing very clear to him, he could easily fall for her all over again. He was already finding himself imagining what it would be like to be with her now that she's all grown up, and that angered him and he could not allow himself to think about her like that, especially after what she'd done.

* * *

The next morning Ashland called a meeting outlining requirements and deadlines they had to meet. Dividing a few employees into two groups, she had Team A that were required to complete the business complex, which was the most time consuming and Team B, a much smaller group, were to complete the estate. By noon, both teams were at work. By the following Friday evening, Jordan knew Ashland had an amazing crew. Within one week, the building was transformed and everything was going so smoothly, it actually made him feel a little more relaxed. However, working with Ashland was awkward and he could tell she felt the same way, so they ended up avoiding each other whenever possible.

"What do you think you're doing?" Ashland asked heatedly a week later as she stormed into Jordan's office without knocking.

"Ashland, what are you talking about?"

"Your new little barney fife security guard would not allow my workers to enter the building today because they did not have badges. Badges they were NEVER given may I remind you. Do you realize we lost a full day's work, which ultimately set us back? And when I asked your wannabe robo-cop why he didn't allow admittance, do you want to know what he said? He said you told him under no circumstances should anyone be allowed to enter without proper identification, then told him you were not to be disturbed again, and he informed me that we should come back Monday since there was no one to make badges or log us in until then."

"Ashland, when *Charley* called me this morning I assumed he was only asking a general question, he never told me people were actually waiting to get in. I promise, I'll take care of this immediately." Jordan casually picked up a piece of paper then asked, "I'm curious to know how you got in if Charley wasn't allowing entrance without proper ID?"

"The head security guard came out to see what all the commotion was. You know you really should have your new recruits better informed," she snapped, and for the first time, Ashland realized they were not alone, and felt completely embarrassed by her outburst. Jordan noticed her discomfort and smiled.

Jordan stood smiling, "Kira, this is Ashland Kendrix of Ultimate Renovations, she is the one responsible for all of the designs you've been admiring all afternoon. Ashland this is Kira Tompkins from our North Eastern Division.

Kira smiled, "Nice to meet you Ms. Kendrix. I really love what you've done to this building. I really hope Jordan decides to contract you for the other divisions."

Ashland smiled politely, "It's a pleasure to meet you as well. I must apologize for my timing. I didn't realize you were in the middle of a meeting, so if you'll excuse me I have a lot of..."

Kira cut her off, "No that's fine. You guys seem to have a lot to discuss. I've got a few things to take care of while I'm in town, anyway. Jordan, remember dinner on Friday, no excuses this time." Kira gave Jordan her undivided attention and looked longingly at him then swiftly left the room.

Ashland didn't miss the look Kira gave Jordan and thought to herself, *Dinner? Yeah right. Oh well. None of my business or concern.* She angrily walked out of his office. She was aggravated with herself that he had been on her mind constantly since their first meeting.

That evening Jordan got home a little earlier than usual, Ashland's Jaguar was the only car parked out front. After pouring himself a drink, he found Ashland in the kitchen writing in a notebook. "Still here, I see," he said casually, as he relaxed against the door.

"I'm actually finished for the day, just deciding on a few changes." She looked down at her watch, "I didn't realize it was so late. I need to be going." She ignored him as she stretched,

"We'll be back here first thing Monday morning and will have to work at the complex tomorrow to try to make up some lost time."

Jordan only nodded, he liked the way her jeans hugged her hips. He thought about her outburst earlier that day and smiled.

Ashland gathered her belongings and said, "See you later."

Jordan took a swallow of his drink, "Why don't you stay and talk with me a while? Just for a few minutes." Jordan was actually surprised that she agreed. "Have you eaten? We could order something. " He added as an after thought.

"Thanks, but I've eaten a little. I'm really not that hungry, but I'll take whatever you're drinking." She really hoped he was drinking something strong. She knew she should leave, but she honestly was not ready to go yet.   "I'm   drinking Vodka, you sure you want some?" He asked with a raised eyebrow.

Ashland laughed, "Quite sure."

Jordan smiled "Follow me then." He led her to the study and opened the double glass doors. "Let's sit outside."

Ashland leaned against the rails, enjoying the evening breeze.

"Here you go." He said holding a glass towards her; she noticed he had mixed some juice in her drink.

When Ashland turned around, she realized he was standing too close for comfort to suit her. Thanking him, he handed her the drink and she took a large swallow as she turned back around pretending to be completely immersed with the beautiful view. She decided to let him lead the conversation. She could tell Jordan still had not moved, because she could smell his cologne. *Damn, he smelled too good.* Closing her eyes. She finished her drink off, "May I have another?" Ashland was surprised at herself for feeling slightly nervous.

Without saying a word, he reached around her to take her glass. She was definitely nervous, his closeness was causing havoc to her body and she was glad when he walked away, but he wasn't gone long enough for her to get control of her emotions. *Damn I've been man free for too long*, Ashland thought as she took a deep shaky breath.

Jordan leaned against the rail facing Ashland as he handed her the glass back, "I would advise you to take it easy on this stuff," Jordan said.

Ashland took the offered glass then turned away looking at the rolling hills in the distance, "The view is so beautiful out here."

Jordan looked at his surroundings for a moment, "All I see is too many trees." He said sitting down in one of the chairs.

Ashland turned to face him, "You never could appreciate the beauty of nature."

"Ashland," he said smiling appreciating her beauty as he stood back up to look briefly at the trees as he turned to ask, "What is so beautiful or even special about trees? All they do is blocked the beautiful view."

"Trees have character," she stated matter-of-factly. Jordan raised an eyebrow as she continued. "Each is individually unique like people. No two trees are made exactly alike. They give us their beauty, provide us with fresh air, and even give a home to the homeless animals. Trees are an essential part of our lives. Damn Jordan, didn't they teach you anything in school over there?" She said laughing.

"Homeless animals?" He laughed because she said it so seriously. They shared a smile as they stood there for a while in silence each with their own thoughts.

"Ashland what happened to us?" Jordan asked quietly needing to know why things happened the way they did.

Ashland thought of a response and nothing came to mind. She wondered with rising anger how he could even ask her a question like that. He was the one who never tried to call to check on her. For all he knew she could have given birth to a son or daughter and he never cared enough to call. *Oh, my God, he was supposed to be a father and he doesn't even care enough to ask about the baby we lost*, Ashland thought all of a sudden. With extreme care, Ashland placed her glass on the table. "It's late and I'm tired." was all she said before she turned to leave. *What happened to us? Huh? Forget about us!* Ashland thought again furiously as she slammed his front door.

Jordan was confused by her sudden anger, which only angered him more.

* * *

Jordan was glad it was Friday and he planned on getting some much-needed rest. He didn't even feel like eating so he cancelled his dinner plans with Kira. He smiled as he thought briefly of Kira, she was nice but he didn't want her getting the wrong idea about them. He could hardly believe how tired he was as he drove home. He knew he had been pushing himself a lot lately, but work seemed to be the only thing to keep confusing thoughts of Ashland away. All he could think of was a hot shower and sleep, but as he pulled into his driveway, he saw Ashland's car and frowned. He looked at his watch and noticed the time. It was only five thirty no wonder she was still there.

Jordan found Ashland in the room, which was to be his gym. She had on headphones and was swaying seductively to whatever she was listening to while working diligently at the wall. Jordan smiled and decided to sit unnoticed so he could observe her fully. He was intrigued by her beauty and admitted to himself he was still attracted to her, but he couldn't get over her killing his child. At the thought of his child, he became angry with himself for the attraction he felt for her. He angrily stood and left the room.

Ashland was walking down the hallway on her way out when she heard a noise from Jordan's study. She immediately stopped in the doorway when she noticed Jordan sitting at his desk deeply immersed in some report he was reading as his machine printed out a fax. She decided to leave before he noticed her, but she didn't move fast enough. Their eyes meet, and the intensity of Jordan's stare made her look away.

"Ashland, come in. Have a seat and tell me how things are coming along." Jordan said without emotion as he laid his papers aside to give her his full attention.

Ashland removed her backpack from her shoulder and sat down in the chair across from him. She immediately began filling him in on the progress of everything. "I guess that's about it for now." She said about twenty minutes later.

Jordan stood to come around to lean on the front of his desk. "We really need to talk," he said seriously, as he put his hands in his pockets.

"About?" She asked with a raised eyebrow.

"Us" he said evenly.

Ashland inhaled deeply as she stood, "Can we do this later? I'm not really up to it right now. Besides, there is no us."

Jordan visibly relaxed and smiled, "Should I make an appointment?"

At his teasing tone, Ashland relaxed a little, but not enough. "Okay. Would you fix me a drink, first? I'm probably going to need it."

Jordan laughed then fixed them both a drink as Ashland opened the balcony doors and stepped outside for fresh air.

"Now, what is it that *we* need to discuss?" Ashland asked after taking a long swallow.

Jordan stood in front of Ashland and finished his drink off, "It's really been a long time for us and no matter how hard I try not to think about us I can't help but to think of us."

Ashland didn't know what to say, so she took his glass and refilled them both. "Okay, so you think of us. I do to at times. Big deal," Ashland said while taking another long swallow.

At her flippant tone, he felt himself becoming aggravated, "Ashland, what happened to us?" For the second time Jordan asked that question.

She thought to herself, *what happened to us? What the hell kind of question was that. Hell you left and didn't come back, that's what happened.* She wasn't in the mood to relive the past and she felt an argument coming on. She finished off her drink. Then looked up and shrugged her shoulders as if to say she did not know.

Jordan's anger flared up he wanted to shake her until she told him why she had refused to talk to him all those years ago and more importantly, why she had aborted their child. For some unexplained reason he needed to know. The longer he stood looking down at her, the more he became aware of how close he was standing to her. He began to notice how full her breast had become. He had not eaten, and knew he was feeling the effects of the alcohol. He wanted her and that infuriated him more because she was the one that had taken away the one thing he had always wanted. A child. He unconsciously took a step back.

Ashland saw the anger and wondered what he had to be mad about. If truth be told, she could care less if he was. She was the one that should be mad. She was the one that was left alone, scared and pregnant. She was the one that went through a miscarriage and had to suffer through her mother's verbal abuse at what they had done. All those broken promises and lies he had told her. He never even called to check on her. He was nowhere to be found. She went through it all completely alone. Now all of a sudden he comes back into her life asking her 'What happened to us?' Ashland became royally pissed, "I really think it's time for me to leave." She unconsciously grabbed her locket.

Jordan noticed the locket once again, and then before Ashland could turn to leave he leaned down and kissed her. She tried to pull away but he grabbed her shoulders and deepened the kiss. She felt so weak she had to put her arms around his neck for support. She was overwhelmed by the arousal he awakened in her. She knew she couldn't make him stop even if she wanted to, which she didn't.

Jordan hugged her tighter against him, kissing her with all the frustration that he had felt over the years. Jordan knew his control was slipping, but it felt so good having her back in his arms. He was surprised at the way his body responded to hers, he'd never felt an attraction this strong before. His chest constricted as she molded her body to his, *God, do I still love her?* He wondered, and then decided it was only because it has

been a while since he'd been with a woman, his body was just
starving for a release. Jordan did not want to lose complete
control so he tried to pull away.

Ashland felt Jordan's manhood pressed hard against her
and got lost in the moment, she could not let him go, she had
not felt this good in a very long time. She deepened the kiss,
moaning as she pressed her body even closer against him while
unbuttoning his shirt. Jordan was lost. He slipped his hand
under her shirt caressing her swollen breast causing her nipples
to immediately become hard and erect. Jordan pulled her shirt
over her head exposing a green lace bra. He kissed her softly on
her lips as he unsnapped it. "God you're beautiful," he said as
he took one erect nipple into his mouth. Ashland moaned and
was lost beyond words. He slowly caressed her back and
stomach as he kissed her other breast, making hot trails as he
began to kiss her stomach while unfastening her jeans. He
caressed and squeezed her buttocks as he pulled them down.
Ashland moaned helplessly as she ran her hands through his
thick hair.

Ashland stepped out of her jeans standing only in a pair
of green lace panties. Jordan closed his eyes and moaned. She
pulled him up to kiss him again. She noticed how hard and
muscular his chest and stomach was. His chest was covered
with jet-black hairs, which thinned out on his stomach
disappearing beneath his black trousers. She moaned kissing his
chest, rubbing his hard muscles as she began unfastening his
trousers, she realized she wanted and needed to feel the man
that Jordan had become.

Jordan's trousers dropped to the floor and he stepped out
of them while Ashland kissed and caressed his stomach. She
pulled down his boxers lightly kissing and massaging his
throbbing erection. *Oh my god*, she thought to herself, *he has
really grown.* He pulled her up to kiss her once again as he
removed her panties rubbing between her legs. He could not
wait any longer. He picked her up to lay her on the lounge chair
and leaned down to kiss her softly between her legs, as he raised
up to enter her slowly, taking her breath away with each stroke.

He could not remember ever feeling this good as they made love on the balcony.

Afterwards when reality sat in, neither spoke, they just stood and dressed. Jordan reached over to softly caress the side of her face as he kissed her on the forehead. Ashland only looked briefly up at him then she quickly left.

Ashland's phone was ringing as soon as she walked through the front door of her house. It was Jordan. She let the machine answer, "Ashland, I'm sorry." There was silence. "It should not have happened, I'm sorry." Then she heard the click of his phone.

"You're damn right it shouldn't have happened," she said as she went to take a long hot shower. She laid on her bed and tried to sleep but it was too early and all she kept thinking about what had happened on his balcony, being with him and against his body had never felt so good. Making love to Jordan was scary. She knew she could easily fall in love with him all over again, a part of her even felt as if she still loved him. She was angry with herself for wanting him the way she did. "Why can't I just get over him?" She yelled as she hit the pillow with her fist. She had never felt that way for any other man, not even Nick. One minute Jordan made her so angry, she could not think straight, the next she was ripping his clothes off. Suddenly, she sat up. She was so caught up with the feeling that she didn't even ask him to use protection. She grabbed her locket and laid back down curled her legs up for the longest time before she fell asleep.

Jordan sat on the balcony after trying to call and apologize to Ashland. He could not figure out what the hell came over him, but seeing that locket he had given her all those years ago did something to him. He could not explain it. He really wasn't sorry he kissed her; he was only trying to get a response from her. To make her talk, yell or even scream at him, anything except standing there saying nothing. He didn't expect things to turn out the way they did, but they had made love and he didn't regret it one bit. He wondered irritably how one person made him so angry then so excited to the point where he would lose all self-control within minutes. She had felt good, too good to be exact. He closed his eyes but all he could see was the image of what had just happened between them.

Jordan stood up and paced. He was irritated that she could still provoke feelings in him. Irritated that he had gotten so caught up in the moment he didn't bother to put on a condom. It would be just his luck to get her pregnant again. *She'd probably abort this one too*, he thought ironically to himself. He angrily thought how careless they were once again, but this time they were old enough to know better. He poured another drink, straight, no ice.

Chapter Four

Ashland woke up early Monday morning so she could check in with her crew at the complex, then leave before Jordan arrived. He unfortunately was the first person she ran into. They completely ignored each other.

The next four weeks went by relatively fast. Ashland kept extremely busy and Jordan kept himself tied up with meetings and paperwork sometimes until late hours into the night. They never saw each other. The fifth week Tylen Alexander arrived in town on a Friday afternoon. He tried calling Jordan's cell, but each and every time he was sent straight to his voice mail. When he called the office, he was informed that Jordan would be in meetings all day. Tylen was annoyed to say the least.

When Tylen arrived at the complex, he was more than impressed. It was the same as the others but this one had a little extra here and there. He liked it, thinking that maybe the other buildings needed a few changes also. He saw a group of people standing by a water fountain and wondered if they were Ashland's employees. When he walked up everyone became immediately quiet and just stared at him. He was used to that because Jordan was a younger version of himself everything was the same except their eye color.

"Excuse me," he asked. "Can someone tell me where I may find Miss Kendrix?"

They looked as if they didn't have any idea who that was. Then one young man said, "Oh Ashland? Yeah she's over at the Estates today."

"Would that be, Mr. Alexander's' Estate?" Tylen questioned.

"Yes sir." The man answered.

"Thank you, young man," Tylen nodded then walked off, now he was getting somewhere.

Tylen was driving through the gates then said, "Well, well, well my boy. I couldn't have done better myself." He was very impressed. There were a few cars out front, but he hoped one of them belonged to Ashland. Tylen thought Jordan's house was magnificent as he searched the rooms looking for Ashland. He had almost given up looking for her until he came to the study and saw a woman through the double doors on the balcony. Even though her back was facing him, he knew it was her.

Ashland turned when she heard someone approaching and prayed it wasn't Jordan, his sudden appearance had brought back too many memories. She was frustrated and had been thinking how stupid she was for having unprotected sex with him again after all that has happened between them. "Grandfather Tylen?" She asked, then smiling giving him a warm hug. "You look wonderful. You haven't aged a day." She said sincerely.

"And you, my sweet kitten, have grown up to be an extremely beautiful woman." Tylen smiled thinking Ashland may just be decorating her own home. Then he noticed she looked as if she had been crying all night long, and wondered what his grandson had done now.

Ashland knew her eyes were red from stress and lack of sleep, so she smiled brightly, "I love being outside but I tell you, all this pollen kills me at times."

"Yeah the pollen is pretty bad down here." Tylen stated, but not fooled. He would talk to Jordan when he got home.

"Would you like a tour? I can show you everything I've done so far," she said with excitement. Decorating was her passion and it was easy to tell through her voice.

Tylen smiled, "Lead the way, my dear." Ashland was the granddaughter he never had.

Jordan arrived home a little after eight o'clock. He noticed Ashland's car and a rental car parked out front. That was strange because after what had happened between them, Ashland was always gone before he got home. He was tired from lack of sleep and didn't feel like being bothered with anything or anyone else today. He was going to find out why the hell she was still here this time of night.

Jordan heard soft music and Ashland's laughter coming

from the Sun Room as soon as he entered the house. The closer
he came to the room he heard a muffled male voice then more
laughter. Jordan was surprised at the anger and jealously he
suddenly felt, and thought *this had better not be what I think it
is, especially in my own home or so help him.* Jordan walked in
the room with his face void of any kind of expression.

"Well it's about time you made it home. I've been
talking this poor child to death waiting on you." Tylen joked.

"Grandfather" He walked across the room to fix a drink
deliberately ignoring Ashland. He was angry with himself for
being jealous. "If you had called to let me know you were
coming I would have been here when you arrived." He said
irritably.

Ashland stood to leave. She knew she was the cause of
his displeasure. "It's late, I'd better be going," she told him.

Jordan didn't say a word he only brought his glass up to
his lips and took a long swallow, his face was still void of any
emotion.

"Jordan, don't be so rude. What has gotten into you,
boy?" Tylen snapped.

Ashland went over and hugged Tylen, "I really enjoyed
your company tonight. Goodnight."

"Goodnight, kitten," Tylen said crossing his legs.
"Jordan be a gentleman and walk her out to her car. It's late."

Jordan only raised an eyebrow.

"Really it's ok I know my way. Thanks." Ashland said
walking out the room.

"Nonsense, Jordan." Tylen raised his eyebrow, daring
him to say something.

Jordan put his glass down and walked out with Ashland.

"You don't really have to," she said when she thought
Tylen couldn't hear.

"But I do. I would get no rest tonight if I don't." Jordan
laughed.

Ashland noticed he sounded tired. She looked over at
him to see if she could read his expression. She couldn't but he
seemed a little more relaxed. When they got to her car, she

looked up at him then regretted it. His eyes had soften, "Goodnight Ashland."

"Goodnight Jordan" She forced herself to get into the car.

She still wanted him. He still wanted her. He shut her door, then stepped back and watched her as she drove away, then rejoined his grandfather inside.

"Well Jordan, catch me up on what's been going on." Tylen said sipping his drink.

For the next hour, Jordan brought him up to date on the process of the company. "As you can tell everything is going along smoothly. Now grandfather, tell me why are you here? Do you not find me capable of starting up this company?" Jordan asked.

"Jordan, I have no doubt in my mind that you can do it. To be honest, probably better than me, even. However, I have been calling you for over a week and I am sick and tired of listening to your voicemail. Do you ever check that damn thing?"

Jordan poured himself another drink, "Want another?" Tylen held out his glass and smiled as he sat studying his only grandchild. "She's getting to you, isn't she?"

Jordan could feel himself getting irritated but knew better than to let his grandfather see. "Who?" Jordan asked casually.

"Don't be coy with me boy. You know who." Tylen said frowning.

"I'm not really in the mood to discuss Ashland." Jordan said quietly.

After Jordan didn't say anything else, Tylen sat back and thought for a minute. He didn't want to see Jordan the way he was when he was forced to leave Ashland all those years ago. Unfortunately, he could see signs that he was shutting himself off from everything except work. He would not allow that to happen again.

"She turned out to be very beautiful, didn't she?" Tylen stated.

Jordan didn't respond so he kept talking.

"She's really good at what she does. I'm thinking about asking her to redo the corporate office." Tylen continued.

Jordan stood up to look out the window.

Tylen chose his next words carefully, "I'm surprised she doesn't have a husband, but then again, I'm sure it won't be long. A smart beautiful woman such as herself doesn't stay single for too long." Then he added, "I wouldn't be surprised if that Nick fellow, oh what is his name. Oh yeah, Balinsky. Balinsky's Fine Jewelry." Tylen paused and took a sip from his glass for effect. "Like I said, I wouldn't be surprised if he hasn't come back into the picture. Yet, I remember reading an article about the two of them dating some years ago, still remained close friends I heard. A very hot item they were."

Jordan turned around then asked with a solemn expression, "Is there a point to this?"

"No point just an old man talking." Tylen smiled to himself.

"Since there is no point I'm very tired and I'm going to bed. I'm sure *Kitten* has shown you where the rooms are. Goodnight grandfather."

"Goodnight my boy." Tylen said cheerfully as Jordan left the room. I doubt he sleeps well tonight, he thought. "I think I'm going to stick around for a while. It's going to be fun watching the two of them." He said out loud laughing. He finished his drink then headed to bed.

When Jordan got to his rooms, he knew sleep would not come easy, so he decided to stay in the sitting area for a while. Finally admitting to himself, he missed Ashland. Then thought he had never felt so much jealousy before until he walked through his front door and heard Ashland laughing, thinking she was entertaining another man. However, hearing his grandfather talk about a relationship that she had, tore away at him even more. Just the idea of someone else being with her and touching, her rubbed his nerves raw. His grandfather was right, Ashland wouldn't be single for too long and that really aggravated him, which made him begin to question himself for even coming to Georgia. He couldn't relax so he decided he needed to get out of the house for a while.

* * *

After leaving Jordan's house Ashland went home and showered but she was restless so she called Kayla and they decided to meet at Misty's Bar and Grill for drinks. It had been a long time since they had been out together.

"Hey girl, over here," Kayla said from a table that had a panoramic view of everyone who came and went, but was also private enough to have a conversation at ease.

"Thanks for meeting me tonight. I really needed someone to talk to," Ashland said sitting down.

"Girl please, I've been waiting on you to call me. I knew something's been up with you, but I know how you are about your private affairs." Kayla took a swallow of her drink. "Anyways, I wasn't about to let you fire my ass for being nosey." Kayla added jokingly.

Ashland loved Kayla like a sister. She had a way of making people laugh and forget about their own problems even when things were not going right in her own life.

"What are you drinking, a margarita?" Ashland asked while motioning for a server.

"Yes, with an extra shot of tequila," Kayla informed her.

"Hi." Ashland said to the server, "Can I get a margarita with an extra double shot of   Tequila? Oh, and bring her another please." After the server left, Ashland said, "I probably need a triple." They both laughed.

"OK Ashland, I've got to run to the ladies room before my bladder explodes. Be right back." When Kayla returned Ashland was sipping her drink and watching a couple argued over by the bar. "Alright now, what's going on, and don't leave anything out," Kayla asked in a serious tone bringing Ashland's attention away from the couple. Three margaritas later Ashland told Kayla all about Jordan, AKA Mr. Whitfield.

"Wow, do you realize you could have gotten pregnant? Damn girl how are you gonna forget about safe sex like that?" For the first time Kayla was concerned. She didn't want to ask

Ashland while she was obviously upset, but that was something a woman needed to think about.

"I know. I've actually been too scared to think about it. I don't have any reason to use birth control since I hadn't been messing around with anyone," Ashland said slowly.

"Well now. Tymera's been bugging me about a baby sister. This is even better; Auntie Ashland can go through all those moods swings and weight gain." Kayla laughed jokingly. "Girl please don't look like that you know I'm only kidding. Everything will be Ok this time." Kayla paused for a moment then added with a wink, "Ashland, you've got me in your corner this go round." Kayla smiled softly. "You know you two need to talk. After listening to everything, not once did you mention anything about his reasons for never calling you."

Ashland knew Kayla was right and it was about time she faced what was really bothering her, which was how Jordan had abandoned her when she needed him the most.

A nice looking dark skinned man came up to the table and asked Kayla to dance.

"Be right back, girl," Kayla said smiling.

Ashland smiled; glad her friend was having a good time tonight. Ashland was surprised Kayla had agreed to dance, because after DeShun dogged her out, she rarely gave men her time. Ashland also smiled because Kayla had used her same words on her.

Chapter Five

When Kayla got home that night, she felt good. She sat down on the sofa and turned the TV on flipping through the channels, when she noticed her answer machine flashing. She figured it was her mom, since she insisted the kids spend time with her this weekend, she pressed play, "Kayla baby, call me." There was no mistaking his voice. She sat back on the sofa and thought about a time that seemed so far away.

Nine Years ago Kayla was crying uncontrollably, frustrated and feeling an overwhelming sense of helplessness, Kayla asked, "God, what have I done to deserve this?" She sat in the dark thinking about her life, wondering why everything seemed to be happening to her. All of a sudden she laughed, "Who really gives a fuck, anyways?" Wiping the tears from her eyes, she went to the bathroom to wash her face. Looking in the mirror, she analyzed her facial features. Her skin was very smooth, clear and even tone. She had a perfect oval face. Of course, it was too long, she thought. The front door opened, "Asshole," she said to herself. Drying her face off, she looked at her reflection one last time.

"Hey baby, what's up?" Deshun said.

Standing in the doorway, she admired his handsome face. He was handsome all right, until she got to know him, then she thought to herself how his nasty attitude made him very unappealing, gradually his rugged good looks seemed to disappear. He was like water from a faucet, hot one minute, and cold the next. On his worse days, he was like an uncontrollable river running wild. To put it simply, he had a Dr. Jekyll and Mr. Hyde personality, just got to play it by ear. She walked right by him without saying a word as he tried to kiss her. He followed her to the living room and sat next to her on the sofa, while flipped through the channels on the television.

"You act like you don't love me anymore. What's wrong? You don't love me no more?"

Looking him dead in his eyes, she said, "Not like I used to. I'm tired. DeShun, I think we need a break from each other."

Leaning back he said, "I guess you've met somebody else you want to get with. Is that what this is about?"

Inhaling deeply she shakes her head, "No, I just need to be alone for a while. I can't handle your mood swings anymore. I'm sick of you coming home drunk starting arguments and fights." Shaking her head, she added, "I bet you don't even remember. Do you?"

Reaching over he tried to kiss her, but she turned her head away and yelled, "Get away from me!"

Grabbing her neck, seemingly applied just enough pressure to show her he was serious, "You gonna make me fucking kill you!" Releasing her he went to get a beer from the refrigerator, and ignored her the rest of the evening. If only he knew how glad she was deep down inside. She was truly amazed by how one person could make her harbor so much hatred.

Lying in bed, she closed her eyes trying not to cry, "Dear God, please help me." She turned over and fell asleep. She started dreaming that she was floating, melting away with so much pleasure, very erotic, very sweet, hot and warm sensations all over her body. She opened her eyes slowly to find DeShun kissing her breast, rubbing her between her legs until she became excited with expectation. He entered her and suddenly came. She lay there watching in disbelief as he stood to pull up his boxers, and then turned on the TV.

"Aren't you going to finish what you started?" Kayla asked softly.

He turned from the TV and said, "You finish it," as he rubbed her leg for a second. "I'm tired," he said, smashing her hopes.

Turning over, she closed her eyes and prayed sleep would come fast. Hurt and frustrated, she thought what a selfish bastard.

She woke up to the sound of the telephone. She lay there listening to him whisper, "I'll call you later, after she leaves."

She closed her eyes and pretended to be asleep. She felt him get up out of the bed and listened as he left the room. A few minutes later, he came and sat at the foot of the bed and turned on the TV. She pretended to wake up, "What time is it?" she asked.

While lighting a cigarette he said, "Seven"

She got up to get a glass of water from the kitchen. She looked at the caller ID as she passed by it. No calls, it figured.

"Kayla baby, bring me a beer," He yelled through the house."

She went back to the bedroom, sat on the bed and drank her water.

"Where's my beer?"

She looked at him with confusion on her face, "What beer?"

Taking the last puff from his cigarette, "The one I asked you to get, damn it!"

Looking innocent, she responded, "I didn't hear you."

Lighting another cigarette he cursed, "You're a god damn lie, but that's alright, I'll get it my damn self."

Standing up she walked towards the door, stopped and turned to face him, letting all her hatred show as she said slowly with venom dripping from each word precisely spoken, "Tell your fucking BITCH to get you a beer." She left the room without waiting for a response.

After taking a long hot relaxing bath, Kayla lay on the sofa and turned on the radio. The phone rang and the clock read eight thirty. "Hello" she answered. All she heard was silence again, "Hello?" She thought, *I'm sick of this shit, all these hang up calls.*

Suddenly the female on the other end said, "I'm sorry I have the wrong number."

Kayla laughed, "Who are you trying to call?"

The female hesitated for a split second, "Larry"

Kayla took a deep breath, "Oh yeah. What number did you call?"

The female hung up.

DeShun walked in the room, "Who was that?"

Kayla clicks the phone off, "Wrong number."

He stared at her a few minutes, "You off today?"

Kayla opened the window blinds, "Yep"

He picked up the remote, grabbed a beer from the fridge, and then went to the bedroom. Out of habit, Kayla wrote the number down from the Caller ID. That damn phone. DeShun answered on the first ring. She looked at the called ID it was Leo. He'll be leaving in a few minutes she thought to herself. Sure enough fifteen minutes later Leo blew his horn.

While DeShun was putting on his shoes, he said, "Hey, I'll see you later, I'm going to ride with Leo."

She smiled, "Goodbye DeShun."

Kayla had taken the day off. Actually, she had requested this day off a month ago. This was the day she had marked on her calendar that if things did not change in their relationship, it would end. She packed his bags, called his mom, and asked her if it was all right for her to bring his things to her house. She was tired and drained, both emotionally and physically.

Before leaving her house, she called Ashland, her closest friend, "Can you guys be here in an hour?"

Ashland was quiet for a minute, "Kayla honey, are you Ok?"

Kayla sat down in the chair, "Yea" she answered.

"We'll be there." Ashland said.

Kayla hung up the phone and left. After dropping off DeShun's bags, she went to the hardware store and bought locks, dead bolts and chains for all her doors and windows. Ashland and their friend Nick arrived, along with his friend Benny, who was the locksmith to change all her locks.

"Honey, you sure you're alright?" Ashland asked with concern.

"Yeah girl, I'm fine. Hi Nicky, Benny." She smiled handing him the hardware bags.

"Yeah, you better get started before DeShun get back." Nick laughed thinking how wild and crazy DeShun got at times towards Kayla. He never figured out what Kayla saw in him.

She deserved much better.

In the kitchen, Kayla and Ashland sat at the table.

"Talk to me." Ashland said.

Kayla smiled, "I've just reached my limit. I can't deal with his bullshit anymore. I'm tired of giving all the time without getting anything in return. All he does is take. He doesn't give a damn about me. He disrespects me, talk about me to his family and friends. Just treats me like shit. I deserve better, I've realize that, finally." Kayla sat back and closed her eyes, tears rolled down her cheeks. "He hit me again and he doesn't even remember. And some fucking bitch is calling my god damn house!" She sat quiet for a minute rubbing her face. "I don't know what went wrong between us. All I know is enough is enough."

"It's all going to be okay, you got me in your corner this go around." Ashland said smiling with a wink.

As Kayla and Ashland sat there, they laughed, cried, shared jokes, confessions, regrets, deepest secrets and emotions, while drinking two bottles of wine, a pint of Alize and four wine coolers before Benny finished with all the doors and windows.

"I guess you two didn't save us any." Benny said.

Nick laughed as he went to the refrigerator and got him and Benny a beer. Taking a long sip Nick held up his can, "Damn, DeShun would try to kick my ass if he came home and found me drinking his beer."

Kayla laughed, "Hell I bought the damn beer." Everyone laughed.

Running faster and faster her heart was pounding harder and harder as Kayla ran, surrounded by wooded darkness, it seemed to have been closing in all around her. Someone was chasing her. She ran faster but it was too dark to see where she was going. The pounding feet were getting harder and closer. She ran faster as the terror and fear built within her. She opened her mouth to scream, but nothing came out. Suddenly she awoke sweating and unfocused trying to figure out where she was. She laughed as her surroundings became familiar. She must have passed out on the couch. She jumped when someone started pounding on her door. Damn it's DeShun. Kayla lay back on the couch, very tense, staring up towards the ceiling as DeShun beat on her door. After about five minutes, he gave up and left. Kayla went to the bedroom then crawled into bed. Smiling, she fell asleep. She had the best night's rest in a long time.

Nine years ago DeShun Smoking a cigarette, DeShun flipped through the channels on the television. Looking back at Yazmeen while she lay sprawled across the bed, he wondered why he was still messing around with her. She was pretty enough, but she really didn't want anything out of life except a man. He shook his head and smiled, thinking she really knows how to treat a man. He walked over to the window thinking of Kayla. Damn she would kill me if she knew. He laughed. She would have to find out first and then again, I could talk my way out of it. Laughing, he walked over to the nightstand and poured himself a shot of tequila. There were three knocks on the door. Damn.

He opened it, "Leo what the fuck do you want?"

Leo looked in the room, "Look my girl keeps paging me. It's checkout time. Just tell that bitch you got to go. I don't need no shit tonight. I got to take my girl out tonight, her folks are coming down, damn, I had forgotten. Either I give you a ride or you get your bitch to drop you off. I'm gone in ten." Leo turned and walked off.

Twenty minutes later, they pulled up in DeShun and Kayla's driveway.

"Hit me up tomorrow, dawg. I promised Yazmeen I'd go eat breakfast with her." DeShun lit a cigarette.

"DeShun, why you fuck with that bitch? Kayla is a good girl. Yazmeen ain't shit. Hell, she's fucking Shawn and Dwight. Any bitch that'll fuck two brothers ain't shit. You keep fucking up and Kayla's going to put your ass out." Leo said.

DeShun raised an eyebrow, "How the fuck you gone tell me some shit like that and you doing the same damn thing?"

Leo put his car in park, "Look that bitch is calling your house now, at least I just fuck 'em and leave 'em. They know what's up. I ain't putting no triffling 'ho ahead of my girl. You are fucking up dog."

DeShun smiled, "Aint nothing like a free meal and some good, hot head. Goddamn, Yazmeen make a nigga crazy with all that licking the booty and shit. I like what she do and how she do it." DeShun laughed.

Leo laughed out loud, "Nigga, you crazy. I'll holla at ya tomorrow."

DeShun got out of the car, "Peace my nigga."

Leo drove off.

Kayla was in the bathroom when DeShun got home.

"Hey baby, what's up?" DeShun smiled as he tried to kiss her.

Kayla walked off. He knew she was mad, but he really didn't give a damn. She could be mad he did what he wanted. It was a wasted emotion on her part. Damn, he thought, Leo was right I probably should spend more time with my girl. Kayla was in the living room watching TV. I guess I'll spend quality time with her tonight.

DeShun went and sat next to Kayla on the sofa. Damn, she looks good tonight, considering her eyes were blood red. Too fucking emotional, he thought. She was wearing khaki shorts and a blue low cut t-shirt. Damn, she got some big ole ass pretty thighs, he thought. Make a nigga's dick hard. Her breasts were swollen, I guess it's about time for me to wear it out again; we hadn't had sex in almost two weeks. DeShun leaned over to kiss her, but all he saw was pure hatred.

"You act like you don't love me no more. What's wrong? You don't love me no more?" Damn, he thought, here she goes starting up that bullshit about needing time apart. God damn, no wonder a nigga cheats. DeShun lost his temper when she turned away from him. Fucking bitch, he thought grabbing her neck. It pissed him off even more that she could make him so angry. Fuck her, he thought and went for a beer, so much for quality time, he thought.

Two thirty in the morning, DeShun was still mad at Kayla for turning away from him. She must be fucking another nigga. Anger took over him. He couldn't sleep so he kept drinking. Damn, he thought, why she has to look so good, I bet another nigga is getting my pussy. He started kissing and rubbing her, wanting her to want him. He was angry at the thought of another man being inside of her. He knew he wouldn't last long and didn't care. Let her nigga satisfy her, he came very quickly.

***

Kayla was surprised at how much she enjoyed living alone with her kids. She had even felt free to actually flirt with a few delivery men that came by her job. That was something she was always afraid to do while she was with DeShun, always in fear he would find out and really act a fool on her; besides, she really didn't want anyone else while she had been with him. He just didn't realize what he had when she was his. Now looking back, she was glad that DeShun was no longer in her life, except from being "a sometime" dad. What surprised her the most was that she didn't miss him anymore. She thought, *I guess there really is a limit how much a person could take from another.* She had to admit DeShun really left his mark on her. The next man she would become involved with didn't stand a chance. She knew she wouldn't mean to, but she also knew she has a fear of being used and hurt again. She was determined to move on with her life, in spite of the fact that Deshun was her babies' daddy. She deleted his message.

Chapter Six

Ashland woke up to the telephone ringing she looked over at the clock it was a few minutes past eleven in the morning.

"Hi Ashland, it's Tylen, I'm so sorry to bother you, but I need a favor."

"OK" she said hesitantly not sure what he might ask of her.

"Jordan was in a car accident last night. He's fine, but the doctor says he can't release him unless someone drive him home and will be there with him."

"I don't think-" Tylen cut her off smoothly before she could say no.

"Ashland, I left out early this morning to pick up a friend of mine. I wouldn't ask, but unfortunately, I'm out of town at the moment." He cleared his throat before continuing. "Well anyway I'll be back tonight. I can't tell you how much I would appreciate it if you go pick him up and hang around the house for a while, so I won't worry." Added, when she didn't say anything, "I promise I'll be there as quick as I can."

Ashland sat up in bed. Damn, she thought, this is just what I need. "Sure Tylen."

"Thanks kitten." As Tylen hung up the phone, he smiled to himself. When Jordan had called him, he was glad he had been away from the house, forcing him to reach him on his cell. Now he was on his way to Florida. A few years ago, he had vacationed in the Bahamas and met an extremely beautiful native woman. Although she constantly talked and asked a thousand questions, he still liked her. Her chatter didn't bother him at all in fact he was quite taken with her. She had called him last week to let him know she would be in Florida for about a month visiting relatives. He wanted to spend some time with her, because she had a way that always made him feel good, almost as good as his dear sweet Leola. Tylen smiled sadly, as he thought of his beloved wife. Taking a deep breath, he pushed his thought towards Jordan. He realized Jordan and Ashland needed to work through their problems in order for them to have some closure to the past and move on with their lives. Hopefully, they would find a way to do it together. Tylen couldn't help but smile to himself he knew he wouldn't be back until tomorrow, late sometime.

Ashland dressed with extra care, although she wouldn't admit it, not even to herself, but it was because of Jordan. She convinced herself it was only to make him wait. She thought, *he was in good hands at the hospital.* She smiled. She had fixed herself the way Jordan had once loved to see her, wearing only a touch of make-up. Her thick dark brown golden streaked hair fell gracefully in curls around her face and shoulders. Ashland looked at her reflection once again and smiled. She had never looked better, her jeans fitted her perfectly and her white button up shirt teased her breast provocatively, guaranteed to make a man look twice. Ashland sighed, turning away from her reflection and walked straight out of the house.

At the hospital, it took the nurse about fifteen minutes for her to find out what room Jordan was in, evidently the nurse was new. When Ashland entered his room she found him fully dressed sitting casually on the edge of his bed flirting with a very pretty nurse, she didn't miss the nurse putting a folded piece of paper in Jordan's shirt pocket. *Probably her phone number*, Ashland thought bitterly. She thought that at least Jordan looked fine he only had a small bandage on his forehead.

Jordan looked up surprised to see Ashland, "What are you doing here?" Last night he had been thinking of her, driving too fast, when he'd lost control of his car. Now here she was looking all tempting, which only angered him.

"Your grandfather couldn't make it, so he asked me to come. Is that a problem or would you rather wait for him?" Ashland asked sweetly.

"Where is he?" he asked as if debating whether or not to wait, trying not to stare at her for too long. Then from the corner of his eye he noticed the nurse watching them closely, he wanted her to leave. He turned to the nurse, touching her arm ever so slightly, smiling very sensual.   "Would you please go and get the doctor so I may get my release papers."

"Of course," the nurse said, leaving the room hoping this woman was no importance to him.

"So tell me, Ashland, how long would I have to wait?" he asked carelessly, all charm seemed to have left with the nurse.

"Well Jordan, he seemed to have left town, he'll be back tonight," she said. She had walked to look out the window to hide her face, because when Jordan touched the nurse she became surprisingly pissed, which Ashland knew it was nothing but straight jealousy.

"Mr. Alexander, I see you're all dressed and ready to go." The doctor smiled looking curiously at Ashland, "Hi, I'm Dr. Hayden. As I told Mr. Alexander before, I cannot release him unless someone will be here to drive him home and be home with him throughout the weekend. He looks good, but you never know. Am I right to presume that person is you?"

Ashland smiled brightly only glancing slightly at the nurse, "Well sort of, I'm just a family friend, I'll be there only until they arrive. I'm sure you realized how difficult he can be at times, so I promised his grandfather I would try to take care of him until he arrives." Then she added, "He's not going to pass out on me, is he?" She smiled, flirting ever so slightly. The doctor noticed, the nurse smiled upon hearing his family would be taking care of him and Jordan only frowned.

"I would hope not Mrs.?" He inquired.

"Just call me Ashland," she answered softly.

The doctor cleared his throat as he looked down and noticed she wasn't wearing a ring, "Well Ashland, just make sure his family knows he needs to get plenty of rest and to take it easy for the rest of the weekend." Then he turned to Jordan, "I would like for you to make a follow up appointment with your doctor. I went ahead and filled your prescription. Just follow all instructions on the enclosed papers. If you should have any severe headaches, nausea or vomiting, don't hesitate to come back here to be checked out immediately." He handed Jordan a bag and his release papers.

Ashland knew Jordan would not make a follow-up appointment, so before the doctor could leave the room Ashland asked Jordan, "You do have a regular doctor, don't you?" She knew when they were younger he would complain when his grandfather made him go for check ups. He had told her once how he hated hospitals and wasn't too fond of doctors, although he never told her why. The typical man she only thought, so she smiled as Dr. Hayden turned and waited on Jordan's answer.

"No" Jordan said stiffly.

"In that case Mr. Alexander I'll expect to see you Monday. I'll be in my office all day. I'll have my nurse call you with a time." He smiled looking at Ashland for a moment, and then left the room.

"Jordan, are you ready to go?" Ashland asked.

The nurse had a wheel chair waiting patiently for Jordan to sit in. The look he gave her forced her quickly apologize, "I'm sorry, but it's hospital policy."

"I'll go pull the car around front while you get situated." Ashland laughed as she left the room.

When they arrived at his house Jordan said, "I appreciate the ride, but I think I'll be ok from here."

"I told your grandfather I would stay until he arrived." She snapped.

"Suit yourself." Jordan said while unlocking his front door. "I'm going up stairs to rest for a while. I'm sure you know your way around, so make yourself at home." He put his bag and papers down on the table then left her standing in the foyer.

Jordan was exhausted and his head was killing him, he had only about two hours of sleep within forty-eight hours, but he had been determined to get out of that hospital. It had taken a lot out of him by just sitting up laughing and joking with that nurse for so long, but knew that he had to look as if nothing was wrong with him. He would never forget when his grandmother passed; he was only eight years old. He had been standing in the doorway of her room watching tubes running from her body as she took her last breath. An eerie feeling and a chill swept over him. He had cried as he watched his grandfather cry while rocking his beloved grandmother. That was the first and only time he saw his grandfather cry. On the few occasions, he had to go to a hospital a chill always came over him. He lay down and closed his eyes.

Ashland watched as Jordan made his way slowly up the stairs. Then she took his prescription out of the bag to read the instructions. She wondered if he was in pain, *it would probably serve his ass right,* she thought of the nurse and wondered if Jordan would call her. She laughed at herself, *why should I care if he calls or not,* she thought then began to read the bottle out loud, "Take two immediately then one every four hours as needed. Take with food." She went to the kitchen to make him a light lunch.

Ashland knocked softly on his bedroom door carrying a tray. After about a minute she opened the door walking through his sitting area, when his bed came to view, she stopped suddenly and asked herself, *why am I really here?* Jordan was lying on his back, shirt unbuttoned with his head facing the wall. He looked so good and vulnerable that she walked over and sat his food tray on his night table, lightly touched his hair. He had forgotten to take off his shoes so she began taking them off.

"What are you doing?" Jordan asked frowning.

"Shush, go back to sleep." Ashland said angrily at the feelings that stirred in her as she got his shoes off.

He touched her back then said, "Lay with me." He looked slightly dazed.

"Does your head hurt?" she asked.

"Yeah" He responded.

"Since you're awake, sit up for a minute," she said

"I'm too tired, just let me get some rest," he said

She got a little irritated because he wouldn't sit up to eat so he could take his medicine. She thought about him and for the life of her, she never could remember him like this not even when he had been sick, he had always seemed so strong to her. She began to worry, just a little. "Come on Jordan sit up just for a minute."

He took a slow deep breath then slowly sat up, "Ok, now what?" He asked.

Ashland could tell he was angry but she ignored it and asked softly, "I made you something special. You wanna taste it?"

"Not really" he said carelessly then added as he tried to lay back down, "What I wanna do is go to sleep."

Ashland grabbed the back of his neck, bringing the cup of broth to his lips, "Drink please."

He took a deep breath to control his irritation and closed his eyes again.

Ashland said a little softer, "Just a little bit Jordan. Dang it's just a simple request."

He took the cup from her and drank slowly. When he finished almost all, she gave him his pain pills.

"Can I go back to sleep now?" He asked irritably while looking totally exhausted.

"By all means." she said satisfied.

Ashland took the dishes to the kitchen and washed up the dishes. After picking up odds and ends throughout the house, she went into the den to read then watch television. She realized it was almost nine at night and Jordan had not stirred and Tylen still had not made it home. She decided to check on Jordan. He was fast asleep, lying on his side, something stirred once again inside of her that made her lie down beside him. She lightly stroked his cheek then closed her eyes and imagined what things could have been like between them if her mother had never interfered with them. She fell asleep and slept peacefully all that night.

Chapter Seven

The next morning when Ashland woke up, she was snuggled under Jordan. Embarrassment flooded her. His skin was very hot, she noticed, which made her forget her embarrassment, thought he was feverish, and needed to take his medicine, so she tried to get up. He pulled her back closer to him. "Don't go yet. Stay a little longer," he whispered.

"But you're so hot I'll go fix you something to eat so you can take your medicine."

"I'm not sick, Ashland," Jordan said while brushing his thumb against her breast as he pulled her closer to his body.

"Oh" was all she said as she felt his manhood pressed firmly against her butt. He laughed softly as he kissed the back of her neck.

"What time is it?" She asked breathless, feeling herself becoming extremely hot.

"I don't know, about six thirty I guess." Jordan whispered huskily.

Ashland sat up so fast he didn't have time to grab her, "Oh my god. Your grandfather," was all she said as she ran from the room.

Jordan had been awake for hours just holding Ashland as she slept. It was nice he thought as he smiled then rolled over slowly on his back, all his muscles seemed to be sore. He suddenly laughed, because knowing his grandfather it would probably be a while before he actually returned. He got up and took a much-needed shower.

Jordan stood in the doorway of the kitchen as Ashland placed his food on a tray, "You won't be needing that tray."

"Don't sneak up on me like that." She snapped.

Jordan smiled sitting down at the table and asked, "Did you sleep well last night?"

Ashland turned to walk away as embarrassment and anger once again began eating away at her for falling asleep in his bed.

Jordan grabbed her, forcing her to sit on his lap as he kissed her neck. "Hey I'm not complaining. You just should have woke me up." Jordan said laughing.

Ashland wiggled free, "Jordan you need to eat." She left the room then returned with his medicine bottle. She took two pills out handing them to him.

"What's this for?" he asked with a raised eyebrow.

"Jordan, don't start. Just take the medicine please, after you eat."

He didn't say anything for a minute, then asked, "You're not eating?"

"Jordan, you know I never eat this early."

"Oh yeah, I almost forgot."

Then she asked, "Is Tylen here?"

"I don't know. I seriously doubt it, though. He would be up and about long before now. You didn't run into him in the hallways, did you?" He teased.

"Very funny," she said. After a moment she added, "I'm going to take a shower in the guest room."

He smiled, "Do you want me to wash your back?"

"No," she said walking off.

Ashland realized after getting out of the shower, she had nothing to wear, so she borrowed a T-shirt and a pair of shorts from Jordan while she started the washing machine. She found Jordan in the study reading some papers.

"I thought the doctor told you to rest and relax?" She asked.

"Don't you look nice," he said smiling.

She ignored him. She thought she looked funny. He thought she looked sexy.

"Do you have anything on up under that?" Jordan asked teasingly. Ashland looked so shocked he couldn't help laughing. "Grandfather called while you were in the shower, he should be here tonight to relieve you of your duties of baby sitting me," he joked.

Ashland stood up to look at his many volumes of books. "Have you read all of these?" She asked.

"Yes," he answered leaning back in his chair as he studied her.

She touched a few books then asked nervously, "Why didn't you ever call me?"

Jordan was about to ask her what she was talking about, but something made him stop and think.

Ashland turned around after she didn't get a response from him. "Jordan?" She grabbed her locket unconsciously.

Jordan noticed the necklace once again and stood up to open the balcony doors. He needed some fresh air. He was a little confused as to her question, but thought this is the moment of truth. Standing in the doorway looking outside he said, "I did call you. I called you more times than I care to remember." He suddenly turned around looking at her hard and dangerous, she took a step back, "The question is, why did you decide to have an abortion? Your mother told me everything," he said so low, she thought she'd heard him wrong.

"What? My what?" Was all she could say.

He took a step forward and said angrily, "You heard me. I asked why did you kill our baby?"

"Kill what?" Ashland was confused, and then became angry with him all over again for all the pain she'd endured. "I was pregnant and alone and not once did you call me." She said hatefully. "I needed you so bad Jordan" She was so angry and hurt she had to fight tears that threatened to fall, "And not one time did you call or write." She jerked the locket from her neck and threw it at him. "I hate you." She said low and menacingly. "I really hate you. And for your information I had a miscarriage six weeks after you left me, you Bastard!" She left the room angrily, slamming the door on her way out.

It really didn't dawn on Ashland what Jordan had said until she got in her car. "Your mother told me everything." The words kept echoing in her head. She had to know. She got her cell phone from the dashboard and called her mother. "Hi daddy. Is mother in?" she asked quietly.

"No baby she's not, is everything alright?" Her father asked with concern in his voice.

"Daddy, no everything is not alright," she said. "Tell me something, did mother tell Jordan that I had an abortion? I know you know the truth." There was only silence. "Daddy please," she begged brokenly.

Marcus couldn't take it, after all these years the guilt was unbearable at times, watching his only child suffer because of one simple mistake. Now listening to his baby beg him for the truth, he wished to God that he had put a stop to all the lies. "I tried to get her not to, but she insisted it was all for the best. It was the only way she could get him to stop calling so much. I'm so-"

Ashland hung up the phone angrily, she felt alone, lost and most of all betrayed. She didn't know how long she was in the car before Jordan came to get her. Jordan opened the car door but she didn't move. "My mother lied to me. She always told me I was a fool for wasting my time on you." She looked up at Jordan with hurt filled eyes. "Why?"

Jordan bent down to her level grabbing her hands he couldn't stand to see her like this. He was just as confused as she was, "I don't know."

Ashland pulled down the sun visor and looked at herself in the mirror, then laughed. "I look a hot mess."

"Yes you do." He pulled her out of the car, "Let's go inside before someone actually sees you like this," he said jokingly. She smiled.

Ashland scrubbed her face clean then went to the laundry room, unconsciously reached for her necklace, but it wasn't there. She leaned against the wall for support. The locket had become a comfort to her all these years. It made her remember the love her and Jordan had once shared, a precious time in her life that was so pure and special that she knew everything was going to be all right. A time no one could ever touch or take away. Jordan had loved her and she loved him, it was that rare, unconditional love that always made everything ok. And that made the locket a reminder to guard her heart from falling so hard in love again.

Ashland sat on the floor, and thought how he had even

called her as he promised; to think all these years her parents had allowed her to think otherwise. She wasn't surprised at her mother, but it hurt so bad to find out her father had lied and allowed her to think Jordan never called or cared. They had allowed Jordan to think she'd aborted their baby. Everything was different now. She didn't even have the locket to hold onto. She had thrown it in Jordan's face. Although she knew Jordan wanted her, it was only the way a man lusts for a woman. She wanted her Jordan back. Ashland put her head on her knees and just sat until the buzzer went off on the dryer. She didn't know what time it was or how long she had been in the laundry room.

Ashland heard voices coming from the Sun Room. Tylen was home. She didn't feel like socializing, so she decided to speak then make a quick exit before anyone had time to stop her. Ashland took a deep breath then entered the room. Jordan looked up and smiled.

Tylen walked over to hug her, "Ashland, hey kitten, thank you so very much for taking care of Jordan." He winked, kissing her on the cheek. "Now," When he turned her around she was face to face with a very beautiful woman, this is my friend Megan. Megan this here is Ashland, the closest thing I've ever had to a granddaughter." When Megan stood up and hugged Ashland. Ashland knew then she wasn't leaving anytime soon.

Everyone was laughing and talking, so she didn't have time to think of anything that had happened earlier. Jordan was quiet. She stood up to fix herself a drink and Jordan walked to stand beside her then asked, "Are you ok?"

Ashland nodded yes, "Does your head hurt? Jordan do you really think you should be drinking?"

"I'm fine," Jordan answered, kissing her forehead softly before he went back to the sofa to listen to Megan and his grandfather laugh and talk.

Ashland decided she didn't want a drink after all, Jordan's kiss and the attraction she felt for him only added more confusion to the situation. "I think I'd better be going. I have a lot of things to take care of before getting home today," she said as she hugged Tylen and Megan as Jordan stood to walk her out. They both were so caught in their own thoughts that neither said a word, she just got in her car and left.

Jordan watched as she drove away. He was confused as to why her mother had felt compelled to lie. Ashland didn't have an abortion he was actually relieved to know this. *Damn*, he thought, *she never even knew about me ever calling her.* This really changed everything.

Tylen and Megan were not in the Sun Room when he returned. Good, he thought. He needed to be alone. He went straight to his study and sat at his desk. He leaned back in his chair thinking of everything that happened today. His head was hurting. He reached in his pocket and pulled out the locket that Ashland had carelessly thrown at him. When she said, she hated him that hurt worst than being hit physically. He opened the locket and read out loud, "I Love you. I'll be back." The locket looked almost as good as the day he'd given it to her. He closed his eyes leaning back against the chair.

"What is going on around here? I can't leave the two of you alone for a day. What in the world did you do? The day I arrived she'd been crying on that damn balcony and tonight she looked upset," Tylen said walking into the room.

Jordan didn't say anything he only walked over to look out the balcony door, squeezing the locket tight before dropping it in his pocket. Wondering why she'd been crying that day.

Tylen poured himself a drink then sat down knowing Jordan would talk in his own time.

After a few minutes Jordan spoke, "I found out today Ashland didn't have an abortion." Jordan turned around his face expressionless, "She never even knew about me calling her."

Tylen thought sadly about all that had taken place and knew it was time to tell Jordan Bianca's true reasons for her disapproval of his relationship with Ashland. "Bianca and I knew each other before you and Ashland met. We had an affair," Jordan looked utterly shocked as Tylen continued to talk, "I didn't mean for it to happen but it did. Then Bianca started calling and coming to the office unannounced, she actually thought I was going to leave your grandmother." He shook his head sadly, "Well one day your grandmother found out, and I saw how much I had hurt her, and so I ended it right away. I am so ashamed of what I did." He closed his eyes and shook his head for a moment then continued, "Bianca was too young to begin with, she was only about nineteen and I was thirty six at that time. My goodness your mother was seventeen, Bianca was young enough to be my daughter." He took a long swallow of his drink, "Bianca was also engaged to Marcus at the time. Bianca was too beautiful, but also too controlling and outspoken; regretfully she is not, shall we say a very pleasant person."

Jordan thought, *No she's the ultimate bitch, is what she is.* No matter how hard he tried, he would never be able to picture his grandfather and Ashland mother together.

Tylen continued to talk, "Bianca always managed to get what she wanted one way or another, no matter the cost or consequences, but I was the one thing she never could get. I honestly do not see how Marcus has made it all these years." Tylen took another swallow from his glass. "At first, I was a little concerned when you started showing interest in Ashland all those years ago. I knew how Bianca was, but after she never said anything about the two of you, I became relaxed with your relationship. I've always thought that Ashland was the one for you. Then after Ashland became pregnant, Bianca came to my office and told me since she wasn't good enough for me, then her daughter wasn't good enough for my grandson. She actually had the nerve to threaten to have you locked up, saying she would find any and every loophole in the system to ruin you. Through you, she'd hurt me, by having your whole life, which meant any and everything you ever touched or any happiness she thought you have, would be ruined if I didn't keep you away from Ashland. Then later Marcus called me to come over to their house to discuss the situation. I wasn't there for too long before Bianca had pissed me off all over again so that's when I convinced you to start your internship overseas." Tylen took a sip from his glass.

"After Ashland turned twenty-one I tried to arrange a meeting between the two of you, but all the lies had you both filled with too much hurt, anger and disappointment. Therefore, I did what I thought I should, I kept in touch with Ashland myself. She was the one that was completely alone after she left home. At least I was there for you," Tylen said.

Jordan opened the doors. He needed fresh air. He felt nauseous, because for a brief moment he thought his grandfather was going to say Ashland was his daughter, but he wasn't born until his mother was nineteen. He was three years older than Ashland. Everything was happening too fast. He thought about all those wasted years. All that anger he felt toward Ashland was not even justified, her mother had caused so much pain. And to think his grandfather had actually slept with Bianca. Jordan didn't want to think any more, his head was throbbing painfully. He needed to take some pain pills but knew he couldn't since he'd been drinking. He knew then he should have listened to Ashland. "Grandfather, I'm rather tired. I think I'll turn in for the night," Jordan said before he left the room.
* * *

As soon as Ashland got home, she called Kayla. "Hey girl, I need you to handle things at the office, I've got to go out of town."

Kayla was quiet for a minute. "Is everything ok?" she asked

"Yes, something has come up. Just make sure everything continues to go on schedule." Ashland said, "I love you, Kayla, I'll be back in a couple of weeks. Bye." She hung up. She knew exactly where she was going.

Chapter Eight

Ashland was at her cabin in the mountains. She and Kayla had stayed there for a week after Kayla had broken it off with DeShun. Ashland loved the serene atmosphere so much that she talked the owner into selling it to her after receiving her money.

Ashland stood on the porch and inhaled deeply thinking how beautiful it was there. She was feeling a little queasy today, praying it was stress and because she had not been eating right, she decided to go to the market later to buy something healthy. She was getting a blanket to relax in front of the lake for a while before going into town when her cell phone rang.

"Hi Nicky," she said smiling as she answered the call.

"I see you finally took a vacation. What brought this on?" Nick asked curiously.

"I just thought it was time to take one," Ashland said.

"You ok?" Nick asked with concern.

Ashland laughed, "Yes Nicky, I'm wonderful and I'm having a very relaxing time here. Don't worry so much about me; you know I can take care of myself." The line was silent for a moment so Ashland added, "Hey, what's up? Why did you call me?"

"Just calling, I can't ever seem to get you completely off my mind." Nick teased then added softly, "You know all you have to do is say the word and I'd be there, no questions asked."

Ashland laughed then asked jokingly, "What would Stephanie say if she heard you say that?"

Nick did not respond, but thought to himself if Ashland gave him another chance there would be no Stephanie.

"Besides, you've been with too many women for me." Ashland laughed.

"Maybe I've been with so many women because I've been trying to get over you. You know I still care about you," Nick said softly.

Ashland knew how Nick felt, but things changed for her

that night she walked in on him and Sheila. Nick was supposed to have been out of town another day so she went to his house to surprise him. She decided she wanted a romantic atmosphere by putting candles and flowers everywhere. He had asked her before he'd left if she'd move in with him. She told him she would think about it, but she had already made up her mind the moment he had asked her because he had slowly made her fall in love with him over the years and she knew they would be good together. Ashland had decided she would give him a night he'd never forget, she had even taken off the locket that Jordan had given her. Unfortunately, she was the one who received the big surprise.

Nick and Sheila had parked their cars inside his garage. Ashland had used the key that Nick had given her early in their relationship, it was the first and last time she had ever used it. Ashland had begun placing a few candles around the living room then decided she'd do the bedroom first. The closer she came to the room, the sicker she was feeling, she knew Nick was home and knew he wasn't alone.

Ashland felt angry, hurt and betrayed as she opened the door to find Sheila performing oral sex on Nick. "You bastard," Ashland said as she stepped into the room slamming the door in the process. Sheila looked terrified then immediately jumped up and began gathering her things then stopped when she realized Ashland was blocking the doorway. "Ashland, I'm so sorry…" Sheila began but stopped when she saw the look on Ashland's face. Nick put his pants on quickly, looking embarrassed and defeated because he knew Ashland would never forgive him.

Ashland had unconsciously reached for her locket but it wasn't there as she stared at Sheila for a few deadly minutes. Ashland's eyes had become angry and small when she dropped the candles and attacked Sheila. Unfortunately, Nick managed to get her off Sheila and held her tight as Sheila scrambled for the door. "Get your hands off me," Ashland told him hatefully. Nick immediately let her go. Ashland only looked at him asking as tears rolled down her face, "How could you?" Nick only stood there because he knew there was nothing he could have said to justify what she had just witnessed. Ashland had become even more furious at him for just standing there, so she took her fist and knocked the hell out of him then said before leaving, "That's for making me fall for your sorry, lying, cheating ass." And that was the end of Nick and Ashland as a couple.

"I'm sorry but I can't go back to the way we were, you hurt me too bad," Ashland said softly.

"I know," Nick said quietly as he cleared his throat.

The line was quiet again then Ashland said quietly, "I'm not sure yet but I think I might be pregnant."

Nick felt as if he was hit with a ton of bricks. He wondered whom she had been sleeping with, because she never mentioned anything about seeing anyone else since they had broken up. Hell for that matter she rarely went out, all she ever really did was work. "By who?" Nick asked slightly breathless.

"Jordan," was all Ashland said.

Nick was angry, "How could you get pregnant by him a second time after the way he left you?"

"Jordan thought I aborted the baby. He was angry with me, and he did call me. My mother lied to him, she lied to us both," Ashland said.

Nick thought of Bianca and shook his head. "I see. Well, call me if you need anything. And I do mean anything, Ashland. I'll talk to you later. Enjoy your vacation."

Ashland closed her cell phone thinking how she hated telling Nick, but felt it was better for him to hear it from her since they'd been through so much over the years. She knew he was hurting but she also knew there was nothing she could do about it. She lay on the blanket in front of the lake looking up in the trees wondering what life would have been like if her mother hadn't… She sat up not wanting to think of her mother. She thought of Jordan, he had left a message two days ago for her to call him, but she didn't because she honestly didn't know what to say to him. She had spent her entire adult life angry with him, wondering why and how he could turn his back on her the way he did. She angrily thought of her mother again then her cell phone rang.

"Girl your mother is driving me crazy. Where are you? She's either calling or coming here three to four times a day asking where you're at. And every time she gives me a new name," Kayla said sounding aggravated. She and Bianca could never get along but Kayla always managed to be respectful to her. It was just something about Bianca that never set right with Kayla.

"Has she now?" Ashland laughed because her mother has never called Kayla by her correct name. She wasn't surprised her mother showed up especially since everything was all out in the open.

"I'm trying my best to be nice with her, but I can tell she thinks I'm lying, coming around here talking to me any kind of way, like I'm gone get intimidated by her and tell her where you're at," Kayla said in such a way that Ashland couldn't help but laugh. *Hell if I knew I still wouldn't tell her,* Kayla thought to herself. "Oh and your boy just left you a message," Kayla added.

"Who?" Ashland asked confused.

"Jordan," Kayla called him out.

"Kayla, what did he want?" Ashland questioned.

Kayla laughed, "He said that he has an agreement with you to complete a job and he expects to see you first thing tomorrow morning."

"Oh really?" Ashland said annoyed because she knew when she left everything was way ahead of schedule, he was probably just mad because she hadn't returned any of his calls.

"Ashland, where are you? I'll just tell him you were called away on some important business," Kayla said.

"Yeah, you do that, and double check to make sure everything is still on track. I'll be back soon," Ashland said.

"Ashland, do you need me to come be with you?" Kayla asked seriously.

"No I'm fine. I just need you to make sure things continue to run smoothly for a little while longer."

"Ok. But listen, I'm very, I repeat very worried about you myself. I don't understand why you don't just tell me where you are. You've been gone for a week now." Kayla said with concern.

"Kayla," Ashland began, but was cut off.

"Ashland, I'll take care of this end. You just need to let somebody in. You always try to deal with everything yourself then you'll tell me about it after the fact. I'm your best friend and I'm going crazy worrying about what's going on with you. It's not like you to take off from work, so I know something is very wrong. Why can't you ever let anybody take care of you sometime?" Kayla said with frustration.

"I'll be back soon," Ashland said, because she knew Kayla was worried about her. She added quietly, "I'm at the cabin."

Kayla thought about all the pain she was in when they were there all those years ago. "Hey I'm here for you if you need me. You know I love you."

"I know. I love you too, Kayla," Ashland said quietly.

Jordan sat casually on Kayla's desk listening to her talked with Ashland. He had thought about everything this past week and finally realized he still loved her and wanted her back in his life, but this time he wouldn't tolerate any interference by anyone, especially her mother. They had wasted too many years as it was; it was time for them to move forward. It had taken him about forty-five minutes just to convince Kayla to call her.

After Kayla hung up the phone she said, "I shouldn't tell you where she's at, because if she wanted you to know she would have told you herself." She was silent for a minute, "I don't really like the idea of her being alone up there, and I guess you two do have a lot to talk about." She looked deep in thought a few more minutes then her eyes became small when she said very firmly, "I warn you, you had better not hurt her."

After Kayla gave Jordan directions, he told her not to tell anyone where she was especially not her mother. He thanked her then got into his rental car and left. He called his grandfather and told him he had to leave town for a week or so and needed him to handle things while he was away. He decided to save time and use the company jet instead of taking the five-hour drive.

Jordan arrived there about four thirty in the afternoon and took a cab straight to the cabin. Ashland was not there so he sat his travel bags down beside the swing on the porch and stood looking at his surroundings. There was a blanket in front of the lake, about one hundred yards in front of the cabin. He smiled looking at all the trees and thought of Ashland and all her homeless animals. It was quiet and peaceful and he understood why she came. He sat in the rocking chair and put his foot up on the railing, as he waited for Ashland.

Jordan was tired; he had not slept much since he found out the truth about everything. Then with Ashland leaving and not letting anyone know where she was, he spent the whole week worrying about her especially after she would never answer or return his calls. He had closed his eyes for only a few minutes when he heard a car pulling up. He decided to stay seated and wait for her, from where he sat, he could see her but she could not see him, and when she got out of her car he thought, she looked so alone.

"Jordan you scared me!" She was carrying two small grocery bags, which she dropped when she reached the porch.

He stood quickly picking up her groceries, "Sorry, I wasn't trying to."

"Well you did! How did you know-well, of course, Kayla," She said annoyingly as she fumbled with unlocking the door. He followed her to the kitchen and sat the bags down. She was silently putting everything away. "Are you hungry? I was going to make a salad, but do you want chicken or anything to go with it?"

"I'm not really hungry right now, how about we go out for a bite later," Jordan said as he watched her closely.

"Sure," she said as she put away the last of the groceries then wiped down the already clean counter tops. "Would you like something to drink?" Without waiting for an answer from him, she opened the cabinet and took out two glasses and poured vodka in one and orange juice in the other. "You can get ice from the freezer," she told him as she handed him the drink leaving the kitchen to go sit outside on the swing.

Jordan joined her. "I missed you," he said quietly.

"I missed you too," she answered softly, then laid her head on Jordan's shoulder, he in turn put his arm around her and they sat comfortably in the swing for about forty minutes without saying a word.

"Where do we go from here?" He finally asked.

"To a restaurant, I'm hungry," she stood up smiling.

"That's not what I was talking about," he said as he reached over and held her hand.

"I know. Be right back." She bent down to kiss his forehead and disappeared into the cabin. Jordan smiled.

They didn't talk too much at the restaurant; it was still early so they decided to walk to the sports bar for a couple of games of pool. They laughed and joked as they played five games. Jordan won all except the last one.

As they walked to her car, Ashland said, "I had a great time playing with you, of course I let you win so you wouldn't quit on me."

Jordan laughed out loud, "Is that right?"

"Yes that's right, I used to beat you all the time, you don't remember?" She said teasingly knowing she really sucked at the game of pool.

"If you remember correctly, when you won you would always jump up and down kissing me," Jordan said smiling.

"So I guess that means you used to let me win just to get a kiss?" She asked.

"Of course I did," he said seriously.

She stepped in front of him abruptly, surprising him by putting her arms around his neck and kissing him. "Now that's for letting me win tonight," she said teasingly.

Jordan cleared his throat and unlocked the car doors and they drove quietly back to the cabin.

"I love this place. It's easy for me to relax here," he said sitting on the steps looking up at the stars. She was quiet for a few minutes then continued, "It was hard after you left, especially after losing the baby. I guess because it was all I had left of you." Then she added with a smile, "Although I did graduate top of my class. I guess I probably wouldn't be where I am today if things had turned out any differently. I wouldn't have Kayla. I guess things sometimes have a way of working for a reason." She took a deep breath, as Jordan sat quietly just listening, "I don't know. I guess it doesn't really matter anymore. My mother ruined everything being so controlling. I guess now she'll come to me justifying everything the way she always does," Ashland said softly. "I'm tired Jordan, I'm going in to shower. You can have the bedroom on the left and the bathroom is straight down the hall."

After Jordan showered, he decided to sit out on the porch in the rocking chair because he couldn't sleep, but was comforted with knowing Ashland wasn't somewhere all alone.

Ashland came out and stood in front of the steps, "I see you couldn't sleep, either." She was thinking he looked good in his black pajama pants and shirt, which was unbutton, exposing his hard chest and muscle toned stomach. *Damn he look sexy with his bare feet up on the porch rails, too bad I'm not feeling good tonight,* she thought devilishly. Then chided to herself because she was once again praying she had eaten something that made her nauseous. She walked down to the lake and sat down on her blanket.

Jordan didn't say anything just thought how fresh she looked in her shorts and t-shirt as he watched her walk away. Ashland had an aura of sadness about her, which concerned him. Jordan gave her about twenty minutes to be alone then decided to join her.

"Why did you come here?" She asked when she felt his approach.

"I knew how upset you were and I didn't want you to be alone. I guess I kind of missed you," Jordan said trying to be as honest as possible. "I guess I could have come back sooner, a part of me wanted to, but I was too angry at you because I thought you had an abortion and I have to admit it really hurt when your mom told me all those things."

Knowing the lies her mother had told made her angry.

She stood up to go inside but Jordan stopped her. He grabbed the side of her face and kissed her softly then pulled away to look into her eyes, "Ashland, none of that matters anymore, I want you back. I want us again."

Ashland took a deep breath and turned away from him to lean on the tree. He reached around her waist and pulled her toward his chest. He kissed her neck and slightly brushed his hand against her breast making her nipples immediately erect. She couldn't breathe so she pulled away.   "We don't really know each other anymore. I'm not the same person and neither are you," Ashland said quietly.

"Yes we are, we've just grown up," Jordan said not liking the way the conversation seemed to be going, but continued, "We can't change any of this, all we can do is move on." He walked to edge of the lake, "I need you, Ashland. I just want to be with you."

Ashland sat down and thought, "He wants me." She smiled, "Jordan how about a game of rummy?"

"What?" He turned around and asked with a frown.

"Cards, we use to play all the time. Please don't tell me that you're still scared after all these years," Ashland said looking up at him smiling mischievously.

"Let's play." He laughed as he followed her inside, she had always been spontaneous and fun, but it never failed to amaze him how quickly she could be talking about one thing this second then flip to something else the next.

They sat on the floor and played four games, Ashland won them all. "Just like old times," She said laughing, "What time is it?"

"Two twenty-five," he said looking at his watch.

"I think it's time to go to bed," She said softly then added when he raised an eyebrow, "Alone. Goodnight Jordan."

"Goodnight Ashland," he responded as he watched her walk to her bedroom.

        ***

The next morning Ashland woke up to the smell of sausage cooking, she ran to the bathroom and was sick. She took a long hot shower then lay down for a few minutes. She finally managed to get up and put on a pair of jean shorts and a black halter-top. The smell of sausage was making her extremely ill. She felt horrible and needed to get out of the cabin.

"Good morning I made breakfast. Are you hungry?" Jordan asked.

Ashland thought he looked so good standing there cooking, "Only if we can eat by the lake."

"That sounds good. You go ahead I'll bring it out," he said smiling as she rushed out the door.

She was lying on her back when Jordan came up, "Is this what you do all day?"

She sat up looking at a tray with two glasses of orange juice and two full plates of food, she was getting nauseous all over again.

He set it down beside the blanket, "You better eat before the bugs get to it."

"Gosh Jordan, you know I don't really eat early in the morning," she said taking a sip of juice hopeful she'd make it through breakfast.

"I know but you look as if you've lost a few pounds lately. You need to eat." He said staring at her for a long moment.

"Why are you looking at me like that?" She was hoping she didn't look like she felt.

"I don't know. You ok?" He questioned curiously.

She grabbed a piece of toast and prayed she wouldn't get sick. "Yes Jordan I'm ok. I've just had a lot on my mind lately." She ate slowly. She asked teasingly after Jordan finished eating, "I see you've cleaned your plate, you want the rest of mine?"

"I'm full," he said taking the plate, "Give it to me and I'll get rid of it for you."

She couldn't say anything when he went inside she rushed into the woods a little ways and threw up what little breakfast she had eaten. Ashland felt a little better but she was scared, "Please don't let me be pregnant." She went back to sit on the blanket then rinsed her mouth out with some of her juice before taking a few sips, being very thankful Jordan was still inside the cabin.

When he returned, he asked, "Are you sick you actually look pale."

"Jordan my dear I don't have on any makeup." She stood smiling, "but if it will make you feel better I'll go put some on." He reached over and kissed her. She kissed him back. They lay down on the blanket just kissing and caressing each other. He wanted her, "I didn't bring any protection."

"We'll just have to be careful, won't we?" She kissed him softly as she removed her halter.

Jordan grabbed her hands as she began unbuttoning his shirt. "Hey" he said softly, "We really need to be more careful." He kissed her then stood, "Right now, I want you too much to be careful." He pulled her up to stand. "Come on put your shirt back on lets go into town for a while."

They ended up at the town's fair. "Jordan, look!" she said excitedly. It was a big pink stuffed elephant. "If you shoot all the bottles you could win that for me."

"What do I get out of it?" He asked teasingly

"You'll have to find out later." She laughed kissing him full on his lips.

Jordan laughed thinking when they were younger he would take her to all the fairs because he loved to see her so happy, at that thought he shot all the bottles. "I guess now you expect me to carry this thing?" She only smiled up at him. Jordan shook his head, "I should have missed one."

They laughed. They spent the whole day in town it was late when they got back to the cabin. "Are you tired?" She asked.

"Not really maybe a little. Why?" He asked smiling.

She began taking off her cloths, "I'm going to take a shower. Do you wanna wash my back?" She left Jordan staring after her as she disappeared through the bedroom door. He decided to join her.

For the rest of the week Jordan and Ashland enjoyed each other having fun spending time together. They woke up early on Wednesday morning the following week, Jordan said, "You know I really need to be getting back. I do have a lot of work to do."

"I know," she said, all snuggly in his arms.

"Are you ready to go back?" He asked rubbing her hair.

"Not really but I need to get back to the office. I don't want to breach any contracts." She laughed.

He smiled, remembering what he had Kayla tell her, "Your mother is still waiting on you I'm sure. Are you going to be alright?"

"I am now." She kissed him rubbing his stomach.

"Where are you going?" he questioned when she got out of bed.

"To pack," she answered.

"Come here I want to show you something before you go," he whispered huskily.

* * *

They finished loading the car and locking up the cabin. "You sure you're ready?" he asked. They were on their way back home so Ashland could have complete closure to her past. Her mother was waiting for her. They had so much fun talking, laughing, and stopping periodically that he took his time driving back. They pulled up in his driveway late that evening.

"Do you need me?" He asked

"I'll call you if I do," Ashland smiled.

Jordan leaned over to kiss her, "Call me, even if you don't," he said getting his bags out of the car and grabbing her as she walked around to the driver's side. I still love you, he thought to himself as he kissed her forehead and opened the door for her.

Ashland went home to shower and change then decided

to go to the office to catch up on what had been happening. She was surprised to see Kayla's car still there, and it was almost six.

"Well hello," Ashland said to Kayla.

Kayla stopped typing and jumped up from her chair to hug Ashland. "I've missed you so much. Don't you ever leave me like that again!" Kayla had tears in her eyes.

"So you told Jordan where I was?" Ashland asked pretending to be upset.

Kayla sat down and said slowly, "Ashland he said you two needed to talk. Girl he just seemed so determined and sincere when he was telling me everything that had happened. I swear I was only trying to help you." She added, "Besides, I didn't want you up there all alone. You didn't leave me alone now, did you?"

Ashland walked around the desk to hug Kayla again, "Thank you."

Kayla didn't say anything for a minute then she screamed, "Oh my god! Tell me everything and you had better not leave anything out."

Ashland told her everything that had happened the past weeks. Everything except the nausea, she would go to the doctor first.

"I'm happy for you two. But when are you going to go see your mother?" Kayla inquired.

"I'm not," Ashland stated casually.

"Why?" Kayla asked curiously, why Ashland wouldn't want to confront her mother.

"If she needs to see me so bad, she'll find me. Ok, now tell me what's been happening around here."

Kayla filled Ashland in on every detail around the office. Then she added, "Deshun stopped by yesterday."

"For what?" Ashland asked her. She prayed Kayla would not get involved with him again after all these years.

"He says he misses his family and wants to see me and his kids sometimes. Well I told him he could see the kids maybe once a month. Have to see how that goes. But I had to tell him I couldn't see him since I'm involved with someone else."

"Now who's keeping secrets? So who is this mystery man?" Ashland asked smiling.

"Remember the night we met for drinks?" Kayla asked and Ashland shook her head yes. "Well Jamison, that's the guy that asked me to dance, well we sorta kept in touch." Kayla smiled wickedly.

Ashland said seriously, "I am so glad you're finally giving someone else a chance. Now when do I get to officially meet him?"

Kayla laughed, "How about you and Jordan meet us for drinks Friday night at Misty's?"

"I'll talk to Jordan and see if he's available but I will most definitely be there either way." They both laughed.

"I see you finally made it back. Why didn't you call me?" Bianca asked neither Ashland nor Kayla heard her walk up.

"Ashland I think I'll call it a day. I'll see you in the morning." Kayla hugged her whispering in her ear, "Call me if you need me. Love you."

Ashland watched Kayla get on the elevator before she said anything. "Hello mother. You're looking very beautiful today," Ashland said, although she knew her mother always looked good.

"Save the small talk. Why didn't you return my calls? I've left you probably a hundred messages," Bianca said angrily.

"The same reason you gave Jordan; I didn't want to talk to you," Ashland stated offhandedly.

Bianca stared at Ashland and thought how she wasn't a little girl anymore; she sat down in one of the lounge chairs. "Ashland you were too young to be thinking about marriage and a baby, my goodness, child, you were only seventeen. I had every right to keep him away from you. I never should have allowed you to see him in the first place."

"I agree, I was too young, but did you have to lie to us? I mean you kept on and on everyday about me being a fool for waiting on him. Telling me he wouldn't do this, he wouldn't do that. But in fact, he was more than willing to marry me and take care of our baby. You just wouldn't let it go, you just had to lie by saying I aborted our baby. It's truly amazing how evil and vindictive you are." Ashland said furiously.

"Ashland I am still your mother. You will talk to me with respect," Bianca said angrily.

"Respect? What do you know about respect? You don't respect daddy. You treat him like he's your personal servant. You treat everyone like crap. But you're right, I do owe you respect just because you're my mother. However, I don't owe you anything else beyond that. And if I am pregnant you'll never get to poison my child with all your hatefulness." Ashland stopped talking realizing what she had just said.

"Pregnant? Did you and Nick…" Bianca was smiling as she began talking but Ashland cut her off.

"That's really none of your business. How many times do I have to tell you that there is no Nick and me? We're over and we've been over for a while now, so just let it go," Ashland said indifferently.

"I am your mother so that makes it my business. And if Nick isn't the father then whose baby you think you might be pregnant with?" Bianca stood asking harshly as her eyes became small looking as if she was ready to battle.

"Mother, have you forgotten that I am a grown woman? I do not need your permission nor do I have to consult you for anything anymore." Ashland stood her ground.

"It's Jordan isn't it? That's why all this has come up again…You're not going to keep it, are you?" Bianca asked incredulously while her face actually began to turn red.

"Mother, to answer both your questions I guess we'll just have to see, won't we?" Ashland said carelessly with a raised eyebrow.

Bianca held her tongue but at Ashland's offhanded remark and the idea of Jordan being the father, Bianca slapped Ashland so hard she fell to the floor hitting the end table in the process. Bianca started for Ashland again, but the look on

Ashland's face stopped her cold when she raised her head up.

"Get out of my building before I call security," Ashland said furiously. This was the first time in her entire life she felt an urge to fight her mother. Bianca grabbed her purse and stormed off.

Ashland stood up feeling woozy as if she was going to be sick. She put her head between her legs until the feeling passed. Her face was still stinging. She knew it had to be swollen. Her arm hurt from hitting the table so hard she just hoped it wouldn't leave a bruise. She went into her office and slammed her door. She was pissed and was curious about why her mother would become violent about Jordan fathering her baby. She wasn't seventeen anymore. She got up deciding to stop by the drug store to get a pregnancy test, finding out once and for all whether or not she was pregnant.

Chapter Nine

When Ashland got home, she went straight upstairs ignoring the ringing phone. She went to the bathroom to take the pregnancy test. She sat on the edge of the tub while she waited on the results; it immediately turned positive. "Shit!" she said out loud. Her phone was ringing again so she got up to check the caller ID. It was her mother, so she ignored the call. "I guess I need to tell Jordan," she said as she picked up the phone then put it back down because she was nervous. She picked up the phone again then dialed Kayla.

"Hello," Kayla answered.

Ashland didn't say anything for a minute, "I'm pregnant."

"Oh no. I'll be over in a few minutes."

Kayla didn't bother to knock. She used the key that Ashland had given her. She ran up the stairs to Ashland's bedroom. Ashland was sitting on the windowsill staring out the window. Kayla went over to her to sit beside her. "It's going to be okay, Ashland." Then Ashland's phone rang and Kayla went to look at the caller ID, "Ashland, its Jordan do you feel like talking to him?" Ashland shook her head no, but didn't say anything. Kayla took a deep breath then picked up the phone.

"Hello, Is Ashland home?" Jordan asked.

"Hey Jordan, its Kayla, she can't come to the phone right now do you want her to call you?"

He hesitated for a moment, "Yeah that's fine. Is she alright?"

"She'll be ok she just needs to rest I'll tell her to call you tomorrow. Jordan, don't worry about her, she's fine." Kayla hung up the phone then saw Ashland's arm when she stood, "Oh my god what happened to you? And your face is all swollen?"

"My mother hit me and I fell," she said simply.

Kayla couldn't say anything else about her mother. She didn't want to think about what she really wanted to do to her.

"Call Jordan…Call him right now he's worried about you. And to tell you the truth, he needs to be here with you. If you don't call him, I promise you I will," Kayla stood with her hands on her hips.

Ashland sat on the bed, for some reason she felt nervous about telling Jordan about the baby. She picked up the phone, "Hi Tylen, it's Ashland. How have you and Megan been?"

"Hi Kitten, we're doing great. We're getting ready to go out to eat, would you like to join us?" Tylen sounded cheerful as usual.

"I think I'll pass this time, I was calling to speak with Jordan if he's still home?" Ashland asked.

"I think he is, hold on for a minute," Tylen said.

Kayla sat beside her and put her arms around her shoulders.

"Hey, I didn't expect you to call until tomorrow. Is everything okay?" Jordan asked

"I just need to talk to you, can you come over?" Ashland asked.

"I'm on my way." Jordan answered slowly then hung up.

"Now" Kayla said to Ashland, "I'll stay until he gets here."

Jordan wondered what happened with her mother. He was walking out the door when his grandfather stopped him.

"So I take it you two are back together?" Tylen was smiling.

"We're working on it." Jordan smiled

"Good, well you better get going you don't want to keep her waiting." Tylen said.

Jordan nodded and walked out the door.

Tylen had a big grin across his face. "Finally," he said out loud.

"Finally what?" Megan asked, walking over kissing him softly.

"Nothing. You ready to go?" Tylen said smiling.

"Whenever you are," Megan answered softly.

* * *

When Jordan rung Ashland's doorbell, it was immediately opened by Kayla, "Come in, Jordan, I was just leaving." Kayla kissed Ashland on her cheek and whispered in her ear, "You can do this. Call me later."

"Goodbye, Jordan." She was out the door before he had a chance to say anything.

Ashland stood nervously, "Do you want something to drink?" She was walking out the room when he noticed her arm. He reached to pull her to him. "What happened to your arm?" He frowned, "And your face?"

"My mother and I got into an argument, she hit me I fell and bruised my arm. It's okay, really," she said with a shrug of her shoulders as she tried pulling away, but he wouldn't let go.

Jordan continued to frown as he caressed her cheek then he let her go. He went to look out the window while she fixed him a drink. Jordan was pissed it took everything he had to maintain his control.

"Here you go." Her hands were shaking she spilled some of his gin.

He grabbed her hands, "Hey it's okay, damn you're shaking." He took her to the couch to sit down. "Here drink some."

She shook her head no.

"It'll calm your nerves." He tried to get her to drink one more time.

She stood up abruptly, "Jordan I can't. I'm pregnant."

He just looked at her as if he did not understand what she had said, "Did your mother know you are pregnant when she hit you?" He asked slowly, face void of any expression.

"I told her I might be," Ashland said. When he turned his glass up and drunk all his vodka at once she asked him jokingly, "Did it calm your nerves?"

"Not really," Jordan said. He made her more nervous by not saying anything, so she stood to get him another drink. He pulled her back down on the couch. He just looked at her strange.

"Are you mad at me?" She asked unsure of what to say because she felt his uneasiness.

"For being pregnant?" He asked her as if she was crazy, "No, of course not. I'm not surprised. We didn't use any kind of protection the first time." He went to the window and put his hands in his pockets, "She hit you pretty hard to make you fall and bruise that bad."

Ashland didn't know what to say, he continued to look out the window. Her doorbell rang. Ashland stood to answer it. "Daddy, what are you doing here? Come in." She smiled weakly then her expression quickly changed when she saw her mother.

Marcus hugged his daughter tight, "Baby, are you alright? Bianca told me what happened." He rubbed her cheek softly then looked back at Bianca with pure hatred in his eyes. He didn't say anything to her.

"Daddy, Jordan's here," she whispered cautiously because Ashland had never seen her father so angry at her mother. Ashland's nerves were so bad she was fidgety.

"Good, I'm glad. Bianca, are you coming?" Marcus walked into the living room without waiting for Bianca to respond. He noticed Jordan standing in front of the window hands in pocket. "Hello Jordan," Marcus said. Jordan turned around and only nodded.

"Ashland, your mother has something she wants to say to you," Marcus said.

Ashland sat in a chair near Jordan.

"I didn't mean to hit you so hard," Bianca said with regrets.

"Damn it Bianca! You should be apologizing for hitting her period!" Marcus was livid.

Bianca cleared her throat, "Ashland dear, I did not mean to hit you. I just got a little angry when you wouldn't tell me if he may be the father of your baby." She cut her eyes briefly at Jordan. He continued leaning against the windowsill with his hands in pockets. His face was unreadable as he watched and listened to everything.

"Why, I ought to slap you myself. You didn't tell me she was pregnant. Are you crazy or what?" Marcus said incredulously. He rushed toward her and raised his arm to hit her.

"Daddy, don't! Please?" Ashland stood pleading for her mother; it was actually for her father. She didn't want him to do anything he'd regret later, because he was all she really had.

Marcus took a step back, "I can't do this anymore. I have sat back and watched you destroy people's lives, your own daughter's for goodness sake, and I have taken things that the average man wouldn't have. You've been angry at me for not being him, angry because he did not want you. Don't look so surprised, I've known all along actually, before I even married you, I just loved you so much that I settled for what I could get, but I deserve more. He shook his head furiously, "I don't know who you are. I don't want to know you or any woman that could hit their pregnant daughter. You disgust me." He turned away from Bianca, "Jordan, I know I can't change anything, but I can not express how so sorry I am for not stepping up sooner. Just take care of Ashland. I hope you two find your way back to where you were before." He walked over and hugged Ashland tightly. "I'll call you," he said to Ashland then he noticed the bruise. He turned back to his wife, "Bianca I'm filing for divorce. It's over." He shook his head then rushed out of the house before he did something to Bianca he knew he would regret.

Bianca stood, "May I use your phone to call a cab?"

"Yes mother." Ashland told her.

Jordan turned back toward the window.

After Bianca got off the phone she said, "Jordan I'm..."

He turned around and looked so threatening she stopped talking.

"I'll wait for my cab out front." Bianca said as she grabbed her purse and walked casually outside.

Jordan walked over and just held Ashland in his arms.

***

Ashland woke up early the next morning; she was

dressed and ready to go to work when Jordan woke up.

"What time is it?" He asked

She sat on the bed beside Jordan, "About five-thirty, I have a lot to catch up on, I need to get an early start." She sounded professional again.

"You okay?" He sat up.

"Have to be I have a business to run." She was hurting inside but staying busy was the best thing to do. Her mother really hurt her this time, but she wasn't about to let anyone else see her down. "Go back to sleep, just make sure you lock up on your way out." She leaned over and kissed him. "Will I see you later tonight?" She asked.

"We got a lot of celebrating to do," he said while putting his hand on her stomach and kissed her softly, "Besides, grandfather probably won't let you leave tonight anyways."

"Your grandfather or you?" she joked then said, "I can't make it tonight I forgot I promised Kayla I would meet her and Jamison for drinks tonight you're invited also."

"Just invite them to the house for dinner and drinks. I'm sure she wouldn't mind."

"I'll ask her. I'll see you later," Ashland kissed him and left.

* * *

Jordan made it to his office about seven. "Hello Mrs. Peterson, How are you today?" Jordan asked his secretary.

"I'm doing fine. Welcome back we missed you around here, although Mr. Alexander is such a pleasure to work with," she said shyly.

"Is he now?" He said grinning. Mrs. Peterson was a widower and a very nice looking woman for her age. He figured she was something back in her day. He could see his grandfather being extra charming to her. Megan had better watch out, he thought. "Is he in this morning?"

"Yes, he was up in his office earlier." She added, "He doesn't have any meetings until one o'clock so you might be able to catch him before he makes his rounds."

Jordan nodded his head and smiled. His grandfather

always made sure his employees were happy and well taken care of. He headed towards the elevator.

"Hi Jordan, Mr. Alexander was just asking about you. Go on in he has been expecting you," his grandfather's secretary said.

Tylen was on the phone when Jordan entered his office, too a sit in one of the chairs in front of his desk. "I see you didn't make it home last night," Tylen said smiling when he got off the phone.

"No I didn't. So why don't you catch me up on everything around here first," Jordan said.

"Not too much going on right now, I have everything under control. I have a lunch meeting at one about the merger you were working on before you left, other than that everything is going smoothly," Tylen said leaning back in the chair, "Will you be free to join us?"

"Where will this meeting be?" Jordan questioned.

"Angelica's," Tylen said

"I'll be there." Jordan stated.

"Now, you catch me up on everything with you and Ahsland," Tylen said.

"Tonight we'll be having dinner and drinks at the house, it'll be just us and maybe a friend of Ashland," Jordan told him.

"Ok, sounds good to me. I'll call Megan and let her know, she loves to cook and she'll be glad for the company." Tylen smiled.

Jordan sat a few minutes then said, "I'm going to be a father, Ashland's pregnant."

"Well, well, well you don't waste any time, do you? So how do you feel about that?" Tylen said obviously surprised.

"I don't know. A little worried, you know she lost the first baby. Otherwise I'm excited," Jordan said.

"Excited? Never can tell with you with the way you never show any emotions." Tylen stated matter-of-factly.

Jordan laughed because Tylen made a valid point.

Tylen thought sadly how Jordan rarely let his emotions or feelings show. "So tell me, how is Ashland?"

Jordan stood and walked over to the window, "She seemed fine this morning, but I'm not really too sure. You know her parents are in town."

"What was Bianca's reaction to the renewed friendship between the two of you?" Tylen asked curiously.

"Not good. Evidently she and Ashland got into an argument Bianca ended up hitting her," Jordan said casually.

Tylen just shook his head unbelieving, "Bianca hit Ashland? Is she okay?"

"She's a little bruised up, but she's fine," Jordan said.

"Bruised up? What did she hit her with?" Tylen asked with a shocked expression.

"Evidently, she slapped her hard enough for her to lose balance and fall. She ended up hitting a table or something, which caused an ugly bruise on her arm. I guess it could have been worse than it was."

Tylen shook his head in agreement thinking about the baby, "Well does she know about the baby yet?"

"Yes, I stood back and listened to her say she got mad because Ashland would not admit that I was the father." Jordan said annoyed.

"So you saw Bianca?" He asked a little taken aback.

"Yeah after Ashland called me and I went over there she told me about the baby, then not too long afterwards her parents arrived. It was interesting to say the least." Jordan sat on the windowsill then added, "It seems Marcus knew about you two all along."

Tylen raised an eyebrow and thought for a moment, "Really? Does Ashland know?" He didn't know why, but it bothered him more for Ashland to know.

"I don't think she knows. She didn't act like it," Jordan said indifferently.

"How is Marcus doing?" Tylen asked.

"He's mad to say the least. After he saw the marks Bianca had left on Ashland, he says he's going to file for divorce. You know at one point I actually thought he was going to hit her. And to tell you the truth I'm ashamed of myself because I have to admit a part of me actually wanted him to. I don't believe in a man hitting a woman, but I stood waiting and I would not have stopped him," Jordan said honestly.

Tylen sat back and thought for a moment understanding how Bianca could set a person off that way. Curiously, Tylen asked, "Jordan, what about Ashland? Do you plan to marry her before the baby is born?"

"Mr. Alexander," Tylen's secretary buzzed in.

"Yes Miranda," Tylen said.

"There is a problem in warehouse number two. They have to shut down the power." She told him.

"Let them know I'll be right there," Tylen said.

Jordan stood, "I'll take care of it. It's about time for your rounds anyway." Jordan grinned and left the room.

Tylen stood up to make his rounds then laughed because Jordan never answered his question.

Chapter Ten

Bianca was pacing the floor in her hotel room, "The nerve of Marcus to embarrass me like that in front of him of all people. Now he can't even answer his phone," she said out loud while picking up the phone to call Marcus again. He answered on the second ring. "Marcus please don't hang up I need to talk to you."

"So talk," Marcus said.

"Not like this, meet me somewhere, please," Bianca asked. After Marcus didn't say anything she said, "Marcus, please don't make me beg."

"I can't, I'm busy tonight," Marcus said coldly.

"Doing what?" Bianca asked with a false sense of jealousy.

"I'm having dinner with my daughter. Is that okay with you?" He said sarcastically.

"Marcus you don't have to be so dramatic," Bianca said with aggravation in her voice.

"Dramatic?" He laughed, "You're something else, you know that."

"Marcus…"

He cut her off, "I'm busy right now. I have things to take care of before meeting *my* daughter. Goodbye Bianca" He hung up the phone.

Bianca looked evilly at the phone not believing how he was treating her. Bianca got dressed to go out.

Ashland was waiting on her father to pick her up. After her father had called her, she tried to cancel her plans with Jordan, but Jordan wasn't hearing it, he wanted her to bring Marcus to his house for dinner as well. "Hi daddy," she said.

"Hi baby, you look beautiful tonight are you ready?" He asked.

"Yes I am." She smiled happily.

"Are you sure Jordan won't mind me being there?" Marcus questioned.

"He's the one that told me to bring you." She kissed her father on his cheek.

Bianca sat in her rent-a-car watching as Marcus and Ashland got in his car and drove away. She followed. They drove up to a very large Victorian style house, she was glad that the gate was open. She turned off her lights as she drove a safe distance behind them. She parked her car in some bushes so it could not be seen as she waited. Bianca became angry when Jordan opened the front door. Another car pulled up and she noticed it was Kayla and a man getting out of the car. Ashland opened the door that time hugging the couple. Bianca was furious, they couldn't invite her, she thought with disgust. "We'll see about that," she said aloud and took out her cell phone.

Ashland's cell rung, she was having so much fun that she answered it without checking the ID.

"Hi Ashland, how are you feeling tonight?" Bianca asked cheerfully.

"I'm okay," she said cautiously as she stood slowly to walk into the foyer. "What do you want?" She asked obviously annoyed.

"Can't I just call my daughter to see how she's doing?" Bianca asked innocently.

"I'm doing fine," Ashland stated.

"I just can't forgive myself for hitting you. I am so sorry. Your father tells me he was meeting with you tonight I was thinking that it would be nice for us to get together as a family again. I think we need to come together, you know that's the only way we can work this out. You know I love you. Are you still home? If you are, maybe I could come over and we could all go out together somewhere," Bianca said.

"Not right now, we're already out. Maybe we can do it some other time," Ashland said.

"Okay that will be fine, but I hear a lot of talking in the background, are you at a party?" Bianca questioned.

Ashland decided to be honest, "Not really we're just having dinner with friends."

"I see." Bianca controlled her anger and asked calmly, "So why wasn't I invited?"

"After everything that happened today, Mother, I don't think the timing is right for all of us to get together," Ashland said to her mother.

"Ashland honey, you're still my daughter and I still love you. So tell me, who is there with you two?" Bianca said trying to sound hurt.

"Jordan, his family and a few friends," Ashland said

Bianca got quiet for moment Jordan's only family was his grandfather. "So I take it Tylen is in town?" She asked casually.

"Yes mother. I really have to go now. Goodbye Mother." Ashland hung up.

Bianca sat thinking for a few moments she then an evil grin and drove away.

Ashland went back and joined everyone in the Sun Room. She smiled at Jordan then sat down.

"Everything okay, baby?" her father asked.

"Yes," Ashland smiled brightly.

"Ashland have you gotten a due date yet?" Megan asked. Everyone stopped talking.

"I went to the doctor today he says I'm about eight weeks. I'm due the first week of January," Ashland said awkwardly.

Kayla noticed then whispered jokingly to Ashland, "You'll be swelling up, getting clumsy, and waddling around pretty soon." Kayla and Ashland laughed. Megan heard and joined in. About forty-five minutes later the doorbell rang.

"I'll get it," Megan said still laughing. "Hello may I help you?" Megan asked smiling.

"Hi, I'm Bianca, Ashland's mother," Bianca said politely.

"Nice to meet you, I'm Megan. Please do come in." Megan was shocked at her arrival but continued to smile. Tylen had told her all about Bianca, but he never mentioned how shockingly beautiful she was, and her cream colored evening gown, which seemed to hug her every curve snugly made her more so. Megan thought she could have easily been on any magazine cover; she didn't even look old enough to have a daughter Ashland's age. Therefore, in spite of everything negative she had heard about Bianca, she was still Ashland's mother and should be welcomed regardless.

"Follow me, we're in the Sun Room as Ashland loves to call it," Megan said brightly.

Bianca wondered who this Megan person was.

"Ashland your mother's here," Megan said graciously, "Please make yourself comfortable and have a seat, we're so glad you joined us. Would you like something to drink?" Megan was the perfect host.

"I guess I could stay for one drink. A white wine please." Bianca smiled charmingly. "Hello everyone, Marcus, Jordan, Katie, isn't it? And hello," she said to Jamison. "I stopped by after talking with Ashland just to say hello to everyone, and to officially congratulate the two of you on your upcoming new arrival." She smiled pleasantly at Jordan not caring in the least when he didn't respond or show any emotions.

"How did you know where we were?" Ashland asked bewildered.

"I do have connections, my dear," She said in good spirits as Tylen entered the room.   "Hello Tylen, it's been a very long time," she said politely.

"Bianca" Was all he could say. He was stunned. He walked over to Megan and sat on the arm of her chair.

Marcus noticed her dress, it was new and she looked very enticing, if things could have only been different, he thought sadly. A part of him resented Tylen but he realized he hadn't been married to Bianca when they had their affair. He knew he didn't have to marry her, he chose to do so, but still it bothered him knowing that Tylen was the one that she had truly wanted for all these years. Bianca never could handle rejection too good. Pushing those thoughts aside, he wondered what Bianca was up to, she was being a little too nice and that meant something was going to happen and he knew it wouldn't be good.

"Now, where were we? Oh yeah, Ashland was telling us that your grandchild will be born in January, I know you're very excited, I know I would be if was my grandchild." She suddenly became excited, "That reminds me, Tylen, you have got to tell them about the time we spent in Mexico." Megan's laughter lightened the mood.

About twenty minutes later Bianca stood, "I have to be going, as I said before I just wanted to stop by to congratulate the happy couple," she said very sincerely as she went over and kissed Ashland on her cheek. "Please forgive me," she whispered loud enough for only Ashland to hear then continued speaking to everyone else, "I know I was an uninvited guest so I'm going to take off now. Enjoy the rest of your evening." Bianca looked breathtakingly beautiful and she knew it as she elegantly walked from the room and left.

"Okay now who's up for a game of spades?" Megan asked to break the silence. Jordan looked at Megan for a moment he was quite impressed with how she handled the situation.

It was almost two-thirty in the morning when Kayla said, "Guys I've had a wonderful time but I do believe it is time for us to go."

"It's late why don't you two stay the night there's plenty of room," Jordan said.

"We'd love to but we really need to be going," Kayla winked at Ashland. "I've had a wonderful time. I am so glad to have met you all," she said to Tylen and Megan.

"Yes," Marcus said, "I do think it's time for us to get going also."

Tylen and Megan stood to walk out with everyone.

Ashland stood and hugged Kayla, "Jamison, I'm glad we had a chance to officially meet, drive her home safely. Kayla, call me tomorrow."

Jordan put his hands on Ashland's shoulders as Jamison and Kayla drove away. "Are you staying tonight?"

"Not tonight, I'm going to go home. But you can pick me up for a late breakfast in the morning," Ashland said.

"I'll be there." He kissed her briefly as she and Marcus got in the car and left.

***

Bianca woke up early the next morning feeling very refreshed even though she didn't get in until about three-thirty in the morning. She had stopped by an old acquaintance's house after leaving Jordan's home last night. Mark Trovelli who was a private investigator she had met here in Atlanta seven years ago while doing research on one of her cases. They had kept in touch over the years, but it had been almost three years since they had actually slept together. Since Marcus wouldn't act right, in her opinion, she had decided it was time to re-new old friendships and Mark had indeed turned out to be very useful to her.

She laughed as she thought about their conversation last night after they had made passionate love. How she casually mentioned her daughter's pregnancy and Jordan, telling Mark how she was worried her daughter might get hurt by him since it had been almost ten years since anyone had even heard from him, and quite naturally a lot can happen in that time. So Mark being himself, suggested he do an intensive investigation of Jordan just so Bianca could feel safe and at ease with her daughter's relationship with him. She laughed at how she had refused him at first; saying investigating Jordan would be invading his privacy. She was just being an overprotective mother and should just mind her own business. She had even cried about hitting her daughter, accidentally of course, and how Marcus was divorcing her because of that. By the time their conversation ended, he had told her to go home and relax, and he would be calling her within the week. Mark would be doing a full investigation of Jordan, Tylen and Megan. "What luck! I could have won an Oscar for last night's performance," she said with an evil laugh as she packed her bags to go home.

True to his word, Mark called Bianca six days later he would be coming out to see her this afternoon. Bianca could hardly wait; they would be meeting at her condo around three today. Bianca had ordered Chinese take-out and was pouring herself a glass of wine when her doorbell rang. She decided to wear only a black negligee because the more she thought of him and his investigation, the more she became sexually aroused. It actually turned her on that he could be easily manipulated into doing what she wanted. "Hello Mark, please do come in." She smiled passionately as she glanced briefly down at his briefcase.

Mark walked in, hugged Bianca while kissing her on her lips. He was forty-five and in excellent shape, his skin was light brown and he wore a full clean cut beard and mustache. He was a very nice looking man.

"Would you like something to eat or drink?" Bianca asked as she took a sip of her wine.

"Let's eat, drink and get comfortable," he said pulling her into his arms, "Then we have a lot to discuss."

After eating and making love they were lounging around on the sofa laughing, talking and drinking wine when Mark said, "To start off, Megan Wallers is just an island girl. Her family owns a restaurant on the shorefront over there. Seems Tylen was on vacation there last year when he met her. She stayed with him about three months after their initial meeting. Then she went back home. She's only been here about a month so far. She spends a lot of time in Florida with family members. Other than that, there's really nothing that concerned me about her. She pretty much worked everyday helping her family run their restaurant."

Mark opened his briefcase sat back then said, "Jordan Alexander," he rubbed his forehead, "he went away to complete college over seas. That, I think, was when he got Ashland pregnant the first time."

Bianca nodded then he continued.

"Well he graduated top of his class at college. His education is very extensive. He speaks French and Spanish fluently. He doesn't speak Japanese but he understands the language well enough to have closed quite a few profitable business deals. Since he started working at his grandfather's company their net worth has increased significantly," Mark stated.

Bianca stood to look out the window as she listened to Mark. She learned from Ashland about all the languages that Jordan spoke. She often wondered how Jordan managed to find the time to spend with Ashland because he was always very serious about his education, always studying and tutoring others.

"He's had quite a few relationships none of them seemed to be serious only lasting two months at the most. There is one female in particular that he had been seen with at a lot of dinner parties over the years." Mark turned a few pages, "Her name is Sierra Sanders, who was CEO of Chambers Lawson which was a black magazine company which had started in Europe about fifteen years ago. She has caused a few disturbances where Jordan is concerned."

Bianca turned to look at Mark and said with interest, "Really?"

"From what I hear Sierra has been physically thrown out from a few well known establishments because Jordan was dining with other women. Jordan threatened to file a restraining order against her. All this took place about five years ago. I'm not sure if that order was ever issued, but some say she convinced him to drop the order a few days later. Rumor has it she didn't want any more bad press for the magazine so she promised to stay away from him. I think she was about to lose her job. Which she did two years later, the company went bankrupt. Today she is the executive director of one of the local newspapers in Cleveland, Ohio."

He looked through a few more pages then asked, "Bianca did you ever meet Jordan's mother Carmen?"

"Not really, I saw her once, very briefly, one day at Tylen's office. My goodness I was nineteen at the time. I heard she and Jordan's father died in a boating accident right after Jordan was born. Why?"

"I spoke with a few older ladies that used to work for Tylen back then. They all say Carmen left Jordan with Tylen and his wife a few days after he was born to run off with Jordan's father Mitchell Maxwell, she was nineteen at the time. They say Tylen never approved of Mitchell, he was known for having a lot of different women. Although Carmen never believed her father when he tried to tell her, she continued to see Mitchell staying out all hours of the night coming home drunk. Tylen later found out Mitchell had her doing drugs. They say when she became pregnant she immediately changed, staying home more. Mitchell would come to see her maybe once a month. They say after Jordan was born, Mitchell went to the nursery, looked at him briefly then walked right back out of the room, and then he and Carmen went to speak to Tylen in his study. Nobody knows exactly what was said, but that night Carmen and Mitchell left on his boat, never to return. Tylen never spoke of Carmen again." Mark continued, "About two years later Carmen got pregnant again, Mitchell didn't want that child either, even though they were married. He gave her the house in Virginia they lived in, child support and he left, rumor has it she hasn't seen him since. After Mitchell left her, she stopped drinking and partying, she actually dedicated herself at being good mother to their second son."

Bianca was shocked, "Carmen is alive? Oh my God, Jordan has a brother? What is his name?"

"Damian Maxwell," Mark responded.

"Does he live in Virginia still? What does he do?" She asked anxiously.

"Yes. He bought a house not too far from his mother. He has a Marina boating company, a popular tourist attraction spot. A very nice young man, he and his mother are very close. The eerie part about it is that he looks exactly like Jordan, he could even pass for his twin." Mark stated.

"Oh my goodness, so you've talked to him?" Bianca was truly stunned.

"Yes, I've spoken with him and Carmen. I even went on one of his tours. She actually helps out with them. She's crazy about her son, Damian. I even went as far to ask her how many children she has. She got quiet for a minute then said just

Damian," Mark said carefully.

"So tell me, what does Jordan know about his parents?" Bianca asked.

"They say when Jordan was about seven he got into a fight with some kid, they say the little boy was so mad that he told Jordan his parents were drug addicts and they never wanted him so they threw him away, that's why he had to stay with his grandparents. Jordan was upset because he had always been told his parents had died in a boating accident. No one knows exactly what Tylen told Jordan after that, but whatever it was Jordan never asked about his parents again." Mark then added, "Mitchell currently lives in Las Vegas."

Bianca was stunned she never expected Mark to give her so much information. Oh my God! Tylen actually lied to Jordan about his parents. She was trying to decide what she would do with all the information when Mark interrupted her thoughts by saying, "I was also told about the affair you had with Tylen when you were nineteen. You got pregnant and aborted his baby."

Bianca wasn't surprised he found out about the affair, but she was speechless when he mentioned the abortion. She had no choice; she wasn't about to risk losing Marcus since Tylen refused to leave his wife. At that time, her hatred was so strong for Tylen that the thought of having a child by him sickened her to the core. Tylen had thrown her love back in her face, so she did what she had to do without any regrets. Bianca wasn't quite sure what to say to Mark so she decided to say nothing as she sat down. Mark sat beside her then kissed her. "Its okay Bianca, my feelings haven't changed for you. You were so young back then, besides, we've all made mistakes," he tried to comfort.

"Thank you, Mark, I needed to hear that." Bianca thought with disgust, that abortion was not a mistake. She smiled to herself and knew exactly what she was about to do. Then she started kissing him. He stayed the night.

Chapter Eleven

Jordan had been feeling very edgy for the past two weeks, so he tried to keep busy at work. Ashland was busy herself because she had just landed a multimillion-dollar contract, which would probably last about a year or so. They had been having problems with her working so many long hours because he didn't think it was good for the baby. After he found out, her doctor had already warned her not to do a lot of strenuous work; Jordan became furious and asked her if she was trying to have another miscarriage. She in return got pissed and left without saying anything to him. It had been almost a week since he'd talked to her. It was a little after five so he decided to give her a call.

"Ashland, I really need to see you," Jordan said quietly then asked, "Are you doing ok? Where are you?" He asked cautiously because he knew he would become angry if she was still at the office.

"I'm home today," she said offhandedly then continued, "I'm fine, but after your little comment I decided I should take it easy for a while."

Jordan relaxed, "Would you have dinner with me?"

"Where do you want me to meet you?" Ashland questioned.

"I'll pick you up. I'll see you in about twenty minutes." Jordan hung up the phone.

Ashland was pleased Jordan had called her even though she was still angry at the hurtful comment he made to her earlier in the week. He made it seem as if it had been her fault she had lost their first baby. She inhaled deeply trying not to get angry all over again forcing herself to think of something else. She's been home mostly and was becoming quite bored. She thought of all the decisions she made this week, she would now only be going into the office two days a week mainly to conduct the weekly meetings and make sure everything was running smoothly. She hired six new workers and promoted Kayla, she got her own office with a secretary. Her doorbell rang interrupting her thoughts.

Before Ashland could say anything, Jordan walked in pulled her into his arms, and kissed her. They greeted each other and he asked is she was hungry. She told him she hungered for him as she him upstairs.

Jordan sat on the side of the bed watching Ashland unbutton her blouse. He smiled as he pulled her between his legs placing his hand on her stomach. "You're going to be showing pretty soon." He kissed her stomach.

"I know" She kissed his forehead while rubbing her hands through his hair.

"I got something for you." He kissed the swell of her breast while he rubbed her pink lace bra.

"Oh yeah," she smiled as she sat on his leg.

"Close your eyes." Jordan reached in his pocket then slid a two and a half carat princess cut diamond ring on her finger. Ashland opened her eyes slowly looking down at her hand, she never expected him to give her a ring. She figured they would eventually get married one day, but she really hadn't thought about it since everything was happening so fast with the baby and all.

"Jordan" Ashland began but he kissed her to keep her quiet.

"Don't talk." He rubbed her leg softly. "Pack some clothes we're going to Las Vegas for a couple of days." Jordan thought for a moment then asked with a touch of uncertainty. "You will marry me, won't you Ashland?"

Ashland was quiet for a few minutes then said, "Yes, I'll marry you."

Three hours later after deplaning Jordan's personal jet, they were checking into the honeymoon suite at the Casino Hotel in Las Vegas.
Ashland felt overwhelmed with everything, and thought the room was beautiful.

"Just like you," he said kissing her, and then added,

"Let's shower and change. We're to be married soon."

"What? Right now?" Ashland asked so nervously, she seemed almost ready to call it off.

"Yes right now, arrangements have already been made. Oh yeah, I never did take you to dinner. Do you want to come back here to rest for a while and order room service, or do you want to go out right after we get married? We'll discuss it later go ahead and take your shower first," Jordan said calmly.

Ashland couldn't believe how calm he was since she was a nervous wreck as she left the room to shower. Jordan only laughed. An hour later, they were married and were sitting at a cozy table in the hotel's restaurant where they were staying. Unbeknownst to them, they were being watched closely by Mitchell Maxwell.

Mitchell had just left one of his lady friend's rooms when he spotted Jordan and Ashland entering the restaurant. He ordered a drink then sat at the bar thinking about the woman he met almost two weeks prior, her name was Bianca Kendrix. She was sitting cross-legged at a black jack table at one of the other casinos when he saw her. She was wearing a very flimsy black dress, the thought of her in that particular dress sent chills through him, arousing him. She was easily one the most beautiful women he had ever laid eyes on, and he had lain his eyes on a lot of beautiful women in his time. He thought Carmen was beautiful but there was something exotic and very overpowering about Bianca's beauty that made him stop to take a second look. He watched her play then later introduced himself. They connected right away. They hung out for five days straight having a real good time together. Sometime during one of their conversations, she mentioned her pregnant daughter and her fiancé, who just so happen turned out to be his first-born son. Bianca was shocked at first everyone believed he and Carmen had died on his boat that awful day he had given Jordan so callously away. Damn, he thought to himself before he asked Bianca if she had a picture of Jordan, he was curious as to how his son looked. She didn't have a picture of them together but she did have one of her daughter. Jordan looks exactly like

Tyler, Bianca told him.

Ever since that conversation with Bianca, he's been thinking about Jordan and Damian on a daily basis. Especially Jordan, he at least had taken care of Damian with child support and a trust fund but with Jordan, he had turned his back on him completely, he didn't even have his last name. Even though he knew he was well off financially, it still bothered him, and to top everything off his own son thought him to be dead. Now after all these years he was finding himself yearning for a relationship with both his sons, but he admitted he was afraid of being rejected by them even though he realized he was the one that rejected them first.

Mitchell took a long swallow of his drink then thought of Bianca once again and how he could not believe their coincidental meeting and the conversation about their children that had somehow brought them closer together. He thought with a smile that was probably the most memorable affair he ever had, usually he forgot about the women after about a day or so, but there was something about Bianca, he couldn't seem to get her off his mind. He briefly thought of Carmen, he still loved her, and all she had ever really wanted was a stable family life. He tried but he knew he could never be that for anyone and he was honestly getting tired of hurting her. Mitchell sat for a long time thinking about his sons, he never saw Ashland and Jordan leave the restaurant.

***

The next day Jordan and Ashland woke up early but didn't make it out of bed until late that afternoon. Jordan had been gambling since five, which was when Ashland left to go shopping. It was almost seven and Jordan decided to join the Black Jack table, there was an empty seat so he took it. The man sitting next to him spoke but looked at him strange for a long moment before he turned away. Jordan suddenly experienced this feeling of déjà vu, but he knew he had never seen the man before. He brushed it off and got into the game for a little while until he felt the need to check on Ashland. She wasn't in the room, so he decided to go down to the bar to have a few drinks.

When he got there, the same man from the Black Jack table was sitting at the end of the bar. He decided to join him. "Is anyone sitting here?" Jordan asked him.

"No, go ahead have a seat," the man said.

Jordan ordered a shot of vodka from the bartender then said to the man as he sat down, "I hope you did better than me at the table." Jordan had lost three hundred dollars.

The man laughed, "Barely, I only lost two-fifty."

The man still seemed familiar to him so Jordan said smiling, "I guess I should introduce myself I'm Jordan Alexander." Jordan smiled as he extended his hand.

The man looked at Jordan's hand briefly before he shook it then he looked directly into Jordan's eyes and said hesitantly wondering if Jordan even knew his name, "I'm Mitchell Maxwell."

Jordan's smile died on his face as he stared at Mitchell for a long moment. Boating accident, Jordan thought of his grandfather and of the little boy from so long ago, *'Your parents were druggies and threw you away because they didn't want you. That's why your grandparents got you.'* He stood and drank all his vodka in one long swallow then turned around and left.

Mitchell watched Jordan walk away and with every step Jordan took Mitchell's heart dropped. It hurt him so bad to watch Jordan's smile fade away when he told him his name. Jordan seemed so relaxed and happy at first, suddenly all emotion seemed to drain from him as his eyes became unreadable. Mitchell ordered another drink wondering how Jordan must be feeling to finally have met his father that he had presumed to be dead all these years.

Jordan went straight to their room and paced the floor. He packed their bags; he had to leave Vegas. He called and made flight arrangements for his private jet. He decided to tell Ashland he wanted to go back to the cabin in the mountains before they returned home. He stood looking out the window when all of a sudden he started laughing and thought he should have known. Looking into Mitchell's eyes was like looking into his own.

"What's so funny, Jordan?" Ashland laughed as she walked through the door, "I know I've been gone for a while but they had a great sale downtown." She noticed their bags packed then said with confusion, "I thought we were going to be here a few more days."

Jordan smiled and walked over to hug her tight and kiss her, debating whether to tell her about his father, but he didn't want to spoil their time together, "I wanted to go to the cabin before we went home." He smiled into her eyes.

"Okay that will be great. I love it up there." She frowned as she looked up at him a moment and asked, "Are you ok?"

"I'm fine but I'm tired of gambling and being alone on my honeymoon, and if we stay here any longer I'm afraid I'll never see you. You'll spend the rest of your time shopping," he said teasingly as he kissed the tip of her nose.

She felt a little guilty for being gone for so long, "I'm sorry Jordan. I'll make it up to you, I promise. So when are we leaving?"

He looked at his watch and said, "In about an hour."

Ashland knew something was bothering Jordan even though he laughed and talked, he was quiet for long periods, especially when they first left Las Vegas. During their stay at the cabin, he seemed his old self again. They had a wonderful time in the mountains neither really wanted to leave when it was time, so they decided to rent a car and take the drive back home instead of flying.

It was about five-thirty in the evening a few days later when they made it back home. Ashland was tired and opted decided to lie down for a while. Jordan needed to get himself together so he chose to go to his study to do some work to keep his mind off the situation. Tylen was sitting at his desk working when he entered.

"I see you made it back. Where have you been? I was getting a little worried." Tylen smiled glad to see him.

Jordan sat in the chair across from his grandfather. He was quiet a few minutes then he said softly, "Monday we went to Vegas and got married."

Tylen smiled, "I knew it was coming." Tylen stood and asked, "Want a drink?" He knew Jordan had something else on his mind.

"Sure" Jordan took a long swallow of his vodka but didn't say anything until Tylen sat back down. "I met my father on Tuesday." Jordan said as he took another swallow.

Tylen looked at Jordan as if he was in a daze. He was completely speechless for a few moments. Then he finally asked, "How did the two of you meet?"

Jordan's face was expressionless as he stared at his grandfather, "I actually sat at a Black Jack table beside him and played. I didn't play too long. I left then ended up at the hotel's bar. I saw him sitting there and decided to ask him how things went after I left the game. I knew something seemed familiar about him when I first saw him but I didn't pay too much attention to that. I introduced myself then he introduced himself. I just stood up and left."

Jordan stood to pour more vodka in his glass and sat back down, "You told me that my mother and father died in a boating accident after I was born. Now I've heard a lot of rumors over the years, which I ignored and never brought up because I knew the subject of my mother always upset you. But tell me, grandfather, did you lie to me? Was that boy telling me the truth when I was seven, did they not want me? Were they really strung out on drugs? Tell me everything grandfather and do not leave anything out. I have a right to know." Jordan looked hard at Tylen, his eyes demanding the truth.

Tylen sat back closing his eyes he looking like a man who had just been defeated, "Your mother had been on spring break from college when she met your father at one of her friend's birthday party when she was eighteen. Right away, she fell head over heels in love. At first, we didn't think too much about their relationship, she was eighteen and we were trying to respect her privacy. One day a couple of my friends, Phil Peters and Dawson Perkins, asked me whom Carmen was dating. I told them and they didn't ask anything else. A few days later I got a call from Phil; they wanted to get together to play poker. They came over to the house and we had only been playing for about ten minutes when Dawson told me he saw Carmen at a party. I didn't think anything of it so I continued to deal the cards. Phil threw his cards in, and standard yelling angrily at Dawson. I'll never forget that night as long as I live. He said, "Tell him damn it. You had better tell him right now because if she was my daughter I would want to know." I had never seen Phil so angry in all the years I had known him. He saw Carmen do a line of cocaine. Carmen had started smoking marijuana and drinking, they say she was doing it all. Everyone knew except Leola and me. We didn't know she had even dropped out of college. See, she was best friends with Phil's daughter, so I figured a part of him feared his daughter was doing the same.

Mitchell was wild, seeing a lot of girls around town, but for some reason he wouldn't leave Carmen alone. We tried everything we could think of to get through to her, but Carmen had become out of control where Mitchell was concerned. That was until she became pregnant with you. When she realized she was pregnant, we took her to the doctor and he had a real good talk with her after her blood work came back and drugs showed up in her system. She immediately stopped all the drug use. She loved you. While she was pregnant, she would read and sing to you. She decorated the nursery and bought clothes for you before you were born. That's why we couldn't figure out why she would leave. Your father would come to visit her about every two weeks or so. We monitored his visits to make sure he didn't try to get her to go off anywhere with him or give her anything illegal. She seemed happy enough with only his visits.

After you were born, we were all so excited. Mitchell came by to see the two of you. He and your mother walked through the gardens for about twenty minutes then they went up to see you. We thought maybe seeing you would make him want to slow down for a while, but we were wrong. Leola was sitting in the nursery when Mitchell walked in, Leola thought he was going to pick you up but all he did was lean over the crib and look at you briefly then he just turned around and walked out. I was in the study at the time. Carmen entered my study followed by Mitchell, as soon as Carmen closed the door Mitchell said, "Mr. Alexander we can't keep him. We don't know what to do for it. A baby? My God, we're still young we have our whole life ahead of us. We can't be tied down and burdened with a child this early in life. You and Mrs. Alexander can have him. We'll try to come around and visit him sometime." I only looked at Carmen not believing what I had just heard, but all she said was "I'm sorry daddy. Please let Jordan know when he's old enough that I do love him." After they left on his boat, I told a friend that Carmen died the minute she stepped on that boat. What I said got misconstrued, the rumor escalated, and Leola and I never tried to correct it. Out of respect, no one brought up Carmen again, and if they did I let them know I didn't care to hear or discuss anything they had to say. We never dreamed she would leave you for him; we didn't raise her to be that way. So that was the last day I ever saw or talked to your mother or your father. Jordan, I am so sorry I lied to you. We never wanted you to know how heartlessly they had acted towards you."

"Thank you grandfather for the truth, I think I'll go check on Ashland now." Jordan stood up and left the room even though it pained him to hear how his parents didn't want him he never showed any kind of emotion.

Tylen continued to sit back in the chair after Jordan left then said aloud, "Oh Leola please forgive me for telling him." His heart was heavy. This was the first time Tylen had cried since Leola died.

Jordan didn't know what to feel. He was angry. He knew he would get over it. It hurt him to hear all the things his father had said, but it only made him appreciate his grandparents more. He had already forgiven his grandfather for lying to him. As he walked up the stairs to check on Ashland, he promised himself that he would never walk out on his family for any reason. He was drained; he just needed to hold Ashland.

Ashland was asleep, so he lay down and held her. He couldn't fall asleep. For a brief moment, he allowed himself to wonder what his life could have been like if his mother had decided to stay. Ashland moved slightly then he pushed the thoughts of his mother aside. His grandparents had given him more than a lot of people would ever have. Now Ashland and his unborn child was his life he would give his child what his parents never gave him, a family with a lot of love.

Chapter Twelve

Ashland was lying in bed thinking how the months had gone by so fast. She was now eight months pregnant and everybody was driving her crazy. Jordan had even hired a housekeeper, Mrs. George, to help out around the house. Ashland thought, *That woman seriously gets on my last nerves, always telling me to eat this, eat that, don't do this, don't do that.* She just wanted to go to her cabin away from everyone.

After Ashland showered and got dressed, she decided to sit in the flower garden. It was a pretty December day not too cold or breezy, she loved being outside first thing in the mornings. Jordan had left for work early as usual. Lately, he's been leaving early every morning. He said he scheduled his meetings as early as possible so he could get home early afternoons. She didn't really understand the logic because if the baby decided to come at nine in the morning the baby wasn't going to wait until Jordan finished his meeting. She felt Jordan was avoiding her; he used to make love to her before he went to work and now he rarely touched her. She was moody today she felt too fat and very unattractive. She didn't want to be bothered with anyone today.

"Good morning, Ashland," Megan said brightly giving Ashland a glass of apple juice. "Would you like me to fix you some breakfast? Mrs. George had to go get peppers from the store. She'll be back shortly."

"No thank you the juice is fine for now." Ashland wanted to be alone and wished Megan would just go away and leave her alone. She knew Mrs. George got on Megan's nerves too, but Megan was just too polite to admit it.

"Ashland, I have something for you," Megan said excitedly as she jumped up and ran into the house returning quickly. She handed Ashland a pretty blue box with a white ribbon. "I made it myself I hope you like it," Megan said.

Ashland opened the box carefully and almost cried. Megan had knitted a baby blue sweater, hat and some little booties for the baby. "Oh Megan I love it!"

Ashland tried to stand but Megan jumped up and hugged her first. "I love you Ashland." Megan said.

Ashland cried, "I love you too Megan, thank you." She felt guilty for her earlier thoughts. "Megan, can we go somewhere? Just to get out of the house. Jordan never takes me anywhere anymore, besides I don't want to be here when Mrs. George returns."

"Sure, I don't think I can deal with her this morning either, she's on a rampage since I bought green bell peppers instead of red ones at the market." They both laughed then Megan added, "Just imagine how she'll be when the baby arrives. We'd better go now or else she won't allow you to leave the premises." They laughed but they also knew it to be true.

Ashland and Megan had a great time together they ended up eating breakfast, then going to the mall and seemed to buy everything they saw for the baby. Kayla even met them at the mall on her lunch. Ashland was happy and felt relaxed, Megan was the mother she never had. Her mother never took her on an all day shopping adventure like this. Bianca never really did anything, she mostly remembers her mother working or fussing about something that she or her father had done. Megan and Ashland ended up at an all you can eat seafood buffet bar for dinner.

Ashland hesitated then asked, "Megan, can I ask you a personal question?"

"Sure," Megan said in between bites.

"I was wondering, you look so young, and I don't know but Tylen appears younger than his age too. I mean, I don't really know what I mean. You really seem so young, yet you act older at times. I don't know. I know you should never ask but I was curious as to how old you are."

Megan started laughing and reached over to hugged Ashland, "I'm not ashamed of my age, I'm fifty."

"Wow, you don't look it!" Then Ashland added, "I wish my mother was more like you." Ashland thought, then asked

Megan another question, "Do you have any children?"

"No I can't have children. When I was twenty two the doctor told me I'd never be able to conceive," Megan said.

"I'm so sorry," Ashland said.

"Don't be, it's not your fault," Megan answered casually.

"Well do you think you and Tylen will get married?" Ashland asked curiously.

"Aren't you full of questions today?" Megan said jokingly, "Seriously I would marry him in a heart beat but I could never replace his wife Leola. I'm happy just the way things are. I love him and that's all that matters," She said honestly. "Oh my goodness, it's almost seven Jordan going to have a fit," Megan said worriedly.

Ashland laughed, "He'll be alright, but let's go."

It was a little after seven thirty when they arrived home. Jordan was pissed, Mrs. George was furious and Tylen was laughing. Tylen saw them pull up and met them at the door to whisper, "Ashland beware Jordan's not too happy with you right now." He kissed Megan and continued laughing as he helped Megan get all of the bags from the car. Ashland went into the Sun Room to wait on Jordan.

"Hi Jordan," she said as he entered the room. He sat down beside her without saying a word. "Did you have a good day?" She asked brightly.

"Ashland, I have been calling you since ten this morning. Mrs. George has been driving me crazy at work worrying over you. Why did you not answer you cell phone?" Jordan asked annoyed.

"Oh Jordan, I'm so sorry I forgot it," she said honestly.

Jordan inhaled deeply to maintain control. Ashland's forgetfulness sometimes drove him insane and he had already been having a very bad day.

"Did you miss me today? I missed you." Ashland reached over to kiss him. "You smell so good Jordan."

Before Jordan could answer, Mrs. George entered the room. "My goodness chile, I've been worried to death. Are you ok?" Mrs. George put her hand over her chest for effect.

"I'm sorry Mrs. George I lost track of time and forgot to take my cell phone with me. It won't happen again."

"Well, Megan should know better. She knows I'm too old to be worrying about you and the baby. She should have called."

"Oh Mrs. George, please don't be mad at Megan. I begged her to take me. I'm ashamed to admit, but I threatened to go without her if she didn't. I've just been so restless being inside all the time. As you can see she took real good care of me," Ashland said.

Mrs. George only made a noise then left the room. Jordan and Ashland laughed.

"Jordan" Ashland said standing slowly, "Come on up to the nursery and let me show you everything we bought for the baby."

Ashland fell asleep talking while lying in Jordan's arms, he thought how good it felt to hold her. Sierra had come by his office today. He had no idea as to how she found out where he was. He should have filed that restraining order against her instead of taking her word that she'd leave him alone. She told him she missed him, even had nerve enough to kiss him then asked if he was positive that the baby Ashland was carrying was his. That's when he put her out of his building telling security never to let her return. He would not allow himself to have doubts about Ashland, and he would not allow her or anyone else to upset Ashland especially while she was pregnant. Sierra was nothing but trouble and he had the feeling she was about to do something. He wondered how she knew about Ashland's pregnancy. Then to make matters worse, his father had called him telling him he wanted to see him, Jordan thought how he only laughed then hung up on his father. He then informed his secretary under no circumstances did he ever want to speak to Mitchell Maxwell again. After talking to his secretary, he found out that Mitchell had been calling at least once a week shortly after he returned from Las Vegas, so Jordan informed his secretary he would be working from home until his baby arrived.

***

Jordan woke up early the next morning. He showered and got dressed and went down to his study to work. When Ashland woke up, she didn't know Jordan was home. She went about her usual routine, but this time she decided to surprise Jordan at the office. She noticed that Jordan's car was home, but she didn't think too much of it, since Tylen's car was gone. Sometimes they would ride to work together. She left before anyone could miss her. When she arrived at the office, she didn't see Tylen's car there, so she thought she'd better call Jordan. She needed to stretch her legs so she got out of the car while she called his cell phone.

"Hello," Jordan answered and she thought how he always sounded so sexy in the mornings.

"Hi baby where are you?" Ashland asked.

"In the study," Jordan responded surprised at her question.

"At home?" She laughed, "I'm in the parking lot at your office. I was trying to surprise you. But I'm the one surprised."

"Ashland didn't you see my car in the driveway?" He laughed asking her as if talking to a child.

"I assumed you rode with Tylen since his car was gone." She snapped. "I'll be home in a little while; I guess I'll stop by the office to see Kayla on my way. I'll see you later." She hung up her phone. Ashland was walking over to get in the car when a very pretty woman came up to her.

"Hi, are you Ashland?" the woman asked.

"Yes I am why?" Ashland asked frowning.

"I'm Sierra Sanders, Jordan's friend. Can we talk?" She asked.

Ashland had a funny feeling about her, "I don't think so I'm on my way to a doctor's appointment." Ashland lied.

"It won't take but a minute. Please, we can sit over there," Sierra said pointing to a bench.

"Ok just for a minute," Ashland said cautiously.

"Well to start off, I am so happy to finally meet you.

- 111 -

Jordan has told me so much about you. I actually feel as if I know you myself. See Jordan and I usually eat breakfast together. I guess he's running late today." Sierra smiled.

Ashland didn't say anything she only sat wondering who she was and what she was talking about.

"Jordan never told you about me? Oh, my goodness I should have known. Yesterday when I left him I was under the assumption, he was going to fill you in on everything. All of us are supposed to get together and have lunch or drinks, whenever his schedule allows it," Sierra said with a slight frown.

Ashland only stared at Sierra without saying a word.

Sierra became nervous, she looked at her watch then said, "I wonder where he's at we're supposed to have breakfast. I'm sorry I thought you knew about me. I love Jordan but he can be forgetful and thoughtless sometimes. He left me to come down here to expand their business, telling me he wouldn't be gone for too long. Our schedules have been so crazy lately we rarely have time to talk to each other at nights, so we usually call each other during the day. You see we're engaged." Sierra held out her hand and showed Ashland the ring on her finger, "Well he told me about you two being such good friends and all. It's nice to have a friend that goes back to teenage years. So is your husband going to meet you at your doctor's office? Oh and I must say, Nick Balinsky is so handsome, I bet if it's a boy he'll look just like him." Sierra jealously heightened as she looked down at Ashland's ring, "Being married to the owner's son of Balinsky's Fine Jewelry does have its perks, doesn't it? Well I've got to run; Jordan will be meeting me at the hotel suite in a couple of hours. We like to spend as much time together as possible when I'm in town." Then she added, "Ashland, are you ok? Do you need me to call Nick for you?" Sierra asked for effect.

Sierra was beginning to get scared. She had been waiting for Jordan to arrive at work because she had planned to go to their house and talk with Ashland. While waiting she saw a pregnant woman get out of the car. She really hoped it wasn't her because this woman was advanced in her pregnancy.

However, by looking harder at her, she realized this was the woman in the picture Bianca gave her. Bianca had paid her handsomely, two thousand dollars to be exact, just to try and make Ashland think Jordan was a liar and cheat. She had even looked forward to upsetting the woman Jordan chose to be his wife. Bianca had given her enough information for her to plant seeds of doubt about Jordan, at least for a while. She was still angry at Jordan because he didn't want her. So, at the time she thought she'd have some fun. Bianca never mentioned to her that Ashland was so far along in her pregnancy. She wondered how a mother could do that to her own child. Looking at Ashland, she didn't think it was such a good idea now. If she didn't need the money so bad she would have told Ashland the truth about her mother.

Ashland only looked at her as if she was in a daze while she rubbed her stomach. Sierra stumbled as she stood up. "Well I got to run. See you later." Sierra nervously looked around and ran off.

Ashland opened her cell phone and called Kayla.

"Kayla speaking, how may I help you?" Kayla said very professionally.

"Kayla come get me, I'm in the parking lot at Jordan's office. I really need you. Please don't call anyone. Hurry ok." Ashland said unemotionally.

Kayla was nervous; she got to Ashland in less than fifteen minutes.

"Take me to my townhouse." Then Ashland added when she saw the worry on Kayla's face, "Don't worry I'm just stressed out right now." Kayla didn't say anything she helped Ashland get in her car. Ashland was scared she wasn't feeling good, she felt sick and nauseous and her stomach was slightly hurting.

When they entered the house and got Ashland settled onto the sofa, she told Kayla everything. "I'll be back in less than an hour. Call Megan and have her come sit with you so I won't worry." Kayla stood up abruptly before Ashland could say one word. Kayla didn't mean to but she was so mad that she yelled at Ashland, "Call her now, Ashland!" Ashland jumped slightly then called Megan as Kayla stormed out.

Ashland knew why Jordan left so early every morning, she knew why he'd stopped making love to her like he used to. He was having an affair. And she was fat and ugly.

* * *

Kayla beat on Jordan front door like she had lost her mind.

"Can I help you?" Mrs. George was irritated at the way she was pounding on the door.

"I need to see Jordan." Kayla said impatiently.

"Well he's busy right now working in his study and can't be disturbed." Mrs. George was surprised at Kayla's rudeness so she decided she could be just as rude.

"Oh really? We'll see about that!" Kayla said with attitude as she pushed herself past Mrs. George. She knew where his study was because she helped Ashland decorate the place. She opened the study door without knocking then slammed it shut.

Tylen and Megan had just returned home when Megan received a call on her cell then quietly rushed out. Later, Mrs. George grabbed Tylen's arm pulling him towards Jordan's study. Tylen and Mrs. George were bewildered, everything was happening so fast.

Jordan stood frowning and was immediately concerned, "Kayla, is Ashland ok?"

"What the fuck do you think? I told your monkey ass in the beginning not to hurt my girl. Now I'm gonna have to beat yo mutha fuckin ass," Kayla yelled as she took off her earrings and heels. The street thug in her came completely out.

Jordan only laughed. "Kayla calm down," he said casually as he tried to put away his paper so he could try and make sense of her anger.

"Let's see if you still laughing when I whoop yo ass!" Kayla jumped across his desk knocking them both over onto the floor as papers flew everywhere. She punched him about five good times before he could grab her and held her down.

Jordan wasn't laughing anymore, he was pissed that she busted his lip and made his nose bleed a little. "Kayla what the hell is wrong with you?" He asked her confused, barely controlling his anger.

"What the hell is wrong with me? What kind of stupid ass question is that? What the hell is wrong with you? Ashland doesn't deserve you cheating on her. You got her crying and shit over yo sorry ass! Hell she was crying over you when we first met. She should have left yo ass alone!" Kayla yelled she was so angry, she was crying.

"I'm not cheating on her, Kayla, I swear!" Jordan retorted back at Kayla.

"Well who the fuck is Sierra Sanders and why the hell is that stank ass ho filling Ashland's head with a lot of bullshit about the two of you being engaged and shit? Ashland don't need no shit right now and you know it. Men ain't shit!" Kayla yelled.

Jordan was so stunned at hearing Sierra's name that he unconsciously loosened his grip on Kayla. She swung on him a few times hitting him up side the head.

Tylen couldn't help laughing out loud. Kayla looked like a mad woman and Jordan looked so comical trying to hold her down. It had sounded like a tornado was ripping the room apart. Jordan and Kayla froze and looked up, Tylen laughed louder.

Kayla jerked away and stood, "You hurt her again and I'll beat yo ass again! You lying mutha fucker!" She kicked him and walked away.

Just as Kayla bent to pick up her shoes and earrings Jordan yelled, "Kayla" The room became completely quiet. Tylen was getting a little scared for Kayla he had never actually witnessed Jordan this angry before. "Where is Ashland?" He asked her so quietly and looked at her so menacingly she unconsciously took a nervous step back before she caught herself. She rolled her eyes and turned to leave. "Kayla," he said barely above a whisper visibly trying to control his anger, "I said, where is Ashland?"

Kayla was thinking a little clearer now that she was calmed down. She realized she may have temporary acted a little crazy by attacking Jordan, but she wasn't stupid and she knew he was more than likely pissed off at the highest level and she was not about to push him any further. "She's at her townhouse," Kayla told him.

Jordan stormed off without uttering a word to anyone.

"Kayla, what in the world is going on? Megan rushes out and you rush in," Tylen asked.

Kayla explained everything. She even apologized for losing her cool. "But dang Ashland's my girl," she said out loud to no one in particular.

Tylen only smiled he liked Kayla. She was a very nice young lady and had a lot of spunk. It warmed his heart to realize that Ashland had a true friend in Kayla, although he did feel sorry for Jamison or whoever if they ever wronged Kayla. Tylen couldn't help but laugh at the whole situation, but upon hearing Sierra's name he immediately became somber. He knew with her in the picture, Jordan would have a whole lot of explaining to do. She always managed to keep a lot of mess stirred up where Jordan was concerned.

Jordan showed up at Ashland's townhouse to talk to her.

"Ashland," Jordan said rubbing her face lightly.

"Don't touch me," Ashland said, she was tired and did not feel like arguing or being bothered with Jordan.

She wouldn't open her eyes but Jordan saw tears falling. He sat back on his heels taking a deep breath while rubbing his face. He leaned up to rub her hair softly. Ashland sat up and pulled away so he couldn't touch her, she couldn't look at him.

"Ashland, I swear to you," Jordan began but Ashland wouldn't let him finish, she thought about what Sierra had said and anger consumed her, she swung at him with her fists, but luckily for him she missed, so he grabbed her wrist, "Damn Ashland, be still, I admit I dated her a few times in the past, but that was it. I swear I haven't seen Sierra in five years before yesterday. Even then, she just showed up unannounced at the office. I didn't talk to her five minutes before I ended up throwing her out. I even told security to never allow her to return. That's why I was home I didn't want to risk seeing her again. You've got to believe me I would never hurt you or our baby."

Jordan sounded so frustrated and very sincere Megan almost left the room.

"Ashland please you've got to believe in me. I don't think I can handle losing you and the baby again," Jordan said softly with barely controlled emotions.

Megan stood up because she believed Jordan, he sounded desperate. She went to the kitchen to see if there was tea in the cupboard. Jordan and Ashland needed their privacy.

Ashland turned her head so she could look into his eyes. Jordan noticed her eyes were red and swollen, he couldn't stand to see her like this, and his eyes almost began to water.

"I love you Ashland with all my heart. I don't know what's going on and I don't know where she's getting her information, but whatever Sierra said to you about us seeing each other is not true," Jordan said as he stroked her face.

Ashland was tired but at least her stomach wasn't hurting anymore. This Sierra person knew too much about her and that concerned her, and she didn't know why she should believe Jordan but she did. Ashland sat up frowning to take a better look at Jordan. She rubbed his face softly, his left eye was red and a little swollen, and his lower lip was busted on the left corner. He even looked as if his nose had been bleeding. "What happen to you?" She asked.

"Kayla," he said, feeling himself becoming angry again when he saw Ashland lips twitch. Megan was sitting tea on the table and when she and Ashland looked at each other, they both lost it. Jordan stood he was furious and didn't see anything funny.

"I see you're back to normal, Megan will you make sure Ashland gets home," Jordan said tightly as leaned down to kiss Ashland then flinched because it hurt his lip to even kiss. Ashland and Megan laughed. Jordan only was becoming angrier by the second, "Don't get home too late, Ashland, drink your tea. I have things I need to take care of. I'll see you when you get home." He was turning to leave when he thought to asked, "Are you feeling ok? Do you need me to stay a while?" Concern for her health showed back in his eyes.

"I'll be fine. Just a little tired." Ashland said. Jordan nodded then left.

Megan and Ashland laughed for a long time. They were still laughing when they got home. Tylen and Jordan were sitting in the Sun Room when they entered. Tylen smiled. He couldn't wait to fill them in on what had happened earlier, "Oh my God you should have seen Kayla jump across that desk."

Everyone laughed. Tylen actually had tears in his eyes. Ashland laughed so hard her stomach hurt, she was still very tired so she decided to go to bed early. Jordan only stood to leave the room saying he would be working in the study for the rest of the evening.

Tylen suddenly said, "Jordan my boy," He paused long enough for Jordan to turn and then he took a swallow of his drink, "Make sure you lock the door. Kayla's coming over later to check on Ashland when she gets off from work." Everyone started laughing. Jordan was furious.

Jordan looked around his study. Mrs. George had straightened the room; papers were no longer everywhere. Jordan had to admit it was pretty funny when he really stopped and think about it. At least he knew he didn't have to worry about Ashland when Kayla was around. Sierra's sudden appearance was bothering him. None of it made any sense. Jordan was determined to find out what was going on.

Jordan's phone rang, "Hello." No one answered. Jordan knew someone was there, he could hear them breathe. Jordan hung up then picked it up again pressing the code to see the last number called. It was the same as before. He was fed up with everything. Someone had been calling and hanging up on him all week. He turned on his computer and decided to do a research on the number. He felt as if his blood had frozen when he saw the name that came up on his search.

Chapter Thirteen

Bianca sat in her hotel room drinking a glass of wine. She was thinking about Marcus. Early that morning she went to the house Marcus was renting trying to get him to come back to her, but she soon realized he had company. It was Parrish Clemmons, Bianca thought how she could not stand her ass, Parrish had told Marcus years ago about one of the partners of the firm that she had slept with, Bianca was mad because damn near everyone had slept with that man, including Parrish. Bianca thought how Parrish was always ranting and raving about how Marcus didn't deserve to be treated that way, Parrish always tried to be a goody- goody, but she was nothing but a ho on the down low. She wished she had never confessed to it during a girl's night out party. Bianca smiled thinking how she wished Parrish had found out about her sleeping with her ex-husband. Even though Marcus eventually forgave her, things were never really the same between them.

Bianca stood by the window looking and thinking about how pleased she was when Sierra told her everything she did, even though she ended up paying Sierra an extra two thousand just to keep her mouth shut. Bianca shook her head as she thought how Sierra had the nerve to storm up in here trying to judge her about her daughter, telling her she was too far along in her pregnancy to be getting upset like that. Bianca knew after everything Ashland had been through over the years, she could handle someone telling her about a man cheating on her. Anyway, if she lost the baby, oh well she could always have another. She had told Sierra if she knew what was good for her, she'd mind her own damn business. Bianca stopped Sierra dead in her tracks when Sierra tried to step up to her. In her most serious tone, she told her, "Bitch, you don't know me like that. Somebody will find your black ass floating somewhere you keep fucking with me." In fact, she had told her it would be to her benefit to disappear for while, keeping her mouth shut in the process or else she would help her disappear forever. Bianca let

Sierra know she wasn't playing any games, and Sierra got the message and left scared half out her mind. "Stupid bitch," Bianca said shaking her head.

Bianca then said aloud to herself, "Jordan, you will probably convince Ashland of your innocence, but it doesn't matter. You'll be faced with a new dilemma real soon. All I have to do is sit back and wait because it's only a mater of time before Carmen gets curious about her firstborn. I only wish I could see the look on your face when you meet your brother." Bianca laughed evilly.

Bianca had flown to Virginia almost two weeks prior and had taken Sierra with her. That girl was in serious need of money, so she was easily convinced to go along. She had paid Sierra three thousand just to pretend to be a reporter doing an article on black business owners. Sierra asked Carmen questions about Damian, and casually brought up her father Tylen, then later Jordan. At first, Carmen pretended not to know who Jordan was then she broke down finally admitted the truth to Sierra. Sierra ask Carmen if she knew she was about to become a grandmother, of course she didn't. Then Sierra ended by convincing her how wonderful it would be for two long lost brothers to come together. Carmen had a lot to think about.

Bianca laughed, she knew Jordan would not be happy, just imagine to start off his father couldn't stand to look at him, his mother gave him up, he grew up thinking his parents had died only to find out that was a lie. Then to find out his mother had another baby that she raised and loved, and as an only child at that, completely wiping Jordan out of the equation. Bianca shook her head because Carmen could have just as easily come home to raise both her boys, instead of waiting around on Mitchell to one day come back to her. Bianca shook her head and laughed madly saying out loud, "You gotta love it!" She hadn't felt so good or laughed so hard in a long time. "Jordan, mommy's coming back home and does she have a surprise for you!" Bianca laughed so hard she cried. Then she said aloud to again herself, "I warned you Tylen to keep your grandson away from my daughter but you just wouldn't listen. Now let us see how bad Jordan can really hurt." She just shook her head, smiled and drank the rest of her wine from the glass, then poured some more.

All of a sudden she thought of Mitchell and her smile softened he really knew how to make a woman feel good, especially for a dead man. She laughed. I guess I'll fly out this afternoon to Las Vegas to see him again, she thought. She was tired of waiting on Marcus to come around.

***

Jordan woke up early the next morning, Tylen and Jordan had a very important business meeting to attend. As usual, Ashland was still asleep when he left, she had gone to bed early saying she was sleepy and tired. Jordan figured she needed to rest more the closer she got to her delivery date.

At ten o'clock, that morning Ashland was still lying down. Megan and Mrs. George went back in together to check on her. Mrs. George had been calling Jordan for the past fifteen minutes on his cell phone, so Jordan excused himself from the meeting after she had called him the fourth time, he was on his way home. He told Mrs. George flatly she would be looking for another job if he got there and nothing was wrong with Ashland. He was sick and tired of her overly dramatic episodes.

"Ashland honey, are you ok?" Megan pulled a chair up beside Ashland's bed and asked as she rubbed her hair gently.

"I don't feel good, please leave me alone, I just want to go back to sleep," Ashland whispered so weakly, Megan could barely hear her.

"Jordan, I think we might need to call her doctor," Megan said when she looked up and saw him.

Jordan quickly walked in the room Megan moved so Jordan could sit down on the bed beside Ashland. He became instantly worried when he had entered the room and looked at her. She looked so pale. He touched her face and said, "Ashland, wake up!" He lightly shook her shoulders. She groggily moaned then Jordan felt something wet on his hips "Mrs. George the bed is wet she might be in labor. Come help me get her up. Megan, call her doctor." Jordan pulled back the covers thinking her water may have just broken.

Jordan could barely breathe, Megan gasped out loud and Mrs. George screamed hysterically, "Oh my God! Oh my God! Oh Lord, Oh Jesus help us please! Jesus" She ran in a circle then straight out the room as Tylen ran in. Ashland's gown was soaked in blood.

Megan managed to regain her composure to dial 911.

Jordan pulled Ashland up to his chest as she moaned painfully. He rubbed her back while softly talking to her. Jordan was terrified. He whispered, "Ashland baby, look at me."

"Don't, Jordan, I hurt when I move. My stomach hurts really bad, please make it stop." Ashland whimpered barely above a whisper. He had to lean closer to hear her, "I hurt." A single tear ran from her eyes. Everything suddenly went black for Ashland.

Jordan was trembling, "Ashland wake up. Ashland don't you dare leave me. Not like this. Ashland. Ashland!"

The paramedics rushed in, Jordan was still holding her, rocking her seemingly lifeless body trying to get her to talk or respond.

Tylen put his hand on Jordan's shoulders, "Son let them take care of her." Tylen said calmly. Tylen wouldn't let Jordan get in the ambulance, "Jordan, she just passed out. You got to let them do their job. Stay with Megan and me. We'll be right behind them."

Megan called Marcus, Bianca and Kayla while they were on their way to the hospital. Marcus was having a late breakfast when Megan called. When Kayla got the call about Ashland, she was dropping off a bracelet at Nick's jewelry store. Nick overheard her call, so he drove Kayla to the hospital. Bianca did not answer her cell so Megan left her a detailed message.

Bianca was on the phone with Mitchell when her phone beeped, she was giving him directions to the hotel where she was staying. He was arriving in Atlanta in less than an hour. She didn't answer the call because she wanted to talk to Mitchell, so whoever it was could leave a message for all she cared. After hanging up with Mitchell, she checked her messages. She re-dialed Mitchell to tell him about Ashland, she was beginning to freak out, so he tried to calm her over the phone, it was no use, but he told her not to worry and would meet her at the hospital. Bianca felt like an old woman. Everything she had done came crashing down on her with full force.

When Bianca arrived at the hospital, she was weary and completely stressed out. Her clothes were wrinkled and her hair was wind blown, Bianca had never left home with so much as a hair out of place and yet she didn't care; her only thought was Ashland and she felt totally to blame. The nurses told her no one had heard anything yet, and then led her to the waiting area to the rest of the family. Marcus and Parrish Clemmons were the first ones she noticed, Bianca just ignored them as they sat holding hands. Guilt was beginning to set in and she sat as far away from Tylen and Jordan as possible. She thought about how ironic it was that she had wanted Jordan and Tylen to hurt. They were hurting and she was hurting right along with them. All Bianca could think about at the moment was how her trifling ways were catching up to her. No one said anything to Bianca, there was really nothing to be said, there was still no word on Ashland. All they could do was wait, and that was very hard. The room remained very quiet.

Kayla could not take too much more of this waiting. She looked around at everyone in the room, Jordan, Tylen, Megan, Marcus and his lady friend, Nick, Mrs. George and Bianca, everyone had one thing in common and that was Ashland. She began to rock back and forth she was terrified. She looked over at Jordan. He sat still and unemotional. Kayla stood and walked over to him. Everyone seemed to hold their breath as Jordan just sat there never acknowledging her presence. He really didn't acknowledge anyone. Kayla bent down, took one of his hands into hers, and squeezed, with her other hand she lightly brushed her fingertips to the corner of his lip where she had hit him, "I am so sorry for hitting you." Kayla looked so small and scared that his heart went out to her.

"It's ok," he said softly then squeezed her hand back. Jordan seemed empty.

"I'm scared, Jordan," she said softly as tears began to fall.

Jordan wiped her tears away. "Me too," he said barely above a whisper. Jordan had unshed tears in his eyes. He was trying to be strong. He could not cry; he was afraid to.

Kayla stood to return to her seat.

Tylen said trying to lighten the mood, "Jordan, why don't you tell everyone about the tornado that came through your study yesterday." Tylen laughed, Jordan and Kayla looked at Tylen then at each other.

"I must say I hope Jamison is a very good man." As soon as Tylen said it, Jamison walked through the door and Megan and Tylen laughed.

"Hi everyone," Jamison walked over to Kayla and kissed her, "How is she?"

"We haven't heard anything yet," Kayla said.

"Tell me Jamison how long have you and Kayla been dating?" Tylen asked mischievously as Megan tried not to laugh, but couldn't help it.

Jamison looked at Kayla confused. Kayla rolled her eyes and shook her head. "Well since Tylen isn't going to give it a rest, Jordan would you like to tell everyone what happen or should I?" Kayla asked.

"I think we should let grandfather do the honors. I'm sure he'll make it more interesting than you and I ever could," Jordan tried to smile.

Tylen told every colorful detail as to what had taken place. By the time Tylen finished everyone was laughing, even Jordan.

Everyone got quiet when the door opened thinking it was the doctor, but it was Mitchell. "Hello Jordan," Mitchell said as he and Jordan stared at each other for a brief moment, Mitchell nodded towards Tylen, then he went straight to Bianca and held her hand. "How is she? Is the baby all right? Are you all right I got here as fast as I could?" Mitchell said to Bianca as he put his arm around her.

"We don't know anything yet, but I'm better now that you are here," Bianca squeezed his hand.

No one said a word. Everyone immediately felt the tension. No one knew who he really was except Jordan, Tylen and Bianca. Jordan stood and left the room. Tylen followed him.

Jordan was in the hallway standing with his hands in his pockets leaning against the wall when Tylen came up behind him, Jordan said, "I don't believe this is happening. How can he act so concerned after everything?" He sounded worn-out to Tylen.

The door opened and Mitchell came out.

"Why are you here?" Jordan asked Mitchell with quiet calmness that he was far from feeling.

"Bianca told me about Ashland and the fact that you are going to have a son. My grandson. I wanted to at least be here for you. I-"

"You son of a bitch!" Jordan said between clenched teeth as he grabbed Mitchell by his collar.

"Jordan, this is neither the time, nor the place for this. Let him go," Tylen said angrily as he grabbed Jordan's hands making him release Mitchell.

Mitchell put his hands in his pockets then continued as if nothing had happened, "Jordan, I know you don't want me here but I had to come. I've heard so much about you and I can't begin to tell you how proud of you I am, even though I can't take any credit for it. You're actually doing something I have always been afraid to do. That is stand up, take responsibility and be a real man. I knew Tylen would do a great job raising you," Mitchell said honestly. Mitchell watched Jordan a moment then added, "From what I hear, Ashland loves you too much to let go."

Jordan wouldn't admit it, but Mitchell said exactly what he needed to hear.

Tylen stood back and listened to Mitchell talk to Jordan. There maybe hope for him yet he thought to himself with a smile.

The doctor walked up, "Jordan come with me please." Jordan held his breath and stood unmoving not sure what to expect. The doctor smiled, "Don't you want to see your son? Considering he's a little early, he's a healthy five pounds and two ounces" Then he added softly, "And your wife. She's going to be ok. "

* * *

Jordan and Ashland named their son Michael Adrian Alexander. When Jordan held Michael, he could not describe the feeling that came over him, he looked over at Ashland where she was resting peacefully, and thought they were both going to be all right.

It was late when Jordan was getting ready to go home for the night, he decided to go to the nursery and sneak one last peak at his son. He couldn't believe what he saw. Mitchell was in the nursery holding Michael. Mitchell was smiling as he cried silently. Watching his father cry while holding his son really touched his heart. Jordan discretely left and went home.

The next day Jordan didn't arrive at the hospital until almost ten o'clock that morning. "I have something for you," he said kissing Ashland as he sat down.

"Oh yeah, what is it?" Ashland asked as he handed her a small box.

"Open it and see," Jordan said as he stood to pick up Michael.

"Oh Jordan I love it. And I love you." She had tears in her eyes. He gave her the locket back, but this time it held a picture of Michael on the right side. She put the locket back on.

"I love you too," Jordan said quietly.

For a moment Bianca went unnoticed in the doorway, she came to visit Ashland and her grandson; she smiled as she watched Jordan give Ashland the locket that Ashland always seemed to hold on to in spite of everything Bianca had ever said. Bianca admitted to herself that she knew deep down Jordan loved Ashland; having almost lost Ashland put a lot of things in perspective for Bianca. She realized how much she had hurt her daughter by keeping her and Jordan apart. Bianca also realized she had been so consumed with her work and Tylen for all these years that she never appreciated Marcus or even Ashland for that matter. She missed Marcus dearly but she knew too much had happened; it was now too late. Bianca was about to turn and leave so they could be alone when Ashland looked up and saw her.

"Hello Mother, come in please," Ashland said smiling.

Bianca smiled as Jordan held his son and she said, "He is so beautiful he looks exactly like you Jordan." Jordan looked up at a smiling Bianca, surprised because she usually never smiled at him. She explained, "Tylen has been showing everyone your baby pictures."

Jordan and Ashland only laughed. Jordan stood up and placed Michael in the crib then left, giving Ashland and her mom some time alone.

Bianca sat in the chair next to the bed, "Well you gave everyone a big scare yesterday, so how are you feeling today?"

"I'll be ok. I'm a little tired and very sore."

Bianca grabbed Ashland's hand, "Ashland I know I've done a lot of things that was wrong but throughout it all I've always had your best interest in mind. I am truly sorry for all the pain that I've ever caused you. You're my only child and I don't know what I would do if I lost you. I love you more than you'll ever know." Bianca had tears in her eyes.

"I know mother. I love you too," Ashland said, smiling as her mother hugged her.

Bianca and Ashland talked for about fifteen minutes more. It was probably the best conversation they ever had.

"Well I have to be going. I have a lunch date with Mitchell." Bianca said smiling. Just as she stood to leave, Nick walked in.

"Hello Nick," Bianca smiled.

"Bianca" Nick said with a nod of his head thinking of what Ashland had said about her lying to Jordan.

Nick tried his best to like Bianca over the years just because she was Ashland's mom, but he always felt uneasiness when she was around, especially after she had made a bold pass at him one thanksgiving day, then apologized blaming it on alcohol. He knew to keep this and his feelings to himself so he always tried to discretely avoid her whenever possible.

Bianca kissed Ashland on her cheek and left.

"Hey sunshine, you look very beautiful today," Nick said smiling as he walked over to the crib. "He's beautiful like his mother." Nick smiled softly at her.

"Everyone else thinks he looks like Jordan," Ashland said looking over at her son.

Nick once had thought Ashland would be the mother of his children. He looked over at Ashland and noticed the locket. Nick was suddenly struck with a sense of jealousy. He still loved Ashland, he always will. He remembered back when they were dating he had asked her about the locket because she always wore it and never took it off. She would always shrug off his questions saying it was given to her a long time ago. Well, one day after they had been drinking a little too much, Ashland had passed out on his sofa, he opened the locket, saw the picture of her and a man, and had read the written words inside, "I love you. I'll be back." Jordan most definitely came back, he thought ironically to himself. When he asked her who the man was, she said it was someone that hurt her really bad and the locket was a reminder never to completely trust anyone again. After that, he tried his best to make her forget that man and that reminder, and he had actually succeeded, until Ashland caught him with Sheila.

"I must admit I'm a little jealous of Jordan. He did something I never could," Nick joked, although he knew it to be true. He sat on the side of her bed and held her hand briefly, squeezing it before letting go.

"And what is that Nicky? Or should I be afraid to ask?" she questioned.

"Win you back and Marry you, of course." He smiled mischievously then leaned forward to whisper softly, "I always thought it would be my baby you'd have one day." He cleared his throat then stood, "Well anyways, Stephanie will be back in town next week I really want her to meet you. Damned if she didn't push up the wedding date. I was informed; we would be getting married in three weeks. All arrangements have been made all I have to do is show up." They both laughed, "Ash, she even planned my bachelor party." He shook his head laughing.

"No she didn't?" Ashland was laughing because she really missed talking with Nick.

"Yes she did," He laughed, "But damn I really do love her." He leaned over to kiss Ashland's cheek and said softly, "I love you too sunshine always will, be happy with Jordan." Nick turned to leave.

Jordan had been leaning against the doorway listening to their conversation. He was to say the least, jealous. It was obvious how much Nick still cared for Ashland. He also saw how fond Ashland was of Nick. Sierra's words returned, 'Are you sure you're the father of your wife's baby?' Jordan pushed that thought aside as he walked into the room. The blood test he had done already confirmed him to be the father. Anyway, Michael looked exactly like him. He only wondered when the last time Ashland and Nick had slept together was.

"Hello Nick," Jordan said casually, but careful enough not to show any signs of jealousy.

"Jordan, hi, we haven't officially met, I'm Nick Balinsky a friend of Ashland. I must say it is a pleasure to finally meet you." Nick's smile was contagious as he held out his hand to shake Jordan's.

"Is it now?" Jordan asked smiling.

"I've always wanted to meet the man that held Ashland's heart captive," he answered honestly.

"Did I now?" He looked at Ashland smiling as he asked. She could only smile.

"Congratulations on becoming a father and marrying the most beautiful woman I've ever laid eyes on," Nick said laughingly.

"Thank you," Jordan said. He didn't know why but he actually liked Nick.

Nick looked down at his watch, "I have to be going I'm

already late for my flight. Stephanie is going to have a fit. Jordan, I'll be back next week, it would be nice if we could all get together. I really want Stephanie to meet Ashland. Maybe if Ashland let you, we can get a few guys together and have a private bachelor's party," Nick said half jokingly.

Ashland laughed, "Nick I've seen videos of your so called private parties. If Stephanie found out you would never get married and Jordan would be divorced," Ashland said half jokingly. Jordan laughed.

Nick said, "Well I guess that means I'd better be going. I'll be seeing you around Jordan, talk to you later Ashland." Nick turned toward Jordan, "Oh one more thing you should know is to be careful. Ashland doesn't like to share her *belongings*, and she would rather go out and get new ones." He laughed when Jordan frowned, "Just don't make the same mistake I did. She'll explain it to you. See you later." Nick left the room grinning.

Jordan came and sat on her bed. "So that was your ex?" He asked still frowning.

"Yeah that was Nicky," Ashland said.

Jordan raised an eyebrow when Ashland called him Nicky, "So what did he mean by that?"

Ashland laughed, "I told him that after he cheated on me. By the way who was your real-estate agent?" She asked with a slight frown.

Jordan frowned at her sudden change in conversation, "I really don't remember his name. Why?"

"Just curious," Ashland kissed him.

"I can see why you like him," Jordan said honestly.

Ashland laughed, "Don't go getting ideas about that bachelor party."

Jordan laughed, "Just remember, I don't like to share my *belongings* either."

Chapter Fourteen

Over the next two weeks, Jordan and Ashland had lots of friends and family at the house. Jordan explained to his wife the fact that Mitchell was alive. Ashland actually liked him. She didn't approve of Mitchell's relationship with her mother because he was still married to Jordan's mother. But one thing was for sure, Mitchell was crazy about Michael. Jordan wouldn't admit it, but he liked Mitchell too or at least was curious about him, Ashland often found Jordan just staring at Mitchell when he held Michael when he thought no one was looking. Tylen took notice as well.

On the fifth week, the house was finally back to normal. It was rare for her to be home alone, but she was when the doorbell rang. Ashland opened the door she was holding Michael, smiling at a woman. "Hello," Ashland said then turned to the man who was standing next to the woman and began "Can I help-" the rest of the question died on her lips as she stared at the man. He looked exactly like Jordan.

The woman brought her out of her trance. "Are you Jordan's wife?"

"Yes, I am." Ashland kept glancing at the man, "Who are you?" She asked the woman, but she was looking at the man when the words came out.

"Hi" The man held out his hand to Ashland and smiled, "I'm Damian Maxwell"

Ashland turned her head slightly and frowned, "You're Mitchell's son." She said slowly.

Damian looked at his mother and frowned slightly he had never met his father. "Yes I am."

"Then you must be Jordan's brother, Hi I'm Ashland, Jordan's wife." She turned towards the woman and smiled.

The woman said, "I'm Carmen, Jordan's mother."

Ashland couldn't think of anything to say she was at a complete loss for words. Jordan and Tylen never spoke of his mother. Jordan had told her his parents were dead, so that's what she had always thought until a few weeks ago. Ashland frowned as she thought there wasn't even so much of a picture of her that she could ever remember, "Please come in." She led them to the Sun Room. "Have a seat make yourself comfortable. Can I get either of you something to drink or eat?"

"No, we're fine," Carmen said then she asked, "May I hold him?"

"Sure," Ashland said she couldn't help but stare at Damian. "I must apologize but you look exactly like Jordan, I mean even the eyes. How old are you?" Ashland said in amazement.

"I'm twenty-eight" He smiled, "Is Jordan here? I must admit I only found out I had a brother two days ago. I'm kind of anxious to meet him." Damian was nervously excited.

Ashland decided she liked Damian. Ashland looked up and saw Jordan standing in the doorway. He was staring at Carmen very oddly. Ashland immediately became very uncomfortable.

Damian stood smiling, "Jordan" They stared at each other for a long moment. They could pass as twins.

Ashland stood to walk over to grab Jordan's hand then said, "Jordan this is Damian, your brother, he just found out about you two days ago." She added nervously, "He's been so excited to meet you ever since." Ashland squeezed his hand tightly as she spoke.

Jordan knew Ashland was trying to keep the peace, he also knew Damian wasn't to blame, they both were almost the same, they had just found out about each other. A brother? Damn. He was trying to get his feeling under control. It was hard but he managed to get a slight handle on things. "Hello" Jordan smiled slightly at Damian. Jordan was stunned when Damian walked over to hug him tightly, and he hugged him back. It was weird, he used to wish for a brother, and to think he always had one. They continued to stare at each other neither seemed to want to look away, until Michael cried. Jordan looked over to who he assumed to be his mother and frowned, he walked over to take his son away from her.

"Hey little fellow, what's wrong?" Jordan asked smiling, turned to Damian, and said, "And this is Uncle Damian." Damian and Jordan looked at each other once again and smiled. Ashland relaxed a little. "Damian" Jordan said, "Would you like to walk up with me to lay Michael down for his nap?"

Damian smiled, "Yes I would." He turned towards Carmen and said, "Mom, I'll be back shortly." Jordan looked at Carmen and frowned when Damian called her mom he had actually felt a huge stab of jealously and resentment.

"Carmen I guess it's just the two of us for now. Are you sure you don't want tea or anything?" Ashland said wishing Megan was here because she always knew what to say no matter what the circumstance was. Then she thought, *I'm going to get Jordan for leaving me with his mother.* Right before Carmen could answer Tylen and Megan entered the room talking and laughing together. Tylen stopped dead in his tracks when he saw Carmen sitting on the sofa with Ashland.

Carmen stood slowly. "Daddy," she said unbelievably as tears of joy began falling from her eyes.

Tylen looked at her then turned and left the room quickly. All the hurt he had felt all those years ago came crashing back upon him.

Megan turned her head slightly then Ashland stood and said, "Megan this is Carmen, Tylen's daughter."

Megan was momentarily struck speechless. Then she gathered her manners very quickly and said, "Hello Carmen, I'm Megan a friend of your fathers."

Carmen sat down slowly and asked, "Where is my mother?"

Megan looked at Ashland and Ashland shook her head, so Megan took a deep breath then said, "You mother passed on years ago."

Carmen began to cry and Megan put her arms around her to comfort her. Ashland left the room to make some tea.

Mrs. George entered the kitchen, "Ashland what are you doing?" She asked in a loud demanding manner.

Ashland jumped before responding, "I'm making some

coffee and tea for our guests."

"I'll do that," Mrs. George said and scooted Ashland from the kitchen.

Ashland looked in the Sun Room where Megan and Carmen were talking. She decided to find Tylen. He was in the study.

"Tylen, are you ok?" Ashland asked.

Tylen smiled slightly, "Yes Kitten, I'm sorry but she looked so much like Leola that I just couldn't take it."

"It's alright. Megan just told her about her mother. She never knew she had passed," Ashland said.

Tylen leaned back in the chair, "I'll be out there in a minute. Please give me a little time to myself."

Ashland nodded and left the room. She was walking back to the Sun Room when the doorbell rang. She was glad for the interruption. It was Mitchell. Great she thought. Ashland smile, "Hi Mitchell, come on in." She had started to warn him then changed her mind. He was the one that created this mess. Let him deal with it like everyone else.

"Hi Ashland, I just stopped by to see Michael for a few minutes. Is that ok?" Mitchell asked.

Ashland thought for a brief second and smiled, "Yes, follow me." She made sure he never looked into the Sun Room. They went straight to the nursery. She opened the door and smiled, "Jordan, Mitchell is here to see Michael." Then added, "Go on in Mitchell. I'll see you down stairs." Ashland immediately closed the door behind him, she was curious but this was their time to be alone.

Ashland knew she shouldn't have left Megan with Carmen but she went to her room anyways. Too much was going on for her right now, and she knew much more was about to come, so she took a very long relaxing bath to help prepare herself for what was to come.

When Mitchell entered the nursery, he was faced with two identical faces, his two sons. Jordan sat down in the rocking chair and thought to himself, this should be interesting. Mitchell looked at Jordan and then at Damian and back at Jordan again.

"Hello father," Jordan nodded.

Damian stared hard at Mitchell. He was stoic. He was angry at his father for leaving his mother. He could not believe Jordan could just sit there so casually. Damn if anyone should be mad, he thought. It should be Jordan. At least, he felt he had his mother.

"Mitchell, how are you feeling today?" Jordan asked as he stretched casually back in the rocking chair.

Mitchell thought how Jordan was the one he had completely discarded, he at least had provided for Damian, yet Damian was the one who didn't even try to conceal his contempt and hatred, and with Jordan, he couldn't seem to ever figure him out from one minute to the next. Mitchell could talk to Jordan but Jordan had a way of looking at him that made him uncomfortable and edgy at times, like the way he was doing now. Mitchell, looking at both his sons, felt Jordan's calm appearance was definitely the more compelling of the two.

"Mitchell, I know it's been a while, but you do remember your other son Damian, Maxwell don't you? Oh yeah I almost forgot you left before he was born." Jordan rocked slightly in the chair. "Damn, I guess I should feel lucky, huh? At least you waited until after I was born before you left and at least I was told you were dead, poor Damian here, had to wonder why his father left and where he was for all these years." Jordan then added recklessly with a chuckle, "Tell us Mitch, who you think looks more like you, me or Damian?"

Mitchell obviously didn't know what to say.

"Well Mitch, tell me what brings you by today?" Jordan asked while laughing.

Mitchell would have laughed under different circumstances at the way Jordan was calling him Mitch, but today was not the day. "As I was telling Ashland I only wanted to look in at Michael for a few moments."

"Damian and I just got him off to sleep. Try not to disturb him, I'm sure you won't though, I'm quite certain you've done it before. You know bending over the crib looking for the briefest of moment and then walking callously back out.

Well tell me." Jordan stood abruptly when he felt his anger began to rise, "Would either of you like to have a drink with me? Mitch, I'm sure you would. Damian, do you drink?" Jordan was trying to keep everything light but his emotions were wearing thin.

"Yeah I do drink. Lead the way," Damian said tightly.

Now, Mitchell knew for certain that Jordan was told of how he had coldheartedly given him away when he was only a few days old.

"Hey Mitch" Jordan patted him on his back and asked, only to add to his discomfort, "I was just thinking, what do you think we should do on Father's Day this year? It's a first for me." Jordan laughed then added when Mitchell never responded, "Well I guess we'll just have to figure something out, won't we?"

As Mitchell, Jordan and Damian descended the stairs, Tylen was leaving the study. He looked up with unbelieving eyes and stood completely still.

"Grandfather, I'm glad you're home. I want you to meet someone," Jordan paused for effect, "This here is Damian Maxwell, your other grandson."

Tylen looked at Damian then he reached over to hug him, Tylen had tears in his eyes as he said, "I never knew." Then he repeated brokenly, "I never even knew."

Damian smiled, "Hello" Then added, "Grandfather"

Tylen hugged him again tightly.

Jordan smiled broadly, "Now let's go have that drink, I think the Sun Room, as my beautiful wife, Ashland, loves to call it, is the perfect place for a drink."

Mitchell thought a drink was just what he needed. *Oh hell*, he thought as he looked at Carmen, *I need the whole damn bottle.*

Carmen saw Mitchell and was visibly shaken. She hadn't seen her husband in over twenty-eight years. He was still a very sexy and extremely handsome man, his hair was still thick and jet black just a slight bit of gray on the sides. He looked very distinguished. She had once loved him, embarrassingly enough more than life itself. She was bothered because he was the last person she had expected to see here. She wondered with jealousy how long he had been in Jordan's life. She had actually been stupid enough to give up her child for him. As she looked over at Jordan, she finally realized she couldn't blame Mitchell at all. It was in all honesty her decision. She had chosen to leave her beautiful precious baby and she had chosen not to go back home out of fear even after Mitchell had left. She could have raised both her boys, but if she did, deep down she admitted to only herself, she feared how Mitchell would've reacted to two boys. She knew she had been waiting on Mitchell to return, afraid if she left, their house he wouldn't be able to find her and she knew he would never go back to her father's house. She was also afraid of what her parents had thought of her, afraid of them turning her away, the way she had turned from Jordan and now most of all she was afraid of Jordan's rejection. She needed Jordan to forgive her, but yet she couldn't forgive herself. Admitting to herself that as the years passed it had become easier to stay away. Suddenly, she was flooded with so many overwhelming emotions. It was as if a dark cloud engulfed her.

Jordan was quiet as he made drinks for everyone. He looked briefly at Carmen; she was staring at him strangely, because he didn't want her coming anywhere near him. After talking with Damian and finding out how Mitchell had left them, he didn't understand why and he doubt he ever would be able to understand why she never came back home or at least sent for him. He thought to himself, he was only two years old at the time. Hell, he could have even just visited them on summer breaks. He took a double shot of tequila to soothe his raw emotions, then another shot. Jordan looked at Mitchell and gave him a double shot too. He left the bottle out on the bar. Mitchell smiled his thanks, but Jordan didn't return the smile. Jordan thought he could deal easier with Mitchell for some reason even though there was still a lot of resentment towards him.

Carmen stood slowly. Damian, Mitchell, her father and

Jordan were all in the same room together. She walked straight to Jordan, hugged him tightly, and began to cry uncontrollably. The room was suddenly quiet as Jordan stood there for a long minute before he decided to hug her back briefly, then just as quickly he pulled her arms from around his neck and left the room. Mitchell was the one to follow him out.

Megan stood and went to comfort Carmen, "Well everyone, why don't we all have a seat. Carmen come sit beside me." Megan smiled brightly, "Damian, Carmen tells me you have a Marina boating company. How very interesting. Tylen, doesn't that remind you of the time we went to Panama?"

Megan was wonderful, Tylen thought, as she started telling them about Panama. He paused briefly to sit by Carmen he put his arms around her, holding her as he did when she was a young teenager, "Carmen everything is going to be fine you just have to give him time. I love you and I forgive you. I'm here for you." Then he continued to talk about Panama. Carmen felt a great weight come off her shoulders; her father at least had forgiven her.

Mitchell followed Jordan to the study, by the time he got there Jordan was sitting outside on the balcony with one foot propped up on the railing. Mitchell sat down in the chair beside him. "It's nice out here," Mitchell said looking around. Jordan didn't respond so he began talking slowly, "When I saw Carmen I knew I had to have her. I fell in love with her the same day I saw her. She was so beautiful and full of life, but unfortunately, I didn't do right by her. I think back on how I openly cheated on her, constantly hurting her and somewhere deep down I think a part of me wanted her to leave me. I knew I could never be good enough for her, so I told her I didn't want to be a father and that I was leaving. It really surprised me that she wanted to come along, because she knew you couldn't come. It was my fault she felt she had to make a choice right then and there." He inhaled deeply, "I let her come with me, but deep down I knew I should not have. She should have stayed there with you and found someone else who really deserved her. But to be honest with you, I was selfish and I just simply loved her." Mitchell took a deep breath, "A year later we married and Carmen became pregnant again. I had the nerve to ask her to have an abortion. Thank God, she refused. I actually tried to settle down for a while but first, I was terrified, and it only got worse the further along she got into the pregnancy. I had to leave, but first I made sure they were taken care of."

Mitchell inhaled deeply and stood to stand in front of the rail, "I was young and wild, but my father only saw me as a complete failure who was out of control." Mitchell thought of his father then continued, "I only wanted to enjoy life. My father loved to party, he made my mother so miserable that she ended up killing herself when I was only fourteen. Unfortunately, I was the one who found her. I found myself being my father and I didn't want Carmen to end up like my mother." Mitchell was quiet for a long moment then continued talking, "Now I look back and I'm ashamed to admit that I simply didn't want any responsibilities. That day I looked down at you, you were so young and innocent I got scared. I was afraid of you. You represented home and stability, responsibilities and growing up. I was afraid of failing and I didn't want to grow up yet, part of me didn't think I was cut out to be a father. I don't think I wanted to raise you because I was afraid you'd end up like me, because I ended up like my father. Now look at me, all the parties are over. I'm old, I'm all alone and I don't have anything to show for myself. Since the day we've met in Las Vegas I thought a lot about the things I've done and didn't do and I honestly think I did the two of you a favor, because Tylen did a hell of a job with you and Carmen did right by Damian." Mitchell felt older than his years at that moment he would have given anything to have a relationship with his sons. Mitchell then asked very slowly, "Why don't you at least talk to her or at least listen to what she has to say. She is your mother."

Jordan sat and listened to Mitchell he was even beginning to understand him a little but when he said, "She is your mother," he felt as if he might explode. She wasn't his mother, his mother died when he was eight. His grandmother was his everything. He still missed her deeply.

"Tell me Mitchell, how does a woman give up one child then dedicate herself in raising the other? I mean really now, I see, but I don't understand, how some men can walk away but I've never understood how a woman could, not after everything she has to go through," he asked with a raised eyebrow.

"Jordan, I don't know." Mitchell was dumbfounded.

"I mean really now, It's not like she didn't know where I was," Jordan persisted then he laughed when he felt as if his emotions were about to take control and said with a raised eyebrow, "And you. Hell, you didn't want me either. How the hell did I manage to get stuck with parents like the two of you?" Jordan shook his head.

Mitchell saw the pain in his eyes. "Jordan, lets get out of the house for a while. Bianca took me to a place called Misty's. It was really nice."

Jordan laughed a little, "Yeah Ashland and Kayla loves that place too." Jordan stood, "Let's go."

Jordan and Mitchell returned two hours later. Although Jordan never stumbled or slurred when he spoke you could tell he was drunk. They both were. Everyone was still there. Carmen was sitting beside Tylen holding his hand. Ashland was sitting on the love seat beside the window holding Michael, Jordan sat down beside Ashland. He kissed Michael then he kissed Ashland, "I love you both you know." When Jordan looked into her eyes Ashland saw pain there.

Ashland rubbed Jordan's cheek and smiled, "I love you too."

Jordan leaned back casually and said, revealing all the hurt and pain he felt all these years in his voice as he spoke, "Carmen, you've finally taken the time after all these years to come and see me, you're a little late, though wouldn't you say? Damn, come to think of it I'll be thirty-one this year, it is a little late for motherly love, wouldn't you say? Damn mother, come to think about it, I believe I was better off thinking you and Mitch were dead."

Mitchell instantly sobered up. Megan whispered something to Tylen then she stood and left the room.

Tylen squeezed Carmen's hand. He had told her about Jordan believing that they were dead for all these years. In addition, how he finally had to tell him the truth. Tylen turned to Damian then said, "Damian, my boy, we have a lot of catching up to do. Let me show you around the house. Jordan has an amazing weight room."

More than anyone Damian understood how Jordan felt, he stood and followed Tylen.

Ashland kissed Jordan then stood, "I'm going to put Michael to bed. Mitchell, would you like to help me? You can stay the night; you really don't need to drive. I'll get a room ready for you." Mitchell stood hesitated for a few minutes then left the room.

Jordan looked carelessly at Carmen. He was drunk and he didn't care, he would tell her exactly what he thought. "Mother, what is it that you could possibly have to say to me after all these years that I could be interested in hearing?" Jordan said hatefully, not trying to hide any of his feelings.

Carmen was speechless she didn't expect him to just forgive her but she also didn't expect him to be so hateful towards her. "Jordan, I-"

"You what Mother?" He cut her off rudely, "Sorry? Didn't mean to hurt me? Oh please don't even think about saying you love me." Jordan stood to fix another drink.

"Do you think you really need that?" Carmen asked slowly.

Jordan looked at her briefly, "Why don't you tell me since you seem to know what I need, or do you? I seem to recall being told my parents were dead, only recently finding out they're not. Now I find out my mother actually left me when I was a few days old, only to have another child two years later, which she lovingly raised. If she had made the time to send maybe a single birthday card or make a simple phone call, or stop by on a holiday, I would have known she wasn't dead. Tell me Carmen, where was my mother? Hell I thought she was dead myself, now out of the blue she shows up on my doorstep asking me if I really need to be drinking." Jordan turned up his glass and drank, "I most definitely need a drink." Then he callously said, "Besides, I often heard you liked to drink and partake in illegal substances. Would you care for a drink? I must apologize though; I don't have any of that other stuff you're so fond of." Jordan knew he struck a nerve, he saw the hurt in her eyes. Carmen stood to leave.

"Jordan, I see that this may not be a good time to talk. I think I should be going. Would you please let Damian know that I'm ready?"

"With pleasure *Mother*," he said insolently as he walked casually towards the doorway to leave the room.

"Jordan!" Carmen yelled so unexpectedly that he stopped and turned around smiling.

"Yes *mother,* did you need something? Although I must say I'm not a child any longer for you to scold," he said with a raised eyebrow.

"Jordan, I've made a lot bad choices in my life. I can't even explain, understand or even justify some of the things I've done." She spoke with firmness, "In all fairness I understand you not welcoming me in your life. I would probably be the same if it were me." Then she added with such conviction as tears ran down her face, that Jordan actually listened to what she said, "There wasn't a day that didn't go by that I didn't think of you. I wanted to come for you, but I was afraid daddy wouldn't let me have you back. I know I'll never know if he would have or not, but I was scared. So I raised Damian thinking he was an only child, I love him, but I never stopped loving you. I swear on my mother. I loved you." Then she asked him firmly, but her eyes pleaded, "I only ask for you to find it in your heart to forgive me. I am not asking for you to forget."

Jordan inhaled deeply, "*Mother,* you come here after all these years and expect me to just forgive you. What is it? Is it your conscience bothering you all of a sudden?" Jordan shook his head and said flippantly, "Hell *mother,* I forgive you, if that's what you come to hear." Jordan left the room.

Carmen sat down and cried for about five minutes, and then Mitchell entered the room. He had been on his way to the gardens as he passed Jordan, who had walked right passed him going to the study, so he decided to check on Carmen. Mitchell sat down slowly beside Carmen and held her tight. He whispered softly, "Carmen I am so sorry for all the pain I've caused you." Mitchell knew he was responsible for everything and it tore away at his heart as he held Carmen. "God help me, I still love you. Please forgive me for everything I've done." Mitchell kissed the top of her head as he held her tight. Mitchell was tormented on the inside, "If only I had stayed with you and raised both our boys together, oh Carmen, what have I done?"

Tylen and Damian stood in the doorway they had come to check on Carmen after they heard the door to Jordan's study being slammed shut, but they stopped and listened to Mitchell console Carmen. Damian was still angry at his father, but after hearing his words to his mother his heart softened a little towards him. They left them alone.

Chapter Fifteen

The next morning Mrs. George made everyone sit down as a family to have breakfast. Damian and Carmen ended up staying the night. "It's a shame you all can't come together at a time like this. In my day, we took the good with the bad. Family stuck together," Mrs. George mumbled to herself as she walked back and forth to the kitchen.

Mrs. George stopped in front of Jordan with hands on her hips, "Jordan is there a problem with your breakfast?"

Jordan only looked up at her with a raised eyebrow.

"Don't give me that look. If you would eat a little you would feel better." She shook her head as she glanced at Mitchell, "All that drinking your head ought to hurt. You know you know better. Ought to be ashamed," She turned away shaking her head and mumbling as she went to the kitchen.

"Jordan, do you have any plans for today?" Tylen asked.

Jordan didn't say anything, so Ashland answered, "It looks so pretty outside that I thought we could have a cook out today. What do you think, Megan?"

"I think that would be wonderful," Megan said brightly, "You can call Kayla and invite them also." Ashland nodded in agreement.

"Ashland, just don't forget to invite Marcus and Bianca," Mrs. George said as she passed by glancing at Mitchell on the way out of the kitchen.

Ashland thought maybe this wouldn't be a good idea after all, as she thought of her mother and Mitchell.

"Who are Marcus and Bianca?" Damian asked smiling at Ashland.

"My parents" Ashland said smiling back at Damian.

"This is going to be a very interesting day I see. Megan, pass me the sausage please. Jordan, as soon as we finish breakfast, I need you to look over a report that I have in the study. It shouldn't take very long," Tylen said. Jordan only nodded.

"So Carmen, would you like to go with Megan and me to the store? We can stop by your room to pick up a few things for you and Damian. Better yet, Mrs. George is right, we're family, and we can just check you and Damian out of your rooms. There is plenty of room here for the two of you. Isn't that right, Jordan?" Ashland said looking firmly at Jordan.

Carmen looked nervously at Damian then Jordan.

Jordan's face remained expressionless as he stood and said flatly, "Yes that's right. Damian and Carmen, as Ashland said, we do have the room. Now if you all will excuse me I have a few things to take care of in the study."

Jordan sat at his desk, pissed at Ashland for putting him on the spot like that and for inviting Carmen to stay. He leaned back in his chair thinking how everything was happening all at once. He closed his eyes for a moment.

"Jordan my boy, are you doing ok today?" Tylen asked grinning.

"What are you all happy about? Oh yeah I almost forgot you got your daughter back."

"And another grandson," Tylen smiled happily.

Jordan smiled for the first time, "Yeah I do like him."

"I'm glad to hear you like somebody," Tylen joked, then added seriously, as he removed two folders from the file cabinet then sat in the chair opposite of Jordan, "Well Jordan we have quite a few things to discuss."

"Let's have it. I'm sure things can't be any worse than they already are." Jordan said coolly.

Tylen only raised an eyebrow, "I had a visitor a few days ago. His name was Mark Trovelli," Tylen handed one of the folders to Jordan, and then continued, "Mr. Trovelli is a private investigator who had been hired to investigate you, Megan and myself. That's the full report of his findings. Very interesting, don't you think?" Tylen sat back and crossed his legs as Jordan read over the report.

"My God, Bianca had an abortion, was it yours?" Jordan asked visibly shocked.

"My guess would be yes," Tylen said unsmiling.

"So who hired him?" Jordan questioned.

"Bianca" Tylen said point-blank.

"Bianca? Damn," Jordan couldn't think of anything else to say.

"It seemed she tricked him by telling him she was concerned for Ashland's welfare. He called her office one day and the secretary told him she would be out for a few weeks. He later found out she went to Las Vegas," Jordan raised his eyebrow, now he was beginning to understand everything. Tylen continued talking, "He followed her down to Vegas. She met with Mitchell and they started having an affair. I think this is what angered Mr. Trovelli. You see they were seeing each other, so Mr.Trovelli had decided first to investigate Bianca before he let me know what was going on." Tylen handed the other folder to Jordan. This folder contained pictures of Bianca and Mitchell in various settings some were bold and explicit. There were pictures of Carmen, Damian and Sierra.

"What is this?" Jordan asked frowning holding up a picture of Bianca giving Sierra money.

"Mr. Trovelli decided to visit Sierra after she returned to Cleveland, Ohio. It took him a while to get Sierra to talk to him, but when she did, she told him everything. You see he had to promise her Bianca would never find out about her talking to him. Bianca had threatened her; the poor girl was scared half to death. Anyway, Bianca paid her to pretend to be a reporter doing an article on black business owners to get close to Carmen. Sierra convinced Carmen a reunion between you and Damian would be the just thing to do. Bianca paid her three thousand dollars just for that." Tylen hesitantly continued, "Bianca also paid Sierra two thousand dollars to convince Ashland that you two were still seeing each other. She even got an extra two thousand to keep her mouth shut."

Jordan leaned back and took a deep breath, "I can't believe Bianca actually had Sierra to do that to Ashland. I wish Bianca could have seen what it did to Ashland."

"Evidently, Ashland loves and trust you more than we all realized," Tylen said smiling, then said, "In a sick way,

Bianca did bring out the truth, but I would say it back fired on her. Did you see how she looked when we all thought Ashland might not make it? She looked a mess, Bianca thrives on her looks, and it terrified her to think she might actually lose Ashland, possibly because of something she had done."

"What do you intend to do with this report?" Jordan asked carelessly.

"I haven't decided I think you'd agree that Ashland should not see what her mother has been up to. They've really been getting along rather well lately." Tylen thought for a minute, "I started to shred everything, but I don't think that would be a good idea. See I don't trust Bianca, not even with her new change of attitude. I really don't think she's genuine. So for the moment I'm gonna just keep it locked away safe and sound." Tylen was truly bothered by the fact that Bianca had actually threatened someone.

Jordan only nodded in agreement then stood, "Well since that's settled I'd better go and throw on some jeans, I think I'll do the grill today."

"Jordan, do me a favor," Tylen asked with a serious expression as he stood.

"Sure, what do you need?" Jordan asked.

"For you to relax and just enjoy yourself today," Tylen put his arm around his shoulders and laughed.

"I will try." Jordan thought how his whole life he had wished for a normal family, a mother, father and a brother, now he had it and all felt was anger and resentment towards his parents, especially his mother. The night he sat in his study, after walking away from Carmen, and thought about Michael, he knew he wanted his son to have a normal family life. So Jordan decided to try his best to push all his feelings aside for the sake of his child. Jordan took a deep breath and tried to prepare himself for the day to come.

***

Jordan was cooking steaks on the grill when Damian came up holding Michael.

"Jordan he looks just like my baby pictures, he's a true

Maxwell," Damian said smiling.

"You mean Alexander, don't you?" Jordan said returning the smile.

"Jordan whether you like it or not your father is a Maxwell," Damian laughed.

"Yes he is, but you're forgetting one very important thing," Jordan said.

"And what is that Jordan?" Damian questioned with a smile.

"We both look like our grandfather, and he, my dear little brother, is an Alexander." Jordan said grinning as he leaned over to kiss Michael.

As Mitchell walked by them and he said, "Well he does have the Maxwell eyes."

"Well Mitch, I guess you're right on that one," Jordan said with laughter.

* * *

Ashland and Kayla had been sitting under the gazebo watching her children, D'Neko and Tymera as they played cards with Megan and Tylen.

"Kayla, did you tell Tylen that they were little card sharks?" Ashland said laughing.

"Tylen said it would only make the game more interesting," Kayla said as she shrugged her shoulders. "Ashland, does he have a girlfriend?"

"Who?" Ashland questioned her with a frown.

"Damian," Kayla said shyly.

"I don't know, he never mentioned one. Why?" Ashland said frowning.

"Just curious," Kayla smiled mischievously.

"What happened with Jamison?" Ashland asked suspiciously.

"His girlfriend stopped by his house while I was there," Kayla said carelessly.

Ashland frowned as she noticed for the first time scratches on the back of Kayla's arm.

"Girlfriend? Damn Kayla, don't worry about his ass, besides it's his loss. And what happened to your arm?" Ashland asked, but she already knew the answer.

"She had the nerve to slap me over Jamison's sorry ass, so I had to whop her ass." Kayla said nonchalantly.

Ashland only laughed, then she smiled when she saw how Kayla was looking at Damian, "He is sexy, isn't he?" Ashland said laughing.

Kayla threw her hair band at Ashland and said, "I'll be right back Ashland."

Damian was laughing when Kayla walked over, "Damian, are you going to let me hold Michael anytime today?" She said flirtatiously.

"Sure," he said kissing Michael as he handed him to Kayla.

Before Kayla could say anything else Tymera ran over pulling on her leg, "Mom I beat grandpa Tylen. I won five dollars."

"Tymera, what did I tell you about taking people's money," Kayla said firmly.

"But momma, I won this money, he lost not me," Tymera whined while holding out the money.

Before Kayla could respond, Damian bent down, "Hello, I'm Damian, and what is your name?"

Tymera looked up to her momma, Kayla nodded and she replied, "Tymera"

"Tymera, what card games do you like to play?" He asked smiling.

"Poker, spades, but my most favorite is tunk. My brother, D'Neko, plays bid wiz too." She said smiling.

Damian was completely shocked he expected her to say old maids or go fish, "Well if you're that good, do you want to play for your five dollars? That is if it's ok with your mom," Damian looked up at Kayla questioningly.

"It's your money honey," Kayla said as she winked at Tymera.

"Come on Mr. Damian," Tymera said walking away, "But don't go getting mad when I take your money too."

Jordan laughed then shut the grill down for a moment. "Well Kayla, I'm not missing this, my money's on Tymera, unless of course D'Neko's playing."

Everyone was standing around the table as Tymera, D'Neko, Damian and Mitchell played tunk.

"Side bet of two dollars on high spades, you want some, Mr. Damian?" D'Neko asked with his baseball cap turned to the back.

"Sure" Damian said in good spirits.

"How about you Mr. Mitchell, Tymera?" D'Neko asked smiling.

Mitchell said yes and Tymera only rolled her eyes while saying, "Just deal the cards D'Neko."

They sat and played twelve rounds, D'Neko won seven hands, Tymera won three,   Mitchell and Damian only won one game a piece.

Tymera stood up putting her hands on her hips as she said with attitude, "He only won so much because ya'll let him cheat and couldn't catch him."

"If I don't get caught that means I didn't cheat," D'Neko looked over and saw a frog and ran off.

"Well Damian and Mitch, good game," Jordan said laughing as he turned to walk back to his grill. Tylen walked with Jordan. "Bianca is here," Tylen whispered mischievously, "I could let Kayla see the report, only the part about Bianca paying Sierra to trick Ashland."

Jordan laughed, "Grandfather that would be a hell of a fight, and I don't think that's a very good idea right now."

Mitchell said jokingly to Kayla before he walked off, "I need to take them to Vegas, especially D'Neko."

Ashland walked over to the grill holding Michael.

Only Damian and Kayla remained at the table, so he asked, "Well Kayla, your kids are something else, where did they learn to play?"

"My family loves cards and that's all they did," Kayla said.

"Is he coming over today?" Damian asked.

Kayla laughed, "I hope not. Bad memories there."

"Well maybe sometimes when you get a vacation you could bring the kids to Virginia to my marina," Damian later said he really liked Kayla and her kids.

"That would be nice," Kayla said softly and smiled.

Ashland said smiling, "Jordan, look, I think he likes Kayla. Don't you think they look good together?"

"He's only being nice, besides, I really don't see why he would like her." Jordan laughed then Ashland kicked him playfully.

"You're only mad because she beat you up," Ashland joked.

Tylen had been standing beside Jordan silently eating a hot dog and couldn't help laughing at Ashland's remark that he accidentally dropped barbecue sauce on his shirt.

Megan walked over then asked, "Would you two like for me to take Michael in?"

"Ok, thanks," Ashland said.

"I think I'll walk in with you two. Careful Jordan, I'd really hate to see Kayla at you again, but Kitten be a dear and make sure you come and get me if any excitement starts up around here," Tylen laughed.

"Anyway, come on Tylen. Enjoy yourselves, I'll watch Michael tonight," Megan laughed as she and Tylen took Michael indoors.

Jordan bent down to whisper in Ashland's ear as he rubbed her back tenderly, "I really need you Ashland. It's been too many weeks already. I don't think I can wait another week if you keep wearing those jeans." He kissed her neck.

Ashland closed her eyes and raised up to kiss Jordan's lips gently as she rubbed his cheeks, "I need you too."

Jordan smiled then pulled back. He was almost tempted to abandon the grill, "Well I guess I'd better concentrate on this food."

Ashland looked down at his jeans and smiled seductively, "Jordan, I see I'm in for a treat. Be right back, I think I'll have a drink. Wanna another beer?"

Jordan nodded as he watched Ashland walk away, and thought how Ashland had already lost all the extra weight she had gained while she was pregnant. Even though her butt was a little thicker and rounder, he loved it. He took a deep breath while flipping the burgers.

"Here you go Jordan, a nice cold beer." Ashland asked, "Does he have a girlfriend?"

"Who?" Jordan asked indifferently.

"Damian, that's who," She said a little annoyed.

"I don't know, but let's find out. Damian" Jordan laughed.

"Yeah?" Damian said looking over.

"Come here please, you too Kayla. Ashland wants me to ask you something," Jordan said laughing.

"Jordan, I'm going to get you for this," Ashland threatened between gritted teeth as she smiled at Damian.

"Damian, Ashland would like to know if you have a girlfriend." Jordan laughed.

Damian looked at Kayla and smiled, "No I don't."

Before anyone else could say anything, Mrs. George was walking over towards them followed by Sierra.

Jordan frowned, "Kayla, you had better not show out. Damian, just hold on to her."

Damian only looked confused but he put his arms around Kayla's waist securely. Kayla wondered who she was, to make Jordan say that, but she had to admit it felt good to have Damian's strong arms around her. She leaned closer to Damian.

Mrs. George said, "Ashland, someone is here to see you." Then asked with concern when she noticed Ashland's expression, "Is everything ok, Ashland?"

"We'll see in a minute," was all Ashland said to Mrs. George. Ashland was pissed. She took a swallow of her drink and thought to herself, *I'm gonna beat Jordan's ass first if he so much as lied to me.*

"Hello everyone, Jordan please let me say my peace and I'll leave, I swear. I know I am the last person in the world you ever expected to see again, so I'll make this brief. Jordan, I am sorry for kissing you and Ashland, I cannot begin to apologize for all the things I said to you. My conscious is bothering me because I was told about what happened to you the day after our little talk. Anyways, I took a big chance by coming here."

Kayla cut her off looking at Jordan evilly, "Kissing you, huh? Oh I know this ain't that-" Damian squeezed her tightly around her waist slightly causing her to catch her breath.

Sierra ignored Kayla, "Well I haven't seen Jordan in over five years. It was all a lie. I am so sorry he's a good man and he loved you even way back when I knew him." Sierra cleared her throat and turned to walk quickly away then turned to say, "I saw your son on the way in, he's beautiful." As she turned back to leave she immediately stopped, she became crippled with fear when she saw Bianca walked out the doors.

"Damian, let me go. I'm gonna bust her ass wide open before she leaves," Kayla said bluntly.

"Kayla, don't forget your kids are here," he whispered into her ear, she only inhaled deeply because his closeness sent chills throughout her body.

Jordan walked over to Bianca quickly, "Bianca, Sierra was just leaving. She only apologized to Ashland for the things she said to her, that's all." Jordan turned to Sierra, "Goodbye Sierra"

She began to walk away quickly then she just stopped.

Jordan whispered to Bianca harshly, "Ashland doesn't know you had any part in it. And I would like to keep it that way."

Sierra was furious, "So I am supposed to be the only bad guy here? If it wasn't for her I would have never known where you were, neither would your mother, brother and father from what that P.I. said. So, don't you think if I can come all the way down here and apologize for my part, she should too? Ashland's not my daughter, and besides that bitch had the nerve to threaten my life if I told." Sierra turned away and left. *Fuck her* Sierra thought angrily to herself, at least if something did happen to her there were plenty of witnesses who knew Bianca had threatened her.

"Awe man, if you weren't Ashland's mother I'd really beat yo ass. How could you?" Kayla was extremely upset.

"Kayla, would you like for me to take you and the kids home?" Damian asked with concern in his eyes.

"Yeah, I think that would be best. I really need to go. Ashland I'll talk to you later," Kayla rolled her eyes at Jordan and it took all she had not to hit Bianca. Damian held her hand tight.

Bianca was having a bad day. She had just walked in on Mitchell and Carmen kissing. When she walked up on Sierra, she thought to herself, *I should have kept my black ass at home today.*

"Mother, please tell me you didn't have anything to do with that and you didn't threatened that woman, did you?" Ashland was furious.

"I could, but I'd be lying," Bianca said quietly.

"Why?" Ashland questioned angrily.

"Your father told you in your townhouse that night he asked for a divorce. I'd been so caught up with myself that I didn't think of no one but myself. I've let my anger and hatred for one man destroy me," Bianca said with complete honesty.

"I don't understand, what man?" Ashland asked frowning she was confused.

"Ashland, I fell in love with a man when I was very young, he was married and wouldn't leave his wife, I became pregnant and aborted that baby, I detested the idea of having his child." Tears fell from Bianca's eyes, "I made you and Jordan suffer because of it. I lied, telling Jordan you decided to have an abortion because you didn't want his child, and in all actuality, it was me that had an abortion. I've lost your father because of all of this. I tried to hurt Tylen through Jordan and succeeded but, I myself, felt the pain of my actions as well. By bringing Sierra here, I almost lost you. Now Ashland, you may not believe this but I do love you, but right now, I think it's best if I go. I'm sorry I made Kayla feel as if she had to leave," she said with regret as she touched Ashland's face lightly then turned to go.

"Mother," Ashland said then only shook her head, she asked baffled, "What does Tylen have to do with all of this?"

"He was the man I fell in love with," Bianca said gently.

Ashland looked at her mother as if she was crazy and asked appalled, "You and Tylen? Are you for real?"

Bianca didn't say anything; she only stood up straighter.

"Then, you slept with Mitchell?" Ashland looked incredulous, "Jordan's grandfather and Father?" Ashland laughed cruelly, "Damn mother! And you called me a little whore when I got pregnant by Jordan." Ashland finished her drink. "No wonder daddy left you. You're not my mother, I've had it with you."

Bianca flinched as if Ashland had slapped her. Carmen and Mitchell had been standing and listening in the doorway. Carmen only walked away. Mitchell did not move, he continued to listen. He was stunned at hearing Bianca had aborted a baby by Tylen.

"You knew everything, didn't you?" She asked Jordan with a raised eyebrow.

"Yes I did," Jordan answered openly.

"And you thought I didn't need to know, right?" Ashland asked heatedly.

"I didn't want you to know what your mother had done," Jordan said, a little annoyed, wondering how she could be upset with him when he had only tried to protect her.

Ashland rolled her eyes at Jordan then looked at her mother with disgust, "You're such a bitch." Ashland stormed off.

At that moment, Bianca vowed to make Sierra regret reneging on their agreement. Bianca thought to herself, *Retribution time*. Bianca was livid and the thought of Ashland hating her was unbearable. She knew she had just lost her daughter and that hurt worst than anything. When Bianca hurt, she became angry and lashed out. *Sierra you better be ready because I'm coming and I'm coming with a vengeance, and I'll make sure nobody will be there to help you.*

Jordan only stood there dumbfounded as he watched

Ashland walk away. Ashland paused briefly in front of Mitchell, "How the hell can you screw my mother while you're still married to Jordan's mother?" She didn't wait for an answer.

Tylen stood on the balcony and witnessed everything. He had finally made it to his bedroom to change his shirt when he had heard the commotion coming from the back yard. It had always bothered him and he had dreaded the day that Ashland would find out about his indiscretions with her mother, only because he loved Ashland just as much as he loved Jordan. So as he looked down at Ashland as Bianca told her about their affair, he felt as if air was being drained from his body. His past sins were slapping him in the face and he only felt embarrassed and undignified all over again.

"Tylen, what's going on? Carmen came into the nursery and said that I should come talk to you before I speak with anyone else. What is it?" Megan asked frowning.

Tylen sat down and said sadly, "Ashland just found out about my affair with her mother and the abortion Bianca had. I guess Carmen didn't know you already knew about that."

"Oh honey, I am so sorry. I know how much it bothered you the idea of her finding out. Try not to worry, she'll realize soon enough that it happened long before she and Jordan were born," Megan said gently as she sat down beside him.

"I guess we'll just have to wait and see, won't we?" Tylen said trying to smile as he kissed the top of Megan's head then added, "I only pray that some good come out of all this." Tylen held Megan and prayed silently that Ashland would be able to forgive him.

Mrs. George looked at Bianca and made a crude noise, the look Bianca gave her startled her, sending waves of eerie chills down her spine. Mrs. George turned away quickly taking the spatula from Jordan, "I guess the cook-out is over. I'll finish this up. Go talk to your wife." She turned away ignoring everyone completely and began flipping the meat.

Mitchell watched as Ashland walked away. He briefly looked at Bianca and actually felt sorry for her. Bianca was beautiful beyond any doubt, but she was all alone. She had manipulated used and tried controlling Ashland to the point of losing her. Hell, she even had lost her husband, he thought to himself as he laughed disgustedly thinking of the life he had chosen. Mitchell suddenly felt scared of being alone and ending up like her.

Mitchell found Carmen in the nursery holding Michael. The sight she presented overwhelmed him to the point that he went to his knees in front of her. She was rocking back and forth singing softly to Michael, he immediately thought of Jordan.

"Carmen, I can't apologize enough for what I've done to you and our boys. Forgive me and let me come home. I swear to you on everything I hold dear, that if you take me back I promise to try my best to make you happy and give our grandson and future grandchildren all the love and support that I should have given our boys. Oh GOD please forgive me for the things I've done," Mitchell said desperately then put his head in Carmen's lap and cried. Mitchell prayed that Jordan and Damian would one day forgive him and that he would be able to build a decent relationship with them.

"I forgive you Mitchell," Carmen said smiling as she cried holding Michael a little closer as she gently rubbed Mitchell's head softly.

Carmen inhaled deeply thanking GOD that part of her prayers had been answered. She sent up another prayer for their family, praying that they would be able to overcome this and all the dark secrets and scandalous lies that have overshadowed their family for so long. She could only pray and have complete faith that confessing hurtful truths would somehow bring everyone closer together.

* * *

Jordan found Ashland in their bedroom pacing the floor with a drink in her hand. "So tell me, why are you so mad at me for not wanting to see you get hurt?" Jordan questioned.

"Jordan, I am not a child, I've taken care of myself without you or anyone else for all these years. I do not need another father!" She said with straight attitude.

"Ok I repeat, why are you mad at me?" He asked beginning to get angry himself.

"Don't you think it would have been better for you to tell me? Oh yeah I almost forgot, let me guess, you conveniently forgot just like you conveniently forgot about Sierra kissing you too?" Ashland said viciously. She finished her drink then poured another. Jordan took it from her. She snatched it spilling most of it. Jordan snatched it back spilling all of it. Ashland slapped him so hard they both were stunned.

Jordan sat on the bed, "Come here." Jordan was tired of arguing. Ashland walked over to stand in front of him. He pulled her down on his lap and kissed her. He unbuttoned her shirt and started caressing her breasts. Ashland moaned and unbuttoned his shirt. They never stopped kissing. He unsnapped her bra as he bent his head to kiss her breast. She unbuttoned his jeans and began massaging his chest and stomach. They both stood and removed their clothes. He gently pushed her back on the bed caressing between her legs in her most intimate area. With his hard stiff erection, he entered her slowly.

"Jordan, what about a condom, you're gonna wear one?" Ashland asked breathlessly.

"I'll be careful," he whispered as he began to move within her. "I love you so much Ashland," Jordan said with a ragged breath.

"And I love you," Ashland moaned.

After making love and taking showers, Jordan said casually as he sat on the side of the bed watching her rub oil over her body, "Don't ever slap me again."

Ashland looked over at him and said casually, "Don't ever snatch anything from me again."

"Do you want to go back downstairs?" Jordan asked.

"Not really. Can't we just forget about everyone for the rest of the day?" Ashland asked.

Jordan nodded and stood to fix them both a drink, "Here."

"Is this an apology?" She asked smiling mischievously.

"Apology for what?" Jordan asked puzzled.

"For being rude when you took my drink," Ashland said with a raised eyebrow.

"Ashland, as you recalled I only took the glass from you. You are the one that snatched first," Jordan said smiling.

Ashland laughed, "I guess, maybe you're right."

Jordan smiled, "Well I guess I'm sorry for snatching your drink." He just stood looking down at her.

"Why are you looking at me like that?" Ashland asked.

"I was just wondering if you're ever going to apologize for slapping me," Jordan said.

Ashland inhaled, "Well, I don't know. You did kiss her so I'm thinking maybe I shouldn't apologize since you did deserve it." She sat on the floor naked, Indian style. "Besides, I kinda liked your reaction. Damn, anger makes you feel so good."

Jordan only stared at her, "You know Ashland I use to wonder if your hair was really brown," He said as he crawled down to the floor kissing her, making her lay back as he kissed and caressed her breasts and stomach. Ashland gasped when he kissed and rubbed her most intimate sensitive spot, making her moan uncontrollably. She spread her legs wider.

"Jordan," Ashland whimpered.

Jordan continued to kiss and suck on her at a steady mind whirling pace.

"Jordan, please don't stop," Ashland begged.

Jordan inserted his finger then another inside of her. Ashland pulled his hair gently as he continued to kiss her in that pleasurable steady rhythm.

"Oh Jordan please make love to me now," she begged as she pulled him up to her, kissing him as she enjoyed feeling his throbbing erection as he entered her slowly again, "God I love you so much," she said.

When he filled her completely she began to scream so he kissed her to muffle her cries of passion, he began to come suddenly, "Shit" he pulled out of her quickly.

"Did you?" She asked nervously.

"A little. Shit. Why aren't you on birth control?" Jordan

snapped.

"Damn Jordan, I haven't gotten my six week check up yet," Ashland snapped back.

"Sorry Ashland, I'm a little scared for you to get pregnant again," Jordan admitted, then added, "I almost lost you, I can't go through that again," he said grimly.

"Jordan," she reached up to put her arms around his neck, kissing him gently, "Don't worry. I'll get on birth control and everything will be ok, besides, nothing probably happened. And we're not going to worry no matter what happens from now on, we're together and no one can tear us apart, as long as we don't let them. We'll deal with our families together." Then she added, "And Jordan, I really am so sorry for slapping you."

"I love you always and forever," Jordan kissed her.

"No matter what," Ashland kissed him back.

Chapter Sixteen

Bianca left the old rat infested building with the sun's powerful rays shining down on her face. She smiled happily. Everything was working out perfectly. The old man with the crooked eyes had come through for her. Bianca sighed as she touched her purse, which contained her new ID, and credit card, life was good. Bianca slipped on her shades and walked gaily to her car.

She arrived in Cleveland and went straight to the local newspaper where Sierra worked. She had decided to drive there, less of a trail on her part. Bianca noticed a young man leaning against a desk talking with an older gentleman as soon as she entered the building. She took a deep breath, adjusted her blouse then sashayed towards them. Both men immediately stopped talking and looked her way.

Bianca put on her most award winning smiles, "Excuse me gentlemen, but could either of you tell me where I may find Sierra Sanders?"

The younger man laughed, "Not really. She just up and quit about a week ago without warning."

"Thank for your time and I do apologize for the interruption," Bianca said graciously then she began to walk away.

"Hey" The young man said to her smiling, "I heard she went back home if that helps you any."

Bianca smiled so seductively that both men were mesmerized, holding their breath as they watched her gracefully leave through the double doors.

"Now my young friend, that is what you would call a woman," the older man said smiling.

* * *

Sierra paced her bedroom. She really hated staying with her mother, she was twenty-eight years old and that woman still seriously nagged the hell out of her, but for now, this would be the safest place. It was the best place to be as friends and family surrounded her, she thought. As many people that came through this house, there was no way Bianca could get away with anything.

"Sierra" Her brother Darius called as he knocked on her door.

Sierra opened her door smiling, "Hey what's up, big bro?"

"Not much, mom was just telling me that you were back, so what happened with that big executive position?" Darius asked smiling.

Sierra thought, *here we go, I'll probably get asked that question a million times before the month is out.* She smiled then answered, "Just tired of being stressed out all of the time. Figure I'd come home and get a job around here some place. Anyway, mom's getting older; she could probably use the help." Sierra asked, "What about you, what have you been up to?"

"Hey I'm legit now. I got a gig at the old plant. The money comes, just not as fast. What went down with Lindsey was messed up, anyway. I haven't been back in the game since," Darius said.

"I know, I'm so sorry about what happened to her," Sierra said with deep sympathy.

"Darius, Sierra, get down here right now!" Their mother yelled.

"Come on you know how she gets, let's go see what Miss Kitty is tripping about now," Darius said as they both laughed.

Katherine Sanders, better known as Miss Kitty ruled her house with an iron fist. She loved the neighborhood kids so much that her house was known as the Kool-aid house. She especially loved her three kids, despite some of their questionable ways, and anyone who dared to even look at them the wrong way got a good ole verbal lashing, and anyone who physically hurt her kids just got a plain ole fashion beat down. Everybody knew Miss Kitty didn't play that, and she had a mind to beat either Darius or Sierra for leaving crumbs on her counter. Hell she had just cleaned two hours ago.

Darius and Sierra entered the kitchen.

"What the hell is this?" Miss Kitty asked while holding a cigarette in one hand and a glass of wine in the other. She had rollers in her head, which was covered with a pair of large white bloomers, and she also had on a very old faded yellow housecoat. "Now I just cleaned this damn house not thirty minutes ago and I only have twenty-five minutes to get ready for work. Somebody had better clean this mess up right now." She left the kitchen.

Darius and Sierra laughed as Sierra grabbed a dishcloth and started wiping down the counters. "Dang Darius, she's still wearing those bloomers after all these years? Why won't she wear any of the night caps I bought her?" Sierra asked shaking her head.

"I don't know, but you have to admit when the rollers, bloomers and housecoat come off, our mother looks good. Some of the guys still joke with me about trying to get with Miss Kitty." Darius said proudly of their mother as he laughed. "Besides, she's not really working. The old folks are having a dance, and she's just helping with entertainment," Darius said laughing.

Sierra smiled shaking her head and thought their mother did look good, and then laughed thinking Bianca or anyone for that matter would be a fool to try and step up in Miss Kitty's house unannounced.

* * *

Bianca sat in her hotel room drinking wine trying to relax. She had just tried calling her daughter, but as soon as Ashland heard her voice, she hung up the phone. Bianca sat and drank more wine. It had been almost a year since Ashland had spoken to her and she and Jordan was about to have another baby. A tear fell from Bianca's eyes as she thought of her grandson, "Sierra you just wait." Bianca said to herself.

What a wasted trip, she thought irritably. "New Orleans, huh?" Bianca then a smile as one name came to mind, Devin Chandler. She smirked as a new plan started formulating in her mind. Watching Sierra squirm was going to be very rejuvenating. Bianca had a lot to do, so she lay down to get a couple hours of sleep.

Chapter Seventeen

Devin walked the woman from his office and watched as she left his bookstore. He could not believe the nerve of her. She was the one needing a job not him. Devin sat at a table and thought, a very gorgeous woman, but much too bossy, too pushy, too outspoken and downright rude for his taste. They hadn't gotten two minutes into their interview when he realized they would not get along and probably could never agree on anything.

"Devin, you have a call," Mrs. Huddle, his part-time employee, said smiling.

"I'll take it in my office." Devin smiled then retreated to his office. "This is Devin, how can I help you?" He said in his silky smooth voice as he looked briefly at the woman's application before carelessly dropping it in the trash.

"Hello Devin, This is Bianca Kendrix. How have you been doing?" Bianca said smiling, as she thought his voice was so different from the last time they had spoken.

There was complete silence for a few minutes. It had been twelve years since Devin had spoken with Bianca. She had helped him when he was eighteen years old. He had been in and out of correctional facilities since the age of twelve stealing and breaking into homes. By the time he was sixteen, he was running game on some of the wealthiest and most influential married women around, charming away their money and breaking their hearts in the process. To Devin it was simply about survival.

Devin's father had been an extremely strong disciplinary force, so much that he was outright abusive, especially towards Devin's mother. One night when Devin had gotten home his father was beating his mother so bad that he actually thought his father was killing her. Devin couldn't take it anymore, watching his mother day in and day out walking around as if she was in a daze, never talking or giving anyone eye contact. She routinely went about her daily chores, cooking and cleaning so not to enrage his father. It was as if Devin had ceased to exist for his mother, she never acknowledged him. Devin killed his father that night. His mother survived that beating, but died one month later from an aneurysm, which left Devin completely alone and devastated.

Bianca had gotten the firm where she worked to help him. They got him off that charge and all of the other charges he had against him. She had even set him up with a job assisting an eccentric old man named Jonathan with his bookstore. Seven years later, that old man died leaving Devin the store, his home and his money. That frugal eccentric old man happened to be very wealthy and without family. He had taken Devin in, welcoming him to his home and treating him as if he were his own flesh and blood, so Devin had vowed to make that man proud of him. Those had been the happiest seven years of his life. Tears came to Devin's eyes as he thought of that generous old man and his mother. To this day, he never knew why Bianca had helped him. Clearing his voice, he asked curiously, "Bianca, what can I do for you?"

Bianca smiled, "I need to see you. Would it be possible for you to meet me tomorrow at three o'clock?"

Devin hesitated slightly, "Ok where would you like to meet?"

"At the coffee house we went to right after the trial," Bianca said smoothly.

Devin sat back and wondered what Bianca wanted. For some reason he had an uneasy feeling about it.

The next day Bianca sat in the coffee house drinking an iced coffee. She wondered how Devin would react to what she was about to ask of him. Bianca spotted Devin right away when he entered the coffee house. He had matured rather nicely, about six one with a deep olive complexion and very compelling dark eyes. His thick black hair had grown long and was pulled back in a ponytail. He was dressed in black slacks and a black silk shirt. Bianca liked the look; she even bet he still looked good in those braids he used to wear. Bianca wasn't scared to bet that Sierra could easily fall for a man like him.

"Bianca," Devin said as he took a seat across from her thinking she still looked the same, beautiful as ever, as if she never aged.

"You're looking good, I take it you're doing well," Bianca said smiling, "Would you like something to eat or drink?" Bianca asked.

Devin motioned for the waitress and ordered a coke.

"I know you're wondering why I asked you to meet me here today. So I'll get right to the point. I need your help with a case I'm working on," Bianca said in a serious tone.

"Bianca, how could I possibly help you with one of your cases?" Devin asked with a frown.

"I really can't go into too much detail, but I need for you to get close to someone, take her out on a few dates. You know get her to confide in you. Make her love you if you have to. " Bianca was cut off.

"In other words, you basically want me to prostitute myself?" Devin asked angrily.

"No Devin, I wasn't saying that at all." Bianca looked contrite.

"Then what are you saying?" Devin demanded.

Bianca felt herself getting irritated but smiled anyways, "Look Devin, It's like this, I have a client who she has embezzled money from. We only need proof. There have been rumors of drug use, which would explain the money issue. I honestly wish I could, but I can not go into too much detail at this time."

"Look Bianca I would love to help you but I don't think I can," Devin said.

"Why not? Are you married? You were a real pro at it in your younger days," Bianca stated matter-of-factly.

"No I'm not married, but I've changed. I don't use people like that anymore," Devin stated irritably.

"Devin, I need your help. I'm really desperate," Bianca said.

Devin sat back and thought how Bianca had helped him so long ago. "Ok Bianca I'll do it. I won't sleep with her, but I will keep my eye on her, at least for a while. Now tell me who this woman is."

"Her name is Sierra Sanders."

Devin knew that name sounded familiar but couldn't place it. Then it hit him the woman he had interviewed for a job. Just great. "This Sierra person just interviewed for a job yesterday, but…"

Bianca smiled, "That's perfect Devin."

"I threw her application away," Devin said grimly.

Bianca stood and dropped money on the table, "So dig it out, I'll call you in a few days."   Bianca had turned to leave then said firmly with a raised eyebrow, "Whatever you do, don't go falling for her."

Bianca left the coffee house and got in her car. Actually, her colleague was working on a case where the woman had stolen the money so it wasn't a complete lie, her colleague did ask for her opinion in how they should go about the case, but Devin doesn't have to know that. She thought to herself as she looked in the mirror, *Ok Sierra here we go.* Bianca smiled and drove away.

Devin was annoyed wondering as he drove back home what he had just gotten himself caught up in.

***

Devin went into his office to take a break; he had almost completed processing his book shipment. So far it hadn't been too busy but he did have to stop a few times to help Mrs. Huddle with a few customers whenever it got busy. He sat at his desk dreading the call he was about to make. He wished he'd thrown his trash out yesterday, but her application had been the only thing in his trashcan. He picked up the phone and dialed her number. Devin frown when he recognized her voice, "Sierra, hi, this is Devin from the book store."

"What do you want?" Sierra said rudely not really thinking because her mother had been working on her nerves all morning.

Devin had to take a deep breath because all he really wanted to do was hang up the phone, "I was wondering if you were still interested in the assistant position?"

"Oh yeah, I'm interested. I can be in today about two to fill out all the necessary paper work. I can actually start working tomorrow," Sierra stated.

Devin gritted his teeth and as soon as Bianca had the evidence she needed he was going to fire her. "Actually two is not good for me. Can you come in about eleven?" he asked

Sierra looked at the clock then rolled her eyes. It was already nine forty-five. "Sure," she hung up the phone without saying goodbye.

Devin hung up the phone and thought, *that woman was something else, how the hell did she have the gall to tell me when she would come in to fill out paperwork. Hell, she's working for me.* Devin knew he would have to set her straight right off.

Devin had just put the last of the books on the shelves when Sierra entered the store. Devin turned his back to her frowning, actually dreading the idea of hiring her. Mrs. Huddle saw his reaction to Sierra and laughed. Devin looked up immediately. Jonathan had told him it wasn't good work ethics to ever let employees know if he had ill feelings toward another employee. He turned and smiled, "Hi Sierra, glad you could make it. Let me introduce you to Mrs. Huddle. Mrs. Huddle, this is Sierra Sanders, she will be working as my assistant."

Mrs. Huddle and Sierra talked while Devin went to his office to get the folder, which held all the forms Sierra needed. Devin was annoyed at Bianca for asking him to help her, and Sierra's attitude really sucked. There was no way in hell he could even see himself seducing her at this point. Devin stopped walking as a thought occurred to him, maybe he should try to make her interested in him, just to teach her a lesson. He laughed, that was a little much even for him. Even when he had used all those women for his own personal financial gain, at least they all got something in return. They had been lonely and he had fulfilled their life making it easier for them to cope with husbands that didn't care or spent time with them.

Devin handed Sierra the folder then turned his attention

to Mrs. Huddle, "I'm going to grab something to eat before you leave. I'll be right back."

"Does anyone else work here besides you and Devin?" Sierra asked as she sat at a table.

"Yes, a young girl named Hannah who's a college student, but she only works three days a week in the afternoons from twelve to four. She's our little Einstein who probably knows about every book in this store," Mrs. Huddle said laughing.

"Do you like it here? Sierra asked curiously.

"I've been working here for over twenty years now and I wouldn't want to be any place else. Devin is wonderful and Jonathan was truly blessed the day Devin entered his life," Mrs. Huddle said with a bright smile.

"Who is Jonathan?" Sierra asked with a frown.

"Jonathan was the man who started this store. God rest his soul." Mrs. Huddle cleared her throat then said smiling after she saw a few people walk towards the register, "Well now you had better get started on that paperwork and I've got to get back to work."

* * *

Sierra sat on the front porch with her mother drinking a glass of wine enjoying the evening breeze. "Momma, are you seeing anyone special?" Sierra asked.

"Why you want to know?" Miss Kitty asked as she took a sip from her glass.

Sierra closed her eyes, "I was just curious. Forget I asked," Sierra said flippantly.

Miss Kitty turned and really looked at Sierra for the first time since she had come home almost two weeks ago. "What made you come back? When you left you swore you'd never come back here to live."

"I don't know, just tired of all the stress that was associated with my job," Sierra said hoping her mother wouldn't ask too many questions. She wasn't in the mood.

Miss Kitty laughed, "Sierra, who do you think you're talking to? In your entire life, you've never let a little stress force you to give up something that you liked doing, hell if anything you've always thrived on it. Always did make me proud." Miss Kitty pulled a cigarette from its box then threw the pack back on the table. After taking a long drag Miss Kitty asked, "This doesn't have anything to do with a man, does it?"

"No momma, it doesn't," Sierra said unemotionally as Jordan came to mind. It had been over five years and everyone still remembers how she had chased after him. God I am still embarrassed at how I acted over that man. Thank God, no one knew about Bianca paying me to cause problems for his marriage, Sierra thought to herself.

Miss Kitty looked at her daughter and smiled to herself thinking, Sierra was too much like her. She wouldn't talk until she was good and ready. Miss Kitty knew Sierra had something heavy on her mind and that bothered her, if some man was messing with her daughter she'd find out. Miss Kitty was pouring more wine in their glasses when her youngest son drove up.

"Hey momma," he said kissing her, "What's up Sierra? You're looking good." Jermaine smiled as he hugged his sister.

"Boy what the hell you doing coming up on me smelling like that shit?" Miss kitty asked.

"Dang it's just a little weed," Jermaine said kissing his mom again.

"Get off me boy," Miss Kitty said but couldn't help smiling because it was hard for her to stay mad at her baby boy for too long.

Sierra laughed then asked, "Who's in the car with you?" Sierra felt the strangest feeling as she looked at the woman in the car, she felt as if she knew her.

Jermaine smiled, "Oh that's just somebody I'm kicking it with."

"You off today?" Miss Kitty asked taking a drag from her cigarette.

"Yeah I am. Why?" Jermaine asked defensively.

"No reason I was just wondering," Miss Kitty said stone-faced as she took a sip of wine.

Jermaine could tell his mom was about to get started about something and he especially didn't feel like talking about his job, so he stood and kissed her, "I just stopped by to say hey, we got to go or else we'll be late. Talk to you later, Sierra."

Miss Kitty sat quietly thinking about her kids. Darius was thirty and she was so happy that he had finally settled down with a real job. Unfortunately, he had to lose someone close to him to realize what he was doing was wrong. It had worried her like hell when he came home and started selling that shit and the damn boy has a college education. She took a big swallow of wine. And now Jermaine was smoking that shit, hell at least Darius had only sold it. Jermaine was twenty-one, and he was still working at that same ole fast food restaurant from when he was sixteen, but Mrs. Millie from across the street had told her yesterday Jermaine had quit. At least he did go to college, part time was better than not at all. Miss Kitty took a puff of her cigarette as she wondered how he was paying his bills, praying he hadn't started selling. Jermaine had even started looking like his father. She took another sip of her wine as she thought with a frown, that lately he had been bringing strange women around her house. That heifer could have at least got out and spoke. Miss Kitty took the last drag from her cigarette, and then squashed it in the ashtray. Looking briefly over at Sierra, she wondered what was up with her. She prayed she hadn't gotten herself in any more trouble, especially over some damn man.

Sierra knew her mom was thinking about something, because Jermaine had left before she could really say anything to him, and her mom had suddenly become awfully quiet. Sierra stood to go inside because she knew her mom would probably start in on her about something. "I think I'm going to bed now. I have a long day tomorrow."

"Doing what?" Miss Kitty asked skeptically with a raised eyebrow.

"I forgot to tell you, I found a job. I start in the morning," Sierra said.

"Where?" her mom questioned.

"At the bookstore, next to the old museum," Sierra said.

Her mom didn't say anything else, so Sierra went inside to get ready for bed.

Chapter Eighteen

Devin had just unlocked the doors when Sierra entered the store. She was right on time.   "Good morning," Sierra said brightly while drinking a cup of coffee. Devin only nodded his head towards her and continued making sure everything was in order for the day. "Excuse me, but aren't you going to show me what you're doing? I've never worked in a bookstore before. I told you that during my interview so I would appreciate knowing everything that's to be done. You'll never know when you may need me to open up," Sierra said point-blank, she was irritated that he couldn't take the time to open his mouth to say a simple good morning.

Devin stopped what he was doing then stood completely still for a full minute, "Sierra, I'll be with you shortly. Right now I need to finish what I'm doing, people will be in soon." Devin then completely ignored her until he completed what he was doing.

"Good morning," Mrs. Huddle said cheerfully, "I brought coffee and donuts; I hope you two are hungry." She winked at Devin, "I brought you a chicken biscuit I know you really don't like a lot of sweets."

Devin laughed relaxing at the sight of Mrs. Huddle, "Thanks."

Sierra only stared unbelievably at Devin, because not even five minutes ago he was looking all dark and moody, now all of a sudden he was smiling. Sierra rolled her eyes at him and didn't care if he caught her doing so. She knew she didn't have experience in a bookstore but all he had to do was show her how things were done and she could run the store by herself, more than likely better than he did, she thought grimly.

After Sierra finished her coffee and donuts, Devin showed her around the store explaining everything from opening to closing. Sierra received a crash course. That night, Devin smiled to himself as he stepped back to let Sierra close out both registers. He grudgingly admitted she would be an asset, he had only explained things once and she caught on immediately. At least he wouldn't have to keep explaining himself. She was good with the customers, especially the children, which really surprised him. Maybe she wasn't as bad as he first thought.

"I really hope you don't expect me to work from opening to closing again, I do have a life, you know," Sierra said annoyingly. She was tired and his ass could have at least closed out one of the registers, she thought to herself.

Devin only laughed, yeah she wasn't as bad as he first imagined. "Come in at one tomorrow," Devin said as he began to turn off lights.

"Listen, you're going to have to make me a weekly schedule because I need to know how to arrange my personal errands," Sierra said pointedly.

Devin only looked at her and shook his head. He intended to give her a schedule, but it was the way she had said it that pissed him off. Devin really couldn't get over her attitude. "Just work tomorrow from one to close then you'll be off the next two days. You'll work Friday and Saturday from one to close. We're closed on Sundays. You'll be off Monday. I'll have your schedule printed two weeks in advance from that point on. You'll have your schedule when you come back Friday." Devin was mad he had planned on giving her Saturday off and letting her work the day shift, but that was before she pissed him off.

Sierra walked out the store without saying a word. When Devin set the alarm and locked the store, he found her sitting on the sidewalk.

"Where's your car?" Devin asked.

"I don't have one yet, my mom dropped me off," she said.

"Where is she at? Didn't you tell her what time you get off?" Devin asked.

"How do I know where she is, she's not answering her phones," Sierra stated irritably.

That's just great Devin thought he had a good mind to

leave her smart ass sitting right where she was, but he knew he couldn't. "Come on I'll give you a ride," he said.

Sierra didn't say thank you or anything to Devin when he pulled up in front of her house. She only dropped some money on his seat when she got out. Devin only shook his head and drove away.

As soon as Devin had gotten out of the shower, his phone was ringing.

"Hi Devin, how are things going?" Bianca asked in a pleasant tone.

"It's not. Listen I don't think this was a good idea. You're going to have to find someone else to keep an eye on her, because we just simply can't get along," Devin was becoming annoyed at the mere thought of Sierra.

"What's wrong, she's not immune to your devastating charm, is she?" Bianca teased she knew all too well how demanding Sierra could be.

"Bianca, it's hard enough working with her. It's impossible to be nice to that woman," Devin said irritably.

"Don't tell me you lost your touch. Here I am thinking that there wasn't a single woman alive you couldn't conquer or control with that smooth tongue of yours. Hell you had me tempted at one point." Bianca laughed thinking how at such a young age he had radiated an abundance amount of sex appeal, she could only imagined what he was like now. At that time, he was a little too young for her to play around with. Bianca laughed remembering she shouldn't lose her focus. *If he wasn't Jonathan's grandson,* Bianca thought cruelly to herself.

Bianca had smoothly challenged Devin's male ego. Once again, she had reminded him of his past, which reminded him of how much she had helped him turn his life around. Devin inhaled deeply saying, "Just call me in a few days." Bianca smiled then hung up the phone.

* * *

It was busy at the store when Sierra got there. She put her things away then immediately assisted with customers.

"Sierra, I want you to meet Hannah before I leave.

Hannah this is Sierra, she'll be working with us from now on as Devin's assistant," Mrs. Huddle said.

Hannah looked Sierra up and down. "Nice to meet you Sierra," she said arrogantly then she turned on her heels and walked away.

The little snotty nose heifer, Sierra thought to herself. Sierra knew Hannah couldn't be any older than nineteen years old.

"Don't let her get to you; she's like that with all the attractive females when she first meet them. You see she has a thing for Devin, so anyone who might seem to appeal to him gets the cold shoulder. Once you get to know her she's a really sweet girl." Mrs. Huddle said as she gathered her belongings to leave for the day. "See you later honey, and remember what I said and don't let Hannah get to you too much," Mrs. Huddle said to Sierra before walking out of the store.

"Well Hannah doesn't have a thing to worry about as far as Devin is concerned, he is definitely not my type," Sierra said to herself.

"You look nice today. Peach is definitely a good color for you," Devin said to Sierra as he passed by to help a few customers.

Sierra didn't know how to take his compliment so she just shrugged her shoulders and forgot about it. Hannah jealously rolled her eyes and continued ordering a book for a customer.

It was almost four thirty and most of the customers had left the store when Devin came up quietly behind Sierra to stand beside her. "Hey, I'm going to grab me something to eat, I didn't realize it was so late and that Hannah was gone. Will you be ok until I get back?" He asked.

Sierra was confused with his mood. He was nice which really bothered her. She liked it better when he was quiet and moody. "I'll be fine," she said flatly.

"Would you like for me to bring you something back?" Devin asked with a smile.

"No thank you," Sierra snapped walking away. She

didn't like him being nice to her. Besides, they were not even supposed to like each other, so why put up a front.

Devin could only laugh at her rudeness as he left the store.

Ten minutes before closing time Devin sat on the stool behind the counter and asked, "Do you want to grab something to eat or drink?"

"No thanks, my brother should be here in a few minutes," Sierra said walking away. A few minutes later, her phone began to ring. "Jermaine you could have called me earlier," Sierra lashed out then angrily snapped her phone shut.

"Is something wrong?" Devin asked with concern.

Sierra stared angrily at Devin, "My brother can't pick me up. Could I catch a ride?"

Devin laughed, "Sure."

"What is so funny?" Sierra tersely asked.

"You. You're what's funny." Devin shook his head.

Sierra was furious. "And why, may I ask, Am I so funny?"

"I have been trying my best to be nice to you, but you're impossible. It's like you have some kind chip on your shoulder, or is it you just simply hate men. I can't be nice to you, you're just a…" Devin stopped talking immediately he didn't want to say anything else out of anger he may one day regret. "Come on, I'll drop you off." Devin started toward the door.

Sierra's eyes became very small, "First of all I'm not a lesbian if that is what you're insinuating. And I'm a what? What were you about to say? Don't act like a pussy now; be man enough to finish it." Sierra was beyond angry.

Devin walked up to Sierra, looked down intensely into her eyes, and spoke so softly that the words came out as if he was caressing her, "You already know what you are."

The softness of his voice stunned and surprised her, but as she repeated his words in her mind, she realized he was right. She knew she was a bitch at times and right now she really didn't care, but she'd be damned if she let any man call her one. "Let's go." She walked past him to stand outside beside his car.

Devin could not get over her attitude as he locked the doors.

***

Friday came slow for Sierra. Since she and Devin argued they simply spoke to each other when necessary, which was perfectly all right with her.

Mrs. Huddle smiled brightly, "Hi Sierra." She picked up her purse, "I'll see you guys tomorrow," she said leaving the store as she thought how easier things had become with Sierra being there.

Devin was busy with customers so Sierra hurriedly went to the employee lounge to put away her purse. Sierra noticed her schedule then frowned. Devin had her working again the following Saturday. She folded her schedule putting it in her purse. *What a prick*, she thought to herself as she went out to assist a pregnant lady.

Hannah looked at Sierra and rolled her eyes. Sierra only laughed because she was acting so childish.

After everything slowed down Devin handed Sierra an envelope, "I'm going to lunch."

Sierra stepped to watch him leave. She opened the envelope and was surprised he paid her more than they had originally agreed, and he actually paid her overtime for the day she had worked from open to close. She sort of felt a little bad for being so rude to him all the time. When he was gone, she straightened the store completely while making sure all the customers were taken care of. When Devin returned Sierra was reading a book to a group of small children.

Devin was surprised at how neat the store was especially for a Friday. Once again, he grudgingly admired Sierra, despite her personality flaw. Devin knew Hannah hadn't done it because she seemed to be allergic to cleaning.

"Why don't you have story time for the children in the afternoons a couple days a week?" Sierra asked later that afternoon.

Devin smiled, "We used to. I would read to them in the afternoons, I just got too busy to keep it up after Jonathan passed."

Sierra looked curiously at Devin as he spoke; he was rather sexy she admitted to herself. Sierra laughed when she realized what he had said, "*You* read to the kids?" She asked with doubts.

Devin smiled, "And what's wrong with that?"

"Nothing. I just find it hard to imagine you reading to small kids," Sierra continued to smile.

Devin laughed, "Pick a day and story time is yours." He walked away to help an old man feeling that was the first time they had actually shared a decent conversation.

Hannah walked up behind Sierra and said, "Don't go getting the wrong idea about Devin. You're *not even* his type."

"Look I'm not even interested in him, not that it's any of your concern, but tell me what is his type, Hannah? Do *you* even know? Don't you think he's a little old for you? Why don't you just go around the corner to the playground, get in the sandbox and wait on someone your own age." Sierra took a deep breath and reminded herself that Hannah was still young, so Sierra decided she wouldn't respond to anything else Hannah might say.

Hannah stared at Sierra for a long moment before rolling her eyes and angrily walked to the other side of the store.

***

The following day Jermaine stopped by the store to let Sierra know he wouldn't be able to pick her up that night. From the store window, Sierra noticed the same woman in the car with Jermaine as he drove away. She had caught the strangest feeling once again as she watched them. She needed a ride home so she called her mom, but as usual Miss Kitty didn't answer, Sierra figured she was probably working late at the old folks home. Sierra called Darius but unfortunately, he wouldn't get off until midnight. She rolled her eyes then walked towards Devin.

"Hey, I was wondering if I could catch a ride with you tonight." She asked.

Devin had actually thought he heard her wrong because

she sounded almost nice, "I'm sorry I wasn't paying attention what were you saying?" Devin stopped typing on the keyboard.

"I asked if you could give me a ride home tonight," Sierra repeated.

Devin smiled at her, "Sure," then he continued typing on the computer as he thought how it was almost scary to see her acting this way.

That night at closing, Sierra asked, "Would you like to stop and get a drink someplace before you drop me off?"

Devin looked at her with a raised eyebrow.

"Look, don't go getting the wrong idea. It ain't even like that," she said rolling her eyes then continued, "I only wanted to buy you a drink to show you that I appreciated you giving me a ride home when I needed it. I also opened my check. Why you paying me so much? Not that I'm complaining."

"Sierra, you may not have experience working in a bookstore, but you got experience. From watching you, I realize you could run this place single-handedly," Devin said seriously.

Sierra was shocked at the compliment he just gave her and was temporarily speechless. She started counting down the registers.

* * *

Sierra took her second shot of tequila, it actually felt good to be back home she thought to herself with a laugh.

"What are you laughing about?" Devin asked taking a swallow of his own drink.

"Me. I never imagined myself working in a bookstore of all places," she said smiling.

"And what's funny about that?" Devin asked smiling back.

"Nothing, I just never pictured it." She smiled then suddenly thought of Bianca. Bianca hadn't even crossed her mind since she started at the store. She ordered another shot.

"You're very pretty when you do that," Devin said softly.

Sierra frowned, "Do what?"

"Smile for a change," Devin teased.

Sierra didn't know how to take that remark so she only laughed. She didn't want to, but she again became aware how handsome he was when he was relaxed laughing and joking. Lately she had often caught herself watching him throughout the day as he interacts with the customers, especially the women. She took notice how he always wore dark colors, always looked good and smelled good. However, unfortunately, all the men she's met so far are either in love with someone else or they're complete dogs, she just wondered which category he fell in.

"A couple more of those and you'll have one serious hangover," Devin said evenly.

Sierra smiled sadly, "I know, but it makes the demons go away."

"What demons?" Devin frowned asking curiously.

Sierra looked at Devin with haunted eyes and briefly debated whether to confide in him, she really needed to talk to somebody. She decided not to and ordered another shot instead. "Not important," she said pushing thoughts of Bianca out of her mind.

Sierra and Devin actually talked for almost two hours. She told him about her mother and brothers, laughing about some of the crazy things they had done as children and Devin only talked about Jonathan. Sierra wondered if he had been an orphan because he never spoke about his childhood. When they left the bar, Sierra stumbled and would have fallen if Devin didn't catch her.

"You ok?" Devin asked softly.

"Yeah I'm fine," Sierra pulled away feeling the unwanted heat arise in her from his touch.

Devin frowned because surprisingly he felt it too.

It was after eleven when Sierra entered her house and an odd almost eerie feeling overcame her. It was much too dark and much too quiet. She took off her shoes so her mother wouldn't hear her on the stairs. She dropped her shoes on the floor beside her bed then went to the bathroom to relieve herself. After washing her hands, she was gripped with a fear so over powering she felt she might pass out. Sierra shook uncontrollably as she ran from her bathroom to check on her mother. Her mom was lying with her back facing the door. Sierra walked slowly to her bed and touched her mother's face softly as she bent over her.

"What the hell is wrong with you? Have you lost your damn mind sneaking up on me at night like that? I could have shot you," Miss Kitty quickly put away her forty-four and sat up. She grabbed Sierra holding her as if she was a child. "Baby, tell me what's wrong," her mother said frowning; Sierra was shaking and crying uncontrollably.

Sierra cried and told her mom all about Bianca. After calming Sierra down Miss Kitty told Sierra to stay with her in her bed for the night. Miss Kitty got up and went to Sierra's bathroom to look in the mirror. *I told you not to FUCK with me BITCH*, was written in bright red lipstick. Miss Kitty walked calmly to the hall closet grabbed a towel then went back to clean Sierra's mirror.

Miss Kitty walked through her house checking all the doors and windows. Everything was locked and secure. She grabbed her cigarettes and sat out on the front porch. Miss Kitty smoked the whole pack. Somebody had invaded her home while she slept. She was furious and somebody had her baby terrified. Somebody was going to pay because nobody fucked with her kids. Miss Kitty stood up putting the last cigarette out in the ashtray. She locked her door and climbed the stairs for bed. Sierra looked so young, helpless and innocent as she slept. Miss Kitty lay down and thought about what was written on Sierra's mirror. Miss Kitty made a strange noise and said softly with vengeance on her mind, "Now I got the bitch. Now it's time to play Miss Kitty style." She turned out the light and went to sleep.

The next morning Miss Kitty held the phone to her ear listening to the recorded message, she had gotten Bianca's work number from telephone directory. She listened to the company directory carefully then pressed Bianca's extension number. It went straight to voice mail, Miss Kitty listened to Bianca's voice waiting patiently on the beep, 'You have reached Bianca Kendrix, please leave a detailed message along with your name and telephone number and I'll return your call as promptly as possible. Thank you and have a blessed day.' Beep.

"Bianca, this is Kitty Sanders and I'm only going to say this once so listen good, *do not* fuck with my daughter ever again and the next time you decide to enter my home without my permission, me and Jack will be waiting on your uppity ass as soon as you cross *my* threshold. Now you have a blessed day Bitch." Miss Kitty carefully placed the phone back in its cradle and walked to her bedroom. She laughed because Bianca would be finding out soon enough who Jack is. Jack was Miss Kitty's Forty-four magnum handgun.

"Sierra honey, it's ten o'clock. Do you have to work today?" Miss Kitty asked.

Sierra's mouth felt like stale cotton, "We're closed Sundays." She rose up slowly, her head was throbbing although not too badly.

"Get up and get dressed while I make you some breakfast," Miss Kitty left the room.

Miss Kitty had just finished cooking when Sierra made it down to the kitchen. "You look nice today. I like it when you pin your hair up like that with those loose curls," Miss Kitty said as she handed Sierra a plate. "I've been thinking, why don't you get your boss to drop you off at nights until you get a car because I've got a lot to do over the next few weeks, Darius is working the second shift and Jermaine is nowhere to be found lately," then added, "I might not be here some nights too."

"You didn't tell them anything, did you?" Sierra asked suspiciously.

Miss Kitty only patted Sierra's shoulders, "No baby, I didn't. Eat your breakfast. Those crazy brothers of yours would only get themselves into a world of trouble. We'll handle this, just the two of us." Miss Kitty smiled. Sierra smiled back, her mom always took care of everything. Sierra sat back and ate her breakfast.

* * *

Bianca was finally relaxed. She got home not even an hour ago. It had been a long week. She took a long relaxing bath, her mind and body was completely drained. She made a cup of hot herbal tea and called to check her messages. "Miss Kitty," Bianca said laughing, thinking she was a true rival, "Much respect to you. I guess it's time I up the ante." Bianca smiled and stretched out. She felt deliriously good.

Chapter Nineteen

Sierra was tired, but was glad to be back at work so she could forget about the home front. The writing on the mirror really shook her up so she was, to say the least, more than happy to arrive a little early at the bookstore. "Good afternoon Mrs. Huddle, how have things been going?" she greeted

"It's been extremely quiet, but it gave me some time to organize a few shelves," she said with a smile then added when she noticed Sierra looking around, "Devin is in the warehouse preparing for inventory." Sierra frowned, wondering why Mrs. Huddle would think she was looking for Devin. She went over to push chairs under tables. Mrs. Huddle smiled as she gathered her things to leave, "You're early, but I think I'll take off anyways. My goodness, I hope this rain stops soon. I doubt you guys get any customers, everyone will probably stay home today, I know I would."

Sierra laughed as she watched Mrs. Huddle run to her car. She almost slipped but regained her footing just in time. "Pretty agile for a little old lady," Sierra laughed to herself as Mrs. Huddle drove away. Sierra inhaled deeply then went to the children's section to reorganize the books.

Devin finished with the warehouse about two o'clock, Sierra was standing in front of the window just looking out. There were no customers in the store, so Devin took it as an opportunity to take a good look at Sierra. She was pretty, too pretty to be honest. Today her hair was parted down the middle and hung straight just past her shoulders. Her skin reminded him of rich honey. He could only imagine how soft it was. She wore a simple blue dress that clung invitingly to her every curve. *Damn*, Devin thought to himself, *it's a shame for anyone to be that fine.* Devin took a deep breath and went back to the warehouse deciding to put together the bookshelf he had bought almost six months ago. He really needed to get Sierra out off his mind. He thought of what Bianca had told him about Sierra, he really found it all hard to believe even with her jacked up attitude.

Sierra was bored. It was almost four o'clock and they didn't even have one customer since she arrived. It's all this rain, she thought. She hadn't seen Devin all day so she decided to at least go and speak with him. Sierra stopped in the doorway when Devin came in her view. His thick hair was pulled back in a ponytail as usual, and he had on a pair of jeans that fitted oh so good and his shirt was unbuttoned. *Oh my God, talk about a brother with a six-pack.* Sierra was a sucker for chest hair, hair lightly covered Devin's chest, and invitingly disappeared in his jeans, *damn* she thought to herself *he had the nerve to be sweating. I really needed to get laid if I'm looking at Devin of all people.* She turned abruptly and went back to the front.

Sierra was sitting on the stool drinking a soda when she noticed Devin standing in the doorway. "Hi," she said, thankful he had his shirt buttoned up.

"You know if you want to take off you can, I doubt if anyone will come in," Devin said putting his hands in his pocket.

"I would love to, but I don't have a ride. I was hoping to bum another from you," she said smiling.

Devin smiled, "No problem." He really wished Mrs. Huddle was still here because for some reason he was too aware of Sierra and that really bothered him. He went back to the warehouse.

By six thirty Devin decided to close the store because it was pouring down outside. They ran to his car only to find he had a flat tire. He was pissed to say the least and he was soaked and wet by the time he finished changing it, and Sierra had the nerve to be laughing. Devin didn't say a word. He was tired, hungry and horny as hell and only wanted to get away from Sierra. She was the kind of woman that would nag a man to death and he had no intentions of acting on any of the thoughts that was going through his mind at that moment, and to top everything off, she actually looked completely naked with her dress molded to her wet body. He started the car and drove off.

"Do you want to come in for a minute, at least until the

rain slacks off?" Sierra asked when Devin pulled up in front of her house.

Devin glanced down to her breasts briefly, "No thanks," he said smiling.

Sierra looked down for the first time and was completely embarrassed, she quickly opened the door and began to run, and then she fell. Devin laughed then jumped out of the car to help her when she didn't get up right away.

Sierra was so embarrassed and very angry that she just sat there a minute before she tried to get up, only to fall again. Devin laughed harder as he helped her up and they ran inside.

"That's not funny," she snapped.

"Actually it was. You just should have seen it from my angle," Devin laughed.

Sierra left him standing in the doorway to go upstairs, when she came back down she handed him a big towel.

"You got mud on your face," Devin said softly as he wiped it off with the towel.

"Thanks," Sierra said stepping back to put distance between them.

"I guess I'd better go," Devin said as he glanced down briefly at her body.

Sierra suddenly panicked at the idea of being in the house alone, "Please stay at least for a cup of coffee or tea."

Devin almost said no but the look in Sierra's eyes changed his mind, "Just let me turn off the car." Sierra smiled handing him an umbrella from the closet.

Sierra set a cup of steaming coffee in front of Devin then sat down across from him.

"Why don't you go cover up or something?" Devin suggested.

Sierra stood and walked away quickly, she returned a few minutes later wearing a big T-shirt and sweats.

"I really do need to get going," Devin said as he glanced at her nipples were poking out very noticeably out of her T-shirt.

"Sierra!" Miss Kitty yelled throughout the house.

"I'm in the kitchen," Sierra smiled.

Miss Kitty entered the kitchen and stopped in the doorway. "Hi mom, this is Devin, he owns the book store. Devin, this is my mom everyone calls her Miss Kitty," Sierra said.

"Hello Miss Kitty, It's a pleasure to finally meet you," Devin smiled and thought with great surprise at how extremely attractive Sierra's mom was. For some reason after listening to Sierra's stories that night at the bar, he expected her to look a whole lot different.

Miss Kitty smiled, "Hello Devin. I'm glad to finally meet you too." She sat her purse on the table.

"Mom, Devin was just leaving. I'm going to walk him to the door. I'll be right back."

Miss Kitty nodded then said, "Devin, I really appreciate you getting her home safe."

Devin smiled, "No problem."

At the front door, Sierra reached for the umbrella but he shook his head.

"I'm already wet. I don't need it," he said.

"At least take the towel," Sierra said.

"It would be soaked before I could get to the car," he stated.

Sierra grabbed his hand, "Thanks Devin."

Devin frowned then asked, "For what?"

"Everything," she said softly.

Sierra looked so tempting when she spoke that he had the urge to kiss her. Devin felt something for her at that moment and he didn't like it one bit. Those feelings that were overpowering him made him turn and walk out leaving Sierra to stare after him.

"Well isn't he a fine one," Miss Kitty said making Sierra jump. "Now, who do you think is going to clean my floor?" Miss Kitty said and walked away smiling to herself thinking about Sierra and her handsome boss. Miss Kitty laughed; Sierra had the nerve to say she couldn't stand him, not even a week ago.

When Devin got home, he took a shower then went to his gym and had himself a good hour workout. He was watching television and eating a sandwich and some chips when his phone rang. He started not to answer when he saw who it was.

"Hi Devin, how are things going?" Bianca asked through a lot of static.

Devin didn't have a chance to say anything because the line was disconnected. "Good," he said to himself. He knew he was indebted to Bianca, but he was actually beginning to like Sierra. He didn't want to get involved in whatever Bianca had going on because something was really nagging him about the whole situation, things didn't seem to add up. He would try to keep out of it as long as he could.

Bianca sat in the hotel suite wrapped in a thick white robe unpleasantly. She was in a bad mood because all this rain and bad weather gave her cell phone a weak signal. She would have to call Devin some other time, but she had a feeling that Devin wasn't going to be much help to her. The only good thing about it was that she could easily keep her eye on Sierra. The bookstore was in the perfect location. It was the last building on the block and stood directly in front of a wooded area. There was a café right across the street, which held a beautiful view of pretty much the whole bookstore. Bianca laughed thinking she almost got caught flattening Devin's tire. He and Sierra had surprised her by leaving early. Bianca had planned on going back to Miss Kitty's house just to leave another message out of spite, and this time it was going to be especially for Miss Kitty.

"Hey Desiree, I'm back, did you miss me? They let class out early because of the rain," Jermaine said.

Bianca smiled at Jermaine, "Baby I've missed you all day. Why don't you let me show you how much?" Bianca purred invitingly. After her initial meeting with Devin, she knew she couldn't depend completely on him, so she decided to work on a few things herself.

Jermaine started taking his shirt off and said softly, "Just give me a few minutes to shower."

Bianca laughed then said softly to herself, "If Miss Kitty could see me now." Bianca picked up her purse and looked at her driver's license Desiree Jones aged thirty-five she laughed, that old man did a remarkable job. Bianca stood to look in the mirror at her reflection, touched the mole below her right eye, and thought it was a good touch. Her make up was flawless just heavier, but along with the grey contacts, she looked damn good. She hated this hairstyle, the brownish blonde color, and the clothes she had been wearing. Bianca laughed as ghetto fabulous came straight to mind, and because she still had every man looking her way at the ripe age of fifty-two.

Bianca laughed when she thought of Jermaine. She had him whipped. There was nothing he wouldn't do for her. He quit his job when she asked him to and started working a couple hours in the mornings at one of the warehouse shipping departments. She even had him going to night school on a regular basis. All she had to do was keep him sexed up, that's how she was able to steal his keys and get a copy made. It was one thing Bianca hated, and that was a young person wasting away their life living too carefree, although that wasn't her only motive in this instance, she needed him away so she could sneak into his mother's house.

"Hey baby," Jermaine said walking into the room then kissing her.

Oh my God, Bianca thought to herself as she smiled seductively, he was young and full of stamina, "Hey yourself."

***

Devin was in his office the next day and was tired, for the last few nights he hadn't been sleeping too well. As of lately, Sierra seemed to be on his mind a little too much. Sierra opened his door and entered without knocking, "Devin there is someone who would like to speak with you," Sierra told him.

Devin nodded his head and said, "I'll be there in a minute." He stood after he finished entering the invoice. When he opened his door, he heard Sierra telling someone he would be with them shortly.

"Devin!" A woman squealed running to him hugging

him tightly, "Oh my god you still look delicious."

The few customers present in the store looked over immediately and Sierra felt a sudden twinge of jealousy, so she walked away immediately to clean off a table.

Devin was temporarily unable to speak. He hadn't seen Lily in almost five years. "Hey lady" he said smiling into her eyes. "It's been a while, hasn't it? How have you been?" He felt a little uncomfortable with Lily around Sierra for some strange reason.

"I've been great. I wanted to see you yesterday but all of the rain kept us indoors," Lily said.

Devin noticed the little girl for the first time. Lily picked her up into her arms.

"Devin, this is my daughter Lilyanne. Say hi to Mr. Devin, baby." Lily kissed the little girl.

Devin felt very uncomfortable as if his airway might close up; the little girl was too small to be his but that didn't keep the possibility off his mind. He and Lily had slept together a few times, but there were never any real feelings between them other than friendship. Lily had wanted more from their relationship, but she was too possessive and much too jealous and he couldn't deal with that. Besides, she had been messing around on her boyfriend and he figured she would have probably ended up doing the same to him.

Lily looked at Devin and laughed, "Calm down, Devin, she's only three. Eddie and I got married right after I left," she said laughing.

Devin relaxed immediately.

"Eddie is waiting on us at my parent's house, we got to get going. It was really good seeing you again," Lily smiled kissing his cheek.

Devin watched as they left the store then began picking up paper off the floor.

Sierra watched them from across the room and actually became jealous again when the woman kissed Devin. She was angrier at herself for feeling that way.

"I'm going to lunch, would either of you like for me to

bring something back?" Devin asked Sierra and Hannah a few minutes later.

Hannah smiled, "No thank you."

Sierra was ordering a book for a customer, so she shook her head no to Devin. She didn't take her eyes off the computer screen until he left. "I have your book ordered; it should arrive in about a week. I will call you as soon as it gets here." Sierra smiled to the lady and watched her leave. Sierra was wondering the whole time if Devin was meeting the woman and little girl someplace. The customers were beginning to leave the store and she began cleaning.

"I can't stand Lily," Hannah said to Sierra as she sat at a table and watched her clean. "When I was fourteen she would cheat on her boyfriend with Devin. Her boyfriend is my cousin Eddie." Hannah stood and went behind the counter to talk on the phone.

Devin was gone for almost an hour because the traffic was backed up from the traffic lights not working properly. When he returned, Sierra was reading a story to a group of small children, and Hannah was standing behind the counter talking on the phone. Sierra never looked his way; she actually avoided him for the rest of the day and only talked when it was unavoidable. Devin laughed to himself because she was the moodiest person he ever met.

Sierra was closing out the last register when Devin came to the counter and flip through a few papers in a folder.

"Today was a good day," he said to her.

"Yes it was," Sierra said quietly. She was confused because she and Devin hadn't gotten along from the first moment they had met, although they did pretty much get along now, it was still no reason for her to become jealous. Ever since Jordan rejected her, she swore herself off the men that brought out her emotions. She didn't want to do anything crazy and embarrassing, but all of a sudden Devin came causing total confusion when she least expected it. Sierra closed the register drawer a little harder than she wanted, then she sat at one of the tables while she waited on Devin.

Devin sat down beside Sierra, "What is wrong with you?"

"Nothing. Are you ready to go?" Sierra was aggravated.

"Not yet. There is one more thing I need to do," Devin said softly.

"Well do it already so we can go," Sierra snapped.

Devin leaned over and kissed Sierra very softly. "Now we can go," Devin kissed the tip of her nose and stood. Now maybe he would be able to sleep since he finally gave into at least one of his urges.

Sierra stood, she was completely bewildered and weakened by his kiss, and she waited at the door for Devin as he turned off the lights and set the alarm. The drive to her house was quieter than usual.

"Goodnight Devin," Sierra said softly as she got out and went inside her house.
Devin sat frowning and watched her until she closed her door. Damn if he wasn't falling for her, he thought before he drove away.

* * *

It was late when Darius dropped Sierra off the next day. She hadn't realized how much she missed spending time with her brother. They spent the whole day relaxing and having fun. Sierra enjoyed her day off but a few times during the day, she thought of Devin and wished she were at the store. Devin's brief kiss the night before caused her to have trouble sleeping and all day she felt as if she had been up all night. When she woke up that morning she called Darius just to talk and was surprised when he had suggested they go shopping; she agreed because she had needed to get out of the house.

Sierra was thinking of Devin when she entered her house that she hadn't heard the noise from upstairs. She went to the living room and turned on the television. She jumped when a radio suddenly blared from upstairs. Sierra went completely still then got up to walk slowly to the bottom of the stairs.

"What the hell! Sierra what's wrong with you? You're trying to wake the neighbors?" Miss Kitty said coming through the doorway. "Did you hear me girl? Why you got that music up so loud?" Miss Kitty slammed the front door.

Sierra stood looking strange at her mom shaking her head, "I didn't do it. It just came on by itself."

Miss Kitty's eyes became small as she pulled her forty-four from her purse. "I'm getting ready to fuck somebody up," Miss Kitty said with a twisted smile. Sierra stood for a minute watching her mom go up the stairs then ran up behind her. The music was coming from Miss Kitty's bedroom. Miss Kitty smiled then opened her door slowly. She went over to turn off her radio. She looked all around her room, her bathroom and her closet. No one was there. She checked all of upstairs. She went back to her room where she had made Sierra stay. She found Sierra sitting on her bed. "Momma, I'm so sorry for bringing you into my mess. I never should have come home. I don't know what I'd do if something were to happen to you," Sierra said softly as tears began to fall.

Miss Kitty was pissed but managed to remain calm. She sat beside Sierra and put her arms around her, "Nonsense, you're my baby and this is where you need to be at a time like this. Don't worry so much, I got this." Miss Kitty stood and put her hands on her hips, "Now, stop all that crying and shit. I can't figure out how the hell you ended up so damn scary." She then walked over to her window and laughed.

Sierra stood up to walk to the window, "Momma, that's not funny."

Somebody wrote on her window *Hello Miss Kitty hope you had a blessed day, and* under her name, there was a smiley face. It was written in the same bright red lipstick that was on Sierra's bathroom mirror.

"Come on baby, let's go to the kitchen and fix us a good stiff drink," Miss Kitty said smiling. She had to admit Bianca had balls, she actually liked that, too bad they couldn't meet under different circumstances. Miss Kitty laughed all the way down the stairs then stopped. Her front door stood wide open. She walked over casually and stepped out on the porch to look around, when she was satisfied no one was there she stepped back inside and closed it. "Come on now. Let's get that drink. Don't go letting Bianca work your nerves. First thing in the morning I'll get the locks changed." Miss Kitty said smiling to Sierra. Miss Kitty really didn't want to change her locks because what she really wanted was to catch Bianca red handed. She couldn't wait to get her hands on Bianca, but for the sake of her daughter, she would change the locks.

The following day at work, Devin had to leave the store for a while; he couldn't put off getting his tire fixed any longer. "Hey, I'll be back later. I've got to take care of some things. My cell number is in the employee lounge if you should need anything."

At eight thirty, Devin still didn't get back and every time she called his cell phone it went straight to voicemail, Sierra was pissed. She couldn't leave the store even if she wanted to because she didn't have a key to lock up. She wasn't able to leave to get anything to eat because no one else was there to watch the store. And someone was calling all day breathing on the phone. It hadn't rung in over an hour and she was glad. Sierra's anger took on a new level, which was definitely beyond words.

She decided to go see if she could find something to eat in the refrigerator in the employees lounge. The refrigerator was empty except for a covered dish. Sierra grabbed the dish. She knew it wasn't Hannah's because she rarely ate anything. However, when she did eat, it was always take-out, and Sierra didn't think Mrs. Huddle would get angry if it was hers. She hoped it was Devin's. She smiled imagining him being stuck there busy with customers without anything to eat. Sierra took the cover off the dish and screamed throwing the bowl across the room. It was something covered with maggots and worms. She was nauseous as she ran back to the front and stopped in her tracks. The front door stood wide open. Sierra was about to be sick, she couldn't go to the bathroom because she had to go through the employee lounge to get there. On weak legs, she ran outside and threw up. When she came back inside she locked the doors, it was already after nine.

Sierra walked slowly to the door that led to the warehouse and looked inside, it was too dark to see anything. She shut the door immediately wishing she had the key to lock it. She went to Devin's office and looked around briefly. Sierra was chiding herself for being so scary. She thought about what her mom had said then started laughing and saying out loud, "How did I get to be so scary and jumpy with a mother like Miss Kitty." She laughed at herself and went to sit on the stool behind the counter. Sierra frowned as she thought of the bowl from the refrigerator could've been a prank. She could hardly wait until Devin returned. She knew she needed to close out the registers, but as she casually looked over at the counter, she stood up cautiously looking around. There was a white piece of paper with *Fuck you Bitch* written on it and it looked like it was written with bright red lipstick. Sierra started shaking uncontrollably because it wasn't there before she went to the back in search of food. Sierra ran into Devin's office locking the door behind her. She picked up the phone to call her mom but it was dead. "Shit," she said because her cell phone was in the employee lounge in her purse.

Sierra looked at the clock when she heard Devin knocking on the door calling her name. It was nine forty-five. Relieved and on trembling legs she stood to open the door.

"I'm so sorry, Sierra, that guy just got done with my car, he had broken a few of my lugs so it took him a while for the replacements parts to come in." Devin looked at Sierra then frowned. "Why are you in my office locked up?" He asked with a frown.

Sierra looked up quietly at him her eyes were blood red she was on the verge of tears, "You could have called me," she said in a strangled voice.

"My cell phone hadn't been charged and when I did get a chance to call all I got was a busy signal," he said frowning.

"You need to keep your damn phone charged. Just take me home," she snapped angrily.

Devin looked around his office wondering what she could have been doing in there. Bianca came to mind as he remembered what she had told him in the coffee house. "Did you close out the registers?" He asked her.

"No I didn't," she angrily snapped.

Devin was already in a foul mood, so he didn't say anything else to her. He went to start closing out and was furious at Sierra for just sitting there doing nothing. He inhaled deeply bringing his attention back to the register, that's when he saw the paper. He picked it up slowly went over and sat beside Sierra.

"What is this?" Devin asked quietly.

Sierra walked over to the other register to start closing it out. Devin stood to finish his register and then simply stood looking confused at Sierra. Her hands were trembling as she counted the money. After closing the register drawer, Devin reached over and pulled her into his arms. Sierra broke down and cried.

"Sierra, come talk to me," Devin grabbed her hand as he headed to the employee lounge.

"No. We can sit in your office," Sierra said.

Sierra sat on his couch in front of the window. "I don't know where to begin," she said in a shaky voice. "It all started about a year ago. I was working as an executive director for a newspaper in Cleveland, one day this lady named Bianca came to see me about a guy that I had dated a few times about six years ago, his name was Jordan." Sierra took a deep breath.
"It all really started when Ashland, Bianca's daughter, and Jordan had been teenagers and had planned to marry. Bianca didn't want that so when Ashland got pregnant Bianca lied to them both. Something happened and Jordan ended up leaving town. Ashland ended up having a miscarriage, but Bianca told Jordan that Ashland aborted their baby. Bianca made Ashland believe Jordan never loved her. They went ten years without seeing or talking to each other. Not too long ago Jordan married Ashland, shortly after she became pregnant again. Bianca hired a private investigator to check out Jordan. That's how she found out about me dating Jordan. Bianca paid me to make Ashland think that Jordan and I were having an affair." Sierra covered

her mouth with trembling hands, shaking her head, as she looked Devin in his eyes, "I swear I never knew Ashland was eight months pregnant until I saw her." Sierra took a deep breath then continued, "I was very convincing embarrassingly enough, you see, a part of me was still hurt that Jordan never loved me, it had always been Ashland that he loved. I was jealous." Sierra said softly.

"I left Ashland and went straight to Bianca and asked her how she could hire me to do that to her own daughter at such a late stage of her pregnancy. We had a big argument. She ended up threatening me. Bianca actually said I'd find myself floating somewhere if I didn't mind my own business. I left promising never to tell and I didn't intend to look back. Then one day that private investigator came to see me, and told me a lot of things about Bianca. He then told me the day following my visit to Ashland, she went into premature labor and almost died. I almost killed that woman and her unborn child." Tears were falling from Sierra's eyes.

Devin sat and thought about how he *had* killed his father, Sierra was lucky she didn't have that burden to carry around. He gave her hand a reassuring squeeze.

"My conscience was bothering me, so I went down to visit Jordan and Ashland and I apologized and confessed my part in everything. When I was leaving their house, I ran into Bianca. We had a few words, so she knew I had broken my promise to keep quiet. The look Bianca gave me..." Sierra stopped talking for a minute, "Well I have nightmares about her doing things to me. I was so scared I quit my job and moved back here."

Sierra looked at Devin with haunted eyes, "Things have started happening around here. The night we went to the bar after you dropped me off, someone had been in my bathroom and wrote on my mirror 'I told you not to fuck with me bitch' in bright red lipstick. Then last night someone broke in again and wrote on my mother's bedroom window in bright red lipstick 'Hello Miss Kitty I hope you had a blessed day.' They even had the nerve to draw a smiley face under her name. Both times it was as if they had a key or something because when my mom looked around there wasn't any signs of a forced entry anywhere and all the doors and windows were locked."

"Today someone was calling here just breathing on the phone. Then when I went to the refrigerator to find something to eat, all I found was a container with something covered with maggots and worms." Sierra looked at Devin apologetically, "I threw it across the room. Later I found that piece of paper on the counter, so I locked myself in here until you came back. You see, Bianca paid me a lot of money to convince Ashland that Jordan was cheating. She also paid me money to keep quiet. Bianca knew she'd lose her daughter if she found out." Sierra stared hard into Devin's eyes, "Bianca also paid me money to visit Jordan's mother and brother to convince them to visit him. The only problem with that was Jordan grew up as an only child, thinking his parents were dead. I have no excuses for the things I've done. I can only say I just had a lot of bills and needed the money." Sierra knew she didn't have to tell Devin about Jordan's mother and brother but she felt the need to be completely honest with him.

Devin was overwhelmed. It took him a few minutes to digest everything. "Sierra, I think we all have done things in life we're not proud of. We can't change our past," Devin said grimly thinking about his own past. He leaned over and kissed her forehead. "Come on, let's get you home."

Devin took Sierra home, talked to Miss Kitty a few minutes then returned to the store. After he cleaned the employee lounge, he went into his office and sat down. He thought about everything Sierra said about Bianca. She lost her daughter and blames Sierra. "What better way to keep an eye on Sierra, through me." Devin was pissed. Bianca had actually tried to use him in her morbid vendetta for revenge. He stood to go home, then something occurred to him, "Maybe Bianca had hoped I'd use Sierra the way I'd used those other women," Devin said thinking about all the women he had made fall in love with him and he just callously walked away and turned his back on them after he had gotten everything he could. "I'm not that stupid young kid anymore," Devin said out loud and left.

Chapter Twenty

Miss Kitty was sitting at the kitchen table when Sierra walked in. After Devin dropped her off, she surprisingly had a good night sleep.

"Hi baby, I see you're getting ready to go to work," Miss Kitty said looking serious.

Sierra smiled but from the way her mom was looking, she knew she was getting ready to talk about something. Sierra got a cola from the refrigerator and sat down.

"Now Sierra, every year I've been going on vacation with a friend, and that time is here again. I am supposed to leave this afternoon, but if you don't feel comfortable here alone I won't go," Miss Kitty said.

Sierra smiled and teased, "You got a man that takes you on vacation every year? Momma, what have you been doing?" Sierra smiled as she reached to grab her mother's hand when Miss Kitty made a noise, "Momma I'll be fine. You go and have a good time. Don't worry about me, remember you changed all the locks, nobody can get in now." Sierra stood smiling and kissed her mom on her cheek, "Now, you have a very wonderful and very sinful time with that man of yours. I'll see you when you get back. Come on take me to work before I'm late."

Miss Kitty handed Sierra her car keys, "I called a cab. I'll be back in two weeks. And you know where I keep Jack." Miss Kitty laughed.

Sierra laughed but was not thrilled at the idea of being in the house alone. She was actually terrified. By the time Sierra arrived at work, Mrs. Huddle had already left.

"Devin, I'm sorry I'm late," Sierra said.

Devin only smiled she was usually early. "You left your purse last night, it's in my desk."

"Oh no," Sierra said running to Devin's office.

"What's wrong?" Devin asked with a frown as he watched her dump the contents of her bag onto his desk.

"My purse, my house keys just everything," she said throwing everything back in her purse then throwing her purse down. She tried to leave his office but Devin wouldn't move from the doorway.

"What is wrong with you?" Devin asked grabbing her shoulders.

"I left my purse here. We just had our locks changed," she said frustrated, then thought to herself, *there is no way I'm staying in that house alone now.* Sierra shook Devin's hands off her shoulders and pushed past him to help customers.

Sierra stood looking out the window when there were no customers in the store. Devin left for a few minutes to get lunch. She declined his usual offer to bring her something back, she was too nervous to eat. Sierra usually enjoyed talking and helping everyone find things they were looking for, but this day she wanted to be left alone. She didn't ask anyone if they needed help, she waited for them to ask. She dreaded each minute that went by because that meant she was a minute closer to going home.

"Good afternoon," Sierra said absently with a forced smile as a woman entered the store. She went to pick a couple of books off the floor as the woman looked around. Sierra went to sit behind the counter and waited on the lady to finish making her selection.

"I hope you found everything ok," Sierra said to the woman as she rung her up.
The woman didn't say anything. Sierra noticed she had very pretty eyes. Her eyes made her briefly think of Jordan's eyes, only his grey was a little darker. Although Sierra thought to herself that the red hair was rather tacky, she didn't make it obvious.

"Thank you Ms. Jones, please come again," Sierra said as she handed the woman her license and credit card back. Devin walked through the door talking with an old man. The woman picked up her bag from the counter only to drop it when she got closer to Devin. He picked it up for her smiling only briefly as he continued to talk with the older man. Sierra laughed because the woman had deliberately dropped it, probably trying to get Devin's attention. There had been something familiar about the woman, she just couldn't figure out what it was, *Oh well*, she thought as she looked at the clock with a frown.

"What are you doing tonight?" Sierra asked Devin at closing after he locked the doors.

"Not much. It's been a long week. I just want to relax tonight," Devin said looking over at her as she closed the register.

Sierra wanted to ask him if he wanted to stop and get a drink.

"What about you, what are you doing?" he asked.

"I'm going to buy a bottle of tequila before I go home," Sierra said smiling. She planned on getting drunk just so she'd pass out. If something happened to her, she didn't want to know about it.

"Oh yeah, I can just imagine Miss Kitty drinking tequila," Devin said laughing.

Sierra laughed, "Very interesting I assure you."

"Devin, would you like to come by for a minute and have a drink, talk or watch a movie?" Sierra asked hopefully.

Devin laughed, "What would Miss Kitty say if she woke up to find me drinking tequila with her daughter late at night?"

Sierra laughed, "She caught me once when I was fifteen. This boy I liked, his name was Darren, had come over and we had drunk a bottle of her wine, well he decided to kiss me at the exact moment my mom had come in the room. Well momma had Jack with her; she had heard talking and thought someone had broken into the house, well as soon as Darren saw Jack he took off running. Darren never talked to me again."

"Is Jack your father?" Devin asked.

Sierra burst out laughing, "No. Jack is my mom's forty-four magnum."

Devin hated guns and thinking of them always gave him the chills then the bad memories would follow. Devin laughed then started walking toward his office, "No thanks, I'll pass on the drink."

After leaving the store and locking up, Devin said laughing, "Tell your mom I said hello." He got in his car and left.

Sierra pulled up in her driveway and sat for a few minutes. She opened the bottle of tequila and took a very long swallow. Her hands were shaking as she got out of her mother's car. As soon as she entered her house, she turned on all the lights and went to her mother's room to get Jack. Jack was gone. She searched her mother's room completely then went downstairs. Sierra went into the kitchen to get a glass and found the back door open. Sierra took a frustrated deep breath and closed the back door. She grabbed her glass, tequila and purse then got back in her car and left.

Devin was watching television when his phone rang.

"Devin, hi it's Sierra, would you come get me?"

Devin inhaled deeply and looked at the clock. It was ten forty-five. "Where are you?"

"I've been arrested," she said.

***

"What the hell were you doing drinking and driving? I thought you went straight home." Devin said angrily as they left the police station.

"I did go home. Then when I got there I went to get Jack, but it was gone. Then the back door was open. I just got fed up with everything and left," Sierra said.

"Where is your mother?" Devin asked wondering why she didn't call her.

"She left this afternoon. Her friend took her on vacation. She won't be back for two weeks," Sierra said.

Devin took her to his house because he didn't want her calling him over in the night. "You can stay here tonight I'll take you to get your mother's car in the morning."

Sierra followed Devin inside his house. He threw his keys on a table in the foyer then went into his living room to sit down.

"Do you always leave your television on?" She asked.

"No I happened to be watching it when you called," he said sharply.

Sierra stood, "Just take me home."

Devin laughed, "I don't think so. It's late and I'm tired. So just sit down, relax and just shut up please." He was really annoyed at her for getting arrested and he didn't really want her at home alone after everything she had told him. He leaned his head back and closed his eyes.

Sierra was restless, "Do you have something to drink?"

"Don't you think that's what got you arrested in the first place?" Devin said angrily as he stood to grab a glass and a bottle of vodka and set it on the table in front of Sierra. "Here drink until you pass out," he snapped then flipped through the channels until he found a movie to watch.

Sierra stood, "Where is your kitchen, I need some ice."

Devin only looked at her with a raised eyebrow.

"Never mind," she said pouring some of the clear liquid in her glass and began drinking.

"Devin, you have a very beautiful house," Sierra said smiling.

Devin only looked at her briefly then continued watching television.

Sierra stood to sit beside him on the sofa, "Why are you being so mean to me?" she asked as she reached for his ponytail. She took the band off his hair. "Don't be so mean, Devin," she said caressing his hair teasingly.

Devin closed his eyes and thought how good it felt to have her hands on him. "Sierra, what are you doing?" He asked annoyed breathing heavily.

Sierra began unbuttoning his shirt and kissed him. Devin stood up, "Sierra just stop, you're drunk."

"What's wrong, Devin? You don't want me?" She said quietly looking down at the bulge in his pants.

"Not like this," Devin said softly. "Come on, I'll show you what room you'll sleep in."

Sierra woke up the next morning and didn't know where she was. The room was white and yellow and the sun shone in brightly. "Devin's house," she said smiling as memory of the night before returned, she stood slowly, "At least I don't have a hangover." She groaned at the thought of getting arrested. Then she smiled thinking about how good it felt to get close to Devin and put her hands in his hair. Sierra stripped down and went into the bathroom to shower.

"You could get lost in this house," Sierra said after finding Devin in the kitchen eating toast and reading the paper. She looked at his coffee; it smelled so good. "Can I have some coffee?" She asked.

"Help yourself," he said never putting his paper down.

"Are you mad at me about something?" She asked.

"Sierra, it's Sunday and it's early, please don't start asking a thousand questions. I like my mornings quiet, so just let me enjoy my one day off," Devin said taking a sip of coffee.

Sierra fixed her coffee and went out his kitchen door to sit outside. Sierra vowed she wouldn't go back in until he was ready to take her home. She didn't have to wait too long before he came out to get her.

"Do you want me to follow you home and check out your house for you?" Devin asked after they got her mom's car.

"No thank you. I'll call Darius, just enjoy your day off," Sierra said sarcastically as she got in her moms car and left.

"Hi Darius, could you do me a favor and meet me at the house? I forgot and left the kitchen door open yesterday. I just want you to check everything out for me," Sierra said.

"In other words you're scared to go inside?" Darius laughed.

"Just meet me there," Sierra hung up on his laughing.

* * *

Bianca was enjoying herself immensely. She smiled as she thought about how she actually went to the bookstore and neither Sierra nor Devin recognized her. She put that hideous red hairspray in her hair just so Sierra wouldn't remember her from being with Jermaine. Bianca squeezed her copy of Sierra's house key and smiled. "Bitch," Bianca said viciously.

"Desiree, who are you calling a bitch?" Jermaine asked

as he sat down with a bowl of cereal.

"I said what a bitch. I broke a nail," Bianca said. She broke a nail but it was when she was in Sierra's house the night before.

Jermaine only laughed.

***

After Darius checked everything out for Sierra, she decided to take a long hot bubble bath so she could relax, but every time she heard the least little noise, she got scared. She was determined not to succumb totally to fear, so she gave herself a facial, curled her hair then pinned it up so loose curls fell teasingly around her neck and face. She then painted her nails then sprayed on her favorite perfume. Sierra lounged on her sofa in her short crème colored silk robe watching television and sipping wine. She felt wonderful and decided to keep herself locked indoors for the rest of the day. Her phone rang she hesitated only a minute before answering.

"Hey Sierra, how is it going?" Jermaine asked.

"I'm good. How about you? I hadn't seen or heard from you in a while, what you been up to?" Sierra asked.

"Just kicking it with my girl. Where's mom?" He asked.

"Her boyfriend took her on vacation. She won't be back for two weeks," Sierra said.

"Dang, I forget about that. All right then I guess I got to get back to work. Tell momma I called when you talk to her," Jermaine said and hung up.

Sierra closed her eyes and drifted off to sleep. Sierra woke up immediately when she thought she'd heard a noise. Sierra laughed because someone was knocking at the door. She looked through the peephole, and then rolled her eyes. "What do you want?" She said frowning while she opened the door.

"I just came by to check on you," Devin said while holding up a bag smiling, "Peace offering."

Sierra stepped aside so he could enter. They walked to the living room. "Have a seat," Sierra said.

"Have you eaten?" Devin asked.

"Why are you here?" Sierra asked rudely as she refilled

her glass with wine.

"I was just a little worried about you," Devin said honestly.

"As you can see, I'm fine. Now don't you think you should leave so you can enjoy the rest of your evening? Remember this *is* your only day off," Sierra said sarcastically as she stood.

"I'm sorry," Devin said. "I admit I was rude. Come on have dinner with me then I'll go," He said taking the containers out of the bag and placing the items on the coffee table.

Sierra sat and took a sip of wine, "Thanks."

Devin smiled handing her a container. She stood to get another glass and poured him some wine.

Devin sat back after he finished eating and looked intently at Sierra, thinking how very tempting and inviting she looked and smelled, he took a swallow of wine.

"What are you looking at?" She asked cautiously when she noticed him staring at her.

"You look really nice today," Devin said softly.

"Come on, I'll walk you out," Sierra stood suddenly.

Devin stood then grabbed her gently around her waist as he looked into her eyes, "I really am sorry for how I acted."

Sierra couldn't say anything, she couldn't even move, she only stood looking into his dark sensuous eyes. Devin kissed her deeply. Sierra sighed a frustrated breath, put her arms around his neck, and kissed him back. He eased her back onto the sofa kissing and caressing her. "I want you," Devin said softly as he nibbled on her bottom lip.

Sierra slowly unbuttoned his shirt breathing heavily as she gently rubbed her hands slowly up and down his chest and stomach. Devin untied her robe and his manhood almost hit the roof as he stared at her.

"You are very beautiful," Devin whispered as he gently took one erect nipple in his mouth gently teasing it with his teeth.

Sierra's pulse quicken as Devin rubbed, massaged and nibbled on her breasts. She closed her eyes as she ran her fingers through his soft thick hair. Sierra hadn't felt this good in a long time. Devin slowly slid his hand down her stomach tantalizing her as he barely touched her most sensitive area.

Devin frowned and stood up abruptly as he heard a loud sound come from the kitchen. Sierra sat up quickly tying her robe as she followed Devin to the Kitchen. Devin looked around then opened the door.

"Go back to the living room and sit down Sierra. I'll take care of this," he said a little harshly.

"What is it?" She asked frowning.

"Sierra, I said go in the living room," he said more angrily than he'd intended.

"No! I want to see," Sierra pushed Devin to look out the door and just stood there. She began shaking violently. Devin pulled her into his arms, "Go back in there and sit down, I'll take care of this," he said gently but firmly.

Somebody had put a dead puppy with a note pinned to its little body. The note was written in bright red lipstick, *you're next bitch!* The puppy looked like someone had hit his little head with something. Sierra cleaned up their uneaten food. She was pacing the floor when Devin returned about thirty minutes later.

"Devin, I can't do this anymore. I'm scared and I feel like I'm going crazy waiting on whatever's going to happen next," Sierra said frantically.

"Why don't you call the police?" Devin said.

"And what? If she's going to get me, nobody will be able to stop her," Sierra snapped angrily. "Where are you going?" Sierra asked as Devin walked past her.

"To pack you a few things, you're staying with me. Now, which way to your room?" Devin asked.

Devin locked Miss Kitty's house and got in his car, Sierra was leaning back in the seat quietly.

At Devin's house, Sierra was pacing nervously when Devin came into the room.

"Just try to relax. We're all locked up with the alarm system on," Devin said smiling trying to make light of the situation.

"Sorry," Sierra smiled weakly. "Can I sleep with you tonight?"

"Come on," Devin said softly then just held her until she fell asleep. Sierra woke up screaming at one o'clock in the morning. Devin held her tight, "Shush. I got you. Nobody's going to hurt you, I promise. You're safe now so go back to sleep."

Sierra kissed Devin as tears fell from her eyes, "Love me," she whimpered.

Devin softly kissed her tears, rubbing her body tenderly as he gently entered her. Sierra was so warm, tight and soft he could barely breathe. Devin had never felt so content, so connected, and completely at peace and whole as he did that very moment in his entire life.

"I think I'm falling in love with you," Sierra whispered.

"Me too," Devin said, but he knew he already loved her.

***

Bianca was relaxing in a Jacuzzi when Jermaine entered. She smiled, "So have you decided on what you're going to do?" Bianca asked.

"Yeah," he smiled, "I'm going to do it. I just wished I could have told my moms at least, you know so she wouldn't worry."

"Just think how proud she's going to be when you get back. Go ahead and finish packing I'll take you to the airport." Bianca pulled some strings and gotten him an internship at a major international corporation in Japan. Jermaine would be gone for six months and was guaranteed a high profile position when he returned. Bianca was happy only because everyone would think he disappeared, wondering if something had happened to him. Miss Kitty is going to have one hell of a fit when her baby becomes missing, Bianca only wished she could be there to see it.

Jermaine was walking away then looked back, "Thanks Desiree."

Bianca smiled sliding lower into the Jacuzzi thinking of Sierra. She'll be crazy before too long, she laughed to herself.

Bianca thought of what she had done earlier that evening. She did not mean to kill the little puppy, but the little mongrel almost bit her, causing her to throw him, he accidentally hit his head on an end table. Bianca frowned as she held up her hands to inspect them. "The little bitch even made me break two more nails," Bianca said to herself as she stood so she could get Jermaine to the airport on time.

* * *

Bianca thought about Devin then said under her breath, "I think you're falling for Sierra's crazy ass." Bianca only wished Devin was still the same heartless playboy because she wanted Sierra to be as miserable as hell. She would have to call Devin, just to make sure Sierra hadn't confessed all her sins. Bianca smiled and said to herself, "Well I'll just have to throw in a monkey wrench."

***

Now that Jermaine was gone, Bianca would focus her attention on Darius. Bianca smiled thinking of Darius, "Now let's see if Darius finds Desiree attractive." She smiled to herself as she headed towards the old plant. "It's dangerous for a woman to be out late at night," Bianca said laughing.

Bianca drove her car and hid it in the woods, and then sat in the woods watching with binoculars, waiting for Darius to enter his truck to leave for the night. Bianca walked down the road, and then smiled as she saw headlights coming her way.

* * *

Darius sat at the table staring at the woman he picked up the night before as he ate a bowl of cereal. She said her name was Desiree and that she had been riding with her girlfriend and her boyfriend when they started arguing, the boyfriend got jealous for some reason. Desiree told him when she tried to defend her friend the boyfriend stopped his car and put her out. It was late and Darius was exhausted so he asked her if she felt safe enough to crash out on his sofa until morning then he'd take her home, since she lived on the other side of town.

Bianca stretched as she sat up on the sofa. She felt his eyes on her.

- 212 -

"Good morning, I hope the sofa wasn't too uncomfortable," Darius said smiling.

"It was fine. Thank you," Bianca said smiling as she stood, "May I use your bathroom?" She asked. Darius pointed down the hall.

Darius watched as she walked away and felt that familiar feeling. "Down boy," Darius said laughing looking down at the bulge in his pants. She was a very exotic woman, especially with those eyes. He stood to wash his bowl out.

"I can't tell you how much I really appreciate everything you've done for me," Bianca said softly.

"Don't worry about it. Are you hungry or anything?" Darius asked.

"No thanks, I really need to get going," Bianca said.

Darius grabbed his keys to take her home.

Bianca sat in Darius's truck and thought to herself, what a perfect gentleman. He was so different from his brother who had been all over her in less than three hours. She smiled to herself as he pulled up to the small house she had recently rented.

"Would you like to come in for a minute?" Bianca asked sweetly.

"I really got a lot of things to take care of before my shift begins. Maybe we'll run into each other again sometime," Darius said smiling.

Damn, how very nice and boring he is, Bianca thought then took the initiative, "Can I call you sometime? It's been a while since I've met a man that never tried to make a move on me." Bianca smiled innocently.

Darius sat and thought for a minute, he hadn't been involved with anyone in almost a year. After losing Lindsey, he hadn't really felt anything for another woman. Desiree seemed nice enough he thought. He gave her his number, because it wouldn't hurt anything.

Chapter Twenty-one

Miss Kitty was relaxing at her beach house, which her friend, Maxim. He had bought the house for her five years ago. Every year she tried to stay there for at least two weeks, she loved it, and as often as they could, they'd sneak away for a weekend here and there.

Miss Kitty's hair was wind blown but looked very sexy as it softly framed her face and combined with her deep caramel colored skin, which was flawless, made her look very exquisite as she lounged back in her chair. At forty-seven, she knew she looked good, especially in her new hot coral colored bikini with her sarong tied around her hips. Missy Kitty wore a size nine, she was a size six until Jermaine was born, but every ounce looked good on her. Miss Kitty flaunted her stuff as much as she could when her children weren't around.

"Hey baby," Maxim said as he handed her a drink.

Miss Kitty thought how she and Maxim had been secretly seeing each for twenty-three years now. Maxim was a forty-eight year old Supreme Court Judge. He was very distinguished looking with his neatly cut full beard and mustache; his hair was still black except for a little grey in his sideburns. Maxim was the most eligible black bachelor around, and he loved himself some Miss Kitty.

At the beginning of their relationship Maxim was the one saying his career would be over if word of their affair ever got out, but somewhere along the way he changed. During their fifth year, Maxim wanted to be open about their relationship and stop sneaking around, but Miss Kitty told him he had worked too hard to get where he was and she wouldn't let him ruin his career.

Maxim was ready to give up everything. Even though her children were grown, Miss Kitty was still nervous. No one ever knew, but Maxim was Jermaine's father, and for all these years Maxim stood back patiently and watched his son grow up from a distance. Hardly ever did he miss football or basketball games, Maxim even went to most of Darius's games and always smiled when he saw Sierra cheering on the sidelines. Maxim took care of Miss Kitty and her children especially after Miss Kitty's husband left them. Maxim was the one that spent thousands on birthdays and holidays. *That should have been my family,* Maxim thought grimly to himself as he watched Miss Kitty relax. Maxim and Miss Kitty had dated first in high school but college had taken him away and when he came back, Miss Kitty was married to someone else.

Darius and Sierra's father, Jacob, had officially left Miss Kitty when Darius was four years old. He continued coming back and forth on visits every three to four months, usually lasting no more than four or five days at a time. Miss Kitty was tired of him cheating on her, lying, breaking promises to their kids, and just not helping her in their upbringing. She herself had even started having an affair and deep down Miss Kitty truly felt guilty after Jermaine was born. Jacob had come around off and on for so long, everyone naturally assumed Jermaine was his son.

The last time Miss Kitty saw Jacob was when Jermaine turned two; she hadn't seen or heard from Jacob in over a year. Jacob had stopped by in a drunken state. He was very angry to find the locks on the doors were changed. Jacob slapped Miss Kitty a few times that night because she wouldn't sleep with him. "You're still my wife," Jacob said, as he tried to force himself on Miss Kitty. That very same night Jacob came face to face with Jack. Miss Kitty said to Jacob, "Now I should blow you away just for having the nerve and sheer audacity to hit me, but since you are my kid's daddy, I'm gonna give you a chance. Jacob, you got thirty seconds to get out of my house before Jack starts talking to you." Miss Kitty started counting and Jacob started running. Jacob's been gone ever since. She and Jacob are still legally married.

Miss Kitty sipped her strawberry virgin daiquiri and thought about Sierra. She didn't really want to leave her alone but her doctor told her a few days ago her blood pressure got too high. He had the nerve to threaten to put her in the hospital if she didn't relax for a while. No alcohol or cigarettes her doctor ordered. *What I wouldn't do for a cigarette right about now,* Miss Kitty thought as Sierra came to mind. She wished Sierra wasn't working so she could have come with her, that way she wouldn't have to worry. She knew Maxim would have understood. She decided against leaving Jack with Sierra at the last minute; Miss Kitty just imagined someone taking Jack from Sierra because she would have been too scared to pull the trigger. She also knew that Devin would be there for her daughter.

"Kat" Maxim said, "I love you."

"You know I love you too," Miss Kitty said as she sipped her daiquiri.

"I've been meaning to ask you if you'd marry me," Maxim said.

Miss Kitty smiled, "I guess it is time I get that divorce." Miss Kitty prayed her children wouldn't be too angry when the truth came out.

Chapter Twenty-Two

"Devin, you have a call," Mrs. Huddle said.

Devin went to his office.

"Hello Devin. How are you?" Bianca said.

"Bianca? What do you want?" Devin asked angrily.

Bianca smiled to herself, "I need to talk to you. It's very important. I'm going to take a flight down today. Can you meet me at the Coffee House about six this evening?"

Devin answered, "No I can't today. Tomorrow morning at ten would be better for me." Devin said.

Bianca thought to herself, *what's one more day.* "Tomorrow it is," Bianca smiled and hung up.

* * *

Devin had gotten up early to drop Sierra off at the store and was already sitting in the coffee house, drinking coffee when Bianca entered and sat across from him.

Bianca laughed to herself because Devin looked as if he could actually kill her. "Thank you for meeting me."

"What do you want?" Devin questioned.

Oh he's mad, Bianca laughed to herself. Sierra must have confessed all after he moved her into his house. Bianca laughed as she watched Sierra in Devin's car looking so terrified. "Devin, you've been on my mind lately. I'm worried about you," Bianca said with a look of concern.

"Stop with the games. Sierra told me everything," Devin stated flatly.

"Everything?" Bianca repeated doubtfully.

"Yes everything," Devin said determined to put an end to whatever Bianca was plotting as soon as possible.

"Really?" Bianca questioned with a raised eyebrow. "I'm surprised she would confess how her boss's wife killed herself when she found out about their affair." Bianca shook her head sadly,   "I should have told you everything, but from the look in your eyes I see now it's too late, you've already fallen for her. You slept with her, didn't you?" Bianca sent up a sincere silent prayer, *Please forgive me Jonathan*. Bianca knew she was about to hurt Devin if he truly cared for Sierra. "Sierra is known for seducing men and her way up the corporate ladder. Even you'd be surprised at the number of men she's slept with."

"Bianca, just stop it. I only have a bookstore. There is not too far for her to go there," Devin stated angrily. He hated the picture Bianca painted of Sierra and at that moment, he hated Bianca even more for forcing him to have doubts about Sierra.

Bianca turned her head slightly to the side, "But there's you. See Sierra's broke. She had an affair with her boss in Ohio. He wouldn't leave his wife so she told the wife about their affair hoping his wife would leave him. Sierra never expected his wife to kill herself and her boss blames Sierra completely. So that's when she stole some of the company's money, quit her job and came back here. This whole investigation is supposed to be kept quiet. That's the only way we know how to find her and catch her. My client wants her locked away, but we have no proof of anything. But everything's changed now," Bianca said. Bianca thought how everything she said to Devin really happened. It all had happened at the newspaper where Sierra worked, but it was some woman named Susie that Sierra's boss had the affair with. That's why it was so perfect, Bianca thought to herself, because the woman's name was never released, Bianca thought.

"What does this have to do with me?" Devin asked as he remembered reading something about a woman killing herself in Ohio after a mistress confessed all, the woman's husband had owned a newspaper. Devin thought irritably, Bianca might very well be telling some truth.

"Devin, you're rich, single and very attractive. That's all she ever wanted, what woman in her right mind wouldn't want you?" Bianca stated the obvious then added, "Well my client could never understand how Sierra turned out that way, from what he tells me her family is very down to earth lovable people. He seemed quite fond of Sierra's mother."

"If you knew all of this, why would you bring me into

this in the first place?" Devin asked angrily.

"Did I not tell you *not* to go falling for her? I only wanted you to keep an eye on her," Bianca said sharply.

Devin just sat back as Bianca continued quietly, "Devin, she almost caused my daughter to die." Bianca had tears in her eyes as she took a deep breath and continued, "She dated my son-in-law years ago, well somehow she found out he got married." Tears continued to run down Bianca's face as she spoke her next words angrily, "After she lied to my daughter, I had to sit in that hospital for hours wondering whether or not Ashland was going to make it. You can't begin to imagine how it feels to think you may lose your child." Bianca wiped her eyes and cleared her voice, "Maybe I'm not the best person to help this man, but I will help him. Sierra has to be stopped, she can't keep going around hurting people," Bianca angrily thought about Sierra confessing all to Ashland.

Devin just sat feeling sicker by the minute because he suddenly thought of what Sierra had said about Bianca's daughter. He didn't know whether to believe Bianca or Sierra they both were very convincing. Devin narrowed his eyes and asked, "Bianca, the way I heard it, you paid Sierra to do that to your daughter. And if Sierra really needed the money, as you keep reminding me, it would make sense, wouldn't you say? Besides, somebody is threatening Sierra. But my guess on that is you'll probably tell me you don't know anything about that. Am I right?" Devin looked hard at Bianca with a raised eyebrow.

Bianca laughed out loud, "Devin, think about what you just said. Why would I do that to my own flesh and blood? My own daughter for goodness sake. Come on now," Bianca said with a look of utter shock and disbelief. Bianca shook her head then added, "As many husbands Sierra has slept with, I'm really not surprised someone may be threatening her."

"Sometimes people do strange things to their kids, and often enough we never understand their reasoning," Devin said softly as he sat back. He felt a headache coming on.

Bianca shook her head sadly and stood to leave, "Well

Devin, I'm truly sorry for you if you believe anything that woman said. I honestly regret ever involving you. All I can say is just keep your eye on her and be careful, because if a richer man comes along, you could find yourself all alone in love. My advice for you is to pull away cautiously, but don't get her too upset. I'd hate for her to do something to sabotage you or the store, because I know how much you and that store meant to Jonathan." Bianca turned to walk away as she thought to herself with a satisfied smile, *now I definitely deserve an Oscar for that.*

"Bianca" Devin said evenly, "Why did you help me all those years ago?"

For the first time Bianca's eyes softened, "He saved me." She smiled sadly thinking of Jonathan and walked away.

Devin sat for a while wondering what she meant by that. He decided to stop and get some lunch and a couple of drinks before going back to the store. By the time Devin returned to work, Mrs. Huddle was gone and it was almost closing time.

"Hey, I missed you today." Sierra walked up behind Devin after the customers left.

Devin pulled her arms from around his waist and stepped back.

"What's wrong?" Sierra asked frowning.

"Nothing. I just don't think we should do that here," Devin said unsmiling.

"Oh yeah. There's no one in the store right now," Sierra smiled seductively as she tried to kiss him.

"Sierra, I'm serious, somebody could walk in and see us." Devin started walking away.

"And," Sierra said.

"And I think it's time I go over some papers in my office," Was all Devin said without looking her way as he went into his office.

"So what have the past two nights been about?" Sierra demanded from his doorway.

Devin only looked at Sierra and shrugged his shoulders. He saw the hurt that turn to anger in her eyes, but he was hurt and angry too. How could she have been such a whore? Devin wondered angrily. Devin looked boldly at Sierra's body and smiled. "What man wouldn't want you, Sierra?" Devin said flatly, although it tugged at his heart to see the hurt in her eyes after he made that cruel statement.

Sierra couldn't say anything. She went to clean the store and didn't say another word to Devin until he pulled up in his driveway. "Devin, leave your car running please. I want to get my things and just go," Sierra stated unemotionally.

Devin didn't want her to go back home after the last message she'd gotten. He didn't want anything bad to happen to her. "Sierra, just stay here tonight. We'll talk about everything when we get inside." Devin said, knowing his mind was still clouded by everything he had learned that day along with alcohol he had consumed earlier.

Sierra looked at Devin with hurt angry eyes and said, "There is nothing more to discuss. I want my stuff out your house right now."

Devin got out of the car and unlocked his front door; Sierra rudely pushed past him and walked angrily up the stairs to gather her belongings. Devin only watched as he had the awful feeling that if Sierra left tonight everything would be over between them and a part of his brain screamed to him saying Bianca had lied. Devin was angry earlier at the idea of Sierra sleeping around with a lot different married men. Devin put his hands in his pockets and leaned against the wall wondering how he could just believe Bianca without giving Sierra a chance to explain herself. Jealousy does strange things to people he thought grimly.

Sierra threw her clothes in her bag as she thought angrily how stupidly she told him she was falling in love with him. Sierra laughed as she remembered his words, "Me too." "Yeah right, you loved me just long enough to get what you wanted." Sierra said to herself as she wiped a tear from her eye. Sierra broke her nail when she jerked her backpack on her shoulders, "Sometimes I really hate men," she said then descended the stairs.

"Sierra, wait a minute, I really didn't mean…"

Sierra laughed, "Yes you did Devin, but it's ok." Sierra walked to his car and waited for him to lock up.

"Do you want me to check the house out for you?" Devin asked when he pulled into her driveway.

Sierra looked over at Devin unbelievably as she pulled her keys from her purse, she wanted to say fuck you, but she got out of the car and slammed his door instead. Sierra didn't care about Bianca or anything, Devin had hurt her, and she had finally given herself to a man after all these years only to get hurt by him. Sierra went upstairs to take a long hot shower. The house was completely quiet that night.

***

The next day by the time Sierra got to work, she already had the house locks changed once again. She had to use some of the money she had been saving towards a car to have an alarm system installed on their house. It cost her a whole lot extra to get it done early that morning, but it was well worth it.

"Good morning Mrs. Huddle," Sierra smiled brightly.

"Hi Sierra," Mrs. Huddle said. "Devin's having a morning I wouldn't say too much to him today if I were you. He's been busy in his office all morning," Mrs. Huddle warned as she patted Sierra's shoulders while preparing to leave. Mrs. Huddle thought about how well Devin and Sierra were getting along, until he snapped at her earlier in the day when she asked him about her. Although he immediately apologized to her, she realized he was very angry about something and Sierra was that something. Mrs. Huddle smiled to herself; she knew they would be ok. He and Mr. Huddle had gone through quite a few trials and tribulations in their time.

Hannah was in a good mood today. She was happy that Devin was angry at Sierra, because lately they seemed to be getting too close. She felt so good that she actually smiled at Sierra.

Sierra was glad that Devin spent most of the day locked away in his office. She went about her day helping everyone

- 222 -

with enthusiasm. She would show him she didn't need anyone but herself. Devin came out of his office about three thirty then went back after receiving a phone call. Sierra forced him completely out her mind, putting all her energy towards the customers. At least he wouldn't be able to say she wasn't a good worker. Sierra rolled her eyes as she thought of Hannah, she seemed to be having such a great day, snickering behind her back, and she even picked up the books in the children's section before she left. "Well at least her little ass cleaned something for a change," she said to herself.

Devin sat unsmiling in his office. A friend of his was checking out Sierra's and Bianca's story for him, it would take a couple of weeks to get back with him. One thing that was certain was the fact that Devin was going to get to the bottom of everything before too long. He sat back regretting how he reacted out of pure jealousy towards Sierra because if she was telling the truth. He knew he was going to have a hell of a time convincing her to forgive him.

* * *

Bianca sat on Darius's bed and just stared at him as he slept. He had only just gotten home, dog tired and all, and he still had energy to go a few rounds. Bianca smiled because she had gotten so caught up with him for the past week that she hadn't even bothered harassing Sierra. At first, she thought of Darius as being boring, but as she became better acquainted with him, she realized he was a strong, sexy, highly intelligent and exciting man who knew how to treat a woman. Bianca could not believe a woman hadn't snagged him up already. For the first time, she was beginning to regret harassing Sierra, only because it would mean losing Darius when he found out. Bianca sat and thought for a minute, if she did everything just right, no one would ever have to find out about her, and it could be blamed on a mysterious jealous wife. What if Darius fell in love with Desiree? She questioned. Desiree didn't exist, and Bianca didn't plan on being Miss Ghetto Fabulous for the rest of her life. *Oh well,* Bianca stood to shower. It was time to give Sierra something to think about. She wrote Darius a note then left.

Sierra was enjoying her day off. One more week her mother would be home. It really hadn't been too bad, no notes or strange noises. Sierra sat back and smiled sadly as Devin came to mind. It had been a hard week ignoring him and completely immersing herself in her job. She was tired and drained all day, and all she wanted to do was absolutely nothing. Sierra showered and just threw on a pair of shorts and a t-shirt and lay around and slept all day.

At about seven o'clock that evening, her doorbell rang. All Sierra saw were flowers when she looked through the peephole. She opened the door, thinking they were from Devin. The delivery woman with a ponytail and shades only handed her the clipboard for her to sign, and then walked away. Sierra took the vase and set the flowers on the table. She picked up the card slowly and read it almost in fear. "Bitch" was all it read. Sierra looked in fear as she noticed that the center roses were black.

Sierra took the vase and went out the back door to trash them. Sierra turned to go back inside but she thought she heard someone calling her name. She turned around just as someone dressed in all black tackled her, knocking her roughly against the brick part of the house. Sierra was hit so hard, it was a moment before she could breathe again. Whoever it was ran away before she could see their face. Sierra stumbled inside the house and locked herself in as she set the alarm. Sierra's head was hurting from the impact on the wall. She touched the back of her head and found she was bleeding. Her ankle was also sprung. Sierra ended up driving herself to the hospital and getting six stitches after she couldn't stop the bleeding. It was after eleven when she got home that night. They wanted to keep her overnight, but Sierra refused. Sierra pulled up as close as possible to her house before she quickly got out. Sierra laughed, "So much for my quiet and peaceful day."

When Sierra arrived at work a little before one o'clock the following day, she was hurting and in an unusual mood. She limped right past Devin to put away her purse and then immediately started helping customers.

"Are you ok?" Devin asked when there were no customers in the store.

Sierra didn't feel like talking to Devin so she figured she'd just walk away, but Devin lightly grabbed her arm.

"Sierra, what happened to you?" He asked frowning.

"Nothing," she mumbled unemotionally before walking off.

Devin only stared at her in disbelief because Sierra always had something smart to say. Devin was beginning to get a little worried. About five thirty that evening, Sierra quietly walked up to him.

"I'm going to take a lunch. I'll be in the break room," she said as she walked away. Sierra was so tired and sore, she thought she might possibly pass out.

Devin knew something was wrong because she never took her lunches only short breaks, and all she did then was sit behind the counter. Devin continued to help the customers. By six forty-five Sierra was still in the back, so he rung up the few customers in the store before going back to check on her. The way Sierra was lying on her side made her hair fall to her face. Devin was shocked as he noticed a small patch of hair missing on the back of her head. When he took a closer look he noticed it was red, swollen and had a few stitches. He left the break room allowing her to sleep.

"Sierra, wake up, it's time to go home." Devin gently shook her.

Sierra turned over slowly her whole body was hurting, she groaned then said, "What time is it?"

"Nine thirty, come on, I'll drive you home," Devin said.

Sierra sat up and looked at Devin in a daze.

"Sierra? Are you ok?" He asked softly.

"Yeah." Sierra stood slowly gathering her bearings then got her purse, she felt light headed. "Devin, I don't feel too good. Help me to the bathroom." As soon as Sierra made it to the bathroom, she threw up.

Devin sat beside her for a few minutes, "Do you want

me to come home with you?" he asked.

Sierra gritted her teeth and prayed for strength, "No I'll be ok. I feel better now." She stood to leave the room. She felt a little better but also little dizzy, so she asked Devin before he got in his car, "Devin, would you please follow me home?"

Sierra got out of her car when she pulled into her driveway and walked to Devin's car. "Thank you. I really appreciate it. I'll see you tomorrow." She walked away before he could say anything to her. She was so tired that she fell asleep on the sofa and never heard when someone tried to unlock her front door.

Devin was tired and couldn't relax; he was worried about Sierra. He picked up his phone to make a call.

"It's me, Devin, you have anything for me yet?" Devin asked.

"Well I have a report you might be interested in. I spoke with Tylen Alexander and he was cooperative. He also gave the name of a private investigator that he thought I should talk to. Give me a few minutes and I'll fax a few things over to you," The man said.

"Thanks," Devin said.

"Oh and Devin, Sierra seems to be quite a handful, especially when provoked I heard, but she's a real looker. All I can say is good luck to you on that one," the man said laughing.

Devin laughed.

I'm going to break it down like this, she's rich, beautiful, intelligent, very powerful and she's one crazy ass bitch. Now you really need to watch your back and stay clear of her. I'll get with you in a few days. There are still some things I need to check out. Oh and about that note written in lipstick that was found at your store, the only finger prints on it are yours." The man said and hung up.

Devin was puzzled as he sat at his desk in his library and waited on the fax. He rubbed his face and laughed as he read the fax cover sheet. 'You're not going to believe this shit,' was all his friend wrote. "I guess I'd better sit for this," Devin said to himself as he sat down and began to read over the pages.

Everything Sierra had told him was true. He was even holding up pictures of Bianca giving Sierra money. Devin shook his head as he looked through the pictures of Bianca and her son-in-law's father. Bianca was a piece of work. From reading the report, Bianca's daughter hadn't spoken to her in quite a while. Devin shook his head and thought it was a shame Bianca hadn't even seen her newborn granddaughter.

Devin felt relieved when he read nothing of Sierra and other men, but was still worried about what Bianca was going to do to her. Devin wondered what he was going to do about Sierra. Devin laughed as he read over a few jealous incidents Sierra had caused over Jordan about quite a few different women. "A handful she is indeed." Devin laughed.

***

Bianca was pissed. Sierra had changed her locks again and this time she wouldn't be getting the keys. Even if Sierra gave Darius a copy that would be too risky for her, Darius didn't drink and he was a light sleeper. Bianca had to figure out what her next move would be. Her doorbell rang interrupting her thought. Bianca smiled as she opened her door for Darius.

"Hey Desiree," Darius kissed her gently.

Bianca was taken aback because she was actually beginning to have feelings for this one. She really wanted to back off. Bianca was just about to tell Darius that maybe they needed to slow down for a while, but he kissed her before she had a chance.

Darius looked deep into Bianca eyes, "I really like you. You're different."

Bianca was surprised at the depth of emotion that she felt. She needed to sit down for a minute to get it together.

"Hey," Darius said as he gently took her chin between his fingers. Darius stood and reached for her hand, "Come on Desiree, let's have some fun, we'll make a day of it. There's a community festival going on a few blocks from my house. Then we'll take a boat ride. What do you say?"

Bianca felt overwhelmed by Darius; their relationship was more than sex. He actually always put her feelings first and that was so foreign to her with a man. Even with her ex-husband, Marcus, Bianca thought sadly. She was so controlling of everything that Marcus never had a chance to do anything for her.

The emotions Darius brought out in her scared her; yet made her all excited inside. Bianca told herself that she deserved to have some fun, at least for a day. That one day turned out to be almost two weeks. Darius took her to so many different places and showed her how relaxed life could really be. Bianca was beginning to fall in love and she hadn't even realized it yet.

One night after Darius got off work and surprised Bianca by just showing up at her door, holding a bottle of wine and one single rose. Bianca was more than a little caught off guard, he usually called first, she almost forgot to put her contacts back in.

"Is this a bad time?" Darius asked as he leaned up against her doorway and handed her a rose.

Bianca couldn't help but smile and invite him in because he looked so sensual and desirable standing there. They ended up lying on her couch just cuddling and talking when Darius surprised her with a question.

"Desiree, why do you wear those contacts all the time? I mean they're super sexy and all, but last week when I came over one night you didn't have them in. I don't think I never would have ever known you wore them. What I'm saying is, baby, you're gorgeous." Darius nuzzled her neck as he said, "Go natural for me sometimes. Your dark eyes are more exotic and more mysterious."

Bianca laughed at herself she was really slipping. "Ok baby. I'll do it sometimes just for you." Bianca was finding it harder and harder to concentrate on Sierra. Darius was taking up too much of her time, so the next day she'd have to make some time to check up on Sierra. Bianca thought to herself, *I don't want you getting the idea and think that I've given up on you.*

"Desiree, do you want to meet my family? It's only my moms, my brother and sister." Darius then said out loud,

"Thinking of Jermaine I hadn't talked to him in a while I need to check up on him to make sure he stays out of trouble."

Bianca stopped moving completely. It surprisingly bothered her that Darius would be worried about Jermaine after everyone realized he wasn't not anywhere to be found, but there was no way in hell she was going to meet with his mother and that crazy sister of his, "Darius, I would love to meet them but it's a little soon, don't you think?"

Darius laughed as he thought of his mom and how she could be somewhat overpowering at times. Desiree was so sweet that she might not be ready for her, "Ok we'll wait a while."

Bianca knew Sierra had seen her in the store, but she wasn't sure if Miss Kitty or Sierra had gotten a good look at her when she was in the car with Jermaine, and she wasn't about to take that chance. It was a little too risky, anyway. She thought of Jermaine, *That little idiot would just go around them without warning him.* She could just imagine the look on Miss Kitty's face if she knew about her and her two boys. Bianca laughed as she turned over and kissed Darius passionately.

Chapter Twenty-Three

Miss Kitty was only home for a week and already she knew something was bothering her daughter. For some reason she didn't think it had anything to do with Bianca. "Sierra what's wrong with you?" Miss Kitty asked watching Sierra, as she sat quietly drinking coffee.

Sierra smiled, "Nothing, just relaxing before I have to leave for work."

"How are things going there?" Miss Kitty was beginning to feel it had something to do with Devin.

"Things are fine mom," Sierra stood to wash out her cup.

"How are things with Devin?" Miss Kitty decided to be direct, then added when Sierra looked at her as if she was about to protest. "Sierra, sit down. Now I know there is or was something going on between the two of you. Baby I felt it the day he was over here in the rain."

"Well what ever 'it was' is over now," Sierra said stubbornly.

"If you say so," Miss Kitty laughed then became serious, "Have you heard from Jermaine? I'm beginning to get a little worried about him. We usually go out to lunch after I get back from my trips."

"Not since before you left, he called and just said he'd call you later." She added, "He's probably with that woman he's been hanging with. He doesn't seem to be able to come around and he has never even been able to pick me up from work not once. I tell you there's really something about that woman that gives me the creeps, which is really weird because I've never met her or even been close to her." Sierra laughed, "She's probably one of those nasty tail strippers he's well known to date." Sierra rolled her eyes.

At the mention of strippers, Miss Kitty made a noise and left the room.

Sierra continued to sit and brood over Devin. Lately it

seemed every other woman that came in the store flirted outrageously with him, he always smiled at her, which only encouraged her more. If she didn't need the job so bad, she would have quit on the spot when a blonde, of all people, had the nerve to ask Devin out to dinner and gave him her number, which wouldn't have been so bad if Devin had said just no. But his ass had the nerve to tell her he was busy that evening but maybe he'd call sometime. "I wish one good looking brother would come up in the store so I could flirt ridiculously with him," Sierra said to herself as she walked upstairs to her bedroom.

* * *

Devin watched Sierra as she talked with Mrs. Huddle. There were so many times he wanted to approach her but the look she gave him always let him know he would only be wasting his time, so he backed off. Just to get a reaction from Sierra, Devin had put up with some of the customers' flirting, being careful not to lead anyone on, well except for that one particular woman. Sierra had looked at the woman in such a way that he couldn't resist telling her he might call. Sierra was actually been jealous, Devin thought with a smile.

Sierra was on the ladder putting a couple books away when a customer walked through the doors. She smiled to herself because she had just wished that a good-looking brother would come to the store. She continued putting the books away then made her way over near him.

"Excuse me. Can you ring this up for me?" His voice was so smooth and his skin was like rich dark chocolate.

Sierra smiled, "Of course. I hope you found everything you were looking for."

"And then some," he said with a smile.

Sierra laughed seductively as Devin walked by. *Now this is what I'd been waiting for,* she said to herself.

"Hi, I'm Lawrence," he said holding out his hand.

"I'm Sierra. It's a pleasure to meet you." She shook his hand.

"Since you're not wearing a ring, I take it you're not

married. Do you have a friend or anything?" Lawrence asked.

"Why do you ask? You're not coming on to me, are you?" Sierra joked.

"That depends on whether or not you'll have lunch with me today?" He said.

"I don't know. It's just me and my boss today," Sierra looked briefly at Devin as he typed on one of the computers. She knew he could hear every word from where he stood.

"It doesn't look too busy right now. Come on we can go to the café across the street and grab a sandwich. You won't even be gone for too long, and I'd really enjoy the company," he said with a dazzling smile.

"You know I would really enjoy that also," Sierra said as she completed the sale. "Devin, I'm going to lunch. I'll be back in a little bit." She went to get her purse then asked sweetly, "Would you like for me to bring you something back?"

"No thank you," Devin said as his fingers continued to glide across the keyboard. Once they were outside, he watched as they crossed the street. He was a little bothered when the man put his hand at the small of Sierra's back. He was jealous, couldn't help laughing at himself, and was relieved when an old lady needed help getting a book from the shelf. He was determined to stay busy for the rest of the day.

Oh my God, Sierra thought to herself as she listened to Lawrence's chatter. Sierra could hardly believe her ears. *He actually acts and talks as if he were god's gift to women. All he's done is talk about himself and his job from the time we've sat down. He is really working my nerves right about now. So what if he was a model with his conceited ass,' cause he's really not that good-looking. Hell, Devin is better looking than he is. God he's worst than most women I know,* Sierra fumed to herself. Sierra looked down at her watch, "I'm so sorry to cut you off, but I really have to get back to the store."

"No problem. I would really hate if your boss docked your pay over a few minutes," Lawrence smiled teasingly.

No he didn't, Sierra thought to herself as she stood and said, "I really appreciate lunch."

"No problem. I would like to do it again sometime. Can I call you?" he asked.

"Sorry, I don't give out my number," Sierra told him.

"Ok Maybe I'll do you a favor and look you up when I'm in town again. I'll take you some place nice," he said.

"Please don't bother, I'm really not interested," Sierra said pointedly as she dropped money on the table and left the café.

Lawrence watched Sierra cross the street, *What a Bitch. But she looked damn good though,* he thought to himself as he looked at her one last time. He was in town for a couple of days and was sexually frustrated; all he really wanted was a booty call, but Sierra would not be it.

Sierra smiled when she entered the store and noticed Devin reading to a group of children. She put her purse away and started cleaning around the store. They worked together the rest of that day only speaking to customers.

***

Sierra had left her wallet in the bookstore on Saturday night. She was in the mall when it occurred to her that she didn't have it. "Hi Devin, I know its Sunday, but I left my wallet behind the counter can you meet me at the store so I can get it?"

Devin was quiet for a few minutes, "I'll be there." He hung up.

"Is there anything else before I lock up?" Devin asked standing in the middle of the store with his hands in his pockets.

"No, that's it," Sierra said coming from behind the counter. As she walked by Devin, he reached for her, pulling her in an embrace.

"Sierra, I've really missed you," he leaned down and kissed her.

Sierra kissed him back then remembered him saying, "What man wouldn't want you Sierra," she quickly broke the kiss.

"Don't. Please," Devin said as he pulled her back and kissed her again.

Sierra couldn't resist and kissed him with everything she had. They ended up making love in his office right on top of his desk.

Sierra was upset at her weakness, so she quietly adjusted her clothes when they were done.

"You ok?" He asked softly while he buttoned his shirt.

Sierra did not respond, so Devin leaned against the desk and pulled her between his legs. "Sierra, look at me," he said putting his finger under her chin. "I am sorry for what I said."

"Anyways, I need to get home and freshen up. I can't go shopping smelling like you," she said sharply.

Devin teased, "What would your mother say about you rushing in to take another shower so soon? Why don't you come home with me? You can shower there. I'll take you shopping afterwards."

Sierra thought about it for a moment, she didn't want her mother to know about them, so she agreed. She left her car parked in Devin's yard while they went to the mall. Overall, they had an enjoyable time together, but Sierra still maintained her emotional distance.

"Do you want to come in for a minute?" Devin asked as they turned into his driveway. He had seen several things he wanted to buy her, but knowing Sierra, he thought she'd have something smart to say, especially after what had just happened between them.

"No, I don't," she said.

"I actually had a good time with you today. Usually I hate the mall," Devin said trying to draw her into a conversation.

Sierra didn't feel like talking and she definitely didn't want anything else to happen between them so she got out of the car. "I have to go, it's getting late," she said looking through her purse for her car keys.

Devin kissed her. "I'll see you tomorrow," he said softly.

Sierra left without another word, she just didn't trust herself around Devin anymore.

The next three weeks went by relatively fast for Devin. Ever since the day they went to the mall, he and Sierra had been getting along better. At work, they were cordial. They laughed and talked with the customers and sometimes with each other. Mrs. Huddle smiled. She knew they would work things out.

Bianca sat in the café and sipped her coffee as she casually eyed the bookstore. Bianca felt gloomy, thinking she was beginning to have guilty feelings concerning Sierra as of lately. She knew she was falling for Darius, but he was so addictive she couldn't give him up, at least not yet. "I can not complicate things," Bianca mumbled to herself as she paid for her coffee and left.

Sierra had been waking up nauseous for the past couple of days, so before going to work, she stopped by her doctors' office to make an appointment, but surprisingly they had a cancellation and got her in. Sierra was almost six weeks pregnant. *Just great, leave it to Devin to be the one to get my ass pregnant*, she thought ironically to herself.

"Hi Mrs. Huddle," Sierra said as she entered the store.

"You ok? You look a little worn." Mrs. Huddle said before leaving.

Sierra only smiled and shook her head and reassured her she was fine. She was anything but fine; she was actually very pissed at Devin. She knew it was not all his fault but she was still mad. The day went by slowly and Sierra stayed to herself most of the day.

Devin did not understand Sierra one bit. He tried talking to her a few times but eventually gave up after she never responded to him. He had never met anyone as moody as her and was glad when the day was over.

Chapter Twenty-Four

As soon as Devin walked through his front door, his phone began ringing.

"Devin, I need to talk to you, can I come over?" The man asked.

Devin waited impatiently for his friend to arrive. His friend demanded that their friendship remain completely anonymous, he only came around if absolutely necessary. It had been like that ever since Bianca got Devin cleared of all charges. They had met when Devin was eleven and he was twenty years old. Devin was hanging out in the streets a lot so one day some older boys tried to jump him, his friend stepped in to help and has been watching out for him ever since. Devin laughed because his friend seemed to have always been covering for him in some way or another.

His friend was the one who showed him how to make money without stealing. That's how he got started seducing the rich women. After Devin was cleared of everything, his friend didn't want them connected in any way, telling him he didn't want him to mess his life back up. They remained friends but they both led their own different lifestyles.

"Devin," his friend said after getting settled and taking a long swallow of his drink, "I have information for you that I didn't feel comfortable faxing. I thought it was best for you to hear it from me, instead of reading a fax." Devin only nodded his head and his friend continued, "To start off Sierra wasn't the woman involved with her boss. It was a co-worker of hers. A woman named Susie."

Devin felt very relieved. "Go on," he said after his friend got quiet for a few minutes.

The man stood to fix another drink. "Bianca was raped one night and Jonathan stopped the man from killing her. I tried, but I couldn't find out who the man was that raped her." He took a long swallow, "Jonathan took Bianca into his home and took care of her until she was well again. Bianca found out she became pregnant by that rape and had her daughter Ashland." The man took a long swallow from his glass, "Bianca was twenty one and had just gotten married and was doing a summer internship at a major law firm. She was determined to get her career started. She asked Jonathan not to tell a soul, he agreed and asked nothing in return, until years later when his daughter came up missing, he called her hoping she could help him locate his daughter." The man paused long enough to stir the ice in his glass before taking a swallow.

"Jonathan's daughter got married then one day just disappeared. Bianca found his daughter, but she died before Jonathan got a chance to see her. Devin, you always wondered why Bianca helped you; well, I just found out that Jonathan was your grandfather."

Devin sat completely still, he was in shock but he didn't reveal any emotion while he tried to figure out why Jonathan never told him the truth. *God I loved that man like he was my grandfather*, why not just tell me the truth? Devin pondered to himself.

He stood to leave because he knew Devin needed to be alone. "Call me if you need anything." The man told Devin on his way out. He didn't think Devin should know the rest about Bianca just yet. He would handle Bianca himself if she so much as hurt a single hair on Devin, or Sierra's head for that matter. The man laughed because he knew Devin was finally in love, and with someone just as stubborn and strong headed as he was.

The man shook his head and thought about Bianca as he got in his car. She was one unbelievable woman. At fifty-two, she was passing for thirty-five. He laughed saying to himself, "Hell, I'd do her." Bianca was one badass woman, he thought to himself, just imagine she was living right here in town. She's screwed Sierra's baby brother and sent him mysteriously away. He laughed because Bianca knew she didn't have to hurt Jermaine or anyone to cause worry.

Now she was screwing with Sierra's older brother. He

laughed because knowing Darius the way he did, he was probably putting it on her, and he had Lindsey all twisted up and crazy in love before she died. He would let Darius have his fun with Bianca a little while longer and hopefully, he would be smart enough not to fall in love. The man thought to himself, on second thought, maybe I'd better school him about Miss Desiree Jones, Lindsey was my baby sister.

***

Miss Kitty sat on the sofa unsmiling as Sierra came into the room, sat down and started flipping through the channels. "Your doctor called with your appointment date. I wrote it on the calendar," Miss Kitty told her.

Sierra didn't say anything she just looked at the television.

"So how far along are you?" Miss Kitty questioned.

"About six weeks," Sierra eyes never wavered from the screen.

"What do the two of you plan to do?" Miss Kitty asked.

"Two of us? This has nothing to do with him unless I decide to keep it, and Momma right now I don't know what I'm going to do. I'm not even sure if I'll keep it. I'm tired, and I've been working all day so just stop bugging me," Sierra snapped before she had a chance to catch herself. She apologized quickly, "I'm so sorry momma. I didn't mean to talk to you like that."

"You had better be thankful your little ass is pregnant, but pregnant or not, next time you mouth off to me like that I'ma beat your ass back into reality," Miss Kitty said dangerously low as she stood and left the house mumbling to herself, "Crazy ass girl, I should have just knocked some sense into her stubborn ass. Talking to me any kind of damn way..."

Miss Kitty drove around for a long time before deciding to go to Devin's house.

"Miss Kitty, is Sierra ok?" Devin asked immediately after opening the door. He opened the door thinking his friend had returned. Devin was still processing the fact that Jonathan was actually his grandfather.

"She's fine. May I come in?" Miss Kitty asked.

"Of course, come on in." Devin said still thinking about everything his friend had said.

"Can I get you something to drink or anything?" Devin asked.

Miss Kitty debated for a moment as she thought about what her doctor had said, "Do you have vodka?" She asked as she pulled out a pack of cigarettes, "May I?" She asked.

"Go ahead," Devin said wondering why she came over. "Do you want juice or anything in it?"

"No. Just ice," Miss Kitty said as she took a long relaxing drag from her cigarette, then she took a long swallow of her drink, and said seriously as she looked from her drink to her cigarette, "My doctor told me I had to give these up." She sat her glass down and looked at Devin. "What do you think about my daughter?" Miss Kitty asked.

Devin stood and fixed himself a drink, *she definitely doesn't waste any time, I see where Sierra gets it from.* Although his mind was still on Jonathan and he didn't feel like listening to any more news or dealing with anything else, he had a feeling he was going to need a very strong drink before this conversation was over. "I think she's a great person. I enjoy working with her," Devin said cautiously.

Miss Kitty sat back and stared hard at Devin, "Devin, don't bullshit me. Not tonight."

Devin took a long swallow and laughed, "I love your daughter, but I'm not too sure what her feelings are concerning me, she gives me mixed feelings most of the time. And I'm sure you know she's rather hard to get along with at times." He spoke honestly.

Miss Kitty laughed, "I figured she was giving you a hard time. She's like me in that aspect, I never did make it easy for a man."

Devin laughed and wondered out of all the women, it had to be a hard headed, opinionated and outspoken one that he'd fall for, and if truth be told, he wasn't sure if he could handle anyone like Miss Kitty. Devin wondered again, why she was there, but figured he would find out soon enough.

Miss Kitty took another long drag from her cigarette and an even longer swallow of her drink. "Well Devin, you and Sierra has come to a turning point. You two need to figure out what exactly the two of you plan to do, the only problem with that is she don't think it concerns you, at least not until she decides."

"Decides about what? You completely have me lost, I have no idea what you're talking about," Devin said with confusion.

"About my grandbaby she's carrying. Sierra has it set in her mind that it doesn't concern you unless she chooses to keep it." Miss Kitty finished her drink off and handed Devin her glass, "Her hormones must be completely off the charts, because that crazy girl had the audacity to raise her voice and yell at me. That fool child of mine actually has the nerve to be thinking about having an abortion. She should have thought about that while she was spreading her legs for you. Can I have another drink?" She asked when he sat there stoic.

Damn she really gets right to the point, a baby? Damn, he thought to himself, if the situation wasn't so serious he would have laughed, Miss Kitty was pissed. Devin took a deep breath and poured them both another drink. Devin sat and smiled at Miss Kitty, "Let's have a toast Miss Kitty. Here's to my upcoming fatherhood." Devin genuinely smiled.

Miss Kitty raised her glass, added with a loud boisterous laugh, "Can you just imagine Sierra as a mother?" She laughed louder, "You'll be the one getting up in the middle of the night feeding and changing diapers."

Devin laughed, but he suddenly felt nervous. What if he turned out like his father? Devin took a very long swallow finishing off his drink. He poured another.

Miss Kitty noticed the look on Devin's face, "Ain't no sense in worrying now, you should have thought about that before you started messing around with my daughter without protection." Miss Kitty sat up laughing and drinking while she told Devin all sorts of things Sierra had done while she was growing up. She did not get home until after midnight.

Chapter Twenty-five

Darius sat outside in his truck on his lunch hour. Lindsey's brother had left not thirty minutes ago and told him quite a few things about Desiree or Bianca or whatever the hell her name was. *That bitch was after Sierra*, he thought to himself. *Then to top everything off Desiree was fifty-two years old.* Darius laughed because his mom was only forty-seven. "Now ain't that a bitch," Darius said aloud. No wonder she didn't want to meet his family. At least she did right by Jermaine regardless of her motives behind it. "That bitch ain't shit," Darius said angrily to himself as he thought of her and Jermaine together. As a thought occurred to him, he got in his truck and drove to Bianca's house.

After leaving Bianca's house, Darius went back to work satisfied. He decided he needed to switch shifts for a couple of weeks, working twelve hour shifts would hopefully make him too tired to beat her ass.

Darius was exhausted when he got home. He had actually worked fourteen hours straight. There was a note on his door and he knew it was from Desiree, "Hey baby just to let you know I stopped by, see you later Desiree" Darius dropped the note in the trash then fell across the bed and slept.

The next morning Desiree stopped by. "You look awful, what's wrong?" she said brightly as he opened the door.

"Just tired, got to work double shifts for a couple of weeks. Hey I'm beat can we talk later?" Darius said holding his temper in check.

"Ok. Get some rest. I'll check on you later in the week." Bianca tried to kiss Darius, but he pulled away. Bianca frowned and wondered if he could possibly be seeing someone else.

It took all Darius had not to strike her, thank God he was really exhausted. "Desiree, Bianca whoever, leave me the hell alone and if you go near my sister or brother again, or come near me again, I'll fuck you up," Darius slammed the door in her face.

"Ok Darius, let's see how bad you can fuck me up," Bianca said out loud as she looked evilly at the closed door. In truth, she was devastated by Darius's rejection. Bianca left thinking it would have been better if he was seeing another woman instead of finding out her true identity.

* * *

Sierra was late for work; she was nauseated and sick. She had felt so bad she almost didn't come to work, but she knew it would pass she had to just work through it.

"Are you feeling ok today?" Mrs. Huddle asked.

"Just a stomach virus, but I'll be fine. I'm sorry I'm so late," Sierra said.

"Don't worry about it, just take care of yourself honey, those can be pretty bad sometimes." Mrs. Huddle patted Sierra's shoulder before she left.

Devin didn't say too much to Sierra that day and since there weren't a lot of customers in the store, he decided to close the store at seven. "Can I talk to you in my office?" Devin asked after closing out the registers and turning out the lights.

Sierra got situated in a chair, with her arms folded and Devin leaned against his desk and asked pointedly, "When were you going to tell me about the baby?"

"After I was certain I would keep it. I planned on telling you," Sierra said wondering how he found out, but figured her mom had to be the one to tell him since she was the only other person who knew besides her doctor.

Devin stared at Sierra for a minute then put his hands in his pockets. "Let me make sure I understand you correctly. You are deciding whether or not you'll have an abortion, but until you decide, it's basically none of my business. Am I correct?" Devin asked.

"Pretty much," she said matter-of-factly as she sat up straighter in her chair.

Devin felt his aggravation with Sierra beginning to rise, "How do you figure my child, that you're carrying, is none of my business?"

Sierra stood abruptly poking Devin in his chest as she

angrily told him, "You're not the one that's going to get fat. It's my body, my decision, my choice. Got it?"

At that point Devin decided anger would get him nowhere with Sierra, so he put his hands on her waist and said tenderly, "Sierra, it's actually my seed and your egg, which makes it our choice."

Sierra relaxed a little against Devin, "Ok what do you want to do? Have it? Ok say we have it. Then what? I get to keep her during the school year and you get holidays and summers? Get real Devin. I'm not even certain I want a baby right now and I darn sure can't afford one. I'm still living with my mom for goodness sake." Sierra sat down and rubbed her head in frustration.

"Sierra, I honestly don't know, but what I do know is that we can't abort it." He kissed her gently. Devin leaned down in front of her, "Hey, look at me" he said grabbing her hands, "It will be ok. I promise. I'll always be there for you and our child."

It was after eight when Sierra and Devin walked out of the store. Something didn't feel right to him. "Sierra, hold up a second," he said as he pulled her back, just as Devin moved her he heard a loud noise then immediately felt a hot burning pain in his left shoulder. Sierra screamed as Devin threw her to the ground covering her body with his.

Sierra frantically called 911 from her cell phone because Devin was bleeding all over her and he wasn't moving. "Devin! Devin!" Sierra screamed.

"I can hear you. Just stop yelling in my ear. Damn you talk too much sometimes," Devin joked weakly.

"Oh God," she groaned as she managed to get him on his back to apply pressure on his wound, he was bleeding profusely. "Devin, we're having a baby remember. You can't leave me now!" Sierra yelled desperately at him trying to keep him conscious. "Do you hear me?" She asked angrily. "I won't let you leave me alone to raise your child. You're not getting off that easy." Sierra was crying. "Devin, please don't leave me. I love you," Sierra pleaded because the blood wouldn't stop.

"I love you too," Devin said softly. He wondered why she was crying covered in blood. He hoped she hadn't been shot too because she was pregnant and he wanted her to have his baby. It didn't matter a son or daughter, he just wanted a healthy baby. Devin thought of his beautiful mother, she deserved so much more in her life. His father was an overbearing tyrant who abused Devin every chance he got when Devin was too young to defend himself. Damn, why did his mother always have to get in the way, that's why his father turned the abuse towards her. Devin thought, *she should have let him discipline me the only way he knew how.* Devin didn't want to go out like this, but then again maybe he deserved to, he did do the same to his own father. Everything suddenly went black.

Sierra sat on the ground as she watched the paramedics work on Devin, and then they rush him off in the direction of the hospital. Sierra vowed to make Bianca or whoever did this pay. "An eye for an eye," Sierra mumbled to herself. Sierra was so numb she didn't remember someone helping her in the other ambulance and drive away.

Sierra sat in the exam room just looking at all of Devin's blood on her. She started shaking uncontrollably. She could hardly wait until her mother got there.

"Honey, don't worry too much, they're working on him. The best doctors are in there with him. Do you need something to help you calm down?" the nurse asked.

"No, she doesn't. She's pregnant," Miss Kitty said to the nurse as she entered the room.

"Oh momma, somebody shot Devin. You should have seen all the blood." Sierra broke down and cried.

"Is there any way we can get her cleaned up?" Miss Kitty asked the nurse.

***

Sierra was admitted in the hospital for overnight observation. She was sleeping soundly as Miss Kitty sat beside her.

"Sierra and the baby are going to be fine. How are you

doing, Katherine?" Their family doctor looked at Miss Kitty with concern.

Miss Kitty smiled sadly and rubbed Sierra's hair, "I'm not the one shot or pregnant scared half to death."

"Last I heard Mr. Chandler is still in surgery. There is still no word," He said quietly, "Come on, she'll be fine. Let's check your blood pressure."

* * *

Bianca completely eliminated all traces of Desiree Jones. She immediately flew home after seeing Darius earlier that morning. On her way to the airport, she stopped by the house she had rented as Desiree to pick up a few things and received a surprise of her own. On her mirror in her bedroom was written in red lipstick, *don't make ME fuck YOU up,* and had a smiley face drawn underneath. She knew it was Darius because she had given him a key to her place. At that moment, all she felt was a great loss and deep regret.

She was tired after she got home, and couldn't get Darius off her mind. Bianca decided to make sure she kept busy. For some reason she missed Darius with a passion, so she decided she would give him some time then she would go and apologize and explain how she only wanted to scare Sierra and didn't really mean any harm.

"Ms. Kendrix, you have a visitor," Bianca's secretary said.

"Send them in." Bianca said and sat back and watched as the tall, dark skinned, well-dressed man entered her office. He was well built and sexy in a rugged rather thuggish way. He wore a very low hair cut almost bald and very thin sideburns with a manicured beard. "Have a seat please," Bianca said professionally, "Now what can I do to help you?"

The man looked at Bianca for a long moment in such a way she felt as if he was trying to see her soul.

"A friend of mine is in the hospital right now fighting for his life. So right now I might be a little on edge and off balanced," he said in a calm, slow and articulate manner.

Bianca looked deep into his eyes and saw anger, hatred, and emptiness there. There was also something else she couldn't name. A chill swept through her body because he reminded her of herself. She waited on him to continue.

"He was shot and I think the bullet was meant for someone else," he said as he watched Bianca's reaction carefully. He saw none, so he added, "I think someone is after Sierra Sanders but they got Devin instead."

Bianca sat as confusion took over her face. "Devin was shot?" She asked unbelieving. Shock and awe by the news was written all over her face.

He leaned up, looked hard at Bianca, and asked, "Did you have anything to do with it?"

"Me? Why the hell would I want to shoot someone, especially Devin? I admit I hate Sierra but killing is definitely not my flavor." Bianca stood and walked around her desk to stand in front of the man, "Look I only wanted to scare Sierra out her mind, you know? Make her crazy. There is no way I would actually shoot someone. Obviously there is someone else out there that hates Sierra far more than I do," Bianca said earnestly.

The man stared at Bianca and actually believed her. "So would you know anyone that hated her more than you?" He asked pointedly.

"I thought I was the only one," Bianca said thoughtfully then added, "What about Devin? How bad is it?" There was true concern for him in her eyes and she felt guilty for lying to him.

"Last time I checked there was no word," he said.

"I said some things to Devin that wasn't true." Bianca took a deep breath, leaned against her desk, and asked, "Do they have any suspects or any idea of who may have done this?" She asked. Bianca saw the look on his face then snapped, "Besides me."

The man laughed, "Nope."

"So in order for me to make sure I don't take the blame for this I'm going to have to do a little investigation myself," Bianca said with determination.

The man laughed because despite everything he knew about her, he still had to admire her determination and drive.

Bianca turned and reached for her phone, "Hey, I need your help, ok?" She hung up the phone then wrote something on a piece of paper, then handed it to the man. "Here, these are my numbers call me in a few days. I'll have something for you then. I'm not taking the fall for this one."

The man stood and left. He would be doing his own investigation and figured he'd have the information long before she would.

Chapter Twenty-Six

Sierra was asleep holding Devin's hand on his hospital bed. Devin didn't want to wake her, but when he rubbed her hair gently, she opened her eyes slowly and smiled.

"Hey," she said softly as she stretched. As soon as the nurses told her he was out of surgery and it was ok for her to sneak in and see him, she did. She had sat by his side for the longest, prayed, and thanked GOD he was all right.

"Hey," Devin said clearing his throat because it felt scratchy.

"I see you're finally awake," The elderly nurse said to Devin then winked at Sierra as she started messing with the equipment that was hooked up to Devin. "I'll let the doctor know you're awake. Be right back." The nurse smiled at Sierra and left the room.

"Why do you have on a hospital gown? You ok?" Devin asked

Sierra laughed, "At the moment this is all I have until my mom brings me some more clothes."

Devin nodded vaguely remembering how she was covered in his blood. It suddenly hit him that if he hadn't pulled Sierra back, she would have been shot and the bullet probably would have caught her in the head. Devin suddenly felt as if he was going to be sick as a cold chill swept over him.

Sierra looked at Devin and smiled, she loved him and he was going to be ok. "Hey, I'm going to go before the doctor arrives. I'll be back later."

"Is the baby ok?" Devin asked before she had a chance to leave.

"Our baby is fine." Sierra turned to leave then said softly as her eyes held unshed tears, "We're glad you're ok." Sierra passed the elderly nurse on her way out and said, "Thank you."

"She looks so much better today. You're a lucky man to have someone who loves you so much. We were all worried about her and the baby after she arrived. The doctor had to admit her she was so upset over you." The nurse patted Devin's hand and smiled at him, "The doctor is on his way in."

Devin smiled at the nurse, considering his shoulder was killing him, he was pleased to know that Sierra loved him seemingly as much as he loved her. He closed his eyes and waited on the doctor.

Hannah stood absolutely still as she listened to what the nurse said. Sierra's pregnant? Hannah thought furiously to herself. She turned around and left the hospital giving the flowers she had for Devin to a complete stranger.

* * *

Sierra was tired but happy that the next day was Sunday; it had been a long week. Sierra was surprised by Hannah because she really helped with keeping the store straight during her shift. Devin made sure she called two other people who had previously worked at the store and asked if they would be interested in coming back. They both immediately agreed to come back after hearing what had happened to Devin, but Denise the younger of the two could only work until Devin was back on his feet. Denise had quit when she had her daughter eight months ago, she and her husband decided she would become a full time mother. Elsie came back on permanently, she was a nosey little lady in her fifties, and everyone loved her.

Sierra turned off the lights in the bookstore and smiled as she thought of Devin. He had been home for a week and already he was restless. All she wanted was a relaxing few hours with him before she went home.

"I'll see you Monday," Denise said.

"Goodnight," Sierra smiled as she got into her moms car and headed towards Devin's house.

When Sierra arrived there, the first thing she heard was Miss Kitty's laughter along with an unfamiliar female's laughter. Sierra went into the living room and could not believe who she saw sitting right next to Devin on the sofa.

The woman stood and walked towards her, "Hi Sierra, I'm Lily, remember we met at the bookstore a while back." Lily smiled then hugged Sierra. "Congratulations, Devin and your

- 250 -

mother were just telling me about the baby."

Sierra could not stand her ass, but she smiled and hugged Lily back. Lily went back to sit beside Devin. That really pissed Sierra off. She walked over to look out the window.

"Honey, why don't you sit down, I know you're tired." Miss Kitty said.

Sierra smiled, "I'm ok." Sierra decided to sit down before she said anything else to her. She took her shoes off as she stretched her legs and wiggled her toes.

Devin watched Sierra stretch and thought how beautiful she was, he could hardly wait until their baby arrived. He stood to go sit beside Sierra, and she pulled her legs across his lap and began rubbing her feet. "Feel better?" He asked her.

Sierra smiled, "Yes it does."

"Well I guess I should be going," Lily said as she stood to leave.

Miss Kitty also stood, "I'll walk you out."

"Ok. Well Devin, you get well soon. I'll see you later. Nice seeing you again, Sierra," Lily said on her way out.

Miss Kitty stood in the doorway as she watched Lily leave. *Something about that girl, I don't like. Sierra really needs to keep her eye on that one*, Miss Kitty thought to herself. She closed the door and headed to the living room. She had been staying with Devin for the past week since that's what she did for a living; take care of sick people, mostly the elderly, but people all the same. Miss Kitty had Darius stay at the house with Sierra so she wouldn't be there alone at nights. She stopped in the doorway and watched Devin and Sierra for a moment. "I think I'm going to go home tonight. Sierra, why don't you stay here with Devin, I know you're probably too tired to drive home, and I really don't think I'm the one Devin needs anymore." Miss Kitty smiled then headed for the stairs to get her things before leaving.

Devin put his hands on Sierra's stomach and said teasingly, "I can't wait to see you fat with my baby."

Sierra laughed then hit him with a pillow making sure

she didn't hit his left side.

"I do love you," Devin said seriously.

"I do love you too," Sierra replied.

Sierra straddled Devin's lap and kissed him softly. "You ok?"

"Yeah," he said as his eyes burned into hers.

Unknown to Devin and Sierra, they were being watched as they made love to each other.

Chapter Twenty-seven

Bianca was in complete shock as she sat at her desk. She had just gotten off the phone with her gynecologist, only to find out she's pregnant. Bianca sat unmoving and thought she was too old to be having a baby. She didn't even think she couldn't get pregnant. She leaned back and closed her eyes because she didn't know if Jermaine or Darius was the father. She picked up the phone.

"Hello Jordan, may I please speak with Ashland?" Bianca asked quietly.

"Hello mother," Ashland said.

Bianca was surprised Ashland came to the phone. Usually, she would be left on hold or heard a dial tone. Bianca was for once at a loss for words. "Ashland. Hello."

Ashland asked suspiciously, "Mother, are you ok? You sound funny. You haven't gotten yourself into anything else, have you?"

"I'm fine. I just called because I love you and I miss you and my grandchild terribly. I need you in my life right now. I'm..."

Ashland cut her off and said, "We'll see when I return. Jordan is taking us with him overseas to see about one of his companies. I'll call you when I get back."

Bianca smiled because this was the first time Ashland had talked to her in over a year.   Bianca asked, "Do you have any idea how long you all will be gone?"

"Jordan said we'll be gone for a couple of months. I'll call you. Goodbye mother." Ashland said curtly then hung up the phone.

Bianca hung up the phone thinking how things would never be the same between her and Ashland. It was all Sierra's fault for talking too damn much. Bianca inhaled deeply wondering what she was going to do. Deep down she knew it wasn't all Sierra's fault, but she had paid Sierra plenty of money to keep quiet. *The little bitch,* Bianca thought of Sierra.

Then suddenly she thought briefly, how Ashland had been conceived then abruptly stood, forcing those thoughts away. Bianca was tired and she felt every bit of her fifty-two years. She left her office for the day.

* * *

"What's wrong with you boy? You've been moping around all quiet for almost a month." Miss Kitty asked.

Darius smiled, "I'm straight just been working a lot of long hours."

"Well go get cleaned up. We're supposed to be at Devin's house in about an hour for a dinner. I have a stop to make, so you go on ahead and I'll see you there," Miss Kitty said before leaving.

Darius had moved back home to make sure Bianca didn't try anything else towards Sierra or his mom. He was hurt, but more than anything else, he was angry with himself for allowing himself to become attached to another woman. Desiree consumed his thoughts, deep down he really missed her, but the woman he missed never existed. Darius laughed because Desiree was nothing but a fabrication. Darius thought of his brother and rubbed his jaw, at least he's doing something with his life now. He had to tell his mom about Jermaine without getting into too much detail so she wouldn't worry about him. Darius had too much on his mind, so he stood to go shower and change, determined to have a good time at Devin's.

Miss Kitty sat waiting on Maxim. Her divorce was finalized and Maxim decided to retire early, now there was no reason for her and Maxim to sneak around anymore. She only wished Jermaine could be there to share in their good news later that evening. Tonight she would introduce Maxim to her family then they would share the news of their engagement. When Jermaine returned home, they both would sit down and tell Jermaine about Maxim being his father. Miss Kitty stood to pace the floor, thinking about how Jermaine would react to that news always made her nervous. "Damn I need a cigarette," she said to herself.

"Now why do you need a cigarette?" Maxim asked

smiling as he leaned against the doorway.

Miss Kitty turned around and smiled, "Just thinking about your son."

Maxim walked over to kiss Miss Kitty, "Come on, let's go. We're already running late."

Sierra answered the door and was surprised when her mom arrived with Judge Evergreen. Sierra stood for a full minute astonished as she just held the door wide open before she realized what she was doing. She smiled and led them into the family area, "Darius, Devin, mom's here."

Devin stood smiling, "How are you this evening, Miss Kitty?" Then he held out his hand for Maxim to shake, "Judge Evergreen, it is a pleasure to meet you. I'm Devin Chandler."

"It's nice to meet you also. Please call me Maxim." Maxim smiled then hugged Sierra, "Congratulations are in order I hear. I know the two of you will make wonderful parents."

Sierra looked from her mom to Maxim then it occurred to her at that moment that he was the same man that she had seen once all those years ago sneaking from her mother's bedroom. *Oh my God*, she thought to herself, *my mother and the Judge*. Sierra smiled barely managing to say thank you.

Darius laughed because he already knew about them, they hadn't really been too cautious when Maxim would come over late at night. Darius kissed his mom and held out his hand to Maxim, "Nice to meet you."

"And it is a pleasure to finally meet you Darius," Maxim said.

"I think this calls for a toast, too bad Jermaine couldn't be here," Darius said laughing as he helped Devin pour everyone drinks. Miss Kitty looked strangely at Darius after his remark.

***

Devin thought it felt really good to be back to work this past week. Mrs. Huddle and Elsie were chattering away with excitement at having Devin well again.

"Tell me Devin, when do you and Sierra plan to marry? You know with the baby coming and all," Elsie asked as she picked books up from the floor.

Mrs. Huddle laughed as she helped a customer.

Devin smiled because he thought Elsie was a sweetheart but a little too nosey and gossipy to suit him. He didn't feel like listening to her preach about right and wrong, so he stood from where he sat and said pleasantly, "I'll let you know as soon as the date is set." He went to his office and shut his door. Ten minutes after he closed his office door someone knocked.

Devin laughed thinking it was Elsie with more questions, and was surprised to find Lily standing there. He stepped out of the office, "Hi Lily, what brings you by today?" Devin questioned.

"I just thought I'd drop in and say hi. Isn't that what friends do?" Lily asked teasingly.

Devin only smiled as he walked towards the counter where Elsie stood. He knew Elsie would tell Sierra about Lily's visit so he wanted to make sure she got everything right. "You remember, Elsie, don't you, Lily?" Devin smiled.

Lily frowned slightly, "Yes of course. Good to see you again," Lily said.

Elsie looked at Mrs. Huddle as she nodded her head slightly. Mrs. Huddle had told Elsie how Lily had been coming around lately to see Devin. *Well she needs to be with her husband and child instead of always up in Devin's face sniffing up round him all the time*, Elsie thought cynically to herself as she smiled sweetly to Lily as she began talking. "Why Lily, what brings you around? I heard you had left town a few years ago. How is that husband of yours and that sweet little girl doing? Next time bring them along with you, I would love to see Eddie and your baby again."

Mrs. Huddle smiled then said from one of the computers, "Devin, could you help me for a moment please?"

Devin laughed as he walked toward Mrs. Huddle because she knew more about the computers than anyone in the store did. "Now, what is it that you of all people need help with?"

"By looking at my watch I realize Sierra is due in at any

moment," Mrs. Huddle whispered.

"And?" Devin asked not liking the feeling he was getting as if he had done something wrong.

"And we both know how Sierra feels about Lily. And I think Lily feels the same way about her. Anybody can tell Lily hasn't gotten over you even after all these years, why else would she keep coming around?" Normally Mrs. Huddle tried to stay out of people's business but lately she was getting bad vibes regarding Lily, it could jeopardize his and Sierra's already unstable relationship. "If that girl keep coming around you, Sierra's bound to get mad and quit *everything* one of these days."

Devin laughed because he knew 'that everything' included him. Devin kissed Mrs. Huddle on her forehead because she was the grandmother he never had. He didn't feel like dealing with Sierra's moodiness today so he'd stay clear of Lily as much as possible without being rude. He began helping an old man on the other side of the store.

Sierra was having a bad day. She woke up late and missed her hair appointment, she was queasy, and the feeling would not go away. *I really hate being pregnant*, she thought to herself. Sierra was later frustrated because she couldn't button up the skirt she wanted to wear. She was beginning to show. She was in a foul mood by the time she arrived at the store, and Lily was the first person she laid eyes on. Sierra went straight to the employee lounge to put away her things, and then immediately started putting books in their proper places. *This is definitely not a good day*, she thought to herself.

Lily saw Sierra and politely excused herself from Elsie. *That woman really talks too much*, Lily thought. "Hi Sierra, how are you today?" Lily asked.

Sierra smiled tightly, "I'm wonderful, and you?"

"I'm good. I just stopped by to see Devin a few minutes before I head out of town," Lily said cheerfully then added, "You don't mind if I ask him to have lunch with me, do you?" Lily asked with a fake smile.

Sierra stared at Lily with pure hatred for the briefest of

seconds then smiled and said sweetly, "Of course not, you two go ahead and enjoy yourselves. Devin doesn't need my permission to eat lunch with a *friend*."

"I didn't think you'd mind, but it's all about the respect." Lily smiled then walked towards Devin.

Devin didn't feel comfortable in going with Lily but Lily kept begging and assured him that Sierra said she didn't mind especially since she was about to leave town. He started to ask Sierra if she was really ok with it, but stopped, thinking he wasn't doing anything wrong and he wasn't about to start asking Sierra or any woman their consent for anything, so he left even though something told him not to.

Mrs. Huddle and Elsie looked at each other wondering what had gotten into Devin and could only shake their heads as they watched Devin and Lily leave together. They knew to stay clear of Sierra, at least until she calmed down.

Sierra was royally pissed. When she told Lily she was ok with her and Devin going to lunch together, she didn't think he would actually go with her. Sierra heard the buzzer in the warehouse and knew it was their shipment of new books. They had been waiting all week for. She decided she would process them because she really needed to keep busy right about then.

Devin returned early from lunch because Lily started acting overly friendly towards him and he knew Lily wasn't worth losing Sierra or his baby. He became angry when he found Sierra working the shipment. "So who brought the boxes up front?" Devin snapped.

Sierra smiled as she continued to put books on the shelf, "Daniel, he's really been a sweetheart to us lately."

"Is that so? And who is Daniel if I may ask?" Devin questioned with a raised eyebrow.

Sierra didn't like his tone of voice or the way Devin was looking at her, "The delivery man, of course, he knows you haven't been here lately and has really gone out of his way in helping out as much as possible around here. He's *really* taken *very* good care of us lately. We can't lift the boxes, and obviously neither can you, so we needed a big strong man like him to bring them up front so we could get the books on the shelves," Sierra said flippantly then walked away to see if any customers needed help.

Devin let out a frustrated breath because first of all, he didn't like the jealous feeling that came over him when Sierra spoke of Daniel. Second, he didn't like the fact that he still couldn't pick up anything over fifteen pounds, along with Sierra's smart remark on his weakness, really messed with his ego, and lastly, deep down he knew Sierra was mad with him for leaving with Lily. He took a calming deep breath then finished putting the books away.

At closing, Sierra counted both registers while Devin vacuumed and cleaned the store.

"Do you want to stop by the house for a while?" Devin asked her.

"Not tonight I'm really tired. I think I'll just go home and get some rest," Sierra said tersely.

Devin stood looking at her for a moment then said, "I'm sorry for going to lunch with Lily. I didn't realize it would bother you so much."

"Bother me so much," Sierra repeated with a laugh, then asked sarcastically, "Why in the world would your going to lunch with your ex-lover bother me?"

Devin was speechless because Sierra just broke it down for him and he realized he would have been extremely angry at her, to say the least, if she had been the one to go to lunch with one of her ex's.

"Well it's late and I'm tired, so are you ready to go yet or what?" Sierra asked annoyed.

Devin leaned down, kissed her, and said sincerely, "It won't happen again. I promise. Come on, stay with me tonight."

Sierra rolled her eyes and said, "Let's go."

Devin laughed as he locked the store.

***

Devin stood looking out his bedroom window thinking about what he was about to do. He smiled as he pulled the box from his pocket and looked at the ring. He was going to ask

Sierra to marry him, but first he would take a shower to relax.

Sierra had already showered and was lying down on the couch reading a magazine when she started craving ice cream. She went to the refrigerator and found nothing sweet. "Just leave it to Devin to have absolutely nothing good to eat. Oh well, I'll just run to the market real fast." She said to herself as she wrote a quick note to Devin explaining her whereabouts.

Sierra hadn't gotten a mile from Devin's house before she saw a car pass the car behind her, and the headlights were fast approaching her. Sierra rolled her eyes thinking people drive too damn fast around here, let them get mad or pass if they wanted because she wasn't speeding up either. She smiled as she thought how good a hot apple pie would taste smothered with ice cream and cool whip. "Some caramel on top wouldn't be too bad either." She laughed, and then all she heard was a loud crash and the sound of her own scream.

Devin sat restless waiting on Sierra. She had to have been gone for almost an hour because he hadn't been in the shower for too long, maybe about fifteen or twenty minutes. He decided to try her cell, but all he got was her voicemail so he left her a message to call. His phone rang so he laughed thinking as usual Sierra was calling to see if he had wanted anything from the market.

Devin frown, "Hi Maxim, what can I do for you this time of night."

"Devin I'm calling from the hospital there's been an accident," Maxim said gravely.

Devin felt light headed, so he sat down and asked, "Sierra?"

"No, it's Darius. Where's Sierra?" Maxim asked.

"She went to the market, but I'm on my way I'll leave her a note for when she returns." Devin disconnected the call and decided it was time to start calling around making sure she was safe, and the hospital was a good place to start.

When Devin arrived at the hospital, Miss Kitty was outside smoking a cigarette. "Are you ok?" Devin asked solemnly.

"I don't know yet." Miss Kitty stated.

"How is Darius doing?" Devin asked.

"We don't know yet. He's still in surgery." Miss Kitty said.

"What happened?" Devin asked frowning.

"He fell through a roof." Miss Kitty stated unemotionally as she put out her cigarette and began walking inside to join the Maxim.

Miss Kitty sat and just stared at the television screen as they waited on Darius to come out of surgery. She was a nervous wreck and needed another cigarette, in a few minutes she would excuse herself for another smoke. "Devin, where is Sierra?" She asked worried.

"She is taking care of something, she'll be here shortly," Devin said trying to keep the worry from his voice. He excused himself to call Sierra's cell again.

* * *

Sierra was shaken really bad. Somebody had deliberately run her off the road. The man in the car behind her stopped briefly to make sure she was all right before he told her to sit tight until help arrived. He said he would try to stop the person who did this. Sierra really couldn't tell because it was dark, but her mother's car didn't seem to have a scratch on it; thank God, her mom drove an older model. The other car had to be pretty messed up, but she didn't know for sure because they kept going. Sierra didn't want to worry anyone since she was ok, so she did what the stranger had suggested; she sat back and waited on the police. Her phone began chiming letting her know she had a voice message. She was about to check her messages but the police had already arrived.

Sierra ended up going to the hospital, at the police officer's persuasion, to make sure the baby was ok. The baby was fine she was only told to take it easy for a few days. Sierra was completely dumbfounded when she went outside to call Devin and there stood her mother smoking a cigarette. "Mom, what are you doing here?" Sierra asked with concern.

"Darius had an accident on his job," Miss Kitty said as

she put the rest of her cigarette out. They went back inside. Darius was very lucky he had missed falling on a steel beam by only inches. He had a head wound but luckily it wasn't serious, a few cracked ribs, his biggest problem was his left leg, he broke it in three different places which was the reason he had been in surgery for so long. The doctor assured everyone that he was going to be all right after a little therapy.

Devin followed Sierra back to his house, after she explained everything that happened. Devin was pissed at her for not calling him, so he decided he would call his friend to help him keep an eye on her. As soon as they got home, they went straight to Devin's bedroom. He was standing on one side of the bed and she was on the other as they removed their clothes. "Sierra, we really need to get a few things straight," Devin said unfalteringly.

"What is it we need to get straight, Devin?" Sierra asked with little concern as she put on Devin's pajama top. She was tired and she only wanted to go to sleep, *Damn, I should have gone home*, Sierra thought irritably to herself.

"You really need to start letting me know what's going on with you," Devin snapped. He didn't mean to be so abrupt but her "I-could-care-less attitude" always rubbed him the wrong way.

"Devin, I don't need to let you know every move I make. I don't remember you consulting me before you and Miss Thang went to lunch today," Sierra said flippantly.

"Sierra, I already apologized for that, I promised you it wouldn't happen again," Devin said tightly.

"I guess next time she comes back to town I'll be all fat and you'll be apologizing for sleeping with her ass, promising that'll never happen again too," Sierra said hatefully.

Devin stood completely still; he hadn't expected her to say anything like that. "Don't start accusing me of things and acting all possessive and insecure on me," Devin stated forcefully.

Sierra only made a noise and got in bed with her back facing him. She didn't mean to say that last part to him, but she was feeling fat already even though her pregnancy was not really showing. She could only imagine how she was going to look in a month or so.

Devin got in bed beside her and put his arms around her. "Sierra, I love you and I only want you and no one else. And all I want you to do is let me know when you need something and I'll make sure you get it. Don't go leaving out all hours of the night, especially for ice cream of all things." Devin laughed and said jokingly, "I'll go shopping tomorrow and buy all that junk food you're craving that's going to end up making you fat."

Sierra turned to face him, "Let's get one thing straight, I'm pregnant and I might get big but I damn sure ain't gonna get fat. Got it?" She angrily turned back over.

Devin kissed her, "Got it." He pulled her closer to him, "I was wondering if you wanted to move in with me?"

"Not really, I thought I got on your nerves," Sierra said flatly. She had never lived with a man and never would at least not until she married.

"You do, but I still love you." Devin reached for something behind him, "Will you at least wear this for me?" Devin opened the box, "Oh and Sierra, will you marry me?"

Sierra was completely caught off guard. She took an unsteady breath, "Wow." The ring was a marquis cut diamond.

Devin laughed, "Is that a 'yes wow' or 'no wow'?"

"Is this because of the baby?" Sierra asked suspiciously. She knew he loved her but she didn't think they were anywhere near ready for marriage.

"Sierra, you're demanding, bossy, pushy and at times you're irritating, annoying and just get on my damn nerves so bad with that smart mouth of yours that you drive me absolutely crazy. But after all that, I would still want you to be my wife, even if you weren't pregnant because when I'm with you I feel whole and complete. It feels good to be with you. I actually miss having you around when you're not here. Besides, you keep me on my toes because I never know what you'll say or do next. And if you marry me, I give you my word of honor that I'll try my best to make you and our children very happy,"

Devin said.

"Ok we'll give it a try and see how it works out," Sierra said. Devin had said all those things with such sincerity she couldn't help accepting his proposal.

* * *

The man thought how he had followed Sierra from a safe distance only to have to watch in horror as the car sped past him running Sierra off the road. Everything happened so fast he was surprised he managed to get the tag number, but unfortunately, they got away when he stopped to check on Sierra. "Let's just see who pops up with this," he said as he held the paper up with the tag number written on.

Chapter Twenty-eight

One month later Devin and Sierra were married. They had a small wedding in Devin's back yard. Everything was perfect except Jermaine wasn't there and Sierra didn't want to get married when she was six months pregnant. She imagined how awful she would have looked in a wedding dress.

Sierra was laughing and talking to Elsie while Devin ran a few errands. She and Devin had been home for almost two weeks from their honeymoon.

"Whose flowers are these? Sierra asked.

"Oh I almost forgot; they came while you were in the back. I put your cookies on the table. I hope you don't mind, but I ate about three, I never could resist homemade cookies," Elsie said.

Sierra smiled wondering who could have sent them, but when she read the card the only thing written was congratulations. Sierra frowned, "Elsie, are you ok?"

Elsie kept trying to clear her throat then suddenly fell against the counter. Sierra called emergency as she frantically tried to help Elsie, unfortunately Elsie died before help arrived. Sierra rushed all the customers away, closed the store and called Devin. Sierra sat on the floor behind the counter and cried until Devin arrived.

"What happened?" Devin asked as he bent down to touch her cheek.

"I don't know we were laughing and talking then she was telling me about the flowers and cookies someone had sent me, she told me she loved homemade cookies then the next minute she couldn't breathe," Sierra told him between sobs.

"Who were the cookies and flowers from?" Devin asked slowly.

"I don't know the card only read congratulations," Sierra said.

"Did she eat any of the cookies?" Devin asked carefully.

"Devin, you don't think…" Sierra began but Devin cut

her off.

"Did she, Sierra?" Devin persisted.

"She said she ate three. Oh Devin, she had already eaten the cookies before she told me about them." Sierra began to panic. "Those cookies were meant for me."

Devin stood, "We don't know if it was the cookies or not, but we're going to find out."   Devin called his friend then the police and explained everything to them. Devin didn't want to wait too long for the results to get back so when he gave the police the cookies he kept a couple to give to his friend to get tested.

Devin's friend called him late that night and confirmed his worst nightmare; the cookies had been laced with poison. Someone was really trying to get Sierra and they had no idea who it was.

Sierra was so upset that she quit working at the bookstore. Devin agreed with her decision thinking she was probably safer at home. Sierra had been home for a couple of weeks and was going crazy locked up in the house all day. She let Devin know before he left for work that she was going to spend the day with Darius.

"Hey big brother, how's it going?" Sierra asked as she entered her mom's house.

Darius laughed, "Looks like you're the one that's big now."

Sierra laughed and threw a pillow at Darius, "Whatever."

"Where is mom? Or do I already know?" Sierra asked smiling, thinking of Maxim and her mother.

Darius laughed, "You already know."

Sierra sat for a quiet minute then said, "Darius, I'm scared, I try to put up a front to Devin, but deep down I'm terrified. I'm even scared to go to the mailbox. Somebody is trying to actually kill me. And the part that terrifies me the most is, it's not Bianca, a friend of Devin's has already confirmed that."

Darius sat up and held her hand, "Hey, have I ever let

anyone hurt you?"

"No, but…" Sierra began.

"Sierra, I might be on crutches right now, but that wouldn't stop me from beating somebody's ass because of you," Darius said with sincerity, and from the determined look in his eyes. Sierra knew he could probably do it.

Sierra smiled as she stood thinking how Darius had always taken care of her and Jermaine while growing up. "How about I cook us something good to eat?"

Darius laughed, "How about we order a pizza or something?"

"Devin eats whatever I cook," Sierra said defensively.

"He just doesn't want to hurt your feelings, I bet you he's probably throwing it out the way we used to. God, I really feel sorry for your baby, Uncle Darius is going to have to teach the poor thing how to effectively ditch dinner." Darius laughed, "Besides Devin's either got a cast iron stomach or he must truly love your no cooking ass to be eating anything you fix."

Sierra laughed and picked up the phone and ordered pizza. She knew she couldn't cook but she gave herself credit for trying. I guess I'll sign up for a cooking class next week, Sierra thought to herself.

***

Jermaine finally returned home, he was actually home for almost two-weeks now. Miss Kitty was nervous, because he was on his way over and it was the day he would be told the truth. She looked down at her a two-carat, emerald cut, diamond engagement ring that Maxim had given almost a month ago.

Maxim sat casually on the sofa watching television, "Kat, would you please sit down. Everything is going to be alright."

Miss Kitty only made a noise and continued to pace the floor.

Darius entered the room and sat down with a solemn expression on his face then said, "I'm sure you both know Jermaine is going to be very angry with the two of you. I would be if it was me."

Miss Kitty frowned, "What are you talking about?"

"Come on now, you already know what I'm talking about. I used to see Maxim here late at night. You see, I would be up because I used to sneak out most nights," Darius said noticing his mom giving him a look that made him laugh but he continued, "Sierra even saw you guys once and told me. I told her to just forget about it because you deserved to be happy with someone, especially after the way dad left us. Besides, I figured Maxim was the reason we had first-rate holidays and birthdays. Somebody told me about Maxim being Jermaine's father years ago."

"Who told you?" Maxim asked curiously.

Darius laughed, "Let's just say a friend that sees and knows all."

Maxim nodded and began wondering how things would have been if the truth had come out a long time ago.

Darius stood laughing, "Well I think I'll go before Jermaine arrives. Oh yeah, one more thing, back in high school some of the guys pointed you out to me one day at a play-off game, I started looking for you after that day. I thought it was cool to have you come to all of our games the way you did." Darius left his mom and Maxim in shock, because they never expected to be caught by one of her children.

Jermaine arrived about twenty minutes later and Miss Kitty inhaled nervously. "Jermaine honey, come here and sit down, there is something we need to talk to you about," Miss Kitty said.

Jermaine sat, which seemed like an eternity to him, as he listened intently to his mom and the legendary Judge Maxim Evergreen, who just happens to be his biological father. *Ain't this some shit?* Jermaine thought furiously to himself. Jermaine never uttered a word; he just casually got up and left.

Miss Kitty cried for the first time in over twenty years. She cried because she knew this was something she could not easily rectify.

Jermaine sat in his apartment and thought about the last six months. He had finally made something of his life that he could be proud of and his mom upped and threw him a curve. He had so many questions but he was too angry to ask. He didn't want to disrespect his mom and as angry as he was when they first told him, there was no telling what he would have said. He laughed thinking his mom probably would have ended up hitting him. He briefly thought of Desiree and wondered what became of her; he really wanted to thank her for everything she had done for him. Jermaine really needed to talk to someone about Maxim and his mom. He thought about calling Sierra but didn't want to get her upset since she was pregnant, so he called Darius.

Darius had been sitting in his truck at the park thinking about his conversation with Bianca when Jermaine called saying he needed to talk to him. Darius didn't have to ask what it was about because he already knew. Bianca had called saying she needed to see him and she would either come to him or he could come to her. He decided to fly down to see her because he didn't want her anywhere near his family ever again. He closed his eyes and leaned his head back wondering what she wanted as he thought how good it felt to hear her voice again, despite all the anger he had towards her.

After leaving Jermaine's place, Darius headed home to pack because he would be leaving out to see Bianca. If everything went as planned, he would be home the next day. He stretched and thought how he was still a little sore from the accident, but he had pretty much healed except for the slight limp. The doctor told him he would probably always have it.

Darius thought back to his conversation with Jermaine. The boy was pissed and rightly so, but Darius still managed to calm him down enough to explain their mom's part in it all. After Darius told Jermaine everything he knew about Maxim's relationship with their mom, he explained how Maxim was a father to them in a sense, even if it was from a distance. He told Jermaine to think about what kind of money their mother earned at work and about all the nice things they received growing up, there was no way she could have managed all that even if she had two full time jobs. Yes, Maxim had seen to it that each and every one of them was well taken care of.

* * *

Bianca had a car waiting on Darius at the airport when he arrived. She really took care of everything, his ticket, transportation and hotel. When Darius knocked on Bianca's door, he was completely shaken at the sight that greeted him.

Chapter Twenty-nine

Devin's friend took a look at the name that belonged to the tag number. He had been watching out for Sierra every since Devin got shot. He suspected a specific person and his suspicions were confirmed one night as he watched her monitoring Devin and Sierra one night through a window. He knew he had to do something fast because now she had killed someone. He stood to leave instead of watching Sierra. He wanted to watch the suspect instead.

The woman paced the floor; things weren't going as planned. She knew Devin wouldn't eat the cookies because he didn't like sweets, but she never expected... "Sierra should have been the one to eat those cookies. What am I going to do? First Devin, now this," she said to herself thinking how terrified she was when she accidentally shot Devin. She was aggravated because in spite of everything she tried, Sierra always managed to come out unscathed. The woman all of a sudden stood completely still and smiled because she knew exactly what she had to do.

* * *

Sierra was petrified as she sat in her mother's car. "Oh my god, momma, I can't believe I'm really having twins."

Miss Kitty laughed, "Honey, you aught to feel blessed having two kids with only one pregnancy." Miss Kitty continued to laugh.

"No, I can't do it." Sierra shook her head slowly and looked at her mother, "Momma, I'm not going to be able to do it. How am I going to take care of two when I have no idea how to take care of one?"

"Sierra, you can do this, remember God puts on us no more than we can handle. You can do this. Devin will be there to help you," Miss Kitty said gently.

Sierra sat back and closed her eyes, *I can do this*, and she repeated to herself, *who the hell am I fooling? I can't do this.*

When Miss Kitty dropped Sierra off, it was almost seven and Devin's car was parked in the driveway. "Bye momma, I'll call you later, thanks," Sierra said as she kissed her mom's cheek.

"What are you doing home so early?" Sierra asked as she entered the living room.

"It was slow at the store so I closed early," Devin said as he flipped through the newspaper.

Sierra went to the kitchen to get a glass of water but the glass slipped from her hands when the baby kicked.

Devin ran to the kitchen after hearing glass break, "Sierra, what's wrong?" he asked when he saw her holding her stomach.

Sierra put Devin's hands on her stomach, "You feel that?" she asked smiling.

"Yeah," he said as he began to smile slowly.

"It feels like the two of them are playing football in there," Sierra laughed as she sat down.

Devin was laughing when it slowly began to dawn on him what she had said. "What do you mean by two of them?" Devin sat down preparing himself for what he knew she was about to say.

"We're having twins," Sierra said.

Devin was shocked but he managed to clean the floor. Sierra sat in silence as she watched him pick up the pieces of broken glass.

* * *

Devin was dreaming. He was taken back to another time and place.

Devin came home late one night, Not again he thought angrily to himself as he heard his mother crying begging his father to stop beating her. For just once, he wished he could come home to a normal happy family. Suddenly, he heard his father's fist connect to her flesh and her begging stopped immediately. There was only dead silence, then the sound of several deadly punches. Devin ran to his room to get the gun he had gotten only weeks before.

"Get away from her or I'll kill you," Devin threatened.

His father smiled cruelly as he stood his full height and began taking deliberate slow steps towards Devin, "Now what the hell do you think you're going to do with that thing? Hell, boy, do you even know how to use it?" his father gloated.

Devin looked at his father unemotionally as he cocked the gun.

"Devin, don't!" his mother cried weakly.

His father laughed then walked back to his mother and kicked her maliciously in her ribs, "Shut up. That's the problem, you're always trying to baby him and not let him be a man." He kicked her again viciously.

Bang, Bang, Bang. Devin began pulling the trigger. Click, click, click was all Devin remembered hearing until his mother managed to crawl to him and stand, gently taking the gun away from him. They looked deep into each other's tortured eyes as she said, "I love you baby. I'm sorry I wasn't strong enough to save you from this." She immediately collapsed to the floor.

Devin awoke in a cold sweat. He hated when those dreams came because they always left him feeling shaky and depressed. He hadn't had that dream in a long time, but he knew why it started back. Ever since he found out he was going to be a father, he was worried and the dreams returned. Worried and scared that one day he'd turn out to be just like his father. Devin laughed thinking of what Sierra would probably do to him if he ever hit her. Devin rubbed his face as he looked over at Sierra sleeping peacefully. He never hit a woman a day in his life, he reminded himself. No, I'm not my father. Devin lay back down and held Sierra as he went back to sleep.

Chapter Thirty

Darius stood dumbfounded in utter disbelief as he looked at Bianca; she looked just as pregnant as Sierra.

"Darius, come in please," Bianca said quietly.

Darius was left completely speechless until Jermaine crossed his mind, "So do you have any idea whose baby it is?" Darius was angry with himself. He was beginning to feel the unwanted stir of excitement. Even in pregnancy, Bianca was still a very exotic sexy woman.

Bianca sat across from him, "It could be either of you."

Darius stood to look out her window and asked slowly, "What do you want from me?"

"I just want you to listen to what I have to say then you can leave," Bianca said.

"I'm listening," Darius said.

Bianca explained every sordid detail to Darius concerning how she had paid Sierra to do some devious things. Darius listened to Bianca and could not believe how someone could be so heartless.

"Well Darius there are a couple of things that I didn't expect," Bianca stated.

"And what were they?" Darius asked.

"You and this baby. Darius, I never expected to fall in love with you and I damn sure didn't expect to get pregnant," Bianca confessed. "I've had a lot of time to think about all the things I've done, and I really can't blame Sierra for my unhappiness. I lost my daughter because of things I have done or paid to have done." Bianca stood to pace the floor, "Believe it or not this baby has put everything into perspective for me. We both know that I'm too old to be thinking about having a baby, but this child was given to me for a reason and I'm slowly getting my life together."

She continued, "I'm in counseling now. There are some things that happened years ago that makes the doctor seem to think that it has a lot to do with some of my problems." Bianca laughed nervously thinking about her rape, "But I think I just have control issues, I always had to get what I wanted and I had to get it when I wanted it, everything just had to go the way I wanted or else there was hell to be paid." Bianca stopped pacing and sat back down. "I really owe your family an apology, especially your sister. I want you to know that's what I plan to do. I don't want you thinking I'm going to harass Sierra because I'm through with that. I have something to look forward to now." Bianca rubbed her stomach thoughtfully.

"I'm so sorry for deceiving you and your brother. Nevertheless, for what it's worth, the time that I spent with you was the best time in my life. Believe it or not Sierra wasn't my main focus when we were together." Bianca smiled sadly, as she thought about the times they had spent together, "Well that's all I wanted to get off my chest. Oh my, I know you're probably tired from your flight and here I am not being a good hostess to my guest." Bianca smiled and stood abruptly, "Can I get you anything to eat or drink?"

"No I'm not hungry right now. What I want to know is what we're going to do about the baby? I think Jermaine and I deserve to know which one of us is the father," Darius said firmly. Darius didn't think Jermaine was ready to face 'Desiree' with everything else that was going on in his life right now, but Jermaine needed to be a man and face his responsibilities if he were the one fathered that child.

"Of course the two of you deserve to know. But right now my plans are to have my baby and be the best mom I can for once in my life," Bianca stated with determination.

"If it turns out to be my child I want visitation rights. I take care of what's mine," Darius said softly.

Bianca only nodded her head in agreement and thought, damned if I'm not still in love with Darius. Bianca knew there was too much of an age difference for them to be together, but she still couldn't help wishing they had met under different circumstances. Bianca truthfully regretted everything she had ever done to Sierra.

Not too long after Darius left, Bianca received a very

disturbing phone call. She had just learned the identity of the person who's trying to kill Sierra. "I guess it's time to make everything right," Bianca said to herself as she grabbed her keys and left.

***

Sierra smiled as she entered the store, she needed to get out of the house so she decided to take Devin to lunch.

"Hi Sierra," Hannah said cheerfully, "How are you doing today?"

Sierra was a little surprised by Hannah's demeanor because she wasn't normally this nice to her. Sierra wondered what was up. "Hi Hannah, it's good to see you again. Is Devin around?"

"He sure is. He's in his office," she said brightly.

Sierra stood completely still for a full minute after opening the door without knocking. Devin was leaned up against his desk with Lily's arms around his neck. She was so angry at Lily's hands on Devin that she never noticed Devin's screw face. Sierra stepped into the room and slammed the door.

Hannah laughed when the door to Devin's office closed. "I can't stand none of their asses," Hannah said out loud. She was wondering what he and Lily were doing in there. "I guess Sierra's finding out," Hannah laughed to herself.

"What the fuck is going on?" Sierra demanded.

Lily smiled wickedly for the briefest second, and then casually turned towards Sierra with a shocked expression on her face. Lily slowly removed her arms from Devin and said unconvincing, "Sierra, it's not what it looks like."

Devin put distance between him and Lily. He was furious with Lily because Sierra would never believe it wasn't anything, even he would have had doubts if he had walked in on Sierra and another man. The words Sierra had said to him came rushing back, *Well I guess next time she comes back to town I'll be all fat and you'll be apologizing for sleeping with her, promising it'll never happen again.* No, Devin thought to himself, Sierra wasn't going to believe him. Damn Lily for coming to the store today.

Lily came into the store saying she really needed to talk to him about something personal. He took her to his office thinking maybe she and her husband had a fight or something and just needed to vent. Venting was the last thing on her mind. Lily started on about how much she had missed him over the years, saying they could start seeing each other again. Devin was completely surprised by her forwardness. He tried explaining he wouldn't hurt Sierra under any circumstances what so ever. She wouldn't listen, so he told her to get out of his office and Lily had just put her arms around his neck and said 'No one has to know. Don't you miss being with me Devin?' That's when Sierra entered the room.

"Sierra, it really isn't what you think," Devin said walking towards her.

Lily smiled, "Well maybe I should go so the two of you can talk. I'll see you later Devin." Lily left the room.

Sierra's eyes became small as she watched Lily leave the room. "Devin, don't you dare touch me," Sierra gritted between her teeth when she saw Devin reach for her.

Devin dropped his hands to his side, "Ok, I won't touch you, but you have to let me explain," Devin said.

"Excuse me? I have to let you explain? What's there to explain? Is it the fact that the two of you were closed all up in your office with her all up on you. Correction, I don't have to let you explain a damn thing," Sierra's words were laced with venom.

"How come you can't just listen for once?" Devin exploded. He was tired, frustrated and didn't feel like arguing.

"So talk. I'm listening," Sierra said sarcastically.

Devin put his hands in his pockets, "When Lily came in the store she seemed to be upset and asked to talk to me for a minute, but as soon as I closed the door she started hounding me about us getting together."

"Is that so?" Sierra said mockingly.

"Yes, that's so. And I told her no," Devin snapped.

"So tell me Devin, was that before or after she was all hugged up on you?" Sierra asked scornfully.

Devin was frustrated, "Why can't you just trust me?" he asked softly.

Hannah knocked on the door then opened it, "Devin, you have a call. I tried to take a message but he said it was extremely important and to tell you it's your friend calling."

"Thank you Hannah." After Hannah closed the door Devin turned to Sierra, "I really need to take this call. Can we talk about this when I get home?"

Sierra was pissed that his call from his friend was more important than their relationship. Sierra stormed from the room slamming his door in the process.

Hannah laughed as she watched Sierra leave.

"The nerve of him, dismissing me that way. I have an important call my ass," Sierra said angrily out loud, as she packed her things. "He can just have Miss Thang for all I care." Sierra heard her doorbell ring and she went down to answer it. Sierra was shocked speechless when she saw Bianca standing in her doorway.

"May I come in for a moment? Please Sierra, I have some information that you're sure to be interested in. It's about the person that's after you," Bianca said seriously.

Sierra hesitated because she didn't see a car out front but she allowed Bianca to enter anyway because she was now curious as to what Bianca had to tell her. Besides, what could she possibly do to me? She's just as pregnant as I am, Sierra thought to herself. "Have a seat." Sierra said slowly.

"May I use your bathroom first? I took a cab over here and unfortunately, the baby has been constantly pressing on my bladder lately," Bianca said smiling.

Sierra smiled then showed Bianca where to go. Sierra was about to sit down when her doorbell rang again.

Just great. Sierra angrily thought to herself. "What do you want?" Sierra said hatefully.

"Sierra, I only want to talk to you for just a moment, to explain things." Lily said.

"Actually there's nothing to explain," Sierra said as she began pushing the door in Lily's face.

"Sierra, wait," Lily snapped as she stuck her foot in the door, "It will only take a minute. I promise."

Sierra inhaled deeply debating whether or not to slam her foot in the door, "Ok Lily, make it fast. I really don't have time for this today," Sierra said closing the door behind Lily as they walked to the living room.

"To begin with there's really nothing between Devin and me, at least not right now," Lily said smugly.

"What do you mean by not right now?" Sierra asked bitingly.

"What I mean by that is that you won't be with Devin for too much longer," Lily laughed.

I am so sick of this Bitch, Sierra thought to herself. "You know what? I want to thank you for telling me there's nothing between the two of you, now I don't have to finish packing since Devin was telling me the truth. Lily, why don't you just leave? I *really* don't have time for this today. Just get out." Sierra stood to show Lily to the door.

"I don't think just yet, Sierra," Lily said as she cocked her revolver.

Sierra stopped in the doorway and turned to stare at Lily in disbelief.

Bianca had just washed her hands and was walking back to the living room when she heard voices. Then to her surprise, she heard Sierra call the woman Lily. *Oh my God. No*, Bianca said to herself as she called Devin immediately from her cell phone.

"Lily, what are you doing?" Sierra asked as if talking to a child.

Lily laughed, "You really are stupid. What does it look like, you idiot? I'm going to kill you. Now come back in and have a seat, let's talk for a minute."

For the first time, Sierra noticed Lily wearing gloves. She became so confused and unfocused she just stood there still.

"I said come in and sit down Sierra. I'm going to count to five and if you're not sitting, I'm going to shoot you. One, two..." Lily began counting chillingly after she spoke each word very slow and precise.

Bianca stood unnoticed looking at Sierra, who was in obvious shock, so Bianca did what she thought was best. In order for her to save herself, she had to save Sierra. Her whole life she had been controlling and just completely self-absorbed. She really didn't care about her daughter Ashland; because after she had found out she was pregnant with Ashland, she didn't really want her. Marcus was the one to give Ashland the love she deserved. Bianca only realized how much she truly loved her daughter after she almost died giving birth to her grandson. Yes saving Sierra would ultimately be her redemption, Bianca thought to herself as she pushed Sierra out of the doorway praying she wouldn't get shot in the process. Bianca felt the burning pain on her side, *Please God, not my baby*, Bianca thought frantically to herself as she collapsed to the floor.

Devin was scared to death as he hung up the phone with Bianca. Luckily, Hannah was still there so he hastily gave her the store key telling her to just lock up when she left. He needed to get to Sierra. He told her she didn't even have to worry about cleaning nor counting down the registers. For the first time Hannah was concerned for Sierra because she had never seen Devin in such a state.

Everything happened so fast that no one ever saw the man come through the front door and shoot Lily. He had been trailing Lily ever since Sierra was run off the road and the tag came back registered in Lily's name. He didn't want to kill her, he only wanted to stop her, she needed to be punished for the things she had done, and Lily would not be facing three murder charges. He prayed Bianca and her baby would survive.

He found out that Lily's husband left her about a few months back, taking their little girl with him. Evidently, he could not deal with the fact that Lily never completely got over Devin. Lily's husband Eddie found this out shortly after they married in a letter she started writing to Devin confessing her undying love for him. It was hard for Eddie to deal with the fact that he was Lily's second choice, but he loved her so much he had managed to deal with it. What Eddie wasn't able to deal with was when he was reading to his little girl and she smiled up at him and said, "Daddy, I met mommy's friend, Mr. Devin, at a bookstore when you were with papa today. She bought this book for me there." Eddie and Lily had a few words that night and a week later, he and his daughter were gone.

Sierra sat on the floor beside Bianca and held her hand to Bianca's side to slow down the bleeding.

"My baby?" Bianca asked breathlessly through a haze of pain.

"Shush, don't talk everything's going to be ok. Your baby is going to be fine," Sierra smiled and said shaken. This was the second time someone saved her life, Sierra sent up a silent prayer for Bianca and her unborn child.

The man bent down beside Sierra, They need to get here fast, he thought to himself as he took a good look at Bianca's appearance. He let out a reassuring smile at Bianca, "Hang tight helps on the way." He then stood to walk over Lily.

"Now what do you think will happen to you in prison?" The man whispered to Lily. He had shot her twice: First, he shot the gun from her hand and then he shot her in her leg just so she couldn't try to get away. "Apply pressure here." He directed Lily's good hand on the wounded spot then found a towel to wrap around her hand. He turned away and left her there until someone arrived.

Chapter Thirty-one

Sierra found Bianca's cell lying on the floor, so as she sat in the waiting room she pulled it out of her purse to call Ashland.

"Hi Jordan, it's Sierra, please I beg of you don't hang up," Sierra cried, "I need to speak to Ashland, it's about Bianca."

"Sierra, what's wrong with my mother?" Ashland asked slowly.

Sierra could hear the fear in Ashland's voice, "There was an accident and she's in surgery right now," Sierra said.

"What kind of accident?" Ashland asked cautiously.

"She was shot. We haven't heard anything on her or the baby's condition yet," Sierra said.

"Baby? What baby?" Ashland asked in astonishment.

Sierra was shocked Ashland didn't know about the baby. "The baby your mother's carrying."

"Just tell me what hospital she's in and I'll be on my way," Ashland told Sierra.

Ashland and Jordan arrived that evening. Bianca was lucky the bullet had somehow passed through her body miraculously missing the baby completely, but her left kidney was grazed which caused blood loss, forcing the baby to go into fetal distress. An emergency C-Section was performed on Bianca and a three and a half pound miracle baby girl was born. Even though the baby had to be put on a ventilator until her lungs fully develop, the doctors were very optimistic because she had a very strong heartbeat.

Sierra and Devin were amazed at how small Bianca's baby was as they looked at her through the window.

"Hello Sierra," Ashland said slowly as she took in Sierra's pregnancy.

Sierra was shocked momentarily to see Ashland and Jordan. "Hello Ashland, Jordan. This is my husband Devin. Devin, this is Bianca's daughter Ashland and her husband

Jordan."

Devin smiled, "Nice to meet you both, I'm just sorry it had to be under these circumstances."

There was an uncomfortable silence for a brief moment, "Well Ashland, your sister is adorable," Devin said as he rubbed Sierra's back.

"Oh my God she is so tiny. Jordan look, isn't she precious?" Ashland said touching the glass window.

***

Darius stood looking at the baby that may very well be his. She reminded him of the picture of Sierra that their mom kept on her nightstand. Whether it was his or Jermaine's there was no doubt in his mind that she was definitely a Sanders. Darius smiled thinking how precious and tiny she was.

Darius was doing a lot of thinking since Bianca saved Sierra's life, so the next time he spoke with Bianca, he decided not to say anything to Jermaine about her being Desiree just yet. Unless the test proved he was not the father then Bianca would immediately have to explain to Jermaine all about Desiree.

Darius awoke early and decided to hit the gym for a good workout, but before going home, he wanted to stop by and see the baby. He was getting on the elevator when Bianca's doctor walked up beside him.

"Mr. Sanders, how are you today? I was hoping you'd be stopping by. I have the results of the paternity test," The doctor said.

Darius only nodded his head and followed him to Bianca's room. Bianca looked up watching the doctor as he closed the door and waited for what he had to say.

Darius drove home and thought of Bianca's little girl. He smiled, my little girl, he thought to himself. Bianca named her Chelsea Symone' Sanders. Darius laughed wondering how his family would react to the news. He wasn't sure how he felt about Bianca but he knew for sure that beautiful precious little girl had stolen his heart the first moment he laid eyes on her.

Darius smiled as he heard Maxim laughing when he entered the house. When his mom wasn't at Maxim's house, he was at hers. Darius was glad that they were happy. He took a deep breath and entered the room. Darius sat quietly until Maxim completed his phone call.

"Hey, where's mom?" Darius asked.

Maxim smiled, "She went to the market. She'll be back soon."

Darius was impatient, "Maxim, can I talk to you for a minute? It's rather personal and I really don't want anyone to know yet until I figure a few things out," he said.

Maxim nodded, "Sure"

Darius looked at Maxim and smiled hesitantly. He sat then stood abruptly. He put his hands in his pockets as he briefly looked out the window then back at Maxim. "I found out today that I have a little girl, her name is Chelsea."

"Are you certain she's yours?" Maxim asked.

"Yes I'm sure, I took a paternity test. Everything is just so complicated right now," Darius said frustratingly.

Maxim leaned forward, looked deep into Darius' eyes, and said quietly, "Darius, just start from beginning and take it slow." He slowly told Maxim the whole story of how he and Bianca met.

Maxim nodded a few times between pauses as he listened intently without saying a word.

"Now I have a little girl by Bianca, who is by the way older than mom, she's fifty-two."

Maxim sat back and wondered about Bianca's mental state. He remembered her in his courtroom once, she was an excellent lawyer and extremely beautiful. He had heard a few comments made about her from some of his colleagues but never anything other than her excellent skills in the courtroom. Although he wasn't surprised by what Darius had just told him, because after everything he'd seen and heard over the years in his court room, rarely did anything surprise him anymore. He really needed to think on this one before he could give any kind advice.

"How about for now you just try to relax and we'll

figure this whole thing out later, together. Come on I'll play you a game of one on one," Maxim said smiling.

Darius laughed wondering if Maxim really knew anything about basketball.

* * *

Miss Kitty only looked at Mrs. Millie because after Lindsey died Darius did not seem interested in anyone else. This is just great. *Lord, please don't let it be one of those whorish ass, weed smoking girls,* she thought feverishly to herself. "Who did Darius get pregnant and are you sure it's his child?" Miss Kitty asked suspiciously, as she put the last bag of groceries in her trunk. Miss Kitty was getting frustrated because she had the feeling she wasn't going to like what Mrs. Millie had to say.

"I really don't know, but my niece works in the lab and she said that the woman was shot when she arrived. She's not supposed to say anything because she could lose her job, but the paternity test results had Darius's name on it along with some woman named Bianca. I just don't remember her last name. From what I hear, if Darius wasn't the father, someone else was going to be tested. From what I heard she'd been messing around with them at the same time." Mrs. Millie shook her head in disgust, "It's a shame when a woman doesn't know who her baby belongs to."

Miss Kitty was finding it hard to believing Darius had a child by Bianca of all people. *I'm going to have a hard time dealing with this one*, Miss Kitty thought to herself. "Well Mrs. Millie I really appreciate you telling me. Now you have a good day." Miss Kitty smiled then got in her car and drove away.

***

Bianca was struggling to get comfortable, but was happy. Ashland and Jordan had just left, although it wasn't what she had hoped for but it was a start. Ashland was relieved to hear that she would be fine.

"Here, let me help you," the woman said to Bianca as she helped her adjust her pillow behind her.

"Thank you." Bianca's smile faltered slightly when she

realized who the woman was.

"So, how are you doing?" Miss Kitty asked displaying no emotion.

"I'm doing fine," Bianca responded.

"My granddaughter is beautiful, ironically she actually looks a lot like Sierra when she was a baby," Miss Kitty said.

Bianca took a deep breath. "To be completely honest with you I'm at a loss for words at this moment, but I can not express how very sorry I am for the things I've put your family through," Bianca said apologetically.

Miss Kitty ignored her apology and sat in the chair beside Bianca's bed. "Well, Sierra told me you actually saved her from getting shot. I thank you for that." Miss Kitty looked hard at Bianca, "But what I came to find out is how did you get my son to sleep with you?"

Bianca sat up a little straighter and said honestly, "I pretended to be someone else."

"OK. So now, I would like to know how you got into my house. Did you steal Darius's keys or what?" Miss Kitty questioned.

"No, I stole Jermaine's keys," Bianca said remorsefully.

"Jermaine?" Miss Kitty's face contorted viciously, "What does Jermaine..." Miss Kitty stopped talking for a second, "Did you sleep with Jermaine too?" She demanded.

"Yes I did," Bianca said, realizing lying there, she was at a great disadvantage and actually began to wonder what Miss Kitty might do.

"You thought Jermaine may have fathered your child also," Miss Kitty said slowly as reality hit her. Miss Kitty then asked, "Bianca, how old are you?"

"I'm fifty-two," Bianca said.

"My lord you're older than I am." Miss Kitty took a few calming deep breaths as she stood, "You better count your blessing that you're laid up in that bed right now, otherwise I'd tear your ass apart before you even had a chance to blink." Miss Kitty turned and left in fear if she stayed a second longer she be all over Bianca and nobody would be able to get her off. She couldn't even begin to understand what made someone like her tick. "Trick ass hoe," Miss Kitty mumbled angrily as she left.

* * *

Jermaine drove up then sat on the back of Darius' truck and watched as Maxim and Darius play a game of one on one. He was surprised Maxim had skills, because Maxim didn't strike him as the athletic type.

"Want some?" Maxim asked throwing the ball at Jermaine after he and Darius finished their game.

Jermaine looked at the ball then spun it on his finger for a minute, then took his shirt off and smiled, "Ok old man you're on."

When Miss Kitty pulled up Darius was watching Jermaine and Maxim play, she sat beside Darius and smiled temporarily forgetting about Bianca.

"Not bad for an old man, huh?" Maxim said after he beat Jermaine by six points.

"So where did you learn to play?" Jermaine was curious.

Maxim looked at Jermaine and smiled, "I played throughout school and a little in college."

"Maybe we can do it again sometime," Jermaine said throwing the ball at Maxim.

Maxim smiled then noticed Miss Kitty for the first time.

"Since you're all out here, I'm sure the three of you won't mind getting the groceries from my car." Miss Kitty stood to go inside. "Oh and when you all get finished putting them away I need to talk to you two," she said pointing at Darius and Jermaine.

"I think your mother's a little upset with the two of you about something," Maxim joked.

"I probably left some dirt on her floor or something the last time I was here," Jermaine said laughing.

"I guess I'd better be going so you guys can talk with your mom," Maxim said after he closed the cabinet door.

"Stay. You're a part of this family too," Jermaine said on his way out of the kitchen.

Darius and Maxim looked at each other with surprise

then followed him to where Miss Kitty was. Jermaine was sprawled across a chair by the time they entered the living room.

"I need to know how in the hell did both of you end up sleeping with the same damn woman and one that's older than me. My God, you're brothers, how in the world did Bianca trick you both like that?" Miss Kitty asked angrily before Maxim and Darius had a chance to sit down.

Jermaine looked at Darius then his mom and laughed, "Calm down mom, I don't know any woman named Bianca. You need to be asking Darius about all that."

Darius leaned his head back and let out a long frustrated breath, "Jermaine we knew her as Desiree Jones."

Jermaine instantly stopped laughing. "You slept with Desiree? Damn Darius what's up with that," he asked his brother angrily.

Darius didn't like Jermaine's accusing tone. He rubbed his face then looked hard at Jermaine and said harshly, "Yeah I did, but at the time I had no idea about you. You see little brother she used you to steal your keys to enter this house to harass our sister. Bianca had a vendetta against Sierra. Then after she got what she could from you she sent you away to make everyone wonder if something bad had happened to you. After you were gone, I became her next target. When I found out what was up, I ended it with her and told her I'd fuck her up if she came near me or any of my family members again." Darius walked to the window, "I hadn't seen Bianca in all this time until about a week ago. That's when I found out about her pregnancy so I took a test to see if the child was mine. I had no intentions of ever telling you about her being Desiree since you already had enough to think about," Darius said looking from his mom to Maxim.

"So is the baby yours?" Jermaine asked.

"Yeah," Darius said quietly.

"Dang Darius I'm sorry man, but..." Jermaine stopped talking as the full impact of what Darius had just said hit him. "You mean that woman that got shot is Desiree?" Jermaine stood to walk over to Darius, "I'm sorry I know you'd never do anything to hurt any of us. Hey, at least she hooked me up with a banging job, now you ain't got to rag me all the time about getting my shit straight," Jermaine said laughing.

Darius laughed, "No I don't, do I?"

"Damn D," Jermaine was shaking his head thinking about what his mom said about Bianca being older than her. "At least we slept with a fine ass old lady," Jermaine said laughing.

Darius laughed, he'd never let anyone know, but deep down he actually cared for Bianca.

***

Jermaine left his mom's house then went home to shower and change then went to the hospital to see Bianca.

"Hello Desiree," Jermaine said smiling as he entered the room to sit beside Bianca on her bed. "Aren't you glad to see me?" He kissed her forehead.

Bianca just stared at Jermaine. He seemed older, but yet, he still looked the same since the last time she saw him.

Jermaine smiled then lay back on the bed to put his arm around Bianca, "I'm not hurting you, am I?" he asked softly.

"No," Bianca said but was feeling uncomfortable having Jermaine act as if nothing had ever happened.

"Good. I wouldn't want anything to ever happen to you not when you and my brother have such a beautiful little girl on the next floor up." Jermaine smiled. "I mean who would be there to take care of that adorable little girl?" Jermaine said pulling her face closer to him. "Darius? No he couldn't he has to work. Mom?" Jermaine laughed, "No, mom, told us know a long time ago that she's not taking care of no grandkids." Jermaine kissed Bianca, "Mmm, you still taste good." He kissed the tip of her nose, "I think Sierra would be the one to take care of my little niece while Darius worked if anything bad should ever happened to you. What do you think?"

"I honestly don't know," Bianca said.

Jermaine laughed, "That's the first time you ever told me you didn't know. Usually you have an answer for everything." Jermaine took a deep breath, smiled, and said very seductively to Bianca as he tightened his grip around her neck. "Don't fuck with my brother as far as his child is concerned, he's always taken care of me and he really will make a wonderful father to his little girl. Oh and before I forget, I am glad that you took the bullet for Sierra because that saved you in my eyes. Now Bianca, I love my sister dearly, and if you ever try to hurt her again, I promise, I'll kill you. No questions asked." Jermaine kissed Bianca softly then released his grip on her. Jermaine stood to leave.

"It's been good seeing you again Desiree. I think I do like your natural eyes and hair better." Jermaine smiled handsomely then left.

Bianca sat staring after him. There was something about his attitude that actually turned her on.

* * *

Maxim and Miss Kitty got married three weeks later. They had a small quiet ceremony at Maxim's home. News of their marriage and Jermaine being Maxim's son spread like wildfire and as soon as Jacob's sister, Helen, heard the news she called him and told him all the gossip she had been hearing.

"Can you believe that wife of yours had the nerve to have a baby that wasn't yours? She all of a sudden upped and divorced your ass for that judge she had been seeing all these years. I wouldn't be surprised if Darius and Sierra weren't your children too. She did date him for a while before he'd left for college. Who knows, maybe they never really stopped seeing each other in the first place. He did have a career to consider," Helen said viciously.

She'd never liked Miss Kitty because she liked Maxim first in high school, but she was too shy at the time to do anything about it. The next thing she knew Katherine and her fast ass was dating him, then ended up marrying her brother of all people after Maxim left for college. By the time she overcame her shyness and went on a few dates with Maxim, he was so infatuated with Katherine and hurt by her marriage that he never really seemed to care about dating anyone for too long. In her opinion, life was a bitch and so was Katherine Sanders.

Jacob remained silent, which made Helen utter a cursed word or two then hang up on him. He sat back as he inhaled the smoke from his cigar then calmly crushed it in his ashtray. Jacob stood and decided that it was time to pay his family a visit.

Chapter Thirty-Two

Bianca sat back as she watched the man leave and close her front door. She slowly stood to go check on Chelsea. She smiled as she watched her baby sleep peacefully. She made sure the monitor was on before she left the room to retire to her own. Bianca sat down on her bed, broke down, and cried. It had been almost thirty years since her rape and this was the first time she could not control her feelings.

The man told her he had debated for months whether to tell her the identity of the man who raped her - The same man who had fathered her daughter Ashland. Bianca was speechless and utterly dumbfounded as he said Charles Chandler. Devin was Ashland's brother. She took a shaky breath as she tried to remember briefly meeting Charles, but as hard as she tried, she could not. The man told her about a close friend of Charles, whose name was Pete, who had spoken to him in confidence. Pete told him about the sophisticated exotic attorney they met on their lunch hour one day and how Charles tried talking to her, but the lady acted as if Charles was scum just because he worked in construction. He knew it hurt Charles' ego but he didn't realized it affected him so badly until the very next day Charles bragged while laughing about raping that uppity attorney and getting away with it. Pete was scared to death figuring if he'd told. Charles could probably kill him and get away with that too, so he kept quiet. After Charles got killed, he saw no reason to drag up the past, since he put Devin and his mom through so much and the young attorney had simply disappeared.

Bianca felt better after she had a good cry. She went and washed her face, "Should I tell Ashland she has a brother? Oh goodness Devin doesn't even know yet," she said to her reflection in the mirror. Soon Devin will because the man said he would tell him. Bianca thought *what if Devin went to Ashland and confronted her.* "I guess this means my dear Ashland that we're going to have a good heart to heart talk and finally be free of all these dreadful secrets." *Devin does need some family, he has no one except for that crazy ass Sierra,* Bianca thought then smiled, *I guess she really isn't that bad.* Bianca laughed out loud as a thought suddenly hit her, "Well Sierra, at least I never slept with your husband."

***

Sierra sat in bed trying to read a book as Devin slept, she was full of energy all day long and now she was becoming restless again. She slowly got out of bed to take another look at their nursery. She was excited and could hardly wait until the babies came. As she walked over to the rocking chair, her water broke. Sierra smiled and turned to get Devin when labor pain struck. "Holy shit," she said between gritted teeth as she grabbed a hold of the crib with both hands until the pain subsided.

"Devin," she said holding her stomach as she stood over his sleeping form, "Devin, wake up…" she began breathlessly as the pain took over.

Devin sat up abruptly, "What's wrong?"

"They're coming, my water just broke." Sierra began to panic so she took a deep breath to try to calm down. She squeezed her eyes tight and snapped, "Just get up and get me to the hospital."

Devin called their doctor and Miss Kitty from his cell on his way to the hospital, he seemed calm as he held Sierra's hand, but inside he was nervous and scared because he knew his whole life was about to change completely.

A few hours later, Sierra gave birth to a five pound seven ounce baby boy and a five pound two ounce baby girl. Sierra was exhausted and relieved it was finally over and Devin was so overwhelmed by the feeling that came over him as he looked at his children. He was speechless as he smiled and held each child. Maxim and Miss Kitty were beaming as they held their grandbabies, Deacon and Devlynn.

***

Several weeks after Sierra gave birth to the twins, Darius had everyone over to the house for a Sunday dinner. He was on vacation and Bianca had reluctantly agreed to let him keep Chelsea for the week. Chelsea was now four months old weighing almost sixteen pounds. She was tiny for her age but she was strong, vibrant and healthy and that was what matter the most.

Darius was sitting by the front window holding Chelsea when he saw a car pull up in the driveway. He watched as a well-dressed man got out of the car and walked slowly up to the door. He had on a hat, which hid his face. There was something about him that was familiar. Darius gritted his teeth when the man took his hat off to wipe sweat from his forehead.

Darius hadn't seen his father since he was a child, except that one time in a club and Jacob was drunk, hugged up with some woman and didn't even recognize his own flesh and blood. Darius left the club in total disgust that night.

"Mom, would you hold Chelsea for a minute?" Darius said handing her to his mom.

"Hello Jacob," Darius said opening the door before he had a chance to knock. Darius stepped out the door and closed it behind him. "So, what brings you by after all these years?" Darius questioned, wishing Jacob would leave before his mom saw him.

Jacob smiled looking at Darius, he was definitely his son, and he was the mirror image of himself. Jacob almost laughed at himself for listening to Helen's accusations about him and Sierra not being his. "Don't you think it's been long overdue?" Anger at Helen's words was actually what brought him home. He was hurt, but wasn't really surprised about Jermaine not being his son, but the idea of Darius and Sierra was more than he could handle, Jack or no Jack he was coming home to find out the truth.

"Right now isn't a good time, so you might as well just leave and come back later." Darius said unsmiling.

Whatever Jacob was about to say died on his lips as he saw the look on Darius's face. He inhaled a frustrated deep breath because he knew what was about to happen.

"And what the hell are you doing here?" Miss Kitty

asked angrily as she stepped outside and slammed the door behind her.

The front door was immediately opened by Maxim, "Kat, don't," he whispered softly as he rubbed the back of her neck. Maxim smiled then held out his hand, "Jacob, it's good to see you again."

Darius was shocked after seeing his mom visibly relax under Maxim's touch, all these years growing up there had been no one, so everyone thought, that could handle his mom, but obviously Maxim could. Darius felt more at ease and thought maybe he should just get it over with and invite him in while everyone was there, "Jacob, why don't you come in for a minute. I'm sure you'd love to see your grandkids."

Jacob nodded and smiled, but before he could enter the house, a car pulled up and the most beautiful exotic looking woman was walking gracefully up the walkway. Jacob was mesmerized as he and the woman locked eyes.

Darius laughed as he watched the two of them exchange looks then thought ironically to himself, this is just what I need, my father and the mother of my child hooking up.

Bianca thought to herself as she looked at the older version of Darius standing before her, *my, my, what do we have here? Since I can't have Darius, I could definitely work with this.* "How are you today, Darius?" Bianca asked as she briefly glanced at Darius, then held out her hand towards Jacob and said seductively, "Hi, I'm Bianca, and you are?"

Chapter Thirty-three

Kayla was still very much pissed off with everything. She couldn't figure out what had possessed DeShun to come by her house and trip when he saw she had company. They hadn't dated in almost ten years and the last time they had been together sexually was when she was about six weeks pregnant with Tymera. Out of all the nights he could have stopped by, it had to be when Damian was over. "His stupid ass," she said as she threw a pot in the cabinet.   Damian was so nice, all he had said to her was maybe we should do this some other time. "Shit," Kayla threw more pots thinking about Damian. They had pretty much started dating after he brought her and the children home from Ashland and Jordan's cook out almost nine months ago. They had been having so much fun together as a family, it was nice to date a man that loved doing things with her children. Damian traveled back and forth from Virginia as often as he could to visit. It was his last night in town before leaving to go back home. "I can't stand his ass," Kayla said thinking of DeShun as her telephone began to ring. She jumped up hoping it would be Damian. She rolled her eyes in frustration, "Hi mom."

"I was just calling to remind you that I'm leaving out today." Her mom, Deidra, said.

"I didn't forget, I was finishing up the kitchen then I'll be right over," Kayla said smiling for the first time. Deidra went away every other weekend with her friends to gamble somewhere. Kayla was grateful to those friends because since her mom started hanging out, she seemed happier now than she had been in a very long time.

Deidra smiled to herself, she wasn't sure how Kayla would react to her dating again, but these last five months with a man who was very nice, and oh so fine was pure heaven. She would continue the charade of pretending to be out with the girls until the time was right. Until then she would continue to enjoy herself.

* * *

"Are we still going to get to visit Damian and his marina?" Tymera asked.

Kayla was sitting on her living room floor alphabetizing her CD's then sighed in frustration, she really didn't know for sure if Damian wanted to see her again after the way DeShun showed his ass the previous night, but Kayla smiled to her daughter, "Honey, as soon as my vacation come up, which is in about three weeks. I just have to ask him when ever he calls if it's still a good time."

"Oh that's ok, mom, he called me and D'Neko this morning right before ma called you. He'll be back Wednesday, he said. I'm just excited about the tours he keeps telling us about, but if he keeps coming down I'm scared we'll never get to go up," Tymera pouted.

Kayla laughed then hugged Tymera excitedly as she thanked God for him coming back. The doorbell rang. "I'll get it," Tymera said.

Kayla closed her eyes tight as she listened to DeShun laugh and talk with Tymera.

"Hey baby, what's up?" DeShun said smiling at Kayla.

Kayla only rolled her eyes ignoring him and continued straitening the CD's. *No, his ass ain't over here smiling up in my damn face after the way he acted last night.*

"Hey where is D'Neko?" DeShun asked Kayla. She continued to ignore him. "Kayla" DeShun began in an aggravated tone.

Tymera sighed rolling her eyes, *here we go again*, "D'Neko come here!" Tymera yelled.

"What do you want?" D'Neko asked after running down the stairs. When he saw DeShun he stopped then walked right passed his dad without speaking, sat on the couch and turned on the television.

DeShun was angry. "Kayla, I need to talk to you in the Kitchen."

Kayla got up and went to the kitchen because she knew what was coming and she at least wanted to shield her kids from most of it.

"What the fuck you been telling my damn kids about me?" DeShun asked.

"Nothing. I don't have to, they see how you are. You rarely spend time with them and when you do, you dump them off with your mom or one of your relatives," Kayla said calmly and quietly, even though she was pissed off with him.

DeShun sat down in the chair, "So where's your nigga?"

"Excuse me?" Kayla asked looking incredulously at him.

DeShun laughed, "You heard me, yo nigga."

Kayla raised an eyebrow and asked softly, "You're not jealous, are you?"

DeShun only stared at Kayla.

Kayla smiled crossing her arms, "You are, but what I can't figure out is why? Are you jealous that he has spent more time with your kids in the last nine months than you have their entire life, or could it be you're jealous at the idea of me being seriously involved with someone other than you?" Kayla laughed.

DeShun sat for a minute and thought about how hard it had actually been for him to hear his daughter talk excitedly about some great guy that did so much with them. He was jealous. This man had suddenly stolen what was his. DeShun knew he had dogged Kayla out back in the day, but damn he loved her and he always came home no matter who he had been messing around with at the time. Even though they had broken up so long ago, it still unnerved him whenever he thought about another man being with Kayla. It didn't bother him when she started seeing Jamison because he knew Jamison wasn't shit and it wouldn't last, but this new guy, he thought, this was different and he was really bothered.

Damn, he couldn't believe how much it aggravated him that Kayla had found someone else to love, he felt as if she would always love him and they would someday get back together. "Kayla, why don't you give us one more chance? I know I messed up a lot in the past, but I've changed. I even got a job now."

Kayla laughed and began to walk out of the kitchen, "I don't think so."

DeShun stood abruptly and grabbed her by both shoulders and hissed, "I don't want him around MY kids."

"Let me go," Kayla said, then laughed, "YOUR kids. When was the last time YOU paid child support?"

"I'm warning you," DeShun began.

"And I'm telling you. You better let go of my moms before I bust you up with this bat." D'Neko said unflinchingly.

DeShun pushed Kayla back against the counter, turned toward D'Neko, and laughed, "Damn boy, you're finally growing up." DeShun casually walked over to D'Neko never taking his eyes off of him and jerked the bat from him. DeShun stood his full height over his son and said forcefully, "Next time you do something like this you better be ready." DeShun threw the bat across the room and left.

Kayla ran to D'Neko hugging him tightly and said half scared with unshed tears, "Don't you ever do that again. I can take care of myself. Do you understand me?"

D'Neko felt his mom shaking as she held him and said, "I understand." D'Neko hated his dad, always have. He couldn't forget that when he was younger his dad only came over when it was late at night and he always heard his mom and dad fight. Sometimes his dad would be drunk and hit her, but his mom was tough but unfortunately, his dad was tougher, stronger and meaner. He had to give it to his mom, she would only cry after his dad left and she never cried in front of him and Tymera. This day, was the first time he had ever seen his mom actually on the verge of tears.

Chapter Thirty-Four

Damian wondered why he was going back to Atlanta to subject himself to that ex of Kayla's. That man was something else, Kayla warned him but it was hard for him to believe everything she said until he finally met him. Damian shook his head thinking he didn't need any more drama in his life because dealing with his parents was more than enough. At least he could always stop to see Jordan and Ashland when he came down, they were cool, he actually couldn't have wished for a better brother, and he was crazy about his nephew Michael and his niece MeShayla who Ashland had given birth to almost three weeks ago. Whenever he pictured Kayla and the kids, he smiled and his heart would swell. He knew he fell in love with them. He loved those kids as if they were his very own. One day they were going to be his family and when that day came, DeShun was going to have a rude awakening.

Tymera and D'Neko had just gotten on the bus and Kayla was running around making sure everything was neat and clean, Damian would be arriving sometime later. Kayla took a personal day off from work and hoped he would arrive before twelve. Kayla had just gotten out of the shower when her doorbell rang. She threw on a red silk robe and smiled excitedly as she opened the door, "Oh it's you. What do you want?" Kayla asked hatefully as she pushed the door up a little.

"Damn baby, I'm sorry about the other day I know how sensitive you are about your kids," DeShun said with an unnatural high.

Kayla frowned pushing the door up a little more, "Are you drunk or what?"

DeShun laughed, "Naw baby, I just wanted to talk to you. Tymera told me last night yo nig-, I mean your friend was coming out today. I just wanted to apologize for how I acted."

"Ok fine, apology accepted. I gotta go." Kayla tried to close the door but DeShun pushed his way in.

"Damn, a nigga can't win with you, can he? I come over

here and try to say I'm sorry and all you do is try to slam the door in my face. What kind of shit is that?"

"Look, I'm running late as it is, I got to get ready for work," Kayla lied she suddenly felt very uncomfortable.

DeShun laughed, "I bet if I had been your nigga you wouldn't be rushing to get to work, now, would you?"

Kayla tied he robe tighter, "What do you want?"

DeShun smiled and touched her cheek softly then became angry when she pushed him away, "Oh it's like that now?"

"Damn DeShun, it's been like that for over ten years now. What's wrong with you?" Kayla asked angrily.

"Damn baby, you always were beautiful especially when you're angry. And red is definitely your color," DeShun said looking hungrily at Kayla.

"Get out, NOW!" Kayla said.

DeShun laughed then reached over and kissed her. Kayla pushed him away and slapped him. DeShun was stunned at first thinking to himself, *I know this bitch didn't slap me*, he knocked the hell out of Kayla, making her fall to the floor exposing her firm well shaped legs and her most private area. Kayla pulled her robed together quickly and tried to run, but DeShun grabbed her by her hair yanking her swiftly back towards him. "Damn, you still look good. Let's see what I've been missing and your nigga been getting," DeShun said harshly.

Kayla panicked and started swinging her fist wildly, she be damned if he would ever touch her again. Kayla landed some very good punches on his cheek DeShun became so enraged he took his fist and hit her up side her head making her fall once again to the floor. Kayla shook her head, she was dizzy, disoriented and terrified, and her past had suddenly crashed into her present more violently than before. She managed to hit and kick DeShun a few more times, but he only laughed angrily as he lost complete control ripping her delicate robe from her body. DeShun had become so livid that when Kayla scratched him across his face he hit her viciously and unzipped his pants then penetrated her ruthlessly, pounding away at her body until he came. Shocked, reality finally set in for him at what he had just done, "Kayla baby I'm so sorry." DeShun stood watching Kayla as she curled her legs up and cried. DeShun stumbled away from her house, he was very drunk and very high. Kayla had never felt so much pain and never felt so degraded in her entire twenty-eight years of life.

Damian pulled up in Kayla's driveway about twenty minutes later and immediately grew suspicious as her front door was partially opened. He walked quickly up her sidewalk, "Kayla!" Damian called out. He took a deep breath, calmed his nerves and braced himself because he heard someone crying. Damian fell to his knees when he saw her naked body curled into a ball on the floor. "Kayla, what happened?" He asked taking his shirt off covering her body with it.

Kayla felt so ashamed she just cried harder. Damian pulled her up in his arms and saw her defeated face for the first time, "Who did this to you? Come on let's get you on the sofa." Blood trickled down her unsteady legs. Damian pulled her chin up with his thumb making her look him in his eyes as he asked her slowly, "Were you raped?"

Kayla looked unfocused and terrified as more tears fell from her eyes, Damian couldn't breathe; the whole left side of her face was bruised. Her left eye was almost swollen shut and her bottom lip was busted. Damian pulled out his cell phone and called the police. "Let's get you covered up." With unsteady hands, he buttoned up his shirt on her and covered her with the afghan from the couch, holding her as he waited on the police to arrive.

* * *

Kayla sat on the hospital bed and touched her lips, and then asked Damian softly after everyone had left the room, "Can I go home now?" It was almost two in the afternoon and she wanted to get home and clean up before the kids got home from school.

"I'll find out." He kissed her on top of her head and left the room. The doctors said it was okay for her to go home.

When Kayla got home, she showered and Damian put her in bed then gave her medicine to help her rest. "Damian," Kayla said with tears in her eyes before he left the room, "What am I going to tell the kids when they ask? I really don't want them to know what happened."

"We'll figure something out. Get some rest." Kayla still looked concerned, so he added, "I'll tell them you slipped down the stairs." Kayla nodded her head in agreement, as he left the room. It was painful for him to look at the way DeShun had disrespected her. He cleaned her house erasing every trace of what happened. Damian thought, *DeShun you had better pray the police get to you first, because if I ever get my hands on you...* Damian laughed because he had never felt so much rage before in his life. He called Ashland to let her know about Kayla and tell her she would need a few weeks off. Ashland was so upset that she rushed over, but Kayla was asleep, as she really needed her rest. After Damian explained everything that happened, he had to calm Ashland down and convinced her to come back later, promising to let Kayla know she'd stopped by. Damian was still troubled at what Kayla told the police officers, he knew if he had not stopped at Jordan's house maybe he could have been there when DeShun stopped by, and none of this would have happened.

Tymera bust through the front door and yelled, "Mom!"

Damian grabbed her, picking her up and smiling at D'Neko as he walked through the front door, "Let's keep it quiet for a while, your mom's resting."

Tymera kissed Damian, "Ok."

Damian sat her down on the sofa. D'Neko asked, "Why is my mom resting, is she sick?"

"She'll be fine. I've ordered pizza and figured we could play some cards after homework. Your mom should be up by then," Damian said. Tymera smiled as she got up to go to the kitchen but D'Neko only looked curiously at him.

"What's wrong with my mom? She was excited about you coming this morning. We usually go to the movies or just out somewhere. Besides, she's never really sick and when she is, she never stays in bed. What's wrong?" D'Neko asked in a serious tone.

Damian thought D'Neko was older than his eleven years, sometimes. It was hard for him to remember how young he really was. Damian knew they were going to eventually see their mom and he hated like hell he had to lie to them, but it was worse for them to know what their father had done to their mother. "Hey Tymera come here. D'Neko," Damian sat Tymera in his lap and pointed for D'Neko's hand to come to him, "Your mom's ok. She slipped down the stairs this morning, so right now she's resting. We'll go up and see her a little later. Ok?"

Tymera's eyes were big, "She's really going to be ok?"

Damian kissed her forehead, "Yes she is, she's a little bruised up, but I promise you two I won't leave until she's all better and back to normal." The doorbell rang and Damian pulled some money from his wallet, "D'Neko would you pay for the pizzas."

D'Neko smiled for the first time.

It was about seven that evening, Damian and the kids was playing monopoly when they heard Kayla moving around upstairs.

"Mom's up." D'Neko said excitedly.

Damian stood and smiled, "I'll be right back. Tymera, why don't you heat her up some pizza and D'Neko can make room for her on the couch." Damian dreaded this moment. He hated that he had to lie to her kids and wasn't looking forward to their reaction when they see her. He knocked softly on her bedroom door, "Hey, the kids are anxious to see you." He walked in closing the door behind him. He put his arms around her and kissed her, "Tymera's heating pizza for you. Do you feel like going downstairs?"

"How bad do I look? Be honest," Kayla asked.

Damian only kissed her gently.

Kayla closed her eyes and asked, "That bad, huh? Well what did you tell them?"

"That you fell down the stairs," Damian said softly.

Kayla took a deep breath and smiled, "Let's go eat pizza

and play cards."

"We're actually playing monopoly and I'm still losing," Damian said laughing, then added, "Ashland stopped by to see you, she's going to call you tonight and come back tomorrow." Kayla's only response was a nod with her head.

Kayla made sure she was still laughing when she entered the living room. Tymera gasped and D'Neko frowned. Kayla kept smiling, "God, do I look that bad? Well this should teach you two never to run down the stairs again." Kayla laughed as she sat down. "God, I'm hungry. Where is my pizza? Don't tell me you guys ate it all."

Tymera stood in front of her mom eyes full of tears, she kissed and touched each of Kayla's bruises softly, "Feel better mom?" Tymera smiled and went to the kitchen to get her some pizza and a coke. Kayla almost cried at the tenderness of the gesture.

D'Neko only stared at his mom then said knowingly, "You look like you've been fighting. Has he been over?" D'Neko asked knowing deep down his father had probably hit his mom again.

"D'Neko, I fell, that's all. Come here," Kayla said. She knew D'Neko was growing up too fast.

D'Neko walked over and hugged his mom, "Ok, if you say you fell, then you fell." He went to sit in front of the television and turned on his playstation, and then said, without taking his eyes off the television screen, "But mom, I know you remember when I got in that fight last month and I tried to lie by saying I fell. You told me I couldn't get a black eye by just falling." D'Neko didn't say too much after that for the rest of the evening.

* * *

Damian woke up early the next morning, looked over at Kayla, and kissed her softly wishing he could take her away from Atlanta. He got up showered, fixed the kids breakfast and made sure they got on the bus. He sat stretched out on the sofa thinking about Kayla and the kids. The idea of another man touching Kayla bothered him, but the idea of someone raping her enraged him to a whole new level. He wanted to always be there for them and make sure they were well taken care of.

"Good morning," Kayla said as she sat beside him on the couch.

Damian looked at her, "How're you feeling?"

"I am so stiff and sore in places I didn't know existed," Kayla said jokingly. Damian didn't respond; he only kept staring at her strangely. "Damian, are you ok?"

"I'm fine, just thinking about you and the kids. I was wondering if you all wanted to come to Virginia for a while," Damian asked casually.

Kayla was completely caught off guard, "I should get beat up more often. Don't be so worried about me. I know how to take care of myself; he just caught me off guard. I stupidly just assumed it was you at the door." Kayla laughed nervously thinking of what DeShun had done. "Don't go feeling all sorry for me, I'm not the only woman this has ever happened to and I seriously doubt I'll be the last." Kayla sat back quietly.

Damian closed his eyes and wondered once again if he had come straight here could this whole incident have been prevented. "I'm serious, why don't you guys come and stay with me for a while, at least while you get better," Damian said.

"Damian you know they have to go to school," Kayla responded.

"Why don't you all move in with me for a while, they could go to school in Virginia." Damian argued.

"What about my job, my house and my mom?" Kayla said.

"You can quit your job. Ashland will understand. You can sell the house and your mom can add Virginia to her list of vacation spots. You win for now. I won't pressure you. But when we get married I'll expect you to move to Virginia with me," Damian said definitively.

Chapter Thirty-five

Deidra smiled as she leaned on the railing sipping her drink.

"Are you enjoying yourself?" He asked.

Deidra smiled, "Very much so."

"Good. You know I've been doing a lot of thinking about us lately and I would like you to meet my daughter. And I am very anxious to meet your daughter as well. Do you think it would be possible for all of us to get together in a couple of weeks?" He asked.

"Yes, I would like that also." Deidra could barely contain her excitement; she could hardly wait for him to meet Kayla and her grandkids.

* * *

As soon as Deidra returned from her trip, she listened to her messages as she unpacked. She frowned thinking how Kayla usually left at least one message complaining about how she needed to get a cell phone so she could be found when needed. Deidra laughed saying to herself, "I guess Damian been keeping you quite busy little lady." She then thought of D'Neko and Tymera and grabbed her keys and left.

When she rang Kayla's doorbell Damian immediately answered it. She didn't miss the surprised look on his face as she laughed. "I know I wasn't supposed to be back until next week but here I am and I miss my babies. Where are they?" She said as she walked through the door.

"Grandma, grandma, you're back!" Tymera squealed as she ran to Deidra and hugged her tightly. "D'Neko's out back and momma's upstairs right now. Come on, we're helping Damian cook on the grill."

"Okay honey, lead the way," Diedra said.

"Hey grandma," D'Neko said as he hugged her tight.

"Hey baby I missed you guys so much," Diedra said as she sat down at the patio table then gasped suddenly when Kayla walked out the door.

"Oh grandma, mommy was running and fell down the stairs," Tymera said quietly.

D'Neko looked up at Damian quietly while holding a pan so Damian could put the meat from the grill on it. At that moment, Damian could not bring himself to say a word or repeat the lie. D'Neko smiled.

Kayla was visibly shocked for a split second, "Hey momma, I'm so glad to see you." She walked around the table to give her mother a kiss.

Diedra just stared at Kayla then looked angrily over at Damian.

D'Neko smiled, "Grandma, Damian got here after mom had her..." he paused slightly to let them know he didn't believe she fell, "accident. He's really been taking care of everything around here." He liked Damian and didn't want his grandma to blame him for not protecting mom from his dad.

"Oh," was all Diedra could say because D'Neko seemed to have grown up over the past couple of weeks.

Diedra and Kayla were laughing and talking in the kitchen as they washed the dishes.

"So, tell me what happened," Diedra said as she dried and put away the last dish.

Kayla sat down and told her mom an edited version of what DeShun had done. Diedra listened intently as Kayla spoke.

"Momma, are you ok?" Kayla asked.

"Yeah, I'll be fine," she squeezed Kayla's hand gently.

"How was your trip? Did anything exciting happen?" Kayla asked laughing as she changed the subject.

"Actually yes, something exciting did happen." Diedra smiled.

"Whatever it is, it has you all glowing. What did you do, meet a man or something?" She asked jokingly.

"Actually yes, I've met someone and he would like for us to meet his daughter. After you're well of course," Diedra said.

"Momma, I'm glad you've finally met someone. So tell me was it at one of those casino tables?" Kayla joked.

"No, we've been seeing each other for a while now. About five months."

"Five months? Wow," Kayla said then smiled, "I'm glad, mom. I can't wait to meet him. He must me something else for you to be dating him."

"He is. Believe me he is," Diedra said.

Chapter Thirty-Six

Kayla and Diedra were sitting at a table inside the restaurant when Kayla saw Ashland enter the restaurant with her father. "Ashland, hey! Over here." They hugged each other. "Hey pops. How's it going?" she asked Marcus as she kissed his cheek.

"I'm meeting daddy's new lady love," she joked as she winked at her father. "Hey mom" Ashland hugged Diedra as she stood.

Kayla rolled her eyes then looked between Marcus and her mom.

"What's wrong with you?" Ashland frowned at Kayla, and then laughed. "Don't tell me. Not the two of you."

Ashland and Kayla laughed then sat down at the table leaving Marcus and Diedra standing quite stunned.

"Mom, are you guys joining us?" Kayla asked then directed her attention toward Ashland, "Hey I think this is cause for a celebration. We are definitely sisters now." She motioned for the waitress, "Hey, we would like two margaritas double shot tequila. I'm not driving, are you Ash?"

"Nope." Ashland grinned and was relieved that her dad met someone who would truly make him happy. She had been worried the whole time as he drove to the restaurant, wondering what kind of woman she was about to meet.

Kayla looked up and asked, "What are you guys having?" She and Ashland laughed again as Marcus and Diedra sat down and placed their drink orders.

***

It was late when Kayla got home but she smiled to herself as she walked in the living room to find Damian, D'Neko and Tymera all asleep on the sofa. Damian was in the middle. Kayla put her purse down on the table and kissed D'Neko, "Honey, time to get in bed," she whispered. Damian woke up. Kayla kissed Tymera.

"Hey, I'll take her up." Damian smiled at Kayla "Come

on little man," he whispered to D'Neko, "Let's get up those stairs."

D'Neko got up sleepily holding Damian's hand as they climbed the stairs while Damian carried Tymera. Damian came back down to sit beside Kayla on the sofa.

"Did you have a nice time?" He asked smiling because he could tell Kayla had been drinking.

"Yes and you're not going to believe who mom is seeing," Kayla said excitedly as she snuggled up beside him. "Damian, I swear you'll never guess in a million years."

"Well tell me who. Anyone I know?"

"Oh my God yes! Ashland's father! Can you believe it? Ashland and I are actually going to be sisters because they are definitely getting married."

"When do they plan to marry?"

"Well they haven't said it, but me and Ashland feel it coming." Kayla laughed.

Damian laughed and kissed her forehead. "I love you."

Kayla sat up and looked very serious, "I love you too." She kissed him, "Make love to me. Please."

Damian kissed Kayla, "Are you sure you're ready?"

"Come upstairs and I'll show you." Kayla stood up, leaving Damian on the sofa and walked slowly up the stairs.

Damian sat for a minute and inhaled deeply as he thought about how his will power had been tested while holding Kayla every single night since her ordeal. Now he was a little scared because he wanted her so bad and he didn't want to hurt her by being too rough. He turned off the lights and went upstairs.

***

Ashland was so happy because she now had everything she had ever wanted, Jordan, two beautiful children and Kayla was now going to officially be her sister. Life couldn't get any better. "Always working," Ashland said to herself as she walked into Jordan's study. "Hey baby. I missed you." Ashland sat on Jordan's lap and kissed him on his lips.

"Been drinking, have we?" Jordan smiled as he wrapped

his arms around her.

"A little," she said then added as he raised his eyebrow, "Yes I've been drinking but guess what? I'm so happy I feel giddy!"

"You're probably feeling giddy because you're drunk." Jordan laughed.

Ashland poked him on his side, "Seriously Jordan, you're not going to believe who daddy is seeing. Take a guess."

"I have no idea." He kissed her, "Your mother," he said.

Ashland laughed, "No, but he is seeing Kayla's mom. Isn't it wonderful! We really are now sisters. Oh my Goodness I can't wait til the wedding!" She laughed.

Jordan sat quietly, which made Ashland nervous, "Jordan, what's wrong?"

He only kissed her.

"Ashland stood up, "Tell me I know that look. Something is bothering you."

Jordan sat back and looked intently at Ashland, "Your mother is here and she needs to talk to you about something."

Ashland smiled as she thought of her baby sister, "What room is Chelsea in?"

"She didn't come this time," Jordan said, without emotion.

"Jordan, what's going on?" Ashland suddenly felt scared. "Is Chelsea alright?"

"Chelsea is fine. She just needs to talk to you," Jordan tried to reassure her.

"I want you to tell me what's going on. Not my mother. Now tell me what she's done."

Just as Jordan began to talk, Bianca entered the room.

"Ashland, I didn't do anything this time," Bianca said as she sat down on the sofa beside the fireplace. "Come sit with me for a while."

Ashland turned to Jordan but he was already standing with his back to her looking quietly out the balcony door. She sat down.

Bianca inhaled deeply and nervously began, "I really

don't know how to begin, so I'll just start talking and pray that I make sense to you. When I was young, I was beaten and raped and out of nowhere, this nice man found me, took me in, and nursed me back to health. Marcus and I had just gotten married and I was away doing a month long internship when it all took place." Bianca laughed nervously, "Marcus never knew about the rape, I never told him because he didn't want me to do that internship in the first place, but you know me, I always have to do things my way. I later found out I was pregnant and when I was told of my due date I knew there was no way Marcus was the father. I let Marcus think that I'd gotten pregnant before that trip and just delivered our baby early."

Jordan stood and watched Ashland's body language as she listened to her mother. Bianca stood to pace back and forth in front of the fireplace, "For all these years, I never knew who raped me, so I just tried to forget what had happened. Well recently, I discovered the identity of the man who raped me and with that knowledge I found out that you have a brother, whom you have already met."

Ashland responded dazed, "A brother? Who is my brother?"

Bianca sat beside Ashland and held her hand gently as she told her, "Devin Chandler is your brother. You remember Sierra's husband."

Ashland shook her head as if in agreement, "Devin," She said slowly. Jordan sat down beside Ashland. "So Daddy isn't really my daddy?" Ashland questioned her mother as tears fell from her eyes.

"Ashland Marcus will always be your father. He loves you so much." For the first time Bianca thought how Marcus would be affected by this and closed her eyes because he didn't deserve the pain he was about to face. She should have been honest with him from the beginning.

"Does daddy know?" Ashland asked in a small voice.

"Not yet," Bianca said.

"Does Devin know about me?" Ashland asked.

"I'm not sure but he should by now. That's why I'm

telling you." She briefly looked up at Jordan. "I didn't want him to just drop by and surprise you with this."

Ashland's face became hard all of a sudden, "Like what happen with Jordan."

Bianca let go of Ashland's hands and stood, "Yes like what happened with Jordan. I didn't want you to find out that same way. I'm here for you, you know that, don't you?"

Ashland stood and faced her mother "You were raped? I'm truly sorry you had to go through that," Ashland said quietly as she thought of everything Kayla was going through and thought how her mother had been through the same thing. She hugged her mother tightly. Everything around Ashland seemed to be moving in slow motion. Ashland pulled away, "But mother, I think it's best if you leave. I would like to be alone with Jordan because I think he knows what I'm feeling and going through right about now better than anyone. Wouldn't you agree?"

"Yes I agree," Bianca said slowly then turned and left their house. Bianca knew right then and there that she was not a good mother. She'd lost Ashland forever and she only had herself to blame. *Oh God Chelsea, would you end up hating me too?* Bianca thought frantically to herself. *I wouldn't be able to handle that. Maybe I should just let Darius keep her to raise, she would probably be better off.* With that thought in mind Bianca knew what she had to do.

Chapter Thirty-seven

"What time are you leaving out?" Kayla asked Damian as she watched him pack his bag through her vanity mirror while removing her makeup.

"I'll leave out after they get home from school tomorrow." Damian walked to the closet.

"Couldn't you stay for a couple more days?" Kayla asked.

"I wish I could, but you know you guys could always come with me. Besides, you know I can't leave mom and Mitchell to run the marina for too long. After a while they'll start all their arguing and it's bound to cause some problems one of these days." He laughed while grabbing a couple of shirts.

"Okay," Kayla said as she went to sit on the bed.

Damian stopped moving, "Okay? Okay what?"

"Okay I want to go with you, because I miss you already and you're not gone yet. And I really don't want to be here without you. " She smiled sadly. "Now, momma has Marcus, so I don't have to worry about her being all alone. I know you need to get back, but could you stay a little while longer? At least let them finish this week out at school and that way I could give Ashland some kind of notice," Kayla said

Damian smiled, "Okay, I can do that. You know I don't have a ring yet but I really think we should plan to get married real soon. You know with the kids and all, I really think we should be a real family." Damian got down on one knee, "Will you marry me?"

"Yes, I think I can do that," Kayla smiled.

***

"What is this?" Ashland asked frowning.

"Gosh, Ash, It's my notice. We're leaving with Damian at the end of this week. I know it's a short notice but I don't want to be without him ever again. It's not official yet, but he asked me to marry him."

Ashland hugged Kayla and cried, "I'm so happy for you guys, now we'll be sister-in-laws."

"Girl stop. Sister-in-law my ass, you're my sister no matter what, besides once our parents marry it's official." Kayla hugged Ashland tighter. Ashland only smiled sadly.

"What is your problem?" Kayla joked.

"I'm going to miss you." Ashland smiled and wiped her tears away.

"Jordan didn't get you pregnant again, did he? 'cause you're acting awfully emotional," Kayla teased

"No, he hasn't. Like I said, I'm really going to miss you and the kids," Ashland laughed and then hugged Kayla tight as she thought about all of the secrets of her mother's past.

THE END

A NOVEL FROM THE BESTSELLING AUTHOR OF "MEETING MISS RIGHT" AND "SEXUAL EXPLOITS OF A NYMPHO"

REVISED EDITION

Neglected SOULS

"Dark alleys, cold and lonely nights just trying to survive... Who can you run to? Neglected Souls made me gasp and grip my heart."
Rashkahna Williams, Best Selling Author of Driven and At The Court's Mercy.

RICHARD JEANTY

NEGLECTED SOULS

Motherhood and the trials of loving too hard and not enough frame this story...The realism of these characters will bring tears to your spirit as you discover the hero in the villain you never saw coming...

Neglected Souls is a gritty, honest and heart-stirring story of hope and personal triumph set in the ghettos of Boston.

In Stores!!!

Jimmy and Nina continue to feel a void in their lives because they haven't a clue about their genealogical make-up. Jimmy falls victims to a life threatening illness and only the right organ donor can save his life. Will the donor be the bridge to reconnect Jimmy and Nina to their biological family? Will Nina be the strength for her brother in his time of need? Will they ever find out what really happened to their mother?

In Stores!!!

Betrayal, lust, lies, murder, deception, sex and tainted love frame this story...
Julian Stevens lacks the ambition and freak ability that Miko looks for in a
man, but she married him despite his flaws to spite an ex-boyfriend. When
Miko least expects it, the old boyfriend shows up and ready to sweep her off
her feet again. Suddenly the grass grows greener on the other side, but Miko
is not an easily satisfied woman. She wants to have her cake and eat it too.
While Miko's doing her own thing, Julian is determined to become
everything Miko ever wanted in a man and more, but will he go to extreme
lengths to prove he's worthy of Miko's love? Julian Stevens soon finds out
that he's capable of being more than he could ever imagine as he embarks on
a journey that will change his life forever.

In Stores!!!

The police in New York and other major cities around the country are increasingly victimizing black men. The violence has escalated to deadly force, most of the time without justification. In this controversial book, noted author Richard Jeanty, tackles the problem of police brutality and the unfair treatment of Black men at the hands of police in New York City and the rest of the country. The conflict between the Police and Black men will continue on a downward spiral until the mayors of every city hold accountable the members of their police force who use unnecessary deadly force against unarmed victims.

In Stores!!!

Just when Darren thinks his relationship with Tina is flourishing, there is yet another hurdle on the road hindering their bliss. Tina saw a therapist for months to deal with her sexual addiction, but now Darren is wondering if she was ever treated completely. Darren has not been taking care of home and Tina's frustrated and agrees to a break-up with Darren. Will Darren lose Tina for good? Will Tina ever realize that Darren is the best man for her?

In Stores!!

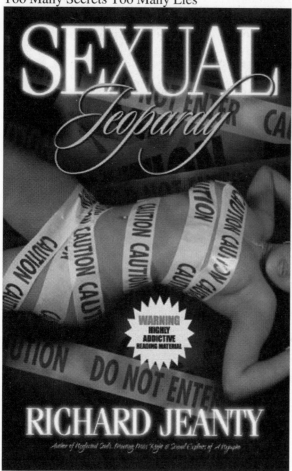

Ronald Murphy was a player all his life until he and his best friend, Myles, met the women of their dreams during a brief vacation in South Beach, Florida. Sexual Jeopardy is story of trust, betrayal, forgiveness, friendship and hope.

Coming February 2008

Malcolm is a wealthy virgin who decides to conceal his wealth

From the world until he meets the right woman. His wealthy best friend, Dexter, hides his wealth from no one. Malcolm struggles to find love in an environment where vanity and materialism are rampant, while Dexter is getting more than enough of his share of women. Malcolm needs develop self-esteem and confidence to meet the right woman and Dexter's confidence is borderline arrogance.

Will bad boys like Dexter continue to take women for a ride?

Or will nice guys like Malcolm continue to finish last?

In Stores!!!

Tina develops an insatiable sexual appetite very early in life. She

only loves her boyfriend, Darren, but he's too far away in college to satisfy her sexual needs.

Tina decides to get buck wild away in college

Will her sexual trysts jeopardize the lives of the men in her life?

In Stores!!!

RICHARD JEANTY

Author of Professional Syde, Mourning Dove, Rogue & Sexual Exploits of A Nympho

INTRODUCES

Me & Mrs. Jones

"A sizzling debut effort from a gifted talent"
— William F. Blue, best selling author of Harlem Gold, Inc.

A NOVEL BY

K.M. THOMPSON

Faith Jones, a woman in her mid-thirties, has given up on ever finding love again until she met her son's best friend, Darius. Faith Jones is walking a thin line of betrayal against her son for the love of Darius. Will Faith allow her emotions to outweigh her common sense?

In Stores!!!

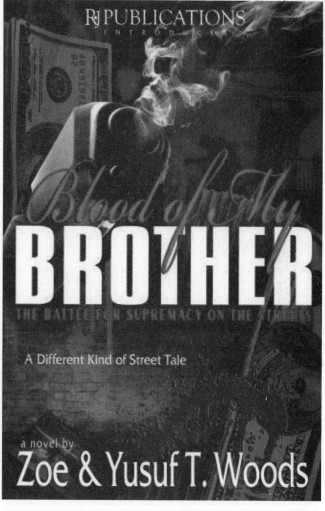

Roc was the man on the streets of Philadelphia, until his younger brother decided it was time to become his own man by wreaking havoc on Roc's crew without any regards for the blood relation they share. Drug, murder, mayhem and the pursuit of happiness can lead to deadly consequences. This story can only be told by a person who has lived it.

In Stores!!!

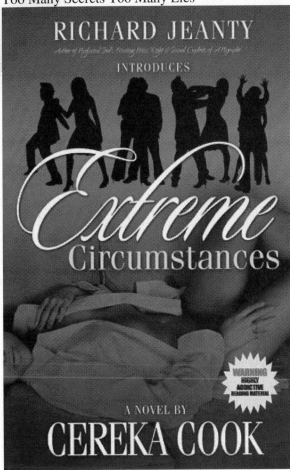

What happens when a devoted woman is betrayed? Come take a ride with Chanel as she takes her boyfriend, Donnell, to circumstances beyond belief after he betrays her trust with his endless infidelities. How long can Chanel's friend, Janai, use her looks to get what she wants from men before it catches up to her? Find out as Janai's gold-digging ways catch up with and she has to face the consequences of her extreme actions.

In Stores!!!

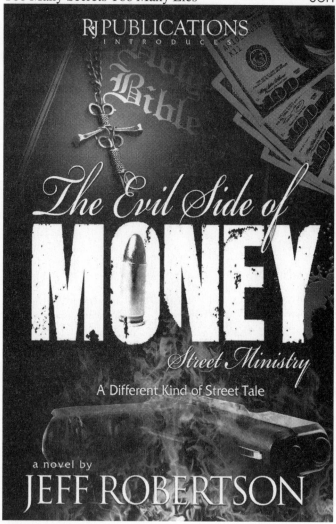

Violence, Intimidation and carnage are the order as Nathan and his brother set out to build the most powerful drug empires in Chicago. However, when God comes knocking, Nathan's conscience starts to surface. Will his haunted criminal past get the best of him?

Coming November 2007

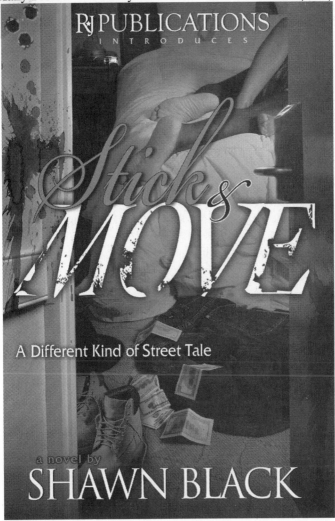

Yasmina witnessed the brutal murder of her parents at a young age at the hand of a drug dealer. This event stained her mind and upbringing as a result. Will Yamina's life come full circle with her past? Find out as Yasmina's crew, The Platinum Chicks, set out to make a name for themselves on the street.

Coming September 2007

Also coming soon…

Ignorant Souls

(The final chapter to the Neglected Souls trilogy)

By

Richar Jeanty

Bloob of My Brother II

By

Yusuf and Zoe Woods

Miami Noire

(The sequel to Chasin' Satisfaction)

By

W.S. Burkett

Cater To Her

W.S. Burkett

Kwame

The Street Trilogy

By

Richard Jeanty

Use this coupon to order by mail

1. Neglected Souls (0976927713--$14.95)
2. Neglected No More (09769277--$14.95)
3. Sexual Exploits of Nympho (0976927721--$14.95)
4. Meeting Ms. Right(Whip Appeal) (0976927705-$14.95)
5. Me and Mrs. Jones (097692773X--$14.95)
6. Chasin' Satisfaction (0976927756--$14.95)
7. Extreme Circumstances (0976927764--$14.95)
8. The Most Dangerous Gang In America (0976927799-$15.00)
9. Sexual Exploits of a Nympho II (0976927772--$15.00)
10. Sexual Jeopardy (0976927780--$14.95) Coming 02/08
11. Too Many Secrets, Too Many Lies $15.00 Fall 07
12. Stick And Move ($15.00) Coming October 07
13. Evil Side Of Money ($15.00) Coming 11/07
14. Cater To Her ($15.00) Coming November 2007

Name_____

Address_____

City_____State_____Zip Code_____

Please send the novels that I have circled above.

Shipping and Handling $1.99

Total Number of Books_____

Total Amount Due_____

This offer is subject to change without notice.

Send check or money order (no cash or CODs) to:

RJ Publications

290 Dune Street

Far Rockaway, NY 11691

For more information please call 718-471-2926, or visit
www.rjpublications.com. Please allow 2-3 weeks for delivery.

 PUBLICATIONS
BRINGING EXCITEMENT, FUN AND JOY TO READING

Use this coupon to order by mail

15. Neglected Souls (0976927713--$14.95)
16. Neglected No More (09769277--$14.95)
17. Sexual Exploits of Nympho (0976927721--$14.95)
18. Meeting Ms. Right(Whip Appeal) (0976927705-$14.95)
19. Me and Mrs. Jones (097692773X--$14.95)
20. Chasin' Satisfaction (0976927756--$14.95)
21. Extreme Circumstances (0976927764--$14.95)
22. The Most Dangerous Gang In America (0976927799-$15.00)
23. Sexual Exploits of a Nympho II (0976927772--$15.00)
24. Sexual Jeopardy (0976927780--$14.95) Coming 02/08
25. Too Many Secrets, Too Many Lies $15.00 Fall 07
26. Stick And Move ($15.00) Coming October 07
27. Evil Side Of Money ($15.00) Coming 11/07
28. Cater To Her ($15.00) Coming November 2007

Name_____

Address_____

City_____State_____Zip Code_____

Please send the novels that I have circled above.

Shipping and Handling $1.99

Total Number of Books_____

Total Amount Due_____

This offer is subject to change without notice.

Send check or money order (no cash or CODs) to:

RJ Publications

290 Dune Street

Far Rockaway, NY 11691

For more information please call 718-471-2926, or visit
www.rjpublications.com. Please allow 2-3 weeks for delivery.

PUBLICATIONS
BRINGING EXCITEMENT, FUN AND JOY TO READING

Use this coupon to order by mail

29. Neglected Souls (0976927713--$14.95)
30. Neglected No More (09769277--$14.95)
31. Sexual Exploits of Nympho (0976927721--$14.95)
32. Meeting Ms. Right(Whip Appeal) (0976927705-$14.95)
33. Me and Mrs. Jones (097692773X--$14.95)
34. Chasin' Satisfaction (0976927756--$14.95)
35. Extreme Circumstances (0976927764--$14.95)
36. The Most Dangerous Gang In America (0976927799-$15.00)
37. Sexual Exploits of a Nympho II (0976927772--$15.00)
38. Sexual Jeopardy (0976927780--$14.95) Coming 02/08
39. Too Many Secrets, Too Many Lies $15.00 Fall 07
40. Stick And Move ($15.00) Coming October 07
41. Evil Side Of Money ($15.00) Coming 11/07
42. Cater To Her ($15.00) Coming November 2007

Name_____

Address_____

City_____State_____Zip Code_____

Please send the novels that I have circled above.

Shipping and Handling $1.99

Total Number of Books_____

Total Amount Due_____

This offer is subject to change without notice.

Send check or money order (no cash or CODs) to:

RJ Publications

290 Dune Street

Far Rockaway, NY 11691

For more information please call 718-471-2926, or visit
www.rjpublications.com. Please allow 2-3 weeks for delivery.

PUBLICATIONS
BRINGING EXCITEMENT, FUN AND JOY TO READING

Use this coupon to order by mail

43. Neglected Souls (0976927713--$14.95)
44. Neglected No More (09769277--$14.95)
45. Sexual Exploits of Nympho (0976927721--$14.95)
46. Meeting Ms. Right(Whip Appeal) (0976927705-$14.95)
47. Me and Mrs. Jones (097692773X--$14.95)
48. Chasin' Satisfaction (0976927756--$14.95)
49. Extreme Circumstances (0976927764--$14.95)
50. The Most Dangerous Gang In America (0976927799-$15.00)
51. Sexual Exploits of a Nympho II (0976927772--$15.00)
52. Sexual Jeopardy (0976927780--$14.95) Coming 02/08
53. Too Many Secrets, Too Many Lies $15.00 Fall 07
54. Stick And Move ($15.00) Coming October 07
55. Evil Side Of Money ($15.00) Coming 11/07
56. Cater To Her ($15.00) Coming November 2007

Name_____

Address_____

City_____State_____Zip Code_____

Please send the novels that I have circled above.

Shipping and Handling $1.99

Total Number of Books_____

Total Amount Due_____

This offer is subject to change without notice.

Send check or money order (no cash or CODs) to:

RJ Publications

290 Dune Street

Far Rockaway, NY 11691

For more information please call 718-471-2926, or visit
www.rjpublications.com. Please allow 2-3 weeks for delivery.

PUBLICATIONS
BRINGING EXCITEMENT, FUN AND JOY TO READING

Use this coupon to order by mail

57. Neglected Souls (0976927713--$14.95)
58. Neglected No More (09769277--$14.95)
59. Sexual Exploits of Nympho (0976927721--$14.95)
60. Meeting Ms. Right(Whip Appeal) (0976927705-$14.95)
61. Me and Mrs. Jones (097692773X--$14.95)
62. Chasin' Satisfaction (0976927756--$14.95)
63. Extreme Circumstances (0976927764--$14.95)
64. The Most Dangerous Gang In America (0976927799-$15.00)
65. Sexual Exploits of a Nympho II (0976927772--$15.00)
66. Sexual Jeopardy (0976927780-$14.95) Coming 02/08
67. Too Many Secrets, Too Many Lies $15.00 Fall 07
68. Stick And Move ($15.00) Coming October 07
69. Evil Side Of Money ($15.00) Coming 11/07
70. Cater To Her ($15.00) Coming November 2007

Name_____

Address_____

City_____State_____Zip Code_____

Please send the novels that I have circled above.

Shipping and Handling $1.99

Total Number of Books_____

Total Amount Due_____

This offer is subject to change without notice.

Send check or money order (no cash or CODs) to:

RJ Publications

290 Dune Street

Far Rockaway, NY 11691

For more information please call 718-471-2926, or visit
www.rjpublications.com. Please allow 2-3 weeks for delivery.

PUBLICATIONS
BRINGING EXCITEMENT, FUN AND JOY TO READING

Use this coupon to order by mail

71. Neglected Souls (0976927713--$14.95)
72. Neglected No More (09769277--$14.95)
73. Sexual Exploits of Nympho (0976927721--$14.95)
74. Meeting Ms. Right(Whip Appeal) (0976927705-$14.95)
75. Me and Mrs. Jones (097692773X--$14.95)
76. Chasin' Satisfaction (0976927756--$14.95)
77. Extreme Circumstances (0976927764--$14.95)
78. The Most Dangerous Gang In America (0976927799-$15.00)
79. Sexual Exploits of a Nympho II (0976927772--$15.00)
80. Sexual Jeopardy (0976927780--$14.95) Coming 02/08
81. Too Many Secrets, Too Many Lies $15.00 Fall 07
82. Stick And Move ($15.00) Coming October 07
83. Evil Side Of Money ($15.00) Coming 11/07
84. Cater To Her ($15.00) Coming November 2007

Name_____

Address_____

City_____State_____Zip Code_____

Please send the novels that I have circled above.

Shipping and Handling $1.99

Total Number of Books_____

Total Amount Due_____

This offer is subject to change without notice.

Send check or money order (no cash or CODs) to:

RJ Publications

290 Dune Street

Far Rockaway, NY 11691

For more information please call 718-471-2926, or visit
www.rjpublications.com. Please allow 2-3 weeks for delivery.